SMOKEJUMPERS SERIES

OMNIBUS

VOLUME ONE

BY EVIE RILEY

Smokejumpers Series Omnibus

Volume One

Books 1-3

Copyright © 2023-2024

Evie Riley

ISBN: 978-1-77357-706-7

978-1-77357-708-1

Published by Naughty Nights Press LLC

Cover Art By Willsin Rowe

HAWKE

SMOKEJUMPERS

BOOK ONE

BY EVIE RILEY

CHAPTER ONE

Twenty-One Years Ago...
Tristan

A HIGH PITCH beeping sound brought me out of my sleep. I knew based on how tired I was that it couldn't be my alarm. It was nowhere near time for me to get up for school. Usually, if my alarm was going off, it would turn off after a minute, but this alarm was going strong and not showing any signs of turning off. It also didn't sound like my alarm. It was a sound I'd never heard before, though.

I let out a groan, knowing I would have to go and figure out what it was. If it was still going off then that meant my parents hadn't heard it.

A coughing fit overtook me, my whole body shaking with the force of my coughs. I had no idea what had caused me to start coughing like I was, but that answer came when I opened my eyes to grab my water from the sidetable next to my bed.

My whole room was filled with the dark grey haze of smoke.

Panic started to flood my entire body as I fought for breath. Every single breath felt like sharp knives were slicing me from the inside out. I couldn't stop coughing, no matter how hard I tried, and the more I coughed, the harder it got to breathe. My eyes were starting to burn from the smoke and I knew I had to get out of there. I didn't know where the fire had started, but I knew I couldn't stay in my room.

I forced my body to move, to get out of my bed. I didn't crawl. I knew I was supposed to, but the smoke was so thick, I was afraid I wouldn't be able to find the door.

I ran my hand along the edge of my bed until I reached the end and then I stumbled, reaching out for my dresser that was next to my door. The second my hand touched it, I felt along the edge until finally, I was able to feel my door.

It was hot.

I knew that meant there was a fire outside of my door, most likely the hallway carpet, but I also knew I definitely couldn't stay in my room. My room was on the third floor, so even if I could get my window opened enough for me to fit through, I couldn't jump. I was too high up. Plus, I couldn't let my parents risk their lives coming upstairs to get me only for me to not be there. The best thing I could do would be to find a way down the stairs and get to my parents.

With more courage than I was feeling, I opened the door and was greeted by fire everywhere. It was on the floor, the walls, and even the ceiling. The whole house was on fire, and for a moment I thought I was trapped. I thought I was going to die in my room, unable to escape. The smoke was just as thick out in the hall, but the light from the fire at least made it so I was able to see somewhat. I knew it was dangerous, but I knew I really didn't have any other choice at that moment, either. I didn't even know if the fire department was coming. I didn't have a phone in my room to call, our only phone was in the kitchen, and if the neighbors hadn't seen or heard our fire alarm, then help wasn't coming.

With that startling realization, I forced my body to move once again, but only this time, I went out into the fire. I moved quickly, everything was hot, so very hot, and I knew if I hesitated or went too slowly it would swallow me whole. I had to move as swiftly as I could.

I could feel the heat on the bottoms of my bare feet and I knew they would be burned within moments. I ran down the stairs, doing my best to jump over large spots of fire. When I reached the second floor, I couldn't believe how bad it was down there. I hadn't met my parents in the hallway or on the stairs and I was afraid that meant they were still in their room. The fire and smoke would have spread to their floor before mine, so there was a very real possibility that they were unconscious from the smoke.

I had to try to get to them.

I had to try and get them out.

I raced down the hallway as best as I could. My foot landed on the ground and a second later it was gone. I collapsed down hard with my foot hanging through the floor.

The fire was getting closer to me now.

A choked scream tried to escape my throat as my left forearm caught on fire. I pushed myself up and tried to get the fire out, but no matter what I did, I couldn't seem to get it out. I knew I needed to drop and roll, but there was fire all around me. If I did what I was supposed to do, what I had always been taught, the rest of me would catch on fire as well. I used my right hand and tried to pat the fire out as I moved to my parents' bedroom. Only, I quickly realized all of it was pointless, because the door had been completely burned away and their room was engulfed in flames. There was nothing left. If they had been in there, they were dead. No doubt about it.

I couldn't allow myself to think of that as the only possible outcome. I had to believe it was feasible that they couldn't get up to me, so they ran outside and called for help.

I promptly turned around and fled back down the hallway. I made sure to jump over the hole in the floor, and once I reached the next level of stairs, I literally flew down them. They were completely covered in fire and I could feel how weak the wood was underneath my burning feet. I could feel the wood giving away as my foot left the last step. I had to get out of there now or I would be trapped inside the house and burned alive.

Reaching the main level of my house, I didn't even take the time to look around. All I could see was the front door, or at least where the front door was supposed to be. It was no longer there and flames surrounded the frame. I didn't care, though, because just on the other side of those flames was my salvation. I would be outside and alive. I would be free from the smoke and the fire. Able to breathe again.

My arm was still smoldering and the pain of the scorched skin and muscle threatened to bring me to my knees, but I knew if that happened, if I went down and gave even another moment's thought to the excruciating pain in my arm and my charred feet, I would never make it out.

I refused to die when I was so close.

Blocking out the pain and the scorching heat surrounding me, I bolted the short distance from the bottom of the stairs and straight through the circle of flames.

The second I was outside, my body gave in and I collapsed onto the cool cement of the walkway at the front of my house. The last thing I saw before everything went black was my neighbor running toward me, and then I felt someone putting a coat over my arm to extinguish the flames.

***

Present Day...

I snapped up in my bed with a sharp indrawn breath, choking as a silent scream caught in my throat. That wasn't the first time I had been woken up by that nightmare. Hell, it wasn't even the thousandth time. One would think that after twenty-one years I wouldn't still be having the same nightmare. I should have been over it, but I guess there was no getting over a trauma like the one I had experienced.

Sometimes, I can still smell their burning flesh. It will strike me out of nowhere and I have to fight back the nausea that hits me like a ton of bricks. I was very tired of having the nightmares, fed up with reliving that night again and again, but I doubted it would ever end. After twenty-one years of having them almost nightly, and they were still going strong, I knew that meant they were not going to stop on their own. I suspected that the nightmares wouldn't end until I got closure, and I knew the only way I was going to get closure would be to find the arsonist who killed my parents and almost killed me.

One wouldn't think it would be possible for an arsonist to go unfound for twenty-one years. There should have been additional fires set after the one that killed my parents. There should have been evidence at other fires that this arsonist was out there, evidence that pointed to who he was and yet, I didn't even know his name. I didn't even know what he looked like.

My obsession with finding my parents' killer had led me to my career of being a fire investigator. I had gone through the Fire and Rescue Academy with the sole focus on becoming a fire investigator.

I took extra classes to ensure that I would be able to work in the investigation department and not be an active fire fighter. I had no problem with investigation work, but I did have a fear of fire. There was no way I would ever be able to run into a burning building every day for the rest of my life. I hadn't even known I was scared of fire until I had to run drills at the academy. I almost didn't make it, but I wasn't going to let my fear stop me from achieving my dreams. I'd pushed the fear down, I'd pushed the panic down, and I'd completed the drills and got through it. Thankfully, without anyone noticing that something was wrong with me. I hadn't risked losing my chance of finally achieving my goal.

I glanced over at the clock sitting on my bedside table and saw that it was four in the morning. The odds of me being able to get back to sleep were slim. I could never get my mind to shut off after a nightmare. Tossing the covers off, I made my way over to my ensuite bathroom. I needed a shower to get the cold sweat off of me. It was a routine that I had long since grown accustomed to. I would wake up, take a shower, then start working. Sometimes if I felt like I needed the escape, I would go for a run. It wasn't often I went for a run, though. I wasn't a natural born runner. I really didn't like it, but every now and then it was the only way I could seem to get my mind to turn off for a little while. So whenever I was in need of a break from the darkness that threatened to consume me or when I needed my mind to see a puzzle from a different angle, I'd go for a run and it helped.

The hot water felt good against my cold skin. I always loved hot showers; there was something therapeutic about it. As if I could wash away the day or the nightmare away and when I came out, it was a fresh start. All of the bad or the trauma was gone and I was a completely different person.

I knew it was just shiny window dressing, I wasn't actually a different person, I was the same person with all of the same problems, but I told my mind I was different with the new vanity update.

I did it all just so I could keep going, go on making it through each day. Some days were harder than others. I wasn't depressed, I wouldn't go that far with it, but some days were certainly harder than others. I knew they would be when I decided to be a fire investigator.

I'd thought they would be hard because it would remind me of what happened growing up. I didn't even think that days could be hard because I had to witness the pain and destruction from each and every fire. Even the fires where no one was hurt or killed bothered me. To know that those people would have to rebuild, that they lost everything, it was devastating. I just needed to figure out how to handle it.

I'd fight through it one way or another.

Once the water turned cold, I climbed out. After quickly getting dried off, I got dressed in some sweats before I made my way out into the living room.

My apartment wasn't very big. I didn't have a need for a large house or condo. I didn't throw parties and I didn't have people over. Hell, I didn't even celebrate holidays.

Holidays used to be huge for my family growing up. I couldn't remember a single

Christmas before the age of twelve where there weren't fifty people over for dinner. Our tree used to be nine feet tall with a hundred presents under it for all of the kids and family members. Christmas was always a big deal, same as Thanksgiving. Even Halloween, my parents would take a ton of photos and all of my cousins would come over and we would all go out trick or treating. It was always a big deal, no matter how small the holidays were.

Everything had changed after that night. I knew things would be different with their death, but I'd never expected for it to change so drastically.

My mother, she didn't have much in the way of family. She was an only child, didn't have any cousins, aunts, uncles, or even grandparents. It was just her and her parents. From what I knew from growing up with them and what my mother had mentioned, they weren't very loving people. They weren't bad people, they just weren't affectionate people.

After the fire, I'd lost my parents, I'd lost my home, I'd lost everything that I had for memories of them. All of that was to be expected, but what I hadn't expected, was losing my family.

My father had a big family with lots of cousins, siblings, aunts, and uncles. My grandparents on my father's side were both alive, too. Every weekend someone was at the house, but that all stopped when he died. With his death, it was like I suddenly didn't exist anymore. I didn't know if they felt like it was my fault somehow or if seeing me only reminded them of who they'd lost. Either way, they disappeared twenty-one years ago. I went from having a huge family with lots of birthday parties and holidays to sitting all alone at the dinner table every night.

I can still clearly remember the look on my maternal grandparents' faces when I told them that I wanted to be a fire investigator. It was the first time in the six years I had lived with them that they showed any emotion. Fear. It was the first and only time they had stated an opinion, that they tried to tell me what to do. They were furious at me for even thinking about being around a fire. They didn't understand that being a fire investigator didn't mean I would be running into burning buildings. I would be the one that investigated when a fire took place to ensure there was no foul play. It was different. But even after explaining it a hundred times, they didn't get it or they didn't care to. When I left at eighteen for the Fire and Rescue Academy, that was the last time I had seen or heard from them. It wasn't my doing, I had reached out plenty of times, but they refused to take my calls. They even moved so I couldn't stop by unannounced. Now, I look at the death notices in the paper every day to make sure they are both still alive.

I had some friends, but I kept them at a distance. I didn't really know why. It wasn't like I didn't know how to have friends. I had plenty growing up and even after my parents died I had some. Not as many as I used to, but more than I could ever need.

I didn't know what happened, but as I got older, I started to lose friends and it was my own doing. I stopped reaching out to them, stopped calling or texting them back. I stopped going out with them. I stopped going out, period. I started to spend all of my time inside and researching.

My apartment was direct proof of my antisocial behavior. I had multiple white boards and bulletin boards that wheeled around. They were all filled with different fires that I suspected were arson, but I didn't have solid proof to bring anything to my Captain's attention yet. I was tracking their signatures and keeping an eye out for any reports of similar fires. When one came up, I would add it to my collection and after three with the same signature, I would finally have enough to bring it to my Captain's attention. I'd done that over two dozen times in the last decade. My work was my life and I wouldn't have it any other way.

I made my way over to the board that I had specifically for my parents' case. Their arsonist was still out there and despite the fact that I knew the chances of him still being active were slim, I was determined to find him. I knew people would probably call it an obsession, hell, it *was* an obsession, but I honestly couldn't think of anything more important to be obsessed over.

Subconsciously, I ran my fingers over the raised flesh of my left forearm where my scars were. It was a habit that I was aware of and yet, I couldn't seem to stop. It happened whenever I thought about my parents or a bad case.

My whole forearm was covered in ugly, multi-colored scars. I had received a third degree burn to it that night. When I had been in the hospital recovering from it, I didn't feel any pain at first, which was the only benefit from having a burn so severe. My feet, amazingly, hadn't been anywhere near as bad as I would've thought they'd be from walking over the fiery stairs and hallways. I'd received first degree burns on the bottoms of my feet and up my ankle on the left side. So yes, I had blisters and pain but nothing like I went through for my arm. That in and of itself was a miracle, I supposed, but one I was grateful for.

The recovery process on my arm was very painful once the burn started to heal. Having to have my burned skin scraped off over and over again as new skin started to regrow was excruciating. The risk of infection was so high, I had to spend two months in the hospital unable to leave or to see people. By the time I got out, I didn't really have anyone to see. My grandparents had even stopped coming by the hospital.

At first they never left.

They would stand outside of my room looking through the glass wall for hours just so they could keep me company. It didn't matter that we couldn't talk, they were there for me. At least for the first two weeks before every day all day turned into every other day for a few hours, until it finally, slowly, dwindled down to nothing at all. At that point, the only people I saw were the doctors or nurses that came into my room to check my arm over and the people walking by.

I used to spend hours trying to figure out who the people were, what their story was. I would look out that glass wall and watch the people buzzing around as if it was my own live theatre. As weird as it was, it kept me sane for those very long two months I spent in the hospital.

Letting out a long sigh, I ran a hand through my hair and shook my head to try to dispel the memories that had crept up on me once more. I made my way into my kitchen. I needed coffee and then I would get back to work. I was going to crack my parents' case, no matter how long it took me.

CHAPTER TWO

Hawke

AT THE SOUND of my alarm going off, I reached over and turned it off without even opening my eyes. I was not ready to be awake yet. I used to love waking up; it was one of the best parts of my day. I used to wake up and roll over to wrap my arms around Paul.

We didn't live together, but we spent every single night over at my place. Paul and I had been dating for two years and it got pretty serious awfully quick. Within two months, he was practically living with me. I had never seen his place, not even to this day. I had no idea what it looked like or where it even was. He was always over at mine. At first, I'd just figured he was a messy person and he knew I was a more clean and organized person so my place is where I'd be more comfortable.

In hindsight, that was my first red flag.

I didn't have a set type, I was more interested in the man's personality, if he was a good person and had strong morals. That was what mattered most to me over body shape or hair color.

Paul was a cop, a good cop. He loved to help people and children. He seemed like a great guy and I quickly fell for him and I thought he'd fallen for me just as fast. We spent so much time together, especially in my apartment.

We used to try and go out on dates, but we could never keep our hands off of each other. In the beginning, I thought it was great that we were so attracted to each other that we couldn't go a single minute without touching the other. Not to mention the sex was off-the-wall amazing. As time went on, though, I quickly discovered that the reason he never took me out on dates was because he was very deep in the closet. That him using sex to make us miss our movie or reservation was just his way of keeping me as his dirty secret. He was using sex to get what he wanted and I had fallen for it. Hook. Line. And sinker.

I wasn't too happy about him being in the closet, but I had tried hard to understand it. To deal with it for the sake of our relationship. I was a firefighter and I understood that the people we worked with were not always open-minded. First responders could be homophobic, more so than people realized. They had no problem saving gay people and protecting them, but they didn't want to work next to one. To most of them, if a man was gay then they would most likely be gawking at them in the shower or when they were changing. They automatically assumed that every gay man wanted every man. They failed to realize that it was the same as it was for straight men. Straight men didn't find every female attractive, and we didn't find every male attractive. Getting someone who was homophobic to understand that though, was like trying to convince a brick wall it was really a door.

My issue wasn't so much that Paul was in the closet. My issue was that he didn't even want to be seen outside of work around me, because I was out and proud. He thought and felt that if people in his precinct saw us together they would assume he was gay as well.

We were *never* allowed to be seen together out in public.

There were no dates, just dinner and a

movie inside my apartment. The blinds were always closed, just in case someone drove by or walked by and just happened to see us together. When we did have to interact at work, which was thankfully, very rarely, he basically ignored me. He would talk to anyone else, going out of his way to ignore me like all the other officers. His image was more important to him than being a decent human being, and for two years I put up with it because he promised me he would come out. He promised me that things would change and we could be together like a normal couple. That he was going to show everyone in his precinct that him being gay didn't change who he was.

It all sounded amazing. It *sounded* perfect. Paul was a man's man. He loved playing sports, he liked to go hunting with the guys, he worked on cars, and he was a gym addict. He was very much the very definition of a *manly* man. He was the perfect example to show people that being gay didn't make you feminine or a fairy. That men could be gay and still love cars and sports. He would have started the long overdue process for the homophobes in the police force to start to see gay men as something more than the stereotype they placed them in. It would have been our chance to have a true relationship like everyone else.

Only after two years, Paul didn't come out.

I lived for two years of Paul and his excuses as to why he couldn't come out yet. At first, he said he was new to the precinct and he wanted to make friends first so they would know him before he came out. Then, it was he got a new Commanding Officer who was homophobic and he had to wait until the guy was transferred. Then, it became he wanted to get his detective shield first so he couldn't have his sexuality used against him. It was just one excuse after the next, and I had quickly started to reach the end of my rope with him.

All of that changed, though, when I went into a local bar for first responders and saw that everyone was celebrating. Paul was there with his new fiancée, Stacey. They had been dating for four years, living together for two. It was a slap in the face to discover that I was the dirty mistress. That the reason I had never been to his place was because he had his girlfriend living there.

I'd felt so sick to my stomach. I'd wanted to yell out right there in that bar that Paul had just fucked me the night before. To whip out my phone and show them the photos of us together. Make him admit that we had been in a relationship, and not just to force him out of the closet, but because Stacey deserved to know. Whether Paul was bi-sexual or not, she deserved to know that her boyfriend, now fiancé, had been cheating on her for two years. That he liked to sleep with men.

What made it come out of left field for me, though, was the fact that he'd always bottomed with me. I was a top, I wasn't a bottom, and I wasn't a switch, I only ever topped. I never expected for Paul to ever be a top with a man or a woman.

He absolutely *loved* being a bottom.

He loved being dominated.

He loved it rough.

To me, I'd never cared for rough sex. I loved passionate sex, but to me that was rough sex. Paul loved it when there were bruises left behind from me holding his wrists or grabbing his hips tightly. I never cared for it, but I wanted to give him the best sex he could have, so I played along. That is something that I definitely wouldn't miss about being with Paul. I wouldn't miss the rough sex and having to always be in control in the bedroom. I loved doing different positions and not just the same ones. I loved laying back and watching my man ride me, but that was something that Paul never wanted.

I was sure that a Shrink would say that Paul needed it to hurt, that he needed to feel like he was being dominated so he could feel good. That he wasn't ready to accept that he was gay, so the roughness allowed his mind to be fooled into what was happening. Or perhaps that he didn't have a choice in the act so it was okay to enjoy it.

It was messed up and I was relieved that I wouldn't have to be a part of that any longer.

After the hurt and anger had disappeared, I started to feel sorry for Paul and for Stacey. I felt sorry for her because the man she was in love with, the man she was set to marry, was living a lie. She was going to marry a man who she truly didn't know. That wasn't fair to her. I knew most people would be mad and angry at her, but it wasn't her fault. I was sure she would blame me if she knew I existed, but it wasn't my fault either. We both didn't know about the other. That was on Paul. Paul was the only one to blame for his betrayal and it was really sad for Stacey because she might have to get divorced. I just hoped they didn't get pregnant. No child deserves to come into a home like the one Paul was creating. A home built on lies and deceit.

I felt sorry for Paul, too. Everyone at the firehouse thought I should still be pissed off at him and trying to cut his balls off. And I had been, at first, but now I thought it was just sad. He was sad and a bit pathetic. He was so afraid to accept who he was that he was willing to be miserable and live a lie for who knew how many more years. He could have been happy. All he had to do was accept that he was gay.

It was the twenty-first century, for fuck's sake.

It wasn't like he was going to be stoned to death in the middle of the street. Yes, he was going to have to deal with assholes inside the force, and some in public, too, there were homophobic asshats everywhere still, but he would find friends like I had who would stand up for him and stand by him. He would at least have a chance at having a real life with a loving and healthy relationship. He was throwing everything away because of his fear and that was no way to live.

I let out a groan as I rubbed a hand over my face and tried to wake up. I had to get to work soon so I needed to get up and start getting ready. I was on day shifts this week and I was thankful for the break from the night shifts. I didn't mind the night shifts, but it made for a long day. I also preferred to not be sleeping all day long and to get to be out in the sunlight. It was also easier to get things done around the house when I was getting home at a decent hour.

Letting out one more groan, I pushed myself up and climbed out of bed. I grabbed a change of clothes and took a quick shower. After grabbing some breakfast, I made my way out of my apartment and took off for the firehouse.

After parking my car on the street, I made the short walk to the firehouse. I was a late bloomer, as the guys like to call me. I was thirty, but I had only worked as a firefighter for five years now. I hadn't joined the academy until I was twenty-five and most people who joined did so between eighteen and twenty.

I hadn't known what I wanted to do for a living. I hadn't known what my calling was. Instead of going to college and putting myself into debt, I'd decided to do different jobs. I'd worked minimum wage jobs and volunteered at other jobs to see what I enjoyed the most. I'd wanted to do something that I loved and I'd wanted to know what that would be before I started my career. I didn't want to be one of these people who went to college and didn't know what they wanted to do so they racked up student debt only to graduate and still not enjoy their career. I'd wanted to be sure that I loved the career that I'd chosen. So I volunteered at various different businesses. I volunteered at a veterinary clinic, a lawyer's office, a restaurant, a day care, a doctor's office, and even a physiotherapist's office. I'd tried all of those different potential careers, but none of them stuck with me. I hadn't felt like they were meant for me. Like they were the type of career I could spend my life in and be happy.

All of that changed one night when I'd been driving down the road and saw a car accident happen right in front of me. Witnessing the carnage shook me to my core.

My reaction even more so.

I had instantly pulled over and jumped out of my car to go over to help the victims from the cars. The crash had very bad and the one car had flipped upside down. I hadn't been able get the woman out, but I'd stayed there on the ground with her, talking to her and trying to help her remain calm and awake until the firefighters arrived.

Standing back and watching them all work, I'd felt mesmerized. They'd all worked together with the ambulance attendants to help secure the woman on a backboard and get her out of the car and off to the hospital. The way they'd interacted with each other and the victims, it felt like a family to me and that was something I'd realized I wanted more than anything. That same day, I had called and asked if I could volunteer at a firehouse to see what it was like to be a firefighter.

I'd gone to volunteer at a firehouse two weeks later and I fell in love.

It was the brotherhood that I wanted. The brotherhood of them all being there for each other, the way they were a family.

I grew up in the foster system. I had no idea who my biological parents were, if they were even alive. I had been passed around from one home to the next my whole life. When I was fourteen, I had been placed in a group home for teenage boys that was more like a jail than a home. I had been abused, neglected, and pretty much left to fend for myself basically my whole life. So to me there was a huge appeal to being a member of a family.

To be a brother in a *real* family.

The idea of running into a burning building never bothered me. It had never even crossed my mind that I would have to be surrounded by fire or put into a dangerous position to help save someone. To me, it was all worth it if I could be a member of a family. Finally, I'd found my calling. A career where my gut told me I would be happy to go to work each day.

I'd signed up for the academy that very same day and I flew through it. The physical aspect of it was very easy for me and I had no problem with the classroom work. I had always been good at school, even if I didn't show up often because of the foster parents. I took everything I could from the academy, aware that any of it could be what helped me to keep my new brothers safe. I took it seriously and I made sure I would be ready for anything that would come my way once I became a firefighter. Once I graduated, I had been placed as a probie in Firehouse Twenty-One and I hadn't regretted a single moment.

"Hey man," Zander said, flashing me a warm smile as he wiped down the driver's side door of engine forty-three.

Zander was always washing the trucks. He loved to keep them shiny and he loved the busy work of it. Zander was a car guy and he loved working on them, even if that was just washing and polishing them. He had two big fire trucks to keep his hands busy and you could find him in the garage doing something with them more often than not.

"Hey, how was the overnight?"

"The guys said it was a pretty quiet night. They were able to sleep most of it away, lucky bastards."

"That's good, though, and hey, maybe it'll be quiet today," I said, flashing my own hopeful smile.

Before Zander could say anything, the alarm from our overheard speaker rang out, followed by the dispatcher's voice over the intercom as they requested our truck for a fire in progress. The second the dispatcher's voice disappeared, Zander gave me a look and I knew what he was thinking.

"You just had to say the Q-word."

"Yup, that was my bad," I agreed, before we ran off to get our gear on.

I really shouldn't have said anything. I knew better than to say the word *quiet* while on shift. All of us knew better because usually, that is when shit hit the fan. This time around it was completely my bad and hopefully, Zander didn't rat me out to the guys. The last thing I wanted to do today was scrub the bathrooms for using the q-word.

We all loaded up and headed off for the fire. I was hoping it wouldn't be too bad, that we could get there before the fire ate up the whole house. It was a toss up on whether we would be able to save the house or not. We always hoped that we could. We didn't want to leave anyone without a home. We knew how devastating that could be and we never wanted to cause someone that pain. Unfortunately, we didn't always have a say in what happened. It really depended on the fire and how hot it was burning.

The second we pulled up to the house, we all could see that the flames were out of control. Local police were already on the scene and trying to escort everyone away from the house. I knew they would have already been evacuating the nearby homes in case the flames jumped to the other houses, too. We jumped out and instantly got to work on getting the hoses out.

"Hawke, Zander, get hose one set up. Jase and Gage, get hose two set up and get it around the back. We need to hit this from both sides," Captain Clark called out.

Zander and I quickly ran and got our

hose started. The fire was burning hot and fast and I couldn't help but wonder if an accelerant had been used. The trick was, house fires could go up quickly with the furniture in the home. It could also burn faster depending on when the house was built. Different building materials could make the house burn faster. Once we got the fire under control, we would be able to go through it and see what the cause was.

With our hose hooked up to the fire hydrant, Zander and I went over to the front door that was engulfed in flames and turned the water on. I was ready for the power of the water that shot out of the nozzle. I was in front and controlling the hose and where the water was sprayed. The power of the water being pushed out had surprised me at first when I was in the academy and now it was a comfort. I knew that as long as that power was there, then the water was coming and we would be able to gain control of the fire.

As the flames started to dissipate, we made our way into the house. I could see Jase and Gage on the other side of the house working their way toward us. The stairs were gone and the top floor of the house had crashed down to the main level. If we had taken any longer to get here, there wouldn't have been anything left. Working together, we were able to get the flames out until all that was left of the house was a wet, charred mess. Zander took our hose back to the truck as Gage and I started to look through the rubble to see if there had been anyone inside. The police didn't know because the neighbors didn't know. The woman who owned the house didn't have a car, so we couldn't look to see if there was a car there. I was hoping and praying that the woman who lived there was not in there. That she had been at work or out shopping when the first started.

"Cap, we got a body," Gage's voice came over our radio.

"Shit," I said to myself.

I hated this part of the job. This was the part of the job that no one could prepare you for. No one could prepare you for finding someone who had been trapped and unable to escape from a fire. There were a lot of ways to die, but to me getting burned alive had to be the worst. Whenever we came across a body in a fire, I always hoped that they had died from smoke inhalation long before the flames got to them. It wasn't ideal, but at least the smoke would make them pass out so they wouldn't have felt any pain as they died. Most of the time, that was the case and I was forever thankful that they could go in a somewhat peaceful manner.

"Copy. I'll call the Investigation Unit. Keep searching for anyone else just in case she had a visitor over," Captain Clark said through the radio.

"Copy," I said back as I silently sent up a prayer that the body would be the only one we recovered today.

CHAPTER THREE

Tristan

PULLING UP TO the crime scene, I already had a bad feeling in the pit of my stomach. Every crime scene brought that same feeling to my belly. I was always waiting for the day that I would come across the same arsonist who had killed my parents.

He was still out there.

I knew in my gut he was.

I couldn't explain it, but I could just *feel* it. He was out there, mocking me with each fire he set.

I had dedicated my life to finding and stopping arsonists, to preventing people from going through the horrific trauma that I had experienced. And yet, I couldn't seem to find one man, the man who gave me my scars and nightmares.

I knew rationally and logically that he was most likely dead. It had been twenty-one years. He wouldn't have been young based on the skill that he used on my home back then. Arsonists tended to either get caught or kill themselves in one of their fires. They didn't tend to be able to dodge the police for very long.

Most people would assume that catching an arsonist was difficult with the fire destroying all of the evidence, and what the fire didn't destroy, the firefighters certainly did. Not that it was their fault, of course. The water was necessary to prevent further damage. The only way to put out a fire was with water, but unfortunately, water tended to destroy any evidence that the fire didn't eat away in its path. Still, a trained eye could read a burned down building and determine how the fire was started and find evidence that pointed to the arsonist.

The psychological profile of an arsonist also did them no favors. Arsonists, even at a young age, they tended to stand out. People remembered them. More often than not, when I had a suspect and spoke with neighbors, family, and friends, they always said the same kind of thing, 'He's always been a bit weird.' It didn't come as a shock or a surprise to people, not like it did with some of the best serial killers. Arsonists didn't tend to blend in and hide well in society, and nine out of ten times, they had their own burns from their earlier days of experimenting.

What frustrated me the most, though, was knowing that I couldn't catch my parents' killer and yet, so far I caught any other arsonist who came into my path. It was frustrating and I would be lying if I said it wasn't affecting my self-confidence.

How was it I couldn't catch one arsonist?

He was just a man and he was out there, and yet I couldn't even put a face to the man.

My newest crime scene was abuzz with life. Onlookers stood on the other side of the yellow police tape. Most of them looked worried and horrified at the destruction of someone's home. Others had a look that told me they were trying to figure out how to leave without coming across as insensitive. It was human nature to want to gawk at something horrible, just as it was human nature to want to get on with life and be thankful it wasn't you.

I ignored those natural human reactions and scanned the crowd to see if I could find one that wasn't natural in the face of destruction such as this. Arsonists loved to see their handy work. They loved to watch the fire grow and consume. All too often they hid away in the crowd to see the end result. Fire starting was a compulsion, an addiction, and not something that could be stopped on their own. Much like a drug addict or an alcoholic, they couldn't stop setting fires without getting treatment. Unfortunately though, unlike a normal drug addiction, arsonists weren't just inflicting pain onto themselves. Their addiction destroyed lives by either destroying a home or killing someone.

Having your house destroyed might not seem like that big of a deal to some. Not when compared to your life being taken or that of someone you loved. However, it was equally devastating to know that every single thing you owned was lost. Yes, it was just stuff, material possessions, but sometimes that stuff had sentimental meaning. Photos of loved ones who had passed, a child's favorite stuffed animal or blanket that they needed in order to fall asleep at night, a dead parent's shirt with their scent that still lingered on it. Those items couldn't be replaced and there was no monetary amount that would ever be enough compensation for them.

Even the annoyance of having to live somewhere else until they were able to rebuild or find a new home could be too much for some people. Most people couldn't afford to start all over again and often they ended up in a shelter with nothing but whatever clothes had been donated to them. There was more than one way for a person to lose their life in a fire and unfortunately, unless a person were lucky enough to have it contained quickly, they were going to lose their life one way or the other long before the fire got put out.

With the fire out the firefighters were working on cleaning up now. Some were getting their tools and the fire hoses back onto the truck and in the proper order. Others, the more experienced firefighters for the station house, were inside the burned out shell of the house and going through it to try and figure out how the fire got started.

Not every fire required an investigator to be on scene for it. Often seasoned firefighters could find the origin of the fire and determine what ignited it without assistance from an investigator. Most of the time it was a candle that had been left too close to a curtain, or someone dropped a lit cigarette into the couch and thought there was no burning ash left behind, or a kitchen fire when someone wasn't being as careful as they should be with things on the stove. Oil fires were the biggest issues when it came to a kitchen blaze. People just didn't take care and didn't realize how quickly things could go wrong when it came to oil and fire, and then of course, many exacerbated the issue by panicking and making the mistake of putting water on an oil fire, and well, that just made everything so much worse. Oil and water didn't mix. Add in a heat source igniting that oil and it just accelerated the fire, made it spread even more when water was added.

Most fires were accidental or they were electrical. Calling an investigator in meant that something more was going on this time around. The sight of the coroner's van only cemented that probability. A dead victim meant that the fire had been placed in one of two categories.

The first category meant it was an accidental fire or a non-human started fire, meaning it was a structural issue such as faulty electrical, and the occupant was not able to get out. They could have been trapped in a room or they could have died from smoke inhalation before they even made it out of their bed.

The other category was arson. That meant someone purposely started the fire and made sure the occupant could not escape.

It was my job to determine which one it was.

For me, most of the time it was either an accident or some type of structural issue. Out of date electrical, a water heater that was too old and exploded, insulation that caught fire from being around a heating source that went against building codes. Seven out of ten times it was not an arsonist, but someone still had to be held accountable for it.

I had helped to arrest over three hundred contractors and developers for their part in a deadly fire. All of which typically had the same excuse every single time: corners needed to be cut because they were on a tight budget and so they hired handymen instead of licensed professionals. Shady contractors cost the world more damage than most people even realized.

I made my way into the mostly burned down house to see Captain William Clark as well as one of his firefighters. The back of his coat said Colton. I had dealt with a lot of different fire houses in the city and it wasn't the first time I'd worked with Station House Twenty-One, but I hadn't worked with Colton before. I hadn't heard anything about him, but it was possible he was newer.

Captain Clark was known to be a tough captain. He was very professional and he was known to be distant. From what I had seen and based on what I had heard through the grapevine, he kept his men at arm's length, but I couldn't hold that against him.

I myself didn't have close friends, or any friends at all. I didn't let the people that I worked with get to know me. I preferred to keep that level of professionalism between us. I didn't want to get involved in their personal lives and I held no interest in having them poking their noses into mine.

Interestingly enough though, Captain Clark had allegedly been recently warming up to his men. I suspected it had to do with his new boyfriend, Noah Riley. He used to be a Federal Prosecutor but from what I had heard he was now a law professor at the University and he helped the Federal Protection Agency with special cases. Up until recently, Captain Clark had been in the closet and when he announced his relationship to Noah everyone at the office began talking about it.

I never contributed to the conversation. Mostly because I wasn't looking to get into a debate about having homosexuals in a First Responders position. Even though it was the twenty-first century, there were still homophobes everywhere. People often still had that stereotype of what a gay man looked and acted like, and it never tended to be a strong, muscular man who risked his life to save people.

I knew that it would be hard for the Captain. Even though he was a Captain, it wouldn't change the fact that people in the fire department would have an issue with him being gay. It would be even harder for those who came out as gay and were ranked lower. Unfortunately, an all men's club was not very welcoming to those who preferred the company of men to women.

"Captain," I said as I walked over to Captain Clark.

"Investigator Cole, it's nice to see you again. Though I wish it was for different circumstances. This is one of my newer guys, Hawke Colton. Hawke, this is Tristan Cole, one of the best fire investigators I've had the pleasure of working with."

Colton, or Hawke, turned around and I was instantly taken back by how attractive he was. He wasn't wearing a helmet so I could see that he had medium length, light brown hair. It had a slight wave to it and my fingers itched to run through it. His eyes were sky blue and he had high cheekbones. Honestly, he looked like he'd just walked off the cover of a firefighter calendar. As if Mr. June was standing right there in front of me. He gave me a warm smile that almost made my knees go weak.

"It's nice to meet you, Inspector Cole," Hawke said as he held his hand out for me to shake.

"It's nice to meet you." I clasped his hand in mine as I spoke. He was wearing his thick firefighter gloves, but even still when our hands touched I felt a wave of heat starting to spread up my arm from my hand. I had felt something like that before, but it was only skin on skin and it was never anything that intense.

Maybe I did need to get laid.

"What do we have?" I asked, trying to move on and forget about the warmth that was still lingering in my body even after he'd pulled his hand away.

"We have one body, a female, most likely the owner of the house. Local PD are asking around and trying to see if our victim was the only occupant in the house. At first glance, it appears that a candle was left on," Captain Clark started.

"Okay, but I'm here so I'm guessing that you decided the initial glance wasn't correct," I said as I took in the room.

Everything was black. The whole place had gone up and I knew that a house could effortlessly burn down without an accelerant being used. We'd come a long way in making safe products for our homes, but fabric was still flammable. Rugs could burn quickly, curtains, furniture. Almost everything in a home could work as its own accelerant without too much difficulty. All it needed was a flame to get them going. It made it very easy for inexperienced fire investigators to suspect arson when it was just a terrible accident. At the same time though, it was easy for an arsonist to use the items in their victim's home to make it burn hotter and faster. They could use what was already in the house to cover their tracks and get away with arson.

It was also a defense attorney's wet dream.

They loved to argue that we got it

wrong, that it was all an accident. It made our job harder, because we had to find additional evidence to make the case stick. Sometimes there wasn't additional evidence, because it was destroyed in the fire. Too many times arsonists got to walk and there was nothing we could do but keep going and hope the next time we could get them.

"Potentially. After the initial search, we started to look at the wiring and electrical boxes to see if they were the source of the fire. There are no obvious accelerants or origin of the fire, the electrical box, though, is telling a different story," Captain Clark said as he walked toward what was left of the back of the house.

"As you can see, the burn pattern is coming from the main electrical box. When we opened it, we expected to find frayed wires, clear evidence that it was overloaded. Only, we found this." Captain Clark held out a small metal rectangular device. It was all melted together, but I could see the different wire circuit built onto the device.

I had seen this before, and it was a signature that I knew all too well. The device worked as an incendiary device. The arsonist would place it within the electrical box and turn it on. It would slowly start to heat up and once it got hot enough, it caused the wires in the electrical box to start to melt and an electrical fire would be set in motion. Most of the time if it was discovered investigators or firefighters just assumed it was part of the electrical box and ignored it.

I knew better, though.

I had seen it before in the fire that took my parents' lives.

The arsonist had used that exact type of device.

"Have you found any type of camera in your search?" I asked.

The arsonist who killed my parents had been able to see his artwork with hidden cameras that he had placed all throughout the house. Finding those cameras had ultimately been the deciding factor on if my parents' fire was accidental or not.

The fire investigator had discarded the incendiary device that they found in the electrical box, the same device that I was currently holding. When he found the cameras, though, he knew something else was going on. They were hidden in places that people wouldn't put a surveillance camera.

The investigator had grilled me in the

hospital about everyone who had been in my house or had access to it. Nothing ever came from it and now the device and everything else sat in a box marked *cold case*, but I was determined to make sure it was marked *closed* one day.

"Not yet, we haven't done a full sweep. Do you suspect we'll find any?" Captain Clark asked, and I could hear the interest in his voice.

"If it's who I think it is, yes. You'll find them hidden within the walls in protective cases. They'll have burnt up in the fire, but you'll find melted plastic where it shouldn't be."

"We'll look through the debris and see what we can find. It's going to take the better part of the day. You won't have my report until tomorrow, at the earliest."

I nodded in acknowledgement of his words. I knew it would take some time for them to comb through everything. Fire was always a mess and firefighters, unfortunately, made it worse. I would be lucky if I was able to get the report tomorrow, it all depended on what they could find. I had what I needed for today, though. I had the device. Now I just needed to convince my boss that this was connected to my parents' fire.

***

Walking into my boss' office, I had already prepared myself for a war. This wasn't the first time I'd come to speak with my boss about a fire that I believed, that I *knew* in my gut, was connected to my parents' fire.

The cameras connected the crime scenes. They were a very specific brand of camera that had been discontinued fifteen years ago. I had been trying to track down wholesale or bulk purchases, but so far I was striking out. There had been over a hundred suppliers for the cameras and they subcontracted their products to other smaller shops. It was a mess and a very long list, but I wasn't going to give up.

The cameras connected my parents' killer to thirty-five other fires that I'd discovered so far. I didn't work every case and not all investigators liked to share. There were also fires that were investigated but deemed accidental. I suspected there were more, most likely they had been closed as accidental because the investigator missed something. I'd like to say that every investigator was a good one, but it was just like every other job. They had star employees, they had the employees that were middle of the road, and then they have the employees that were just there for the paycheck and didn't care.

"Tristan, what brings you in?"

My boss, Captain Damon Amaro, was thirty-eight and had been on the job since he was eighteen. He was a good man, single and no kids. He worked a lot and he didn't care for the political aspect of the job. Not that I could blame him. I never enjoyed having to play nice with others, either. I was also very bad at it. It's why I would never make Captain. I didn't see the point in kissing someone's ass. If I was good at my job, then it shouldn't matter what social skills I had. My promotion shouldn't be connected to how many parties I went to or how many times I play golf with the boys. Not that I play golf. Hell, I couldn't hit a golf ball if my life depended on it.

"A fire at 1583 Bartlett Street is going to be marked as arson. This device was found in the electrical box," I started as I placed the evidence bag down on his desk.

"How many people know about these things," he asked as he examined the device.

"Captain Clark is looking now for any cameras. I suspect he will find at least ten like the other crime scenes." I stopped as he held his hand up and cut me off.

"You don't know that. We've had this conversation before, Tristan. Not every arsonist who uses this device is the same arsonist that killed your parents. I don't have to tell you the likelihood of this being the same arsonist."

"I understand that, Captain, but if the cameras are found and it comes back as the same cameras from the other thirty-five cases, that's a huge coincidence that you can't ignore," I countered.

"Even if I were to entertain this farfetched idea, you have to look at the facts, Tristan. Thirty-five cases with cameras that were sold by a lot of stores and suppliers. Not all of those fires had this device used, and there have been other fires that did use this device and there were no cameras. Even if I considered this theory the only way it could be the same arsonist is if he started in his early teens for the fire at your parents' house or he's well into his sixties now. You know the odds on that. We've discussed this. Every time cameras are found you try and see a connection to your parents' murder. I can't keep having this dialogue with you, Tristan. It's time you finally dealt with what happened to you growing up. Now, do I need to put you on administrative leave so you can get some help, or will you finally go and speak to a therapist?"

He was never going to believe me. I knew that, I did. No one was ever going to believe me because he was right. Arsonists typically didn't tend to live that long. If they didn't get arrested, their own fire killed them. And this arsonist was changing up his method all the time, but the one thing that stayed consistent was the cameras.

The guy had a huge body count and I knew he wasn't going to stop until we caught him. He was too smart to get eaten by his own fire. The only way to stop him would be to finally catch him. And the only way my boss or anyone was going to believe me was with irrefutable proof and it was on me to find it.

"No Sir, you don't need to put me on leave. Now if that is all, Sir, I have paperwork."

He didn't want to believe me. That was fine. I would prove it, because I was not going to allow the man responsible for my parents' death, for the death of fifty-eight people, to go unpunished. They all deserved justice and I would make sure they got it, even if it killed me.

CHAPTER FOUR

Hawke

IT HAD BEEN one of those days where all I wanted to do was go and get a stiff drink. Twelve-hour shifts were always hard, but it was worse when your shift started with a dead body.

There was this old superstition of sorts that every firehouse had. If your shift started off with a successful fire—meaning the house was saved and no one died or was hurt—then your shift was going to be easy. If your shift started with a failed fire—meaning the house was destroyed or someone died—then your shift was going to be a nightmare and make you beg for the end of the day to arrive.

Today had only solidified the superstition in full force.

EVIE RILEY

After the fire this morning, we had been going non-stop all day. There was a factory fire that burned so hot we lost the building completely and eighteen people had to be sent to the hospital for minor burns and smoke inhalation. Before we even made it back to the firehouse, we were sent on another call for a car crash that involved ten cars and a transport truck. The transport truck driver had hit a car that, according to witnesses, had cut the truck off and the truck driver couldn't stop in time. That driver we had to literally scrape off of the road. The truck driver was fine, but the truck went up in flames. The other cars were total losses and every person in the cars, all twenty of them, had to get some form of medical attention. And all of that was before lunchtime. After twelve hours, I was more than ready for a drink. Thankfully, I had a whole bottle of whiskey at home calling my name.

I headed out and made my way to my truck. Tomorrow was my day off and I was looking forward to the break. Twelve-hour shifts weren't easy. I had gotten used to them, for the most part, but sometimes it wasn't easy getting through the long shifts. Being a firefighter was just like any other job in that sense. Some days the hours flew by and others the time crawled by, it felt like you had been there for twelve days without an end in sight. Today had been one of those felt like forever days and I was looking forward to spending the day tomorrow just relaxing and recuperating after the trying day today.

What I had not expected was to see Investigator Cole standing next to my truck. He looked tired, drawn and disappointed maybe, but I could also see the determination in his eyes even from my short distance away. It was clear something must have happened and he must need some type of help from me. I couldn't help but wonder if it had to do with the body we found this morning.

I was still having a hard time with what I had seen. It wasn't the first time I had seen a dead body in a fire, of course. Hell, it wasn't even the thirtieth, but for some reason the image of her body was trapped in my mind. I knew it had only just happened roughly twelve hours ago and my mind still needed time to process it, but for some reason I felt like I would carry the woman's death with me for the rest of my life.

I was usually pretty good at moving on from a bad fire. Not holding on to any of the images or the people. Every firefighter was taught to not carry the victims with you, whether they survived or not. We didn't check up on patients, we didn't follow up with any of the investigations unless we were asked for assistance. That had happened before where we needed to take a fire investigator back to the crime scene and help walk them through it again. But we had always been taught to see the crime scenes as just evidence. The bodies are evidence, the destruction is evidence, and none of that needs to have an emotional attachment to it. More often than not, I could keep myself objective and distant from the crime scenes, from the deaths, and yet this time around I was having a harder time. I couldn't help but suspect that it had something to do with Investigator Tristan Cole.

The man was very attractive; anyone would have to be a fool to not see that. It was more than just his very attractive face and body. There was something in his eyes, a pain there. I could tell he was trying to hide it, trying to continue living his life as if he was like everyone else, but I could see it.

How could I miss it?

I saw that pain in my own eyes every time I looked at a mirror. It was the pain from a hard upbringing. The pain from not belonging anywhere, not feeling love like all of the other children did. It was not easy to live with and it often left me feeling like there was this giant hole in my chest. For the longest time I felt like I was never going to belong anywhere. That everyone could see the hole inside of me and they were all judging me for it. It took a long time before I was able to finally feel complete. Sure, there are days where I still feel like there is this huge piece of me missing, but for the most part, I finally felt whole. Being a firefighter and having brothers in my life had helped me greatly. Based on the look in Tristan's eyes, though, he didn't have anyone in his corner to help ease the pain he felt.

"Investigator Cole, what can I do for you," I asked once I was close enough.

"I'm sorry to drop by unannounced. I need some off-the-books help. All of the other investigators who I've spoken to have all said that you are one of the best firefighters they have worked with. They actually said they were surprised that you weren't an investigator yourself."

"I prefer the work on the front line."

I never thought I would ever be good at investigative work, but I had learned pretty quickly that I was observant and that helped in investigations. I was also good at reading people. Both of which was a direct result of growing up in foster care. If you weren't good at reading people and being observant, then you were at a great risk of being hurt. I had been hurt plenty of times before I learned that lesson.

It wasn't unusual for other fire investigators to speak with me about a case they were working. They would ask me to review their case file or walk through the crime scene to see if something was missed. I didn't mind doing it. When a crime had been committed or when a terrible accident occurred, everyone involved deserved to know the truth. If I could help them discover the truth, I was all for it. However, I did prefer to work in the firehouse alongside my brothers. I loved going into the fires and helping to stop them and save lives. That was who I was and I wasn't about to change that for a desk job, even one as important and rewarding as fire investigations.

"So I've heard. I have also heard that you are very good for someone who has been on the front lines as little of a time as you have been. People say you were born to be a firefighter. You have a knack for seeing patterns, for spotting things that other investigators have missed or overlooked. I'd hoped perhaps you would consider lending me that skill set with a case I am working on."

I'd suspected he was there for help on a case, but it still hurt to hear my suspicions confirmed. I would have been very interested if he'd wished to see me outside of work for a more personal matter. I didn't know if I was ready for a relationship after my latest disaster of one, but I was very much interested in getting back on the horse, so to speak.

I had a feeling Tristan had one hell of a horse to hop on.

Of course, this very sexy man just wanted me for my mind, typical story of my life, and there was a very good chance Tristan wasn't even gay. I didn't know much of anything about him. Nothing, really. I hadn't asked around about him or anything, but when I did work with other investigators none of them had ever mentioned anything about him, either. A good number of investigators had spoken about others, gossiped, really.

It was funny, in high school people told themselves that the gossiping would stop once they graduated, only to find that it didn't ever stop. It actually got worse as an adult. The problems that the other students were gossiping about in school were minute compared to the adult problems they had. Because of that, the gossip usually spread faster and it could be like trying to walk through a minefield without a map.

"I'm always happy to help out with an investigation. Is it the one from this morning?"

"It is. Amanda Rollins, thirty-five, single, no kids. She had a younger sibling but she died in a car accident five years ago. Her parents are both alive and are local. I have already spoken with them and they are hopeful for answers," Tristan started.

"Do you have any leads?"

Arson was one of the funny crimes, not that killing someone in a fire is funny, but it could be both personal and distant. An arsonist could target a home because they had a grudge against someone or the person represented someone else they had a grudge against, much like a serial killer killing only middle-aged redheads. However, arsonists could also target a home because it was convenient and easy to get to. They didn't always have an agenda of killing someone, often it was just an unfortunate side effect from the fire. An arsonist's only goal was to make a big fire and watch it eat everything in its path. Ms. Rollins' arsonist could be either option, and the first step to an arson investigation was to determine whether it was an opportunity or personal.

"Sort of, it's a bit complicated. My gut is telling me that Ms. Rollins was another victim to a long-time arsonist that I have been trying to find for the past fifteen years. There are possibly thirty-five additional arson cases that are connected to him. I have been working on these cases for years and I could use some fresh eyes on it. I'm hoping you might be able to see something that I can use to point me in a direction of who this arsonist is."

That was interesting. If he'd been working on catching a single arsonist for fifteen years that meant one of two things. One, either the arsonist was incredibly intelligent, so much so that he was able to operate for so long without ever getting caught. Or two, he didn't exist and Tristan was chasing an invisible man. I didn't know him well enough to know if he was after a ghost or a real person, but either way I couldn't turn him down. He deserved to know the answer and if this arsonist was real, we had to stop him before someone else was killed by him.

This time it was one woman, but the next time it could be a whole family, and that wasn't something I could allow to happen.

"I'm always happy to give the Investigative Unit a hand. I can meet you tomorrow at your office, if you want."

"I actually hoped we could meet at my apartment tonight. I know it's short notice."

It was very short notice and I wasn't certain I wanted to go over to his place tonight. I wanted that drink of whiskey. Hell, I wanted five of them, preferably with pizza. The last thing I wanted to do was go over to his place and look through case files of dead people.

And yet, that seemed to be the one thing Tristan really wanted to do.

I could say no. Tell him that I could go by tomorrow and we could look them over. However, I suspected that even if I said tomorrow he would just go home and look through them himself all night.

It was the last thing I wanted to do, but I knew it was the *right* thing to do.

"I'll follow you," I said and nodded.

"I appreciate it," he said, flashing me a small friendly smile.

I hated that a tiny smile from the man brought warmth to my heart and lower. Spending time with Tristan was stupid on my part. Dangerous even. I would have to make sure we got this case wrapped up quickly before I ended up catching feelings for the man. Something I suspected would end about as well as my relationship with Paul. Even if Tristan was gay, he was most likely in the closet like Paul was.

I didn't want to put myself into that position again.

Even if he worked for the Investigations Unit, I knew that it would be just like working on the front lines. The environment would be no different to someone working as a police officer or firefighter. Nope, I refused to be in that position again. I couldn't go through feeling that way any longer. I couldn't sit back and suffer like a dirty secret, and not in the *fun dirty* kind of way. The kind of dirty where if said secret came to light, the only thing I'd be left feeling was shame. I couldn't go through that twice, no matter what.

Tristan headed over to his car and I climbed into my truck. I sat there and looked into the rearview mirror as I waited for when he was ready to head off. As I sat there, I could feel my body getting tired. The exhaustion from the day was setting in now that I was sitting. I was once again questioning if going over to Tristan's place was a good idea tonight. My body and mind were tired and in desperate need of a break, not to mention sleep. Going to Tristain's and looking over old case files was not going to give me the rest I needed, but I did have tomorrow off. With any luck, it would only take a few hours and I could be back home tonight for that drink that I wanted. I could sleep in tomorrow and do all of it with a clear conscience knowing that I had helped Tristan, hopefully, find a lead on his arson case.

I cranked the key and turned my truck on, pulling out onto the road behind Tristan. With any luck, tonight would go smoothly and I would be home before I knew it.

CHAPTER FIVE

Tristan

AS I MADE the drive to my apartment, I couldn't help but start to question if I was making the right call. I had wanted some fresh eyes to go over the past cases and from what I had heard about Hawke, he was a great set of eyes. He was relatively new to the fire department, so he hadn't had time to build a political agenda or deep alliances with anyone. From everything I had been told, he was a man who wanted to help people and had no problem telling someone the truth. I guess I needed that more than anything right now. For someone else to look over these cases and either tell me I was onto something or I was insane. I didn't even know what result I was rooting for.

Maybe my Captain was right. Maybe I

was seeing connections that weren't really there because I wanted so desperately to find the man responsible for my parents' death. I didn't know anymore.

I knew the cameras were used in all thirty-five cases that I had discovered so far. I knew that they were from a discontinued line fifteen years ago. I didn't think it was a coincidence that they were present in all of those cases. I knew anyone could purchase them, at least fifteen years ago they could, but what would be the odds of these people having these cameras in their homes without it being connected to the same arsonist?

That was why I needed a new set of eyes. I needed someone to tell me that they believed me. That I was not crazy or seeing things that just didn't matter. I didn't know if Hawke would be my saving grace, but I was really hoping he would be.

Hawke was something else, too. Everyone that I spoke to about him all had nice things to say. A first-class guy who was looking to help people, do something good in this world. He hadn't been in the department for long, but what he'd managed to do in that short time had been impressive.

He was impressive.

I didn't trust people often; it took a lot for me to build a deep level of trust with someone. And I never trusted anyone without knowing them, but for some reason my gut was telling me I could trust Hawke. I wasn't certain I was ready to listen to my gut on that just yet, but I was willing to bring Hawke in and see what he could pick up.

A few investigators had said it was like his parents knew he would be observant, and that was why they named him Hawke. I wasn't too sure how observant Hawke would be, but I was willing to give him a shot. After all, it wasn't like I had anything to lose at this point. Either I found evidence that would allow me to keep investigating these fires with my Captain's permission. Or I didn't find any evidence and I was right back to where I started. I could only go up from here and it was worth the shot.

I knew my Captain would not tolerate it all for much longer. He was already at the point where he wanted to put me on leave for therapy treatment. If that happened there was no telling what could happen to my career. Once you got a report like that in your file, it followed you everywhere you went. Every time I was up for promotion, it would be there. If I were ever being investigated, it would be there and would be used against me. I would become the *unstable investigator* and that was a legal risk waiting to happen. I couldn't let that happen, which meant Hawke was my last chance to find something that I could use as evidence to prove my theory.

When I arrived at my apartment, I parked in the first spot I could find on the street. It wasn't until that moment that I realized I would be having Hawke in my apartment. I didn't have people in my apartment. I didn't have friends. I didn't have coworkers who would come by to drop off files or have coffee.

I liked being alone.

I was good at alone.

When I was alone, I didn't have to try and explain myself. I didn't have to justify my actions. I didn't have to try and explain to anyone why I didn't have photos all over my walls or proper furniture for company. I also didn't have to deal with any of the pitying looks when they saw my boards for my parents' investigation. I hadn't been planning on having Hawke over to my apartment, but it just made sense to meet at my apartment as opposed to my office or a bar. Hopefully, Hawke wouldn't ask too many questions and we could just go over the files.

Letting out a sigh, I admitted to myself there really was nothing I could do about it now. I climbed out of my car and strode over to the entrance of my apartment building. I glanced down the street and saw Hawke's truck pull into another parking spot.

The area that I lived in wasn't the best and I really hoped Hawke wasn't the type to question everything. I didn't need to live in a nice area. I didn't need to have fancy furniture and decorations. I just needed my work and a place to do it in. I was simple in that sense and I was perfectly fine with it. The more people someone had in their life the more distractions they had, and I couldn't afford to have any distractions in my hunt for my parents' killer.

Hawke climbed out of his truck and made the short walk over to me, with a short nod as he approached. I pulled open the front door, letting him enter the building in front of me, and we made our way over to the stairs in silence.

I was relieved when he didn't say anything about the lack of elevator or what the place looked like. I knew the apartment building wasn't the best, but it could have been a lot worse. There were no dirty needles, bugs, or mice in the building, so that was something at least. Maybe that wouldn't seem like much to most people, but to me that was all that mattered. Places like this, the neighbors didn't want to get to know you. They didn't want to make awkward and unnecessary small talk in the hallways. They liked to keep to themselves and that was exactly what I wanted.

When we arrived at my apartment, I unlocked the multiple locks that I had before I walked in and flicked the light on. I knew my living room left a lot to be desired, but the only thing that really mattered was my working boards.

"Are these the cases?" Hawke asked as he eyed the boards.

"I have the individual case files, but yes, they are the cases. Thirty-five of them spanning over twenty-one years. I've been working on them for fifteen years."

"And how long have you been working for the investigative division?"

"Fifteen years. Since I was eighteen."

"Most of these cases are closed. Why are you looking into them?"

I could hear the skepticism in his voice. I couldn't blame him for it. Most had been closed marked accidental. The investigators believed that the fires were started from faulty electrical wires or a space heater. Something that wasn't caused by an individual. My gut told me that they were wrong, though. That all of these cases and possibly more were connected to the same arsonist who killed my parents.

I spoke as I went over to the crime scene photos that still haunted my nightmares. "They were my parents. The case is still unsolved and when I became an investigator, I started to look into it. The original investigator marked in his report that he found these small hidden cameras throughout different parts of the house." I pointed out the multiple photos of the devices on the board. "He assumed they were security cameras, but they weren't. We never had any. My parents never believed we needed a security system. Most of the time they never locked the door. We lived in a safe neighborhood. The kind of neighborhood where everyone knew everyone. There were never cameras. The investigator never found a cause for the fire, so it's been left as unsolved and sits in the cold case room."

I did everything I could to keep the emotions out of my voice. I didn't want

Hawke thinking I was running some type of vendetta. Or that I was the kind of victim who couldn't let it go, who couldn't accept that accidents happened and we all had to find a way to move on.

My Captain had already suggested that my parents most likely purchased the cameras for security and had just never told me so I wouldn't worry or be scared. And maybe they would have purchased something like that without informing me, but I knew my parents. I wasn't a little kid when they'd been killed. I was twelve. I had been old enough to understand the need for a security system. That just wasn't the life we lived.

Someone had started that fire. Someone had put the cameras in and someone had killed my parents, almost killing me. I wasn't crazy. There was simply no way there could be the same connection in thirty-five cases and for it to be a coincidence. I just couldn't, wouldn't believe that. The odds of that even happening were astronomical. I was right, I knew I was. I just needed someone else to believe it, too.

"I'm sorry about your parents," Hawke said in that pitying tone that I hated.

"Don't. Don't do that. I don't need pity. I don't need that tone and that look in your eyes. The one that says, '*oh that poor guy, can't move on from his parents' death.*' I don't need it and I don't want it. I'm not holding on to something that isn't there. I'm not trying to see patterns that don't exist. I've just hit a wall and I'm hoping a fresh set of eyes will help me see around it."

I didn't do pity and I sure as shit wasn't going take it from him. I didn't know what his life was like, but I did know that he didn't come across to me as someone who understood how much life could suck.

I'd had a perfect life, up until I was twelve when the world decided it was time to swallow me whole. I was still waiting for the gate to open so I could finally leave Hell. It was why I was hunting down this arsonist so strongly. If I could catch him. If I could finally get justice for my parents, myself, and everyone else this man had hurt, then maybe, just maybe, I could find some peace at last. I could finally get out of the hell I had been trapped in since I was twelve years old.

Hawke held his hands up in a mock surrender as he spoke. "Hey, I'm not judging and I sure as shit am not pitying you. I don't know what it's like to lose my parents, especially in something like this.

Fuck, I don't even know what it feels like to have parents. I couldn't imagine having them and then losing them like that. I do not pity you, but that doesn't change that I'm sorry you had to lose them. I'm always happy to help, especially if you think this guy has been setting fires for twenty-one years. I don't know how much help I'll be, but I'm always willing to listen."

I couldn't contain the mental sigh that flooded my mind. I shouldn't have snapped at him like that. My emotions were more tightly wound than I'd thought. I was obviously closer to the edge then I'd thought. I knew I needed to get a grip on myself before my Captain saw it too, and I was given a one-way ticket on the Shrink train.

I also picked up on the fact that he'd said he didn't know what it felt like to have parents. I didn't know anything personal about the man but now I couldn't help but wonder what his life had been like.

Did he not know what it felt like to have parents because they were never there?

Did he grow up with a family member or in the foster care system?

Or did he have parents and they were just checked out?

I knew from some kids at school that they'd had parents who didn't even talk to them for weeks. That always felt so odd to me.

How could your own parents not say anything to you for weeks?

My parents and I had always talked. We talked at breakfast at the table every morning. We talked at dinner at the table every evening. On weekends we would hang out and talk, watch movies together. We were a family that enjoyed spending time together, so anything else always felt so weird to me, and sad.

As much as I wanted to know Hawke's story, I knew now was not the time. I had to focus all of my efforts on solving these cases. Anything other than this case right now was irrelevant and unimportant.

"I'm sorry for snapping at you, that was unprofessional," I said to try and clear the air.

"It's all good. What makes you think they are all connected?" Hawke asked, keeping his voice even and professional. The air had been cleared and we could get back on track.

"The same cameras that were in my parents' case are in all of these cases. And these are just the ones that have reported about finding the cameras."

"We found cameras at Ms. Rollins' place," Hawke stated as he turned to look at the other crime scene photos.

"Ten of them. All of the cameras can be traced back to the same brand that was discontinued fifteen years ago. Some of the cases the fire appeared to be started from an accident. A lot of them are assumed to be an electrical fire, but the same device that was discovered at Ms. Rollins' home was discovered in twenty of the other cases. I suspect it was also at the other fifteen, but the investigator or firefighters didn't know to look for it. Most people just assume it's part of the electrical panel and ignore it," I explained.

"All of the cases except your parents' were marked accidental and closed. What made your parents' case different?"

"Investigator David Hopkins was one of the good ones. If a fire was caused by an electrical accident, and someone was killed, he went after the last electrician who touched the house. He came from a long line of contractors and it infuriated him that unlicensed electricians worked on people's homes. My parents had an electrician, Skip, in two weeks before the fire. They wanted to update the kitchen lighting. Hopkins brought him back to the house and made him walk through the whole place and looked at everything. When Skip explained what he needed to do to the electrical box to change out the cords, he noticed the device and told Hopkins that he needed to be looking for an arsonist."

"And Hopkins believed him?" Hawke asked, slightly skeptical. Not that I could blame him. Just because one electrician said something didn't belong, that didn't mean he was right.

"Hopkins brought the device to his father, who had been a licensed electrician for thirty plus years. His father said the same thing, that the device would never be used by any electrician, licensed or otherwise."

"Okay, and you said the device can cause the wires to overheat and start a fire. Is that something that anyone can Google?"

"Today, yes, but not twenty-one years ago. I have always suspected that the arsonist had electrical training to be able to make the device. The parts are untraceable, even the parts that aren't fully destroyed."

"What about the houses or the people? Was there anything that connected them to each other?"

"No. Completely different areas of the

city, lifestyle, family situation, some were killed and others were badly burned."

That was the frustrating part, because I couldn't find anything that was similar between the cases. The only thing that truly connected them all was the cameras. It was a weak link and I knew that was why my Captain wasn't interested in reopening the cases and telling the city we had a serial arsonist. I needed something more solid. Something that couldn't be explained away by a mere coincidence.

"So the only thing that connects them is the cameras and these devices in the homes they were found in."

"I know it's not much to work with, and I know people assume I am reaching, looking for my parents' killer in every case that I come across, but I find it very odd that these cameras are in so many homes. Homes that friends have said didn't have any security cameras or system in place. I have called every security company in the city and they didn't have any customers under their names. There was no reason for those cameras to be there," I explained.

"Where does their footage go, do you know?"

"The company is no longer around. I

have been trying to track down the wholesalers that could have had some left over, but they all distribute to other stores. So far, I haven't been able to get a list of customers or even all of the stores that might still have some in stock. What little information there is about the cameras online, it states that the cameras don't record footage, you can only watch it live. They were popular for doorbell cameras and nanny cams."

"Until new technology showed up on the scene. It makes sense though, that these cameras would still be used. There's no way to trace them back to a server. And there is no one that has had access to all of the homes?"

"I have checked mail carriers, delivery drivers, friends, coworkers, contractors, the kid that shoveled their driveways. There is no one that had access to all of these homes." And that was beyond frustrating. I knew it wasn't going to be easy, but I had been hoping for something.

"I don't know how much help I'll be, but I do agree with you. It's too much of a coincidence that these outdated cameras are in so many homes. One or two, sure, but not thirty-five. I thought arsonists don't last this long, though?"

It was a huge relief that Hawke was seeing what I was. It only confirmed what I had hoped, that I wasn't losing my mind. I knew we had one hell of a climb ahead of us though, but at least we could make that climb together.

"Typically they only last a few years, five at most before they are caught either by police or by their own fire. It is rare for someone to last twenty-one years. He would have had to have started young or he's in his sixties and still starting fires. It's also possible that he has an apprentice that he's taught his trade to and they have taken up the mantle."

"That's true. They do love to teach and share with each other. But if it is two arsonists, that's going to make finding them even harder."

No truer words. I had never had a pair of arsonists before. Arsonists were narcissists. They only cared about themselves and they never shared trade secrets. That was, until they were more seasoned. When they started to feel like the walls were closing in on them or they were getting too old to keep starting fires, they took on someone young and moldable to teach so they could live out their desires through a patsy. That was my fear, that the man who killed my parents was teaching someone else, and based on the case files, this was a deadly pair and neither of them were going to stop until they were caught. The best I could hope for was that the teacher was dead and we just had to worry about the apprentice. Still, I was hoping this was the work of one arsonist. That would make everything simpler for the investigation and court proceedings should we get that far. Arson was hard enough to prove in court, the last thing we needed was them both trying to pin the fires on the other person.

"The strongest case we have is Ms. Rollins'. It's the newest and the freshest. If we can find something in her case that we can then link to another, we can establish an evidence pattern."

"Let's get started then," Hawke said flashing me an easy smile.

"Pizza?" I asked as I pulled out my phone.

"I never say no to pizza," Hawke said with a playful grin and a wink that made my stomach flip flop and heat fill my veins.

I needed his help to try and find my parents' killer, but now I was starting to second guess spending this much time with him. I was potentially putting myself in a situation that I wasn't going to survive emotionally. It was too late, though. I needed help and so far, Hawke was the only one with an open enough mind to help me. I just had to be careful. I had to keep things professional and not let his perfect smile throw me off my game.

I could do that.

After all, how hard could it be?

CHAPTER SIX

Hawke

"OH MAN, THESE cases are all starting to blur together," I said, feeling weary as I rubbed my burning, overworked eyes for what felt like the hundredth time tonight.

I was used to working long hours. I was used to running off little to no sleep. But what I wasn't used to was working those long hours and then trying to read tiny print for five hours straight right afterward. This was going to be more challenging and exhausting than I had originally anticipated, that was for sure.

We had nothing but the cameras and the devices that were discovered in most of the homes. It should have been enough, but Tristan's Captain wanted something more. He wasn't convinced, not that I could blame him too much. It could be a coincidence that these homes all had the same cameras in them. They could be explained away, and without any survivors any good defense attorney could get them thrown out as evidence. The same could be said for the device. We could have ten electricians that would testify the device was not standard and the defense could have their own electricians who explained it away. We had no suspects, no motives, no connections, nothing that would give us a pattern to present to his Captain to get these cases reopened.

His Captain was going to be another challenge. He wasn't my Captain, but that didn't change that he was a captain and out-ranked the both of us. Even if I didn't work for him directly, I still had to listen to him.

Tristan didn't say that his Captain had ordered him to stand down, but it was implied and we both knew it. His Captain was not looking to have these cases reopened and I knew it was a combination of him believing that Tristan had lost his mind and was chasing ghosts. But he was also worried about the ramifications of reopening these closed cases, cases that were closed as accidental, and having them investigated for arson. It wouldn't stay quiet for long and eventually, the press would get word about it, bringing questions and potentially embarrassment to the department. If Tristan was right, and my gut was telling me he was onto something, it wasn't going to reflect well on the department and that was something the Upper Brass never handled well. It would be nice to say that the Upper Brass wouldn't want to sweep this under the rug, but they would if they could get away with it. They would arrest this arsonist for Ms. Rollins' death and allow the others to remain closed due to accidental fire. No one would be any of the wiser except for the people involved in the investigation.

It was a bit shady, but the Upper Brass were all political-minded people and they focused on making sure the person above them was happy, and at the top of that pyramid was the Mayor. People would think that the Mayor would want to make sure the city was safe, that the people he represented were safe in their homes especially. However, if the crime rate went up while he was in office, it didn't look good for his re-election.

After all, who would want someone in office who would lie and hide things from the people?

"I'm sorry, I know it's getting late and you just worked a twelve hour shift," Tristan said apologetically, his concern and understanding clear in his red-rimmed eyes.

He didn't have anything to be sorry for, though. He didn't ask for this arsonist to be this big of a pain in the ass. Usually, he would have a team helping him, but with his Captain not looking to investigate he was on his own.

Or more accurately, we were on our own.

That was okay though, because I was confident that we would solve this case, one way or another. Even if we couldn't get the arsonist on the other cases, we could get him for Ms. Rollins' case and that would get him put behind bars for life. The other victims would get justice by proxy, which was not ideal, of course, but it was better than nothing. Not very comforting to the surviving victims or the deceased victims' loved ones, but unfortunately justice didn't always come with a straight arrow. Sometimes you had to accept the roundabout option.

"It's fine. I can tell you have been pulling double or triple shifts working on this case, too. It can't be easy on you to have to go through all of this on your own. To repeatedly look at the crime scene photos from your parents' fire."

I couldn't imagine having to go through my parents' file, to see their crime scene photos, to see their charred bodies. I couldn't decide if it made him incredibly strong or incredibly disturbed. He literally had their photos pinned to a board in his living room. He would see it every time he walked into the room or sat on his couch.

The room was another thing. I didn't need to be a therapist to know that he was going through something. There were no personal items in the room. I didn't know if he had anything in his bedroom, but I suspected not. The furniture was old and clearly bought second-hand a very long time ago. The place was small and the area he was living in was one-step above criminal. It felt like someone that didn't know what a home was, which didn't make much sense because from what I'd read about his parents, they came across as loving people. No one had a bad thing to say about any of them, which was rare.

I could relate to him struggling with making a home for himself. When I aged out of the foster care system, I didn't know what to do. I had spent so many years dreaming about having my own place, that when it finally happened I had no idea what to do. I had no idea how to turn an apartment into a home.

I can still remember my first apartment, it was a studio apartment about five hundred square feet in the most disgusting building I had ever been in still to this day. There were mice, cockroaches, and dirty needles everywhere. I woke up with new bug bites every day. At the time though, it was my own personal Heaven, because no one was trying to hurt me. I didn't try to turn it into a home, nor the next five apartments after that.

When I finally got my house that was when I wanted to make it into something real. I wanted to turn it into a home, my first home, and it took me a good couple of years before I finally figured out how to make it a real home.

It seemed like Tristan was going through that himself. The file never said what happened to him after the fire. I knew he was twelve at the time of the fire, but that was all I knew.

A deep fear spread through my body at the thought that he might have been placed in the foster care system as well. It would explain why he was having a harder time adjusting. It didn't seem like he had many friends. None of the investigators that I had worked with before had ever mentioned him. Keeping to himself was a classic sign that someone grew up in a foster home. Foster homes could get pretty rough and sometimes it was safer to stick to yourself and keep your head down. Now I had more questions and none of them were about any of these case files.

"I'm used to operating with little sleep," he said with a small shrug as he pulled his sleeves up just slightly.

He wore a long sleeved shirt, but that slight pull was enough for me to be able to see the raised scars that were around his left wrist. Before my mind even registered what I was doing, I reached out and gently took his left wrist in my hand. I felt him flinch for a second at the sudden contact, but he didn't pull his wrist away. I carefully pulled his sleeve up further and I could see the scaring covered his whole left forearm.

"You were there," I said softly as I looked into his eyes. I didn't let go of his wrist though. I wasn't ready to give up the contact for reasons I wasn't prepared to think about.

"There's that tone again," he said softly

as well.

I could tell he didn't like pity, not that I was giving him pity right now. I would never pity him. He was one of the strongest men I had ever met. He survived a fire that took the lives of his parents. A fire that odds were he wasn't going to make it out just like his parents never did. And instead of letting that dictate his life and destroy him, he'd dedicated his life to hunting down arsonists. It also made sense why he was so determined to solve his parents' murder. It was almost his.

"You'll never get pity from me, Tris. You're a survivor, the last thing you deserve is pity for it," I said with complete strength to my voice. I was not going to tolerate having him think that I pitied him for any of this. He was a survivor and that made him courageous.

"People don't know. I'd like to keep it that way."

"They won't hear it from me. Can I ask why you kept it a secret?"

It wasn't any of my business and I would completely understand if he didn't want to answer me. It was obviously a very painful night for him physically, mentally, and emotionally. It was probably the worst day of his life and having a constant reminder of it wouldn't have been easy. Knowing that he was there, and not just standing outside in horror as it happened, but actually in the house, it made a lot of sense why he was struggling. Why he lived well below his means; why he didn't have anything personal in this place. He didn't just lose his parents at the age of twelve, he almost lost his own life, and as a reward for surviving he had a scared arm that would always bring up those painful memories.

"I don't like pity and I don't like looks of sympathy. I got it enough when I was in the hospital. When people see it, they look at me with pity and then they ask me what happened. I don't need to tell the story a hundred times. It's just easier to keep it hidden," he answered with a small shrug.

"I get that. You shouldn't have to feel like you have something to hide. You shouldn't have to deal with all of the questions or looks. At the same time, I get why you are hiding it, because people will ask. People are naturally curious and they don't often think twice about asking someone a personal question. It's still not fair to you, though."

I knew from speaking with other fire survivors on this job that oftentimes it was the questions that they were constantly being asked that were the hardest part of recovery. Everyone always looked at the scars. They always assumed what happened. They made up stories in their mind and then they went and asked what happened to see if they were right. Survivors had no choice but to either keep the scars hidden or deal with the looks and questions for the rest of their life. It wasn't fair, but life rarely was. Even still, knowing that it was happening to Tristan, it made me angry. He didn't deserve to go through that level of pain. He didn't deserve the constant reminder and having to always keep it hidden or be subjected to harassment, even if the harassment wasn't malicious intent.

"Life never is. My Captain knows about me being in the fire, but that's it. I know my coworkers could know, they are used to being around people with scars from their investigations. But I don't want to be the investigator who is there because they are chasing their own justice. I don't want them to question my reason for being an investigator."

"Would they really question it? I mean, I know of guys who are firefighters that had been in a fire growing up. It's what made them decide to be a firefighter in the first place. Aren't there other investigators who have been through something similar?"

It wasn't unheard of for there to be a firefighter that had personal experience with a fire before they were on the job. Sometimes it was them in the fire and others it was a loved one that was hurt by a fire. That close call or encounter was what fueled their desire to be a firefighter. To help people survive something that had affected their own life so deeply. I couldn't imagine it would be a problem for the investigator division.

"Maybe. I don't know. It's not something that I have asked around about. I keep things professional, it's easier that way."

"I can understand that. I'm different in that sense. I grew up in the foster care system. I spent eighteen years being distant and trying to keep my nose clean, head down, and just get through each day. When I got out and got my first real job, I wanted to know everything about everyone I worked with. I like building personal connections. I don't have a hundred friends, I have a lot of acquaintances, but the close friends that I have, I know everything about them and the other way around," I said as I ran my thumb along the bottom of his wrist. I really should've let go of his wrist, but I couldn't bring myself to do it. He wasn't pulling away and I took that as a good sign.

"So you're close to the guys at the firehouse?"

"They're my brothers. That was my thing. After being on my own for so long, after not having a family, I wanted one so badly. I went from job to job just trying to find one that would fit and give me that family I was craving. Then I just happened to be in the right place at the right time when a car accident occurred. The one driver was trapped and I stayed with them until the EMT guys and firemen showed up. I remember standing off to the side just watching them work after that. The way they helped the victims. They way they interacted with each other. But at the end, when everyone was taken care of, they had warm smiles on their faces and a few of the guys gave each other a side hug. I could tell they were a family and I wanted that more than anything. I did a drive by at their station a few days later and I fell in love with it. The fear of running into a burning building wasn't enough to keep me away and I signed up that day," I explained, flashing him a warm smile.

"People at work say the firehouses are all like family. I wasn't certain I believed it. It's nice to hear that it's true. I'm happy that you found a home," he offered, returning the smile, but I could also see the longing in his eyes.

Tristan might not be ready to have a home, but he wanted one and that was a good sign. It meant that he still had dreams. That he had the desire to have more in his life than just case files. I was not a therapist in any shape or form, but I knew PTSD when I saw it. I had seen it from veterans and from guys on the job. Fire had a way of bringing trauma and Tristan had gone through a fire that killed his parents. Hell, the house was basically dust by the time the firefighters got it under control. Everything he had would have been destroyed. He had nothing but the memories of his parents and unfortunately, those fade over time.

"I know we just technically met and you have no reason to trust me at all, but if you ever wanted to talk about what happened, I'll always listen. Or if you ever want to not be alone, to just sit with someone in the quiet, I'll be there for that, too."

I knew from my own experiences, both

growing up and since being a firefighter, that sometimes people just needed someone to sit with them so they didn't feel alone. It wasn't about opening up and talking about what was bothering them, it was simply about having someone there. I suspected that Tristan didn't have anyone to do that with him.

"I appreciate that. I'm not really good with people," he admitted, and it surprised me slightly. He worked with people all the time, from coworkers to surviving victims and their loved ones. He didn't come across as someone who didn't like people or interacting with them.

"That surprises me. I didn't get that vibe from you."

"I used to be very social. I had a big family, no siblings, but a lot of cousins and uncles and aunts. They were on my dad's side. Everything was a big deal, holidays, birthdays, even accomplishments, anything to bring everyone together. I had a bunch of friends at school. I was almost never alone."

"And then the fire happened," I stated.

"And then the fire happened. I went from being the fun, popular guy at school to the orphan with the weird looking arm. People who I thought were my friends didn't even come see me in the hospital. The ones who stuck around, they treated me differently, like I was made out of glass. It was just easier to fade everyone out. To keep anyone new at a distance. There's a fine line between being friendly and being dismissive of others. I always try to walk it. Honestly, I don't think I even know how to be social anymore."

"You've been through a lot. You lost your parents and your friends at an age that was pretty vital to your social skills and mental health. It's natural that you would have a harder time with social situations, with being around people and having close friends. We didn't go through the same experiences, but growing up I kept people at a distance, too. I was the orphan kid who couldn't afford new clothes or school lunches. I didn't let people get close to me, either. Sometimes it just takes the right people at the right time to make you come out of your shell again. You said you had a lot of family, what about them? Are they not local?"

Having friends leave when life gets hard was pretty typical at any age, but especially at the young age of twelve. Pre-teens and teenagers were not emotionally and mentally equipped to handle something like what Tristan went through. Though it sounded like he had a lot of family so he wouldn't have been subjected to the foster care system.

"I don't know what happened. One day everyone was there, and the next it was just me and my grandparents. Everyone just... disappeared. Even when I was in the hospital for two months afterward recovering from the burn, no one showed. My grandparents even stopped coming by after two weeks. It was just me and whatever nurse was on duty. We used to go days not saying anything. It was weird and hard at first to adjust to it. I was so used to my parents and how they were. My mom never cared if we made a mess cooking, got flour everywhere. My grandmother though, everything had to be clean and perfect. It felt like a museum compared to a home. I didn't understand it at first, but as I got older I understood that seeing me was a reminder of everything they lost. No one likes to have a reminder of the worst day in their lives staring back at them," he said with a small shrug.

I could understand it. I'd seen it plenty of times in the foster care system. From the kids who were given up because they were a product of rape, to the kids who were given up because their parents were dead and the family couldn't handle it. Unfortunately, when tragedy happens the children can be pushed aside because it's too painful to see the resemblance in them. It wasn't fair, and it often left the children with more trauma they had to work through as adults, but people didn't tend to think about the big picture. All they could see was the small picture in front of them and something had to give. It was hard to know what would have been better for him, to stay with his grandparents who didn't know how to deal with their own loss and trauma, or for him to be given over to foster care. It was a coin toss and there was no way of knowing how it would have ended up.

"I'm sorry. That wasn't fair to you. Loss does things to people and sometimes all they can do is focus on the things they can control. That doesn't make it hurt any less on your end. You have the chance now though, to build your own family. When you're ready, I am sure you will find some great people who would love to be a part of your family."

"Maybe. It's getting late, we should call it a night," he said, and I could see him distancing himself again. We had opened a deep wound tonight and now he needed time to try and close it up again.

"Definitely. Why don't I message you tomorrow and we can pick this up. We could both use some sleep and we might see something tomorrow that we missed," I said as I pulled my hand back and stood up.

I could see the raw pain in his eyes as he fought to get it back under control. He needed some time and space to be alone and that was exactly what I was going to give him. Tomorrow, I could come back over and we could keep pushing through the case files. I hoped we would find something that we could use. If this dragged on for too long our arsonist could hit another home and that was the last thing we both wanted.

CHAPTER SEVEN

Tristan

I DON'T KNOW what I had been thinking, opening up to Hawke like that. I didn't talk about my past. I didn't talk about my childhood, not the fire or anything that came after it. It wasn't like I was ashamed of any of it; I just didn't want to talk about it. I didn't want to remember what happened in great detail. Not that I couldn't recall every single second of the horror from that night. It would be impossible for me to forget what happened to me, what had been stolen from me.

I would have loved to forget.

Sometimes, I thought it would have been better if I'd had some type of head trauma or if I had forced the memories into the dark recesses of my mind to protect myself. I had heard it plenty of times from surviving victims that they just wished they could remember what happened. That not remembering, not knowing, was making them go crazy from the unknown of it all. For me though, all I wanted to do was forget. I wanted to forget what the smell of burning flesh smelled like. I wanted to forget what it felt like to look at my parents' bedroom and know that there was nothing I could do to help them. I wanted to forget what it felt like to have my chest being tight and on fire at the same time as I fought for each breath in the thick black smoke. I wanted to forget everything, but I couldn't.

I remembered that night in vivid detail, so much so that I didn't even need the crime scene photos to help me recall even the smallest details. It seemed fitting that I would remember the night that changed my life forever. A night that destroyed everything that I knew of family, friends, and myself.

I didn't talk about it, so why the hell did I tell Hawke so much about it. I never talked about my time in the hospital or what happened to my friends and family. I kept that to myself and whenever someone asked about it, I would just smile and say they were great. That I couldn't have recovered without them. It was a lie, but I knew that's what people wanted to hear. They didn't truly want to know what my life was like afterward. They were only being socially polite by asking.

It was the same thing as a stranger asking how you were doing. You never tell them that your roof leaks and you just lost your job. You tell them you are fine and move on. That's what I should have done with Hawke, but for some reason my mouth didn't listen to my brain.

Talking with Hawke felt like talking with an old friend. One that knew you growing up and knew all of your secrets. At the same time, he felt like a hypnotist. The calm sound of his voice put me in this weird trance where all I wanted to do was open and share my deepest and darkest secrets. It was very odd and not like me at all. I wasn't certain how I felt about it.

"Jesus, fuck," I said as I rubbed my hands over my face.

I was exhausted and I knew I needed to sleep. I was barely sleeping anymore and I knew it was going to make my mind sluggish and I could potentially miss something that I usually wouldn't. I needed some serious sleep, but I honestly had no idea how I was going to accomplish that tonight.

My sleep patterns had always gone up and down. I could go months without a single problem and then my insomnia would act up and I was back to sleeping a few hours every couple of days.

I knew a therapist would tell me it was PTSD from unresolved traumatic issues from the fire. That being a fire investigator was only making it worse and the best course of action for my mental and emotional well being would be to quit. It was why I didn't want to be ordered to see the company Shrink. I knew what he would say and the very last thing I needed was it on record that I was a walking ticking time bomb that the fire department needed to get rid of. I knew this job was hard, I knew that going in, but I had made the decision to risk everything just to find justice for my parents. I was not about to let anything stop me and that was more true today than it had been when I'd first started.

Letting out a sigh, I stumbled to my feet and made my way into my bedroom. I doubted I would be able to sleep for very long before the nightmares would hit, but I had to give it a shot at least. It was something I was trying to make a habit of doing. Trying to sleep even when I knew my mind would not allow me to. I figured if I tried and it didn't work, then I could give myself a break with knowing that I had at least tried and didn't just give up right away. It was a battle, but I felt better knowing that I had at least shown up to the battle and tried to come through on the other side.

I quickly got ready for bed and turned my bedside lamp on. It was dim enough that it wouldn't keep me awake, but it was bright enough to allow me to see the room.

Yet another reason why I couldn't date anyone.

No man would be able to understand that I couldn't sleep in the dark, that I was like a child in need of a nightlight. It wasn't sexy and it certainly wouldn't make a man want to spend more time with me. It definitely didn't make them want to date me. Not that I was looking for a date anyway.

I crawled into bed and tried to get my body to relax as I closed my eyes. With some luck tonight, the exhaustion that was wreaking havoc on my body would finally allow me to fall into a deep sleep.

***

The hot water washed over me, cascading

down my body. I had my head tilted down, but my eyes were closed to prevent any water droplets from getting into my eyes. My left hand was pressed flat against the shower wall, but not even now did the cool tile disrupt my moment of peace. I moaned as a wave of pleasure shot up my spine. My right hand worked away at my hard dick.

It wasn't often I would feel the need to pleasure myself, but when I woke up this morning with a raging hard on, I couldn't ignore it. I had tried, but it wouldn't go back down. The four hours that I had managed to sleep for were filled with dreams. I was used to having nightmares or weird dreams, it was very common for me. What wasn't common was for me to have multiple sex dreams about someone. I didn't even wake up in between, they just flowed from one scenario to another, each one getting hotter than the last. Hawke was haunting me, but instead of him flickering my lights, he was bringing me to new heights in pleasure.

I couldn't stop thinking about the dreams. I couldn't stop seeing it. They played behind my eyes with perfect clarity. I could remember every single touch, every press of his lips on my skin, every single time he slid into me. The way his mouth felt wrapped around my dick. It all felt so real, as if we had already done it and my body was remembering our time together.

Only, we had barely touched and certainly nothing sexual. There was no reason for my body to be reacting this way. I had more self-control over my libido than this, and yet here I was jerking off for the third time in the past hour and it still didn't feel like enough. I hadn't even felt like this when I hit puberty.

I had never been a very sexual person. I could easily go years without sex, and I had without a second thought about it. I had never felt like this before. No matter how many times I came, I still needed more, I wasn't sated and I had no idea how to be.

I let out a deep moan as I came once again. Not much came out and I was pretty certain the well was dry at this point. I placed my forehead against the shower wall and fought to even out my breathing. The heat from the water was starting to go to my head and I was feeling very light headed. I knew I needed to get out, but I just needed a second to catch my breath before I could move. I was supposed to be seeing Hawke later on today and now I had no idea how I was going to pull this off.

Would I get hard by just seeing him?

Would seeing him pull all of my dreams from last night back into my head?

I couldn't afford to be distracted, not when the best chance of catching my parents' killer had presented itself. I needed to focus all of my attention on getting this arsonist off the streets and in jail where he belonged.

Letting out a sigh, I pushed myself up and reached down to turn the water off. I looked down and saw that my dick was already half-hard again and I couldn't help the scowl that touched my face.

"Fuck off," I muttered, before I climbed out of the shower and grabbed one of my towels.

I was ignoring my dick. It had had enough fun for the next few months. I was stronger than this and not about to spend anymore time indulging in something as frivolous as self-pleasure.

After quickly drying off, I made my way into my bedroom to get dressed. I didn't have any plans of going anywhere today. I didn't have work officially, so there was no need for a suit. I grabbed a pair of blue jeans and a black t-shirt. Just as I finished getting dressed my cell phone went off. Instantly, my heartbeat increased and I hoped that it was Hawke that was calling me.

It was ridiculous, because there was no need for him to call me. I had to get a grip on myself. I wasn't going to let a pretty face disrupt my life. He wasn't the first good looking guy that I'd had to work with. I had to focus and stop thinking of him like some lovesick teenager.

I picked up my phone and saw that it was work. I already knew what this was going to be about. There was only one reason I would be called on my day off.

"Investigator Cole," I said, already going over to my closet to pull out a change of clothes.

"Engine fifty-seven is calling for an investigator. Three dead in a fire at 467 Wilton Street. They found an electrical device in the electrical panel. You have an open case with the same device," the dispatcher said.

Every fire investigation dispatcher had access to all open cases. They didn't have the specifics, but they could see the investigator's name and the cause of the fire. It was designed that way so if there was an arsonist operating in town, they could easily get the case files over to the right investigator. It wasn't perfect, there had been plenty of overlap with similar signatures and MOs, but for the most part it helped to keep things organized.

"I'm on my way," I said, before I ended the call.

Letting out a sigh, I pulled up Hawke's number and called him. I wasn't certain if he would be awake or not. We had wrapped up late and I knew he still had to drive home. I was hoping that he would be awake and already have had a cup of coffee. After three rings a very groggy voice answering told me that I had indeed woken him up.

"Colton."

"It's Tristan. I am sorry to wake you up. I just thought I would let you know that there was another fire at 467 Wilton Street. There's three dead, and they found the same device in the electrical panel. I'm heading out now."

"Shit. He just struck yesterday. The gap in between fires was months apart," Hawke said, sounding more awake now. I could hear rustling and I knew he was getting up.

"I know. It could be a coincidence, but I doubt it. I'm getting ready to head out now. I'll have more information once I arrive on scene."

"What firehouse was it?"

"I don't know. The dispatcher said it was Engine Fifty-Seven on scene."

"All right, I know one of their guys, I'll give him a call and get him to start looking for any cameras in the walls."

"I appreciate it. I'm guessing I'll see you there."

"I'll be there within twenty."

"See you then." I said, before I ended the call.

I couldn't help but stand there and look down at the black screen on my phone. More often than not when I got the call to head to a fire to investigate, I would feel anxious in a sense. Well, more like anxious dread. I didn't like seeing the dead bodies, and each fire I had to investigate, I knew it would be devastating to a good number of people, even if no one had died.

This time around though, there was no dread, no anxiety. In its place was a warmth at knowing that I would be getting to see Hawke sooner than I had been expecting.

That feeling sickened me for two reasons. The first, I didn't want to look forward to seeing anyone. I wanted to go through life on my own without having to deal with someone else. I didn't want to have to deal with more disappointment and not being good enough for someone else's love. The second, I was looking forward to going to a fire where three people were dead, just so I could see a man.

It was sick and wrong.

I needed to get my head back on track. I wasn't going to let Hawke come into my life and ruin everything I had worked so hard for. I wasn't going to let him tear down all of the walls I had carefully constructed around my heart and mind.

With that determination, I quickly got changed and grabbed my wallet, phone, keys, and badge before I headed out. I had an arsonist to catch and I was not going to let him slip through my fingers again. Too much was riding on finding him, on stopping him, and now I had another three reasons to find him. The body count was climbing and if we didn't stop him soon, he was going to lose all control and there was no telling how many lives would pay for my shortcomings.

CHAPTER EIGHT

Hawke

I PARKED IN the first spot I could find around the crime scene. There was police tape up to block off the main area and keep any cars from passing through. Engine Fifty-Seven was still there and I knew they were going to be there for the next few hours as they worked their way through the destruction. I couldn't see the house clearly, but I could see the top of it and it was a very usual sight for me. The house was still standing so I had to give the guys credit, they'd worked hard to keep the house and to prevent the fire from jumping to one of the nearby homes. It was not as easy as people thought it was to keep a fire under control, especially when the houses were so close together. One gust of wind in the wrong direction and it could blow the embers into the roof of the nearby house. Most people wouldn't think embers would be enough to start a fire, but with roofing materials, that was all it could take. Roofs weren't designed to prevent fire, they were designed to prevent water from getting into your house. Shingles could very easily catch fire, especially if they were old and dried out. The rubber matting underneath that is designed as a water barrier became a deadly accelerant when it melted. It was a dance that every firefighter had to perform when we were working with houses very close together. A dance we didn't always accomplish.

I got out and made my way toward the crime scene tape. I held up my badge as I ducked under the tape. I scanned the area to try and see if I could find Tristan. I doubted I'd beat him here but anything was possible.

I saw the Coroner's van was still here and I knew that the crime scene would be too busy inside taking photos of the bodies before they could be moved. I still didn't know more than what little Tristan had told me on the phone. I knew there were three dead, but I had no idea if they were adults, children, or a mix of both.

I was hoping they were adults.

It would be terrible for three adults to lose their lives, but it was worse when it was children. Children dying in a fire was a whole new horror, one I was never able to handle. No firefighter could handle the death of a child, especially in a fire. The fear of being trapped in a fire was traumatic on every level, but to know that a child had faced that fear all alone, it was unspeakable.

I still couldn't believe that Tristan had gone through that himself. That at twelve years old he'd lost his parents and almost his own life in a fire that was set by an unknown male. He didn't have closure and I wanted that for him. I wanted to be able to help him heal from the open wound. I knew he wasn't fully healed. I could see it in his eyes. He was fighting and trying to be okay, but I could see it. He needed his parents' killer caught. He needed it in order for him to finally heal and move on in his life. He was standing still and it wouldn't get better until he could close that part of his past and start looking toward the future.

I headed inside the house and started to look for Tristan. It didn't take me very long before I found him. He was talking to Jase, the guy that I had called to search for the cameras. We went through the Fire

Academy together and I knew he was a good guy. We would often grab a beer when we could. We tended to work opposite shifts though, so it wasn't very often we could meet up and share war stories.

I paused for a moment as I gazed at Tristan and my heart skipped a beat. Even his profile called to me, to my heart, and I had yet to figure out why.

I'd had plenty of dreams last night, wonderful and sinful dreams of the man. I was no stranger to sexy dreams. I was a man, after all, with a very healthy sex drive. However, the dreams from last night had felt so real. They felt more like memories, but I knew that wasn't even possible.

This morning I'd tried to dismiss it as a fluke. Convinced myself that I must have been around him at some point on a case and that was why he felt so familiar, why I was so immediately and intensely attracted to him. But I could no longer fool myself. I couldn't ignore how familiar he felt any longer.

I knew most people didn't believe in soul mates, but I did. I believed wholeheartedly that when people died they eventually were reborn and they met the same people they had in their past lives, especially the person they were destined to be with. I knew it sounded silly, like a hopeless romantic, but I truly believed it.

I had come across people who are some of my best friends now, all because they felt so familiar to me when I'd met them for what I knew was the first time. There was just a gut instinct that drew me to them, convinced me they belonged in my life.

And that was just it, the same gut instinct had kicked in and I realized at that moment that Tristan felt like an old love. It felt like my body knew him on a deeper level and I needed to take that into account. I simply couldn't ignore it anymore. I didn't want to, truth be told.

I *needed* to know more of this man.

The trick was I had to be very careful. I had to tread carefully with this because I had no idea if he was gay and if he was, I didn't know if he was out. I couldn't go through another relationship with a man who was in the closet. I couldn't handle being a dirty secret again. It had destroyed parts of my soul, parts that I was just starting to get back, and I couldn't endure it again. Not even if that meant that I would miss out on the chance to be with Tristan. I had to do what was right for me and being kept as a secret wasn't a healthy lifestyle for me.

Even if Tristan was gay and out, that didn't mean there wouldn't be obstacles. He was clearly struggling with the traumatic experiences of his life. That was made very clear to me after learning about his family and friends after the fire. He was undoubtedly used to being on his own and having something or someone there to be strong for him, to allow him to be vulnerable and not strong all the time, to help him through the pain and heartache, that entire concept was completely foreign to him. He wasn't going to let his walls down very easily and it was going to take some serious work to break through them. However, even knowing all of that, my heart was still telling me it would all be worth it.

That the work and potential frustration would be worth it.

I could see the pain in his eyes as we talked last night, but I could also see a longing for more. He *needed* more. He wanted to be happy and healthy, he wanted to move past his rocky history and get on with living, and as long as that spark for life was still in his eyes, that was all the hope I needed.

I waited until Tristan gave a nod to

Jase and then Jase turned and strolled off to speak with some of the other guys. Tristan turned toward me and our eyes locked. I could have sworn I saw a flash of heat briefly go across his eyes before they were locked down once again. I made my way over to him, flashing him with a warm smile as I spoke.

"Morning. What do we know?"

"Engine Fifty-Seven arrived on scene just after eight this morning. The house was already consumed in flames. Local police were evacuating the nearby homes. Most were empty though, with people having to get to work. Homeowner is Shelby Lewis, thirty-seven with two kids. A ten year old boy named Chris and an eight year old girl named Katie. Local police reached out to next of kin, Shelby's mother, Grace. She informed them that Shelby and the kids had been home for the past two days, all were sick from the flu. Grace was supposed to spend the night on the couch, but her daughter told her that she was feeling better and she didn't need to. Grace is a mess and currently blaming herself, believing that if she'd stayed she would have woken up in time to save her daughter and grandchildren."

"Fuck," I said as I closed my eyes for a

second to calm my emotions down.

It was bad enough when it was children, but to know that they were supposed to be safe tucked away in their beds. They were sick and just staying home from school. If they hadn't been sick, they most likely would have been up and getting ready for school. They would have noticed the fire before it became overwhelming.

"They never made it out of their beds. Engine Fifty-Seven didn't initially suspect arson, but when they started to do their walk through while they waited on the Coroner, they noticed that every smoke detector in the house had their batteries pulled. An officer asked Grace about it and she was adamant that they were functioning. She said two weeks ago she had to personally change the one in the kitchen because it wouldn't stop beeping. She said her daughter was very careful with anything that could start a fire. She didn't have candles, no incense burners, she didn't have curling irons, or space heaters. Her biggest fear was a fire starting. She didn't even use the built-in electric fireplace that came with the house. She even had extra smoke detectors installed in each of the kids' bedrooms."

"Why the paranoia?"

It was common for people to be afraid of fires. I had come across lots of people who made sure there were no accelerants or open flames in their house. I knew plenty of people who'd switched their gas stove out for an electric one. It wasn't that uncommon. But it was not common for people to go to the extreme by adding more smoke detectors in the house. To not even want to risk a curling iron being left on. There had to be a story there.

"They used to live in Texas, her husband was a firefighter. According to Grace, he was very paranoid about anything that could start a fire. He had twenty years on the job and that paranoia got worse after they had children. He died seven years ago in an industrial fire that took out him and eight others before they were able to get it under control. Shelby and the kids all moved back here to get help from her mother. According to Grace, Shelby became terrified of fire after that. She said she was never the same again. She wouldn't even park her car in the garage in case a fire started and the gas tank blew."

"Okay, so she had a reason to be paranoid. It also works in our favor, though. We've both seen it where people pull the batteries out of their smoke detectors, especially the one by the kitchen. But someone that paranoid, they don't pull all of the batteries from their smoke detectors. She would have had extra batteries for when they died. Someone had to have physically pulled them, but the question is when. If they have been home sick for the past two days, they wouldn't have had anyone coming in to do any work on the house. And they wouldn't have been able to get access to every room."

"Exactly. They had to have been here before they were sick, but within the past two weeks since Grace changed the batteries in the kitchen detector. They would have also had to have been here within the window for the electrical device to be planted in the electrical panel for it to go off at the right time."

"That is what I don't understand. There's no timer on it, so how does our guy know when it will cause a fire and if someone will be in the house when it happens?"

That's what was bothering me. There was no guarantee he would ever get someone in the house when the device started the fire. There were no timers on the device. There was nothing that would indicate he held any control over when a fire would start.

So how was he able to time it right to get victims?

"I don't know. I think there is more to the device then we can see. The ones we have been able to recover have been pretty much melted into nothing. My guess is there is some type of coding, or liquid that he uses as a timer. As it gets hotter the coding or the liquid starts the fire once it reaches a specific temperature. If he knew the flash point of the materials he uses, he would be able to roughly time when a fire would occur."

"Best way to do that is to practice. Maybe we should be looking for smaller fires that were nothing. Fires that didn't even warrant a call to the investigation unit."

He had to have started somewhere and if he needed to perfect his device, he had to practice with it. He would have to have used it in a real setting and timed how long it took to get the right combination down.

"That's a good idea," Tristan said as Jase walked back over to us.

"We found this in the little girl's room," he said as he handed a small black rectangular device over to Tristan.

"Where in the room?" I asked.

"Across from the bed in the corner," Jase answered.

"It's a camera," Tristan said as he looked at the device closer.

"Like a nanny cam or is someone watching this little girl?" Jase asked, both disgusted and angry. I couldn't blame him, there was really nothing good that could come from a camera in a little girl's room.

"Depends on if there are more cameras all around the house," Tristan answered.

"We're looking in every room. I'll let you know if we find others," Jase said with a nod before he headed off.

"That one doesn't look like the other cameras from previous fires," I stated what I knew we were both thinking.

"I know, but it can't be a coincidence. If there are more cameras in the house, then it has to be the same guy. He must have made a change for some reason."

"Thirty-five fires, each with ten cameras, that's three hundred and fifty cameras. That's a lot of cameras that are no longer being made. Maybe he finally ran out and couldn't get anymore," I suggested.

The cameras were fifteen years old. There couldn't have been that many left out in the world. Even if they didn't get sold, most places would have tossed them as dead inventory. They would take the loss, because they could use the space for items that would sell. It worked out better for them. This guy couldn't have that many of these cameras left and eventually, he would have had to make the change.

"It could explain why he hit so quickly after the last time. He wanted to test out the new equipment. I'll send it to the crime lab and see if they can determine what brand it is. He wouldn't have ordered them online. That would leave an address, name, and a credit card number. He would have wanted to get them in person and paid with cash. We might luck out on security footage at the stores if they are willing to give it over without a warrant."

"They might have an IP address that they feed the footage to. Would he have really stuck so soon just to test out some cameras? Wouldn't it have made sense for him to do a controlled burn with them somewhere instead of risking them failing?"

It made more sense for him to do a controlled burn on a piece of land with a shed or something than an actual house.

There was no telling how well the cameras worked under that level of heat. I couldn't imagine an arsonist wanting to risk missing out on watching their work live in action.

"You're assuming he would have a place to do that. Most people don't have the land to build a house to do a controlled burn. This camera isn't as badly burnt as the previous ones. They must have a higher heat level tolerance. That means they would have worked longer for him. Whether this was a test or not, they definitely passed and that doesn't bode well for us."

"How so?" I asked, slightly confused. I would have figured the camera being in better shape was a good thing. We might be able to track it down to a store and find this asshole.

"Because arsonists are compulsive. They have to burn things, they have to start fires. In the beginning they do it in different ways, trying to determine what way made them feel the best. Like drug addicts trying different drugs until they find the one that gives them the best high. These cameras, it's like going from black tar heroin to china white heroin. He's feeling a whole new high, most likely the best high he's felt since his very first fire.

He's going to be chasing that even more now."

"That works in our favor though, doesn't it? He's chasing that high, he's not as careful and he slips up. This could be the house that catches him. This could be his mistake."

I knew from volunteering at soup kitchens and community centers, that drug addicts who were chasing their high often got sloppy. The more desperate they were for that high, the more erratic they became and the more mistakes they made. If our guy was desperately chasing the high he got from this fire, he might make a mistake. He might have made a mistake with how soon he hit this house. I couldn't imagine he had enough time to plan everything out this time around. Not when he usually goes a few months in between fires.

"It's very likely. We need to dig into Shelby's life. It's possible he has been here before. I'll get the camera to the crime lab. Why don't you search the database and see if there are any small fires that could fit with our guy. I will reach out to a cop friend of mine for the intel on Shelby."

"Sounds good. Meet at your place?"

"Um... yeah, okay."

He didn't sound too sure and I couldn't help but wonder if there was a hint of a blush touching his cheeks or if it was simply the heat of the day making them ruddy. I quickly dismissed it, not wanting to let my mind get away from me. We had to focus on finding this arsonist before someone else got killed. Once he was arrested, then I could always entertain the idea of being with Tristan in a romantic capacity. I still had no idea if he was interested in guys or not, maybe I would need to try and slip it into the conversation somehow. For now, we had an arsonist to catch with a body count going up.

I gave him a nod before I headed out. I was hoping that I would be able to find an older fire that would have something we could use to connect to our guy. Arsonists get better with age and experience, if we could find our guy from when he first started out, we might be able to nail him. Arson had a statute of limitations for ten years, but a death in a fire counted as murder, and there was no time limit on that. Every victim that this man had killed, injured, or destroyed their lives, would still be able to get justice. Now we just needed to find him.

CHAPTER NINE

Tristan

AFTER GETTING BACK into my car, I quickly pulled out my phone and placed a call to Detective Jonah West. I had come across him a few times professionally and I liked how he was a straight shooter and that he cared about people.

Some detectives that I had worked with in the past only cared about their own cases, and even that might be a stretch. They didn't want to take on more cases and they held zero interest in helping with a fire investigation. Most detectives wanted cases that were easy and quick to close, and if there was one thing about arson, it was a long and tedious process to investigate. The fire destroys evidence and any that might be left behind gets destroyed by the firefighters. Most detectives tended to avoid getting a fire case. I'd even seen some trade cases just to get rid of their arson case.

"Detective West," he said, picking up after three rings.

"Detective West, it's Fire Investigator Cole. Do you have a moment to talk?"

"I always have a moment for you, Tristan. How have you been?" Detective West said, his voice warm and welcoming.

"I have been well, thank you. I caught a serial arson case with multiple bodies on his tally. The most recent is a single mother of two young children. All three are dead. They never made it out of their beds."

"I'm sorry. What do you need?" he asked, more than willing to help. It was one of the reasons why I would reach out to him when I needed some police help.

"I think my arsonist finally made a mistake in picking this victim. He just hit yesterday and generally he has a cooling off period of months, but he hit the next house within twenty-four hours of the last fire. I think he knew her. She was paranoid about fires, her husband was a firefighter in Texas and he was killed seven years ago in a fire. My victim had installed extra smoke detectors in her house, but every single battery was removed before the fire was started."

"So he's been in the house. Any work done on the house recently?"

"Not that the mother of the victim knew about. I got the impression that they were very close. The victim moved back from Texas after her husband's death. I have the report from the officer who spoke with the victim's mother. According to her, my victim was focused on her career and her children. She didn't date. She wasn't ready and didn't know how her children would feel about it. She worked at a marketing firm, BizBeep."

"What's her name?"

"Shelby Lewis, thirty-seven. Kids were Chris, a ten year old boy, and Katie, an eight year old girl. They were home the past couple of days all sick with the flu."

"All right, I'll dig into her and see what I can find."

"I really appreciate the help."

"Always. I'll be in touch in a bit."

"Thanks," I said, and ended the call.

With Detective West looking into Shelby and her life, I was hoping he would be able to find someone who was around that we could connect to Rollins' house or her life. We needed something that connected both homes, because I found it hard to believe that this hit was completely random. He had to have been in their homes to set up the cameras, plant the device in the electrical panel, and for him to know that Shelby had extra smoke detectors that would have ruined his plans.

That didn't scream random to me at all.

This man was in both of their lives. He was either older and responsible for the previous fires, or he was younger and working as an apprentice to the original arsonist that started the fire at my parents' home. I wasn't certain which option it would be. Neither one would be common, but it was the only working theory I had. I couldn't see it being a coincidence that these cameras were used in all of these fires and it wasn't connected. Even Hawke found it hard to believe, which only helped to make me feel more confident in my theory.

With any luck Detective West would be able to find us someone that we could dig into and get him caught before he strikes again.

I cranked the ignition on my car, shifted it into gear, and started to make my way to the crime lab. I needed to get the camera into the hands of a professional and find out everything I could about it. And maybe, just maybe, it would be more traceable than the previous cameras.

***

I made my way through the crime lab to the Digital Forensic Division. I had been there a few times, but it wasn't very often I needed to see Hank. He was the best Digital Forensic Expert I had ever dealt with and often helped me with the previous arson cases that involved the cameras. He didn't tell me I was crazy or seeing things. He just focused on the evidence and didn't speculate on the case at all.

I enjoyed that part.

Sometimes forensic experts wanted to get involved in the case. They wanted to follow it until there was an arrest and conviction. It wasn't a bad thing exactly, but I didn't appreciate someone questioning me the whole time. There was such a thing as too many cooks in the kitchen and often the forensic experts believed they were the only cook who mattered.

Hank wasn't like that. He had enough on his plate so he was more than happy to examine the evidence and then classify his work as complete before moving on to the next file. It was a good part of why we got along so well.

I knocked on the glass door to his lab to alert him to my presence before I turned the knob and opened the door. I strolled in quietly so I didn't disturb his concentration and waited patiently beside his desk. I knew he'd acknowledge me when he was ready. We'd been through the same cycle a few times, after all.

He was staring at a computer screen, and I could see he was reviewing footage from someone's security camera. He was always busy and I hated interrupting him, but it was important and I knew he wouldn't mind too much.

"Cole, tell me this is quick," Hank said, and I could hear the tension in his voice.

I didn't know what he was working on, but I could tell by the stress lines around his eyes that he was working on something major and time consuming. Whatever the case he was working on, it must have been footage heavy. I knew there had been plenty of cases where he had to comb through months' worth of security footage to try and find suspects and evidence. Hank often got headaches from spending hours staring at a computer screen without breaks. One of the major downfalls of the job, and his determination to be one of the best at it only added to the issue. Once he got started he was like a dog with a bone and wouldn't quit until he'd found what he needed.

Most people thought being a digital forensic analyst would be and easy job, but it was a lot of work and brutal on the eyes. One small miss and it could mean the difference between either finding or missing critical evidence in a case.

"I hope so. I have a new camera that was found at a crime scene. MO is the same as the arsonist that I have been chasing, but he changed up the cameras. I was hoping you would be able to tell me more about it," I said as I held up the clear plastic evidence bag with the camera inside of it.

He let out a small sigh before he held out his hand and I passed the bag over to him. I wasn't sure if he liked me or not. It was hard to tell with him. He was always professional, but he didn't do the whole small talk, social thing like most of the experts here did. He also didn't go on rants to prove how smart he was, another common trait in this building.

I knew a lot of the people who worked here were highly intelligent nerds and didn't have much experience in the way of normal social interactions with average people. So I never took it personally when they felt the need to over explain something technical. I never cared to hear about all the technical tests they did on whatever piece of evidence they had from one of my cases, but I dealt with their need to explain anyway. I didn't need to hear about the process to get there, I just needed to see the results. Hank understood that and it made me respect him even more.

I stayed quiet while he worked away. I knew if this was going to take a whole lot longer he would have shooed me away and told me to come back later. The fact that he hadn't told me to leave meant that he wouldn't have to do extensive tests on it. The camera was in a bit better shape then the previous ones I'd brought him to review and I suspected that was just due to the advancement in the materials being used for cameras now. Even plastic has come a long way in the last twenty years. It was roughly thirty minutes later when he finally peered up at me again.

"This one is newer. Model Z by Giget; made within the past three years. It's very popular in the private detective circle, but it has also been used as a nanny cam and pet camera. People don't tend to use them for home security, though, because the mount that comes with them doesn't last very long. These kind are designed to be used for short periods of time and usually placed in some sort of housing or container as opposed to being mounted on a door or a wall."

"Okay, how does it work?"

"A person can watch these feeds live, but they also connect to their own private server. When someone purchases them, they also purchase a server that will store the data on it. The server does not connect to the Internet, which is why it's popular with PIs. They don't have to worry about someone hacking their files. It's done all remotely, but the owner does have to activate the camera and connect them wirelessly to the server. They'd have to do that online through the camera's app, either on a computer, tablet, or a smartphone."

"And how far can the server be from the cameras?"

I was very interested in the private server. If we could find a suspect we could get a warrant to try and find the server. We might not be able to link him to all of the cases, or even my parent's case, but we could at least get him in jail for three counts of murder, a life sentence, and it would at least get him off of the streets.

"To make sure the connection stays, typically the owner wouldn't go further than two miles from the house. Any further and they would risk the connection fading in and out. It's bluetooth connected, so it doesn't give them too much leeway."

Two miles, which meant this time around he had to be in a vehicle or close by somewhere in order to watch the feeds. We could pull street cameras and see if we could find a car that we could connect to a suspect. We would have to run the license plates of any car that had been hanging around too long, which could be a few, but if it meant possibly finding the bastard then it was more than worth it.

"And I'm assuming this server is a black box?"

"Yes, like a portable hard drive. They will most likely have a password on it."

That was a given. "How popular is popular?"

I was almost afraid of what his answer would be. If private detectives were using it, I knew that meant there could be tens of thousands of people who had purchased them. Private detectives were just as talkative as normal cops. They all liked to share trade secrets and give advice on the newest tech to make the job easier. There was no telling how many stores sold them and their customer lists.

"Millions are made a year. They're cheap and they have a fairly decent video quality to them. But, I was able to extract the serial number and traced it back to one store. Spy Guy." He said the name of the store with a small smirk turning up the corners of his lips and I knew he was proud of himself.

That was why I loved Hank. He knew how to get results and he could do it fast. I had never been able to get a serial number on any of the cameras before. They were too melted to ever be able to get anything off of them. I now had a store, a single store, where I could potentially get security footage from and a customer list. That could be the break I needed, the intel that finally gave me a real suspect that I could dig into.

Shelby Lewis was going to be this arsonist's biggest mistake and I was going to make sure of it.

"Thank you Hank," I said, flashing him a warm, grateful smile.

"Go get this son of a bitch," Hank said, before he swung back to stare into the computer monitor he had been working on when I came in.

I headed out of the building and made my way back down to my car with a new pep in my step. I could feel my body tingling with excitement. I was getting somewhere. I was finally getting closer. I could almost taste it now.

The second I slid into my car I hit the browser and pulled up Spy Guy on my phone to find its location. It was a good twenty minutes away, but it was open and that was all that I needed. It was owned by Seth Rogers, and based on the reviews it was a good place with a very helpful owner. I hoped like hell that was true and Mr. Rogers was more than willing to cooperate without making me get a warrant.

I tossed my phone down on the passenger seat and cranked the engine with a smile on my face. Pulling out into traffic, I headed off for Spy Guy.

***

Damn it!

Of course he wasn't going to play ball. Nothing was ever easy. I finally had a real break and Mr. Rogers didn't feel comfortable violating his customer's privacy by allowing me to have access to his security footage or customer list. As if his customers were real spies and not a bunch of middle-aged men following people for a living.

The gadgets in his store were all geared toward catering to the lifestyle of James Bond. Mr. Rogers had found a way to make a very good living by playing into the compulsion that his customers had about being real life spies. I would hate to see the private detectives who shopped at that store. Their hourly fee must be insanely high, not to mention how they likely preferred to handle contact with their clients. I would never understand some people.

Either way, I wasn't getting what I needed without a warrant. Thankfully, that would be easy enough with what Hank had found on the camera. I grabbed my phone and rang our Assistant District Attorney Joseph Barba. He worked specifically with the Fire Investigation Division and he was the prosecutor who would handle the cases once they were cleared for court. We had worked together many times and spent many long nights putting the finishing touches on a case before court the next day. He was a good man and he wasn't afraid to go after the cases that were questionable. He gave each case his all and he made sure he put every ounce of strength and energy into getting guilty verdicts.

"ADA Barba," he said, as he picked up the call.

"Barba, it's Cole. I need a warrant for security footage and a customer transaction list for Spy Guy. Store owner's name is Seth Rogers."

"Probable cause?"

"A fire this morning at 467 Wilton Street killed thirty-seven year old Shelby Lewis and her two kids, a ten year old boy and an eight year old girl. Cameras were discovered all around the house. I took one of them back to the crime lab. Hank was able to get a serial number off of it and connect it back to the inventory that Mr. Rogers received. Unfortunately, Rogers is requesting a warrant before handing anything over to protect his customer's privacy. He deals with a lot of private detectives and wannabe spies."

"I'll start working on the warrant, you should have it within a few hours. Who do you want me to call when it's in?"

I could issue a warrant and do a seizure of the evidence. The trick was more and more recently in court defense attorneys were questioning the chain of custody. As a fire investigator, I could not arrest anyone and had no formal clearance to obtain evidence. I could examine evidence as it pertained to my case, but I couldn't be the one to physically collect it. At least not without risking the case in court, which I wasn't about to do. It was a small annoyance, because it meant there had to be someone else, someone in law enforcement, who would have to collect the evidence and record it before I would be able to get my hands on it. It was an extra step and I really didn't like having a middleman, but I couldn't risk it. Not with this case.

"Detective Jonah West. He can serve the warrant and collect the evidence. He is already been briefed on the case and running the victim."

"I'll send it his way once it's in. Anything else?"

"No, that's it. Thank you."

He ended the call and I tossed my phone back onto the seat with a sigh. I had nothing that I could do right now. I was stuck waiting on warrants and evidence. I knew the only thing I could do at that point was to go back to my place and start going over the new crime scene. Maybe something would be different with this one compared to the others and it would give me a new lead that I could chase down. I also didn't know when

Hawke would be showing up and I didn't want to not be there when he arrived. With nothing left to do, I turned my car back on and started to make the drive back to my apartment.

CHAPTER TEN

Hawke

IT WAS A few hours later when I made my way back up to Tristan's apartment. It still bothered me that he lived in an apartment like this. He was too nice and not the kind of a man to live in a dump like this place. I really hoped that once this case was closed and he was able to get justice for himself and his parents that he would see he could have something better in his life.

That he was worth something more.

I had no doubt that he had feelings of low self-worth. The way his grandparents handled raising him after his parents' death was not what a traumatized child needed and it clearly had a lasting impact on Tristan. Hopefully, closure would be enough to give Tristan a new outlook on life and bring him some peace.

I knocked on his door and waited for him to open the door. I had sent him a text letting him know that I was on my way. I wanted to make sure he was home before I just showed up.

The door opened a few moments later and I could see that Tristan was exhausted. He looked tired yesterday, but the dark bags under his eyes were getting darker. I had noticed earlier that he appeared worn-out, but I figured it had to do with going to bed late and being woken up early. Hell, I was weary, too, and I had chugged a cup of coffee on my way over to the new crime scene. I had bounced back though, and it appeared that Tristan had only grown more drained as the hours ticked by. He moved back so I could walk in as he spoke.

"I appreciate you coming back. I know you are tired and probably want to be home on your day off."

"Don't worry about it. I normally just sit on my couch and tell myself I should clean as I binge watch all of the shows that I've missed all week."

"Do you ever clean?" he asked, flashing a small smile.

"When I run out of dishes. And that is one hell of an accomplishment, believe me, because most of my dishes are paper or throw away pans," I said, with a smirk turning up the corners of my lips.

I had no problem with cooking or doing basic chores, but there was just something about dishes that I couldn't stand. It's why I had a dishwasher and a healthy supply of throw away dishes. I only wished frying pans or pots could be throw away as well.

"Wow, that is an accomplishment."

"What about you?" I asked as we went and plopped down on the couch.

"I like doing dishes. I like the peace and the repetitive motion to it. It helps me think, or not think, depending on what I need."

"I get that," I said gently, before I switched to a more joking tone to try and put a smile back on his face. "You know, if you ever run out of dishes to wash, I can pretty much guarantee you that my sink will have a bunch that you are welcome to indulge yourself in."

Tristan gave a huff of a laugh before he spoke. "Deal, but you have to do my laundry."

"You don't like laundry? That's the best adult chore. You just stick it in and forget about it. It practically does itself."

"Until you have to fold it or hang it up.

Or worse, iron something."

"Ooooh, yeah I see your point on that one. I don't have to iron anything unless I have to wear my dress uniform, which is thankfully, almost never. And I almost never hang anything up. I just shove it in a drawer."

"Your life skills are impressive," he teased.

"They really are. You should see me in a grocery store. I can get in and out within fifteen minutes," I said, flashing him a big smile as he chuckled slightly.

"It's official, you have mastered adulting better than me."

"I'll give you some pointers," I said with a playful wink before I moved the conversation back on topic. "So, I went back and searched through a lot of fires that were mostly deemed nuisance fires, but nothing really popped. I spoke to some old timers, and they didn't remember any fires that appeared to be practice runs. But, a retired captain, Captain Atwater, he remembered three cases where they found close to a dozen cameras all over the house and one was even an apartment."

"An apartment?" he asked, confused and surprised,

I had also been shocked, because up

until now our guy had always hit a house. Most arsonists did homes or warehouses just because they were easier. Going after an apartment in a building had a lot of risk and they couldn't control the fire as well. As much as it contradicts logic, arsonists liked control. They liked to be in command of the fire and watch as it ate everything in its path.

"Fifty-eight apartments, a hundred and thirty occupants with a mixture of adults and children. It was twenty-five years ago. I went and pulled the file, it was classified as an electrical malfunction and the owner was charged with various negligent charges, and received five years probation. The apartment building itself was made out of cement, but the apartments were wood, so it went up pretty quick. Sixty-five people were injured from smoke inhalation, minor burns, second degree and third degree burns, and broken bones from being pushed or stepped on. And by some miracle, no deaths. Multiple fire houses combed through the building and Captain Atwater remembered one of the apartments where the fire originated from having these small cameras all over the place. He assumed they were security cameras or some kinky sex thing."

"He's never hit an apartment before. That could be his first real fire. Did they have any suspects, anyone they talked to?"

I could hear the excitement in his voice, not that I could blame him. This was the first time we were getting a better picture of the arsonist. There was a very real chance that the apartment building fire was his first attempt at arson and just like most serial criminals, they strike in their comfort zone first before branching out. When someone was a serial criminal, whether that is a killer, rapist, arsonist, thief, whoever, they always committed their first crimes in their comfort zone, meaning their neighborhood. They felt safe there, they knew the routines of their neighbors. They knew the back and side alleys, the escape routes. It was all familiar to them, making them feel safe enough to finally do the one thing they had been craving. Once they built their confidence up, they got smarter. They no longer shit where they eat, making it more difficult to trace them back to their area.

"Unfortunately, no. They assumed it was electrical. The fire originated in the electrical panel, but they couldn't pinpoint exactly whose it was by the time the fire had burned through the apartments. He didn't remember them ever mentioning someone of interest and he never looked at anyone. I tried to find the file, but it was in the thousands that had gotten destroyed ten years ago from a flood. Captain Atwater was pretty new to the job back then, and most people didn't listen to him, but he did say he always had a weird feeling about it. He had a hard time believing that it just went up by itself."

"Why the feeling?"

"He chalked it up to being a new guy and being suspicious of everything and everyone. But, he said the building owner never wavered in his claim of being innocent. The contractors and electricians who had a hand in building the apartment building, they all checked out. They were all licensed and they only hired licensed employees. They had been around for fifteen years with not a single complaint. Captain Atwater said it never seemed right to him that out of fifteen years of building homes and apartment buildings, that this one went up due to a mistake. It simply defied logic. They also passed multiple inspections along the way and everything was up to code. At the time though, no one was interested in looking deeper and took it at face value.

There was a good number of injuries, but no one died."

It wasn't surprising that no one wanted to look too closely at a fire that didn't have casualties. Fires were hard enough to investigate, but when you talk about ones that large, it was a nightmare that could take months to comb through. Twenty-five years ago, there just weren't enough fire investigators to handle the full city. Back then, if it quacked like a duck, looked like a duck, then it was a duck and no one dared to make it into something else.

"We don't have a suspect, but we have an area now that we can cross reference when we have a list of suspects. Hank, the Digital Forensic Expert at the Crime Lab, was able to tease out a serial number from the camera. It came back to an inventory at Spy Guy, a go-to spot for private detectives and wannabe spies. I went to see the owner, but he demanded a warrant. I have ADA Barba getting that and he will issue it to Detective West who will collect the security footage and customer list. Once he has it, he will send it my way. Hopefully, that will give us something."

Hurry up and wait, basically. We couldn't do much until we could get our hands on some more evidence. The security footage and customer list would be very helpful. We could cross-reference the customers with the address of the apartment fire. Until we had that evidence though, we were sitting around doing nothing. There wasn't anything we could do, which meant I should leave, but that was the last thing I wanted to do.

"I'm sure it will. You must be feeling excited to finally be close to cracking this case. You've been working on it for over a decade now."

"I don't think excited is the word I would use to describe how I'm feeling. This is as close to a real lead that I've had since I started, but I've had times where I thought something would give me a lead only for it to not work out. I learned a long time ago not to hope and just to wait for the results."

I could understand that, but it was also sad at the same time. Everyone deserved to have hope, even if it was just a small piece of it. I could understand why he didn't want to hope. He had been doing this for over ten years, and that would take a toll on anyone. It was only natural that he wouldn't want to allow himself to anticipate finally having some success, that he would want to keep himself guarded from the potential disappointment and hurt. This wasn't just a simple arsonist that he had been hunting down. This was the arsonist who had killed his parents and left him permanently scarred. There was a deep personal and psychological connection to catching this man. If he never caught him, he was never going to have closure. He was never going to be able to move on and finally heal from it. It would break him the rest of the way and that wasn't something I ever wanted to see.

"I can understand you not wanting to open yourself up to potential hurt and disappointment. I know how important this case is for you. How important it is for you to find the man responsible for your parents' death. I'm going to do everything I can to help you get justice for them. You're not doing this alone anymore," I said warmly as I took the chance and placed my hand on his knee.

I had no idea how he would respond to physical touching. We hadn't touched outside of a handshake and that was through my work gloves. He didn't come across as someone who enjoyed his personal space being invaded, but I hoped this was okay.

I wasn't blind. I could see that he was

attracted to me. I was attracted to him and I wasn't one for ignoring my own feelings. I didn't know if I wanted to jump into a relationship, not with it still being close to my last relationship. However, I was open to taking things slow and seeing where it went. We could start off with a light relationship and if it grew then great, but if it didn't there was no harm, no foul. It was completely up to him, though. I wasn't going to push. He had complete control and we could play at his speed.

Tristan turned more toward me as he spoke. "I really appreciate everything you have done to help me. I know this isn't your job and you have no obligation to help me. It means a lot that you've helped me and believed me about these cases."

"I'm happy to assist. You have good instincts and because of them, I have faith that you will solve a lot of cases and put this arsonist behind bars where he belongs. You could have taken the easy way out and ignored these cases. But you didn't. You're doing something very brave by facing the emotional pain connected to these cases to get them justice. That's not easy and most people wouldn't be willing to do it."

He might not think that what he was doing was brave, but it was. I didn't know many people who would be willing to put themselves through the level of hurt this had to cause to get justice for strangers, for his parents. He brought up the trauma every time he looked at one of these cases. That didn't allow a wound to heal over and it definitely wasn't easy to live that way. He shouldn't have to live that way. It was one of the main reasons why I was willing to help him. He had been going at it alone, forced to be strong all the time, it was about time he had someone else in his corner. Someone who he could count on, rely on to be there for him when he needed a breather. Someone that could be the strong one when he couldn't be, and I was happy that he'd chosen me.

"It's the right thing to do."

To him, it truly was that simple. He was remarkable. He had every reason to hate the world, to want to ignore everything wrong in it and live his own life. And yet, he was working to try and give justice to people, to help put dangerous people behind bars. He was reliving his own childhood trauma to help others and he had no idea how remarkable he truly was. He had no idea how special and amazing that made him.

"You're amazing, Darlin'. I just wish

you could see it for yourself."

There was a flash of emotion that went through his eyes, but I wasn't able to pinpoint exactly what emotion it was. I suspected it was a mixture of surprise, confusion, and self-loathing, but I couldn't be certain. I hated that he didn't see how special he was. I hated that his grandparents, people who were supposed to love him and lift him up, had ignored him and torn him down. I was sure they hadn't realized the repercussions their actions would have on him. I was sure they were grieving at the time and having to bury a child was never easy, no matter the age. I understood all of that, but while they were wrapped up in their own grief, they allowed their grandson to be mentally and emotionally neglected. Something that was going to take a long time to repair in him.

Tristan slowly leaned in toward me and I was instantly surprised by the action. I knew what he was going for, but I didn't expect it. It was clear that we were both attracted to each other. It was easy to tell with the way his gaze was constantly traveling down to my lips. I couldn't tell you how badly I wanted to grab him and kiss him, but I was afraid he wouldn't react well to that.

I didn't pull back and I didn't really move in. I was afraid that if I moved in to meet his lips that he would pull back. That he would be snapped out of the moment and I would miss my chance to taste him.

When our lips finally touched, a jolt of electricity shot through my whole body. I instantly pressed my lips harder against his. I wanted to make sure that Tristan knew I wanted this just as badly as he did. I moved my hand over and placed it on the bottom of his jawline on his right side, deepening the kiss as I licked at his lips, seeking entrance.

Tristan gave a soft moan like he was all too happy to open his mouth and allow our tongues to dance together. He tasted amazing and he was no longer shy. The uncertainty he had when the kiss started was long gone and Tristan was not afraid to go after what he wanted. I loved the confidence he now had.

The soft purring moans slipping from his throat were driving me insane. I was already hard and I suspected he was as well. The sexual desire that sparked between us was consuming the both of us and I knew neither one of us wanted it to stop.

All too soon, I had to pull back so we

could catch our breaths. I didn't pull back very far though. We stayed close and I lightly pressed my forehead against his.

"Wow," Tristan whispered on a breath.

"I know. We should probably stop." I said the words, but I really didn't want to say them. I wanted to give him an out, though. I wanted to give him the chance to pump the brakes if he needed it. I really hoped he didn't need it, though. Stopping was the very last thing I wanted right now.

"Do you want to stop?" he asked, and I could hear that he was worried about me regretting this. Regret was not an emotion I experienced right now. It was the furthest thing from what I felt.

"Fuck no," I answered, honestly.

"Good."

Tristan placed his hand on the back of my neck and pulled me back in for another kiss. All of the control was gone now on both of our ends. Now that we had established what we both wanted, there was no stopping us.

Tristan pulled me down so he was lying on the couch and I happily fitted myself between legs that he willingly opened to accommodate me. Our new position only fueled our need as our dicks pressed against each other. Tristan moved his hands down my back and over to my jean-clad ass and pressed me down against him, forcing more contact between our dicks.

I ground my hips against his and we both let out a deep moan as we rubbed against each other. I knew it had been about two months since the last time I had sex, but based on how hungry Tristan was, I was willing to bet it had been much longer for him.

His hips met mine as we both ground and thrust against one another. I needed to feel more of him, though. There wasn't nearly enough contact with him through our clothes. Before I even had a chance to pull back, Tristan spoke.

"I need to feel you inside of me."

That one sentence sent electricity racing through every nerve in my body and it landed straight in my groin. For the rest of my life, I would never hear a sentence sexier than those few words sounded coming from his kiss-swollen lips. I placed my hand on the back of his neck and pulled him up as I spoke.

"Bedroom."

I pressed my lips against his as Tristan guided us down the hallway to his bedroom. We continued to kiss, only pulling apart long enough for us to remove the other's shirt before our mouths were back on each other. Thankfully, the trip to his bedroom was very short and by the time we reached it we were both fumbling on the other's belt and pants. The very second that I could, I shoved my down his boxers and I finally got to feel his hot, engorged dick against my hand.

Tristan let out a long, drawn out moan at the contact of finally having skin on skin and he quickly followed my lead and then it was my turn to let out a deep gravely moan as he wrapped his fist tightly around my already throbbing cock.

There was no way I was going to be able to control myself with him. He felt too good and the needy moans he was making were killing me. I was trying to control myself. I was trying to take it slow, but I felt like my whole body was going to burst into flames.

I walked him back toward the bed, both of us stepping out of our pants and boxers as we moved. Tristan fell onto the bed and backed up until he was lying on his pillows and I followed. I had no choice but to break the kiss so I could speak.

"You got stuff?"

"Top drawer," he said as he pointed to his bedside table.

I quickly reached over and pulled out the bottle of lube and a condom before I turned my attention back to the delicious looking body waiting for me. He looked so good. He was thin, but he had some muscle definition. Nothing crazy, but I could tell he tried to stay in shape. I suspected he was a runner based on his leg muscles. I saw a flicker of self-consciousness as he moved his left arm up toward his pillow to try and hide it. As if he thought if I saw his burn that would ruin everything.

I wasn't about to let him get away with that.

I reached over and took his left hand in mine and turned it so I could see his arm. Before he even had a chance to say anything, I pressed my lips to the back of his hand and kissed my way all the way up his arm, across his shoulder, and up his neck, before I lightly bit on his earlobe and spoke as I started to travel down his chest.

"Don't ever feel like you have to hide from me. You're beautiful, every single inch of you."

Tristan let out a soft moan as I kissed my way down his chest and over his stomach until I reached his glorious dick nestled in a thatch of dark curls. The slit was already dripping with precum and I knew it wouldn't be long before he was coming in my mouth. My mouth watered at just the thought of what Tristan tasted like. I looked up at him as I ran my tongue along his shaft, pausing just before the dripping head of his cock, causing his breath to hitch as he watched me.

"Oh God, just when I thought you couldn't get any sexier," he said, as he locked his eyes on mine.

I smirked before I took his tip into my mouth and sucked on it, causing him to let out a hiss. I moaned my appreciation as his unique flavor burst over my tongue and I finally got to taste him. Just as I'd suspected, he was the perfect blend of sweet and salty.

I wanted more.

I *needed* more.

I took him all the way down to his base and I couldn't help but let a grumbly moan tumble from my throat as I felt his hardness slide over my tongue. I felt Tristan run his hand into my hair and I could tell by how tense his hand was he was doing everything he could to keep himself from thrusting into my mouth.

I continued to work his cock as I flicked open the lid of the tube of lube.

Slathering the slick liquid on three of my fingers, I moved my hand to pluck gently at his puckered hole. He relaxed and pressed back against my hand with his unspoken request, and I gradually inserted my index finger bit by bit into his tight ass. I didn't know how long it had been since he had last been stretched and I didn't want to just jump right in with two fingers. I was glad for my control and the presence of mind to be vigilant and careful with him as he gripped around my finger. I paused for a moment to allow him to get used to the intrusion. The last thing I wanted to do was hurt him or cause him any pain.

When his muscles relented, allowing me movement once more, I slowly worked my finger in and out of him, keeping my mouth wrapped around his pulsing shaft. He was still so very tight but with the combined pleasure of my mouth and fingers, he started to loosen up until he was back to moaning and whimpering for more.

Once I felt like he was ready, I added a second finger and began to truly stretch him out. I was relieved when Tristan started to wiggle his hips to get more of my fingers inside of him. He was starting to really loosen up and become comfortable with me. I added a third finger and began to look for his sweet spot, that one place that would make him scream. The second my fingers ran over it, Tristan gave a loud moan as he thrust his hips up, pushing his dick even deeper into my mouth. I moaned at the sensation of his dick pushing further into my mouth and I continued to rub circles over his sweet spot.

"Oh fuck, you're gonna make me come," he warned, but I had no interest in pulling my mouth off. I had to taste him and I was not going to stop until I got it.

It was only a moment later when Tristan's hips snapped up and he gave a hoarse cry as he came hot and hard down my throat. I moaned as his sweet taste flooded my mouth. I easily swallowed what Tristan had to give me as he continued to twitch.

Once he stopped pulsing, I removed my fingers from his hole and pulled my mouth off of his dick. Tristan instantly pulled me in for a passionate kiss. Our tongues danced with each other and he moaned as the taste of his essence flooded his own mouth.

I reached over for the condom and easily slid it on as our tongues continued to dance with each other. I felt Tristan opening his legs up wider for me as I lowered myself between his legs. I pulled back from the kiss and moved my hand down to my dick as I lined up to his hole. Tristan angled his hips up and I placed my hands on the back of his thighs to lift his hips up more. I placed my tip against his pucker and slowly pushed in.

I wanted to pound the hell out of him, but I knew I had to go slow at first. Even though I had stretched him, he was still so very tight and I didn't want to hurt him. Slowly, I moved inch by inch, watching as my dick disappeared inside of him until I was buried balls deep. Tristan wrapped his legs around my hips and I placed my forehead against his as we both tried to catch our breaths.

"Holy shit, you feel fucking amazing," I whispered as I fought not to move.

"So do you. So big, so fucking big. I'm good, move," Tristan said with need dripping from his voice.

I didn't need to be told twice, not when it felt this good. I pulled out almost all of the way before I pressed back in, causing us both to moan. I went slow at first, but once I felt him truly starting to adjust to my size, I didn't need to hold back.

"So good, Baby. So tight."

Tristan's hands went to my back and

his nails dug into my skin as I snapped my hips hard and fast, pushing all of my dick deep inside of him. Tristan angled his hips once again, and I started to look for his sweet spot. I knew I hit it dead on when he let out a scream of pleasure.

"Fuck yes," Tristan moaned through panted breaths.

I moved my hand over to Tristan's dick and I started to jerk him off in time with my thrusts. Both of us were a writhing moaning mess. Neither one of us could seem to get enough of each other. I never wanted this to end. Being inside of him, it felt like we had done this a million times. He was home to me and I never wanted to be anywhere else.

"I'm so close," he mewled, his fingers gripping my biceps so hard I was sure to have bruises tomorrow. I didn't care. I loved it.

"Me too. I want to feel you come. Come for me, Darlin'," I ordered as I picked up my pace.

I could feel his legs shaking from the pleasure coursing through him. After a few more thrusts, Tristan let out loud, keening cry.

"Hawke," he called out as he came hard once again, jet after jet of jizz escaping his slit as his dick twitched and pulsed in my fist.

The tightening of his walls around my dick was enough to push me over the edge. Electricity raced up my spine and I snapped my hips forward, going as deep as I let myself go.

"Tris!" I groaned as I erupted inside of him.

Tristan's legs fell from my hips and he collapsed back against the pillows, boneless and with a half-lidded, sated look crossing his features. I dropped down over him before I leaned in to press my mouth against his. We were both out of breath, but neither of us were ready to lose the physical connection to the other.

I brought my hand up to the side of his face as we continued to slowly kiss, our tongues tangling once more. I knew I would have to let him go eventually, we were both going to need some serious sleep after this, but for right now, I was more than happy to simply kiss him and hold him as our bodies calmed back down.

CHAPTER ELEVEN

Tristan

AS QUIETLY AS I could, I climbed out of my bed and grabbed some sweatpants and a t-shirt before I made my way out of my bedroom and back to the living room. The glowing clock on my stove told me it was just after two in the morning. I had only slept maybe an hour, assuming I was that lucky.

I was used to not being able to sleep. I was used to having my mind racing with different thoughts. Tonight they weren't racing because of past memories or a case, though. Tonight, I couldn't get my mind to turn off because I was mentally freaking out about having sex with Hawke.

This was all kinds of bad.

We were working together. We would

still see each other even after this case was closed. I'd never slept with anyone who was connected to my job, because I didn't want that awkwardness at work. I shouldn't have done it. I can normally keep myself in line and yet, for some reason with Hawke, I couldn't resist him.

Once again when he'd touched me it felt like a fire had exploded within my body. And once again he felt familiar. I had never been with him. I hadn't met him before this and yet, my whole body was reacting to him like I had known him my whole life. It was ridiculous and made zero sense. No matter how much I try to ignore it, my body didn't want to listen.

I had to put distance back between us. I had to get my mind focused again. I couldn't let Hawke's presence distract me. I couldn't let him break down all of my walls. Last night was a slip up and it wasn't one I could allow to happen again.

Letting out a sigh, I plopped down on my couch. I glanced at my phone and noticed that Detective West had sent me the evidence that he'd collected from Spy Guy.

I opened my laptop up and pulled up Detective West's email. I had to focus on what truly mattered—catching my parents' killer. I couldn't afford to let

Hawke distract me again. Too much was riding on me finding this arsonist. Too many victims were counting on me to solve their case and get them justice. I couldn't let a pretty face distract me any longer. Even if he made me feel things I had never felt before.

***

It was nearing four in the morning when I heard footsteps coming toward the living room. I looked over and saw Hawke standing there in just his jeans as he leaned against the doorjamb into the living room. It took all of my strength to keep my gaze on his and not to let my eyes wander down over his very toned chest and stomach. The man was ridiculously sexy. He was sexy to the point where it just wasn't fair.

The man was all muscle, including a delicious six pack that made my mouth water. There wasn't an ounce of fat on him and don't even get me started on his strong thighs and amazing looking ass. He was sex on a stick and it was not fair. Not because I couldn't sleep with him again, but because there was nothing I could do in a gym that would ever make me look as good as him.

I didn't even have a one pack.

I wasn't chubby or out of shape, but I was flat. I didn't work out. I hated the gym. It was why I always ran outside. Running was the only form of exercise that I enjoyed doing, to an extent, and it didn't give me tight-as-sin abs. I had some muscles on my arms from just typically lifting at crime scenes, and my legs were in good shape, but I was nothing compared to him.

I couldn't stop the flood of images that invaded my mind as I tried to not oogle him. My mind apparently had other ideas, though, because all I could see was our time together just a few short hours ago. The pleasure that he'd brought to my body was unlike anything I had ever felt before. Sex had always felt okay to me, but it was never something that my body craved, at least until Hawke showed up in my life.

We'd only gone one round last night, but I could have gone for another six and still wanted more. I wasn't used to that. I wasn't used to craving someone.

To being horny.

I knew it was stupid, because I had been a typical hormonal teenager, but even then I had never been too interested in sex. I always figured that was just my personality. Not everyone was interested in sex. Not everyone spent their time in the shower masturbating. Plus, I had a lot going on with the fire and adjusting to life without my parents at that point. It was only logical for sexual activity to take a backseat.

Now it felt like this monster inside of me had woken up after being in hibernation for fifteen years and it was starving. As if there was no amount of food that I could feed it for it to finally be happy and satisfied. Even sitting there, I had to fight with my growing erection. Just the sight of the man was enough to make me want to get down on my knees or bend over for him.

I felt like a bitch in heat.

It was pathetic and I was above that behavior. Now I just needed my dick to understand it.

"Sorry, did I wake you?" I asked.

"No, I rolled over and you weren't there. You've been looking more tired each day, and I figured you were having a hard time sleeping. Now I've confirmed that theory. Do you want to talk about it?"

Talking about my screwed up mind was not something I wanted to do.

Not now. Not ever.

Thankfully, I had something that

would work beautifully to change the topic without coming across as emotionally damaged.

"Detective West sent me the customer list and security footage from Spy Guy. I've just been combing through it."

"I'll make some coffee," he said, flashing me a warm smile as he strolled over to the kitchen. The fact that he already knew where my coffee was kept should have bothered me and yet, it felt right somehow. Something else I chose to ignore. I was getting very good at ignoring what was happening between us. At least, my emotions about it.

"Anyone pop?" he asked as he got the coffee maker going.

"Not yet. There's audio, but so far it's a bunch of guys who think they are all James Bond. I've been going through the customer list, but it's only debit and credit cards. He doesn't keep track of cash transactions, so we might not get him that way. I'm hoping we can get him on camera. Spy Guy has a website, but you can't order online so he'd have had to go in to get the cameras."

"And we're sure it's not the owner?"

"Everything about him is clean. Detective West looked into him, but he doesn't think he's our guy. He also has an alibi for the Rollins' fire. He was out of town. Credit card transactions put him two hundred miles away at some spy conference. He didn't get back until yesterday morning."

"He's definitely out, then. It would also be stupid for him to use cameras from his own inventory since they could easily be traced back to him. My guess is it's a new customer. If our guy knew about these cameras before, he would have made the switch even if he had some of the old ones left." He brought over two mugs of hot coffee, handing me one. He even knew how I took it.

How could it be possible for someone to know me so well after such a short amount of time?

We'd barely even spoken about anything personal and yet, he had paid enough attention to notice what I put in my coffee, just like I knew what he put in his.

He sat down next to me and I could feel the heat from his body. It was doing nothing to calm my own body, or my desire to reach out and feel him. It would be so simple, too. I could run my fingers over his leg, down his back. Hell, I could straddle his lap and I got the impression he would be all for it. I had to force my mind to inform my body to not move. It should have been simple, but I felt like my body was fighting me. As if I was drowning and it was taking everything I had to not breathe in the water. It shouldn't be this hard, and yet, it was.

"You know, normally I have a feeling about cases. I can get a rough idea of who the arsonist is. The places he picks, the people he targets, how he does it, if he leaves people alive or kills them. Are the targets empty or have people in them. I can get a profile and a picture of him in my mind. This time, though, I can't *see* him. I don't know if it's because he's smarter than me or because I can't get past the emotional part of the case this time around," I admitted as the security footage continued to play in the background for us to watch.

"He's not smarter than you. Yes, you are emotionally connected to the investigation, but sometimes I think that can be a good thing. If you weren't emotionally connected, would you still be investigating these cases? Would you have suspected it was an arsonist? Would you have connected the cameras? Sometimes, being emotionally involved can lead to disaster, but then there are times when that connection is everything to the case. All of those people will have a chance at getting justice because of your connection. I don't see that as a disadvantage, Darlin'."

And just like that I felt better.

What the hell was it about him that made the voices in my head go quiet?

My grandparents were never mean to me. They never raised their hand to me. They never belittled me or put me down. They weren't terrible people, they were just absent mentally and emotionally. And yet, I couldn't help but feel like I wasn't good enough. Whenever I couldn't solve a case in a reasonable amount of time, I felt like I was failing, like I wasn't good enough. I wasn't smart enough, quick enough, to stop the arsonist before his next fire. I had never been able to silence the voices but a few words from Hawke and they were gone.

I didn't understand any of it. I shouldn't feel connected to him. I shouldn't feel this relaxed around him. I definitely shouldn't be talking about my past or my feelings. I swore to myself I wouldn't. I swore that I would keep the walls up and be nothing but professional with him, but there we were. I had gone against my own promise to myself and fallen for his beautiful eyes.

The sex had been epic, and I couldn't say I regretted it. I should, though. I should be kicking myself for ever even allowing it to happen. I couldn't, though, because it had been the best night of my life. It was a sad fact, because at my age having a one-night stand shouldn't qualify as my best of anything, but it was.

It was better in person than it had been in any of the dreams that still haunted me. I needed to keep my distance from him, but I didn't want to and that didn't scare me as nearly as much as it should have.

"Look, about last night," I started, but Hawke cut me off.

"You don't have to say anything," He started, but it was my turn to cut him off. I had no idea what he was going to say. I was honestly too afraid to hear it, because if he said it was a mistake I was going to lose every ounce of courage I had managed to scrounge up.

"I don't regret it. In truth, it was the best night I've ever had. I'm not good with social situations. I used to be, but after the fire my world got so much smaller and now I don't know how to make it grow. What I do know is that I like being around you. I'm really terrible at this, though. I don't do relationships, mostly because that would mean I'd have to be vulnerable and I'm really not good at that part." I let out a soft sigh before I continued. "Look, what I'm trying to say is, I don't see last night as a mistake. I understand if you do."

"I don't. I don't regret a single second of last night. I don't see it as a mistake. I was worried you might see it that way and I couldn't handle hearing you say it. I can't tell you how happy I am to hear you say it wasn't a mistake. And for the record, I am terrible at relationships, too. I just got out of one not too long ago. We dated for two years and the whole time he was in the closet. I kept telling myself that he wasn't lying about coming out, that the excuses he made were justified. It took two years of being a dirty secret before I'd finally had enough and left. So, I'm not really good at this either, but I'm willing to learn with you."

My heart started to flutter in my chest at his words. This was stupid, I shouldn't be reacting this way to him, but I couldn't help it. Just hearing that he didn't see last night as a mistake, that he wanted to potentially see where this could go, it made me feel excited, hopeful, and those were two emotions I hadn't felt in many years.

"I'd really like that," I said, flashing him a warm smile.

God, what the hell was it about this man?

He gave me a sexy smile as he turned and started to close the gap between us. I didn't even hesitate to move in and the second his lips touched mine, I let out a soft moan. I had never really liked kissing, but the way he did it, the way his lips felt against mine, I was quickly becoming addicted to it.

All too soon, though, he was snapping back and looking at the computer as he spoke.

"I know that voice."

I looked over at the computer to see who was speaking. I didn't recognize the voice softly playing in the background or the image. They weren't talking about anything really, the man was just asking Mr. Rogers for his order. Apparently, he had called it in.

"Who is he?"

"That's Taye Amaro. He's a firefighter at Station House Seventeen."

"Amaro? My Captain is Damon Amaro, are they related?"

"Taye is Damon's older brother."

Holy shit.

There was no reason for Taye to be

buying anything from Spy Guy. His name also wasn't on the transaction list, so he obviously paid in cash.

It would also explain why my Captain didn't want me to look into any of these cases. Why he was happy to let them be closed to accidental or go into the cold case box. Taye would know how to start a fire with being a firefighter, he also would have access to test houses. He could have started a fire for them to run drills and no one would be the wiser of it.

"That's the camera." I said, as a medium size box was placed on the counter and Taye pulled one of the small packages out of it.

"Based on the package size, there's got to be easily a hundred cameras inside that box. We only found ten. How far back is this?"

"A week. I started at the most recent and was working my way back. If he is buying that many, my guess is that means he'd already bought some before to test it out. He could be testing them at the firehouse in the burn house. I don't know anything about him. Have you worked with him?"

There were plenty of firefighters that I had never worked with nor seen before. I only went to places where arson was suspected. If they didn't suspect any foul play, then there was no need to have a fire investigator there. With Hawke being a firefighter, he was more likely to have worked with Taye or seen him at the fire bar—a bar that catered only to first responders.

"I haven't worked with him, but I've seen him at the bar. We've talked a few times, but I don't tend to stay around him long. People tend to give him a wide berth when they can. He's a bit... fuck, I don't even know. He's got anger issues, and he has an issue with authority. That's why he's only a Lieutenant even though he's forty. He's odd, and when I've been around him I get a bad vibe from him. He has some friends, guys who are a lot like him and others who respect him because he's a legacy. Both him and his brother are firefighters, obviously, but so was his father, his grandfather, and his great grandfather. All of them joined the Fire Department at eighteen and were Captain or higher ranking. Taye is the black sheep."

"It would make sense if he was an arsonist. They tend to be socially odd. They don't like authority and can have anger issues. Being around fire, it would have helped to ease his compulsion and obsession with it. He's forty, so he would have been fifteen with the apartment fire."

"Is that possible? It seems like he would have been too young to be able to get away with a fire like that."

It was too young.

Not too young to set a house on fire, but it was too young to take on an apartment building like that. Someone would have noticed him. He wouldn't have been able to build the device and get away with it. He wouldn't have known about putting cameras up. It was why I believed so strongly that it was two people.

A mentor and mentee.

It was looking like Taye was the mentee and now we needed to find the mentor, assuming he was even still alive.

"He would have been. Even if he lived there, it would have been too complicated for him to pull off by himself, especially with it coming back as accidental. My gut is telling me that he's the apprentice; we need the master for older fires. Do you know of any stressors in his life? Something that may have made him snap?"

"I don't know him that well. I know ten years ago his father died in a fire on the job. Apparently it was a really bad fire. His father, Henry, was a Station Chief with House Forty-Two. They were called to a storage facility fire. It was supposed to be simple enough, but the place was filled with smoke and his men kept getting turned around. One of the storage units was storing propane and it all went up. The Chief went in and he never came back out, along with two of his men."

"That would be enough to push his desire for fires into overdrive. You don't just walk up to someone, though, and ask them to teach you how to get away with arson. He must have found his teacher somehow, maybe someone who was close to him already and had seen the signs."

"He's a firefighter though, why would he need a mentor to begin with? It's not like he wouldn't know how to start a fire or how to control one. He doesn't seem to have the personality type to be submissive either."

"Which would mean that the original arsonist approached him. He had to have been in Taye's life to know that Taye would be interested in starting fires. He's gotta be in his personal circle."

The trick was going to be finding that person. Neither one of us knew Taye, really, so if we started asking people at his fire house about him, it would start to raise red flags and questions would be asked. We could spook him and lose him forever or worse, force his hand to do something incredibly dangerous and put even more people at risk.

"We can't ask any of his friends or him without tipping him off. How good of a man is your Captain?"

I let out a deep breath before I spoke.

"I don't know. I mean, he's always willing to help with a case. He wants our cases to be closed and to get to the truth. I've never had a problem with him. At the same time though, he didn't want me looking into these cases. He doesn't believe they are connected. I thought maybe he was against it because he truly believed I was seeing shit, but now, I don't know. Maybe he suspected it was his brother and he's been trying to cover it up."

"He is the only one out of his family so far to not be a physical firefighter. He's like you, he went straight into investigations right from the academy. Maybe that was by design so he could cover up the fires connected to Taye or this mentor."

I wasn't liking any of this. None of this was playing out well in my mind. Either my Captain was involved and he knew what his older brother was doing and covering up his crimes, or he didn't know and I was going to have to fight him tooth and nail with evidence that his brother was an arsonist who was responsible for multiple deaths.

On top of all of that, they were legacies. That came with a level of respect that most people didn't receive. Taye being arrested for arson could destroy that legacy. When people heard the name Amaro, they wouldn't think about all of the good the family had done. It would be all about the fires and the people Taye had killed.

"Either way, I have to talk to my Captain. I have to see where he stands. It's the only play we have. Taye has easily a hundred more cameras. That's ten more fires, ten more chances of someone being killed. We don't have time to play this one close to the chest or slow walk it."

"Do you want me to go with you?"

"No, it's better for me to do this one-on-one. Thanks, though," I said, flashing him a warm smile at the offer.

"I have a shift in a couple of hours. I can ask the guys at the house if they know Taye. They've been around longer than me, they might have worked with him."

"Be careful, we don't know who could

be close friends with him."

"Always. Why don't I make us some breakfast and we can keep going over the footage. Maybe there was someone else that bought a bulk order of the cameras," he offered.

I gave him a nod of acknowledgment, and he headed back into my kitchen. I knew I wouldn't find another customer who was buying the cameras in bulk, but it was something I had to do to ensure I could prove without a doubt that Taye was the only one to purchase the cameras.

I knew my Captain wasn't going to be happy about any of it. He wasn't going to want to admit to what was right in front of his face, not that I could blame him. Taye was his older brother; he wouldn't want to think that he could be responsible for someone like this. He was going to be hard to convince, but I had no choice but to convince him. Too much was riding on the line with this case. I just hoped I could get my Captain to see what I saw. If I couldn't, I didn't know what I would do.

CHAPTER TWELVE

Hawke

I HEADED INTO the Station House and made my way straight to the main area where the kitchen and living room was. The house was pretty cozy considering thirty guys all lived in it in opposite shifts. We tried to get along with the guys on the previous shift. Not moving things around when we know it drove one of the other guys crazy. We made sure to only eat the food in our fridge and not their fridge. We tried to keep it as civil and peaceful as we could.

It might sound silly to have to have two fridges or to keep the living room in the same position, but when you are trying to keep things civil with thirty people in one house, those things help to prevent war.

For the most part, it was all men there.

We'd had a couple female paramedics, but they were floaters and typically only filled in until we could find a permanent replacement. Paramedics came and went a good chunk of the time. Last year we had twenty of them in one year. There was even one shift where I started the day and it was one guy, but by the end of my shift it was another one. Sometimes it was a revolving door around there.

I walked into the kitchen area and saw Zander cleaning up some dishes. I could see that the dishes annoyed him and I knew that meant they weren't his dishes he was washing. So either it was one of the guys on our shift who'd dumped them and run, or the guys from the other shift hadn't done their dishes. A huge pet peeve that Zander had. I couldn't blame him. We were all supposed to be responsible for our own cleanup.

"Who are we killing?" I asked with a smirk as I slid onto one of the bar stools at the counter.

"They're pigs. I get it, the shift was busy and they didn't have time in between calls to eat and clean up. But then one of them could at least stay and do their fucking dishes. We're not their maids and if any of us pulled this shit, they would be leaving them in our bunks," Zander snapped and I knew the frustration had been building for a while.

Things between the two shifts did come up and unfortunately, as humans we had personalities and those personalities didn't always play well with each other. There had even been a few times where I'd seen Cap going toe to toe with the other shift's Captain.

"I know, and I agree with you. I can send Sinclair a text letting him know that we don't appreciate the mess and to make sure it's cleaned up next time. In a very polite and non-confrontational tone," I offered, flashing him a warm smile.

I didn't care about confrontation, but often I was the one who had to play peacekeeper with the guys. Get a bunch of alpha males together and trap them in a house, and it didn't always end well. Every house needed guys like me who could play mediator and try to keep the alphas from tearing each other apart.

"You can let him know that the next time they want to leave their dirty fucking dishes everywhere, I'm putting itching powder in their bunks," he seethed.

"So many swear words and the shift just started," I teased.

Zander was very friendly, when someone didn't piss him off. He did swear though. Like, a lot. Sailors would be proud; some would even be offended by the words that had come out of his mouth. He was rough around the edges and when I first started there I was a bit worried about him. He was the definition of an alpha male. He was also a ladies man and I was worried he would have an issue with me being gay. He didn't care, though. We'd even had conversations about my sex life. It took a special man to be straight and not even bat an eye at sex talk with a gay man.

"Fuck off," he said, chuckling.

I gave a snigger. I decided to ask him about Taye before the others came in, or before that bell went off and we had to leave. "You are a frequent flier at the fire bar," I started, but he cut me off.

"Seems like there's an insult in that."

"There's not, just an observation." He didn't need me to tell him he was a manwhore. He already knew. In the time I had known him, he'd slept with close to a hundred different women. Sometimes multiple women in a single night.

"Mhm, and where is this observation going?" he asked, still dubious.

"Taye Amaro, you know anything about him?"

"He's not gay and if he is, he's so far

deep in the closet he's living in Narnia. He's a homophobic asshole. Stay the hell away from him," he answered with an edge in his voice.

"I'm not interested in him like that. There's a chance he's connected to a series of fires. A friend of mine who is investigating the case asked if I knew him. I told him I would ask around the house with the guys. I know you frequent the same bar, though."

"That's not surprising. He hides it well, but I can see the darkness in his eyes. He's completely fake, but every now and then, when he thinks no one is looking, his mask slips and people see the devil that he is. If your friend thinks he's connected, then he probably is. Good luck finding anyone that truly knows him, though. He has a different face for each person he sees. He only shows fake interest with people who could get him somewhere or make him feel special."

"I've always gotten a bad vibe off of him. I've kept a distance between us and I don't tend to go to the fire bar very often. You ever hear any stories that he's told? Anything about a fire that maybe he was too interested in?"

I doubted he would be dumb enough to talk about one of his own fires, but one never knew. He was arrogant enough to believe he would never get caught. Arsonists loved to relive their fires, it was why so many preferred to record it now. It allowed them to see it whenever they wanted and experience the thrill again without having to rely solely on their memory. Memories faded over time and they got spotty. They were easy to mix up if someone were trying to remember specifics, especially if they were responsible for multiple fires. Those little facts, little memories, they were what arsonists lived for, what they cherished. He would want to remember them, relive them, as often as he could in any form that he could.

"Nothing specific, really. He talks about fires on the job, always the ones that most of us never want to talk about. For him, it seemed like the more gruesome the better. The ones with horrible burn victims, alive and dead. He never talks about the accidents, the rescue calls. Even when the victims are mangled, he never cares about it. He only likes the fires and he has no problem spending hours talking about it. I don't know if this is true, but Keith from Thirty-Fifth, he did a fly by at House Nineteen when Taye was there. He swears that

Taye had a scrapbook of some of the most horrific fires. He would look at them before going to sleep. Something is definitely off with that man."

Couldn't argue that. It all fit though, with who an arsonist was. If he did have a scrapbook, that could help Tristan with his case. It was quite possible that Taye had a scrapbook of the fires he started, little tokens to help him relive the fires when he wasn't able to watch the videos.

It was something that Tristan would be able to look into and hopefully find. That was assuming he would even be able to get Taye brought in alive. Most arsonists would go down in a blaze of glory, literally. They were not above setting themselves on fire to escape prison. They didn't care who else was killed in the process, and what scared me was that person very well could be Tristan.

"Thanks, I'll let him know. It's all preliminary right now. And obviously, he needs to be careful given that he's a firefighter and a legacy. I'd appreciate it if you didn't mention this to anyone."

"You don't even have to ask, Brother. Tell him to be careful, though. People don't like Taye and everyone might not be all that shocked by him starting fires, but that doesn't mean they will ignore the red wall. If he's going to go up against Taye, he better make sure there is no wiggle room with the evidence or someone could turn on him."

And that was my other fear. I was terrified that Taye was going to turn on Tristan and finish what his mentor had started. I was also terrified that the fire department was going to turn on Tristan after having Taye arrested.

Tristan didn't run into fires, so it wasn't like he had to worry about his fellow brothers leaving him in a fire. But he was still out in public. He went onto crime scenes and to the bar. They could go after him outside of work, where they wouldn't be followed or watched. It was extremely dangerous for him, and I was very worried about how easily all of it could blow back on him.

I knew it could also blow back on me, too, but I wasn't worried about myself. I knew my brothers at the house had my back, even if they might not agree with me. They would never let anything happen to me. I also knew they would believe the evidence and they'd know that I would never go after another firefighter unless I was one hundred percent certain he was in the wrong.

"He's being careful and he has a

detective helping him with gathering evidence. He's not going to go after Taye unless he has solid evidence against him. He knows what's on the line."

"Good. Be smart."

The look he gave me told me everything I needed to know. He knew I had my hand in the proverbial cookie jar, but he wasn't going to try and convince me to take it out. He would support me through it no matter what, and that was one of the reasons why I loved him. He always had my back, whether I was right or wrong it didn't matter to him. If I was going to battle, he would be standing right next to me ready to go. Zander was a ride or die man and everyone needed a man like that in their life. I just hoped that we would both get through it unscathed.

I also hoped Tristan and I could get enough evidence to put Taye in prison and be able to start making a real go with whatever was going on between us. I was leaving the ball in his court and I really hoped he was going to serve it back to me. Only time would tell, and I had no choice but to wait and see what time had in store for the both of us.

We just had to get through the investigation first.

CHAPTER THIRTEEN

Tristan

I HAD MADE the walk to my Captain's office plenty of times in the past fifteen years, but I had never felt this nervous before at just the thought of seeing him. A Captain was supposed to be a firefighters' first line of defense. He was supposed to be the one person who would have their back and be there for them. He was supposed to help them and support them.

At least, that was what a Captain was supposed to be.

I had learned from other investigators and firefighters that it wasn't always the case. There were plenty of Captains and Chiefs who didn't have their team's back. Who didn't care to help. They sat in their office and did the work they had to do and ignored the work they didn't have to do.

They didn't stick their necks out to fight for what was right. They didn't risk their careers by doing what was right. They were interested in doing what they had to do to get by and get their paycheck, and not a lick more.

Captain Amaro was a good man, we didn't have many issues between us. I knew he wasn't happy about me having these cases, but I didn't know why. At first, I figured it was because he didn't believe me. That he thought I was seeing something that wasn't there. Now, with this new information, it was very possible that he didn't want me looking into these cases because they were connected to his brother. I really hoped that wasn't the real reason.

I was taking a huge risk going to him right now. If he knew that his brother was starting these fires, he could tip him off. He could try and discredit me, ruin my career, just to keep these cases swept under the rug. I would have to fight all on my own.

Yes, Hawke was helping me, but there was only so much he could do. He wasn't an investigator. He was a firefighter. We played in the same world, but we were not playing the same sport.

There was no short supply of tension

between the firefighters and the investigators. The firefighters tended to think investigators weren't real firefighters because they worked behind a desk and didn't go into a blazing inferno. They also assumed investigators were stuck up and that we thought we were better than them. Other investigators thought the firefighters were idiots, for lack of a better word, because they were constantly destroying evidence or overlooking a clear sign of arson and ruling it themselves as accidental. There was no short supply of ego on either side and it often led to conflicts and confrontations in the field and outside of it. I really hoped this wasn't going to blow up in my face, but I was keeping myself realistic at this point.

I knocked on my Captain's closed door. I waited until he granted me permission to enter. I sucked in a deep breath, bracing myself for the war that I was about to walk into. I opened the door and immediately closed it behind me.

I could see a quick flash of annoyance flicker through his eyes, not that I could blame him. We had gone a few rounds recently over these cases and I knew he already assumed that was why I was here. He was right, but that didn't make this any easier.

I didn't sit. I wanted to be standing and have some form of authority and power to my stance. He wasn't going to make me feel like I was wrong. He wasn't going to make me feel like I was crazy or out of line. Not this time. I had the evidence and this was going to happen, with or without his support.

"Investigator Cole, what do you want?"

He seemed stressed. The mountain of paperwork on his desk told me that he would be working all night to try and get it done. I knew he had been taking on more work because there were fewer Captains currently in the investigation unit. It happened, people moved, people get promoted, people left. The Upper Brass also didn't have the time to promote someone or knew who they might want to promote. The result was the rest of the Captains or Chiefs got the extra work to try and cover the person who had gone. They had no choice but to fill the gap and unfortunately, it resulted in a lot of work that the remaining people had to take on. I knew he was overworked, so I didn't take offense to his dismissive tone or that he seemed annoyed that I was there.

"I need to tell you something and I need you to be open-minded, Sir. I need you to understand that I wouldn't be coming to you with this if I didn't have solid evidence to back up what I'm claiming," I started, but before I could get much further he cut me off.

"If this is about those ghost cases you have been working on, the same cases I told you to shut down, you can walk out that door right now. I'm done with this, Cole, and I will not tell you again. We have enough cases in our backlog, I don't need you chasing down ones that are already closed."

We did have a large backlog, also a result of not having enough investigators, but the city wasn't looking to hire anymore. I knew this was going to be an uphill battle with him. I had mentioned these cases too many times to him and he was finally reaching his breaking point. But I couldn't walk away. I was way past that point and he needed to hear what I had to say, whether he liked it or not.

"Shelby Lewis, the fire at 467 Wilton Street yesterday. Her and her two young children were killed in a fire that was started by a device placed in the electrical panel. The same device that was responsible for starting the fire at Ms. Rollin's home two days ago. The same device that has been connected to thirty-five other cases. All thirty-five cases plus the most recent two cases, had cameras installed in the homes. All of them without those cameras being installed by the homeowners. The fire at Wilton Street, every battery was pulled from all of their smoke detectors," I continued, but once again he cut me off.

"I don't want to hear about any of these past cases. I'm sick to death of having to tell you the same thing. Having cameras in their home doesn't mean they are connected. They were investigated and solved."

I didn't let him finish. I continued on as if he didn't even interrupt me. I had to get this out before he kicked me out of there. The last thing I wanted to do was get into a shoving match with my Captain.

"The fire on Wilton Street had cameras, but they were newer. I took one of the cameras to Hank and he was able to get a serial number off of it. It traced back to the inventory at Spy Guy. Barba was able to get a warrant for the security footage and customer transaction list. Detective West served the warrant and I have spent the night going through security footage. Only one person used cash to purchase the cameras that were placed in the home." I pulled out the photo and placed it on his desk as I delivered the deadly blow. "Your brother. Taye. He purchased roughly a hundred of the small spy cameras."

He stared at me, now giving me his full attention. Gone was the anger from his eyes as he took the photo and looked at it. I knew what was coming and I had no way of giving him more proof than this. All I could do was hope I could get him to see the circumstantial evidence was too much to be a coincidence. I needed his help and I really hoped he would give it to me.

"He could have bought them for the firehouse. This doesn't prove anything," he rebutted as he tossed the photo back down onto his desk.

"He could, but that doesn't explain how one of the cameras he purchased ended up in a house that killed a widower and her two young children," I countered.

"They could have been stolen. You have no proof that he was there."

"With all due respect, Sir, you are not that stupid." I knew that was going to piss him off, but I didn't have time to tiptoe around the chain of command.

"Excuse me?" he snapped.

"Stop thinking like a Captain and start thinking like an investigator again. You used to be one of the best investigators in the fire department. There are multiple fires all with the same MO, all with the same cameras put up. One or two, maybe a coincidence, but thirty-seven, that we know of, that's a pattern, a signature and you know it. I found an old apartment building fire from twenty-five years ago with the same device and cameras found. I think it was the first fire to this arsonist. No one died, but he most likely lived there or knew someone who did. I know it wasn't Taye, he was too young, but I think whoever started the older fires mentored Taye and Taye set the last two fires at least. He switched the cameras, most likely because he ran out of the other ones. They were discontinued fifteen years ago. These new cameras came with a server that isn't connected to the Internet. He would have that server somewhere with him. He has footage of the fire as he watched it."

"You don't know it's him. You only have him on camera purchasing small cameras. He could have used them at the firehouse. And I'm not saying these older fires aren't connected to each other, but we have no way to prove that. I understand it's personal to you with your parents' case, but we have no way to get evidence to reopen closed cases and investigate them for arson."

"Which is why I am pursuing the most recent cases that we have. It's a mentor and an apprentice. Taye is that apprentice and he could give us his mentor who we can speak with. You know arsonists like to lay claim to their work, they brag, we could get the cases closed if we get a confession. I know this is your brother, Cap. I don't like this anymore than you do. I don't want to stand here and tell you that your older brother is an arsonist. That your family's legacy is going to be destroyed by this. I don't want it to be a firefighter who does this, but the evidence is too hard to look away. You know he wouldn't need to purchase that many cameras for the firehouse. You know that no one would steal the cameras and use them to start a fire. And you know your brother, better than anyone. Are you really going to tell me, tell yourself, that there were no signs growing up? You know the signs of an arsonist; you know his behavior. You need to be honest with yourself so we can stop him before anyone else gets killed. He's already got at least four people that he's killed, including two children. I can stop him, but I can't without your help, Cap."

I really didn't know if he would. I prayed that he would, because I needed his help, I needed his support. He might be the only one who would be able to lead me to someone who could be the mentor in the relationship.

I could see the pain behind his eyes, the torment and conflict. He knew something, but he didn't know if he could admit to himself or to me. What I was asking him to do wasn't easy. I was asking him to betray not only his older brother, but his family's name. When this came out, it was going to be huge news and it wouldn't be long before every firehouse knew about it.

Before the Upper Brass knew about it.

This was going to cause him problems. He could very well be under investigation for it, too. It would be hard for people to believe that he knew nothing about what was going on. This was his only chance though, to prove that he was serious about his job, even if that meant that he had to help get his own brother arrested on arson charges.

He let out a deep sigh before he sat back in his chair and looked at me, meeting my eyes.

"Taye had always been odd growing up. He was six when he set fire to the carpet in the basement. It was small and our father was home and easily put it out. My mother was worried. He didn't really have friends and he wasn't social. She was worried that Taye's interest in fire was more than just a boy being a boy. My father thought that it was a good sign. He thought he was born to be a firefighter and he would make small controlled fires in the backyard with Taye. As he got older, Taye started to become disturbing. Around other people he was normal, but when he was home it was as if a switch had been flipped. I was terrified of him. We shared a room and I would spend all of my time out of it, even sleeping on the couch in the living room just so I didn't have to sleep around him. He got good at faking it around people."

"I've heard he has an issue with authority," I said as I absorbed everything that he had told me. It was all fitting with what an arsonist's profile was.

"Started with our father. The older he got, the more he wanted to do larger fires. He didn't want to have to wait for when my father was around for it. They often fought, sometimes physically. Taye barely made it through the fire academy, and the only reason he did was because my father and grandfather pulled some strings. He's never had respect for authority figures. He has always been very good at putting out fires. He's never held any fear of them. He's even done reckless things to help save someone."

"I know your father died in a fire roughly ten years ago at a storage facility. How has Taye been since then?" I suspected that was the stressor and Taye caused all the fires in the past ten years. I had no solid proof though, so I didn't want to bring that up just now.

"I saw him at our father's funeral. He seemed to be struggling and he was unstable. I justified it as him being upset over our father's death. Our mother had passed two years previously from cancer. I've barely seen him in the past decade. It's normally when we are going to the same conference or we happen to be at the same bar, and even then we only talk a small amount of time. I don't like being around him. He was close with our father. Our Dad seemed to be able to keep Taye in check, at least to a point. I think he always knew, though. He used to bring Taye in when he wasn't on shift to help run drills at different firehouses. He would have him set up the fire. I know our parents fought about it often. My mother didn't like that he was around fire so much and that our father was encouraging it. I think she always knew that he was born broken. My father only cared about fulfilling the legacy. It made it easier for him to ignore the signs or explain them away."

He ran a hand over his face and I could see that he was growing more tired as this conversation went on. I hated that I was adding to his stress, but there truly was nothing I could do about it. I needed some insight and answers and he was the only one who could give them to me.

"I'm sorry, Cap. This isn't how I wanted this case to go."

"It's not your fault. I should be the one apologizing. I shouldn't have dismissed your instinct with these cases. I should have taken the time to listen to you. Maybe if I had those people would still be alive, those kids would still be alive. We could have ended this years ago and maybe stopped Taye before he started his first fire. What do you need from me?"

I was relieved that he was willing to help me. That we had gotten over the initial shock and denial. Still though, that didn't ease my concerns that he would reach out to Taye and give him a head's up. They didn't appear to have much of a connection, and he seemed to understand how dangerous and sick his brother was, but that didn't change that sometimes blood was stronger than anything else in this world. All I could do was hope that he wouldn't reach out to Taye and tip him off.

"Was there anyone in his life that could have taken him on? Someone taught him about the cameras and the device. He would have been older, maybe had been burned himself."

"No, no one comes to mind, but like I said, we weren't that close. Captain William Clarke, he works out of the Twenty-First, they worked at the same firehouse ten years ago. He might have a better idea for you. You're going to speak with Taye?"

"I will be. For obvious reasons, you can't be involved in this, Cap. We need it clean for court."

"No, I understand. I'm not looking to put my hand in the cookie jar. He used to hide things in our bedroom in the closet under a floorboard. Old habits are hard to break, you might find the server there. Be careful though, he's not one to shy away from a fight and I don't need to tell you how dangerous arsonists are when they get backed into a corner," he warned.

"I know. I'll be careful, Sir. I'll make

sure to go with a detective when I go and speak with him."

I wasn't about to put myself in a dangerous position. Besides, I had to have a detective there when he was being questioned to make it official. I also wasn't stupid. I was not about to walk into a dangerous situation with an unstable arsonist. Most tended to set themselves on fire to avoid going to jail. I wasn't about to put my life at risk like that.

"I need a favor from you."

"Of course." I assumed this was the part where he asked me to do this as quietly as possible.

"Pull the case file 45721, it's the fire from the storage facility that killed my father and two others. Taye, he was acting very differently at his funeral. Emotional like I had never seen him before. I could smell booze on his breath so I dismissed it, then. But looking back, he seemed guilty. This mentor, you suspect his first fire was an apartment building. It's possible that Taye's first fire was the storage facility. It was closed and marked accidental due to a short in the HVAC system. I've never had a reason to believe otherwise, but..." He opened his arms slightly toward his desk, his features twisting in resignation.

"I'll pull the file and look into it. The only way to get a solid answer might be through Taye, though."

"I know. Be careful."

"Always," I said, giving him a small nod before I turned on my heel and strode out of his office.

I now had someone else to speak to and hopefully, Captain Clarke would be able to give me more intel on Taye and who was around him ten years ago. I needed to try and find this mentor. I didn't even know if he was still alive, but if he was I had to find him. Getting to speak to him might be the only way I would be able to get justice for all of the people who lost their lives to him.

The only way I would be able to get justice for my parents and myself.

I made my way out of the building and toward my car. I pulled out my phone and dialed Detective West. He wasn't going to be happy about this, but I knew he would have my back on it.

"Detective West."

"Hey, it's me, Tristan. I have a suspect on those arson cases for you. Lieutenant Taye Amaro. He works out of Station House Seventeen."

"A firefighter? You think he's behind

all of these fires?" Detective West asked, obviously shocked, and I could hear the worry in his voice.

You didn't go against the blue line for the police, and you didn't go against the red line for the firefighters. They were brothers and they had no problem closing ranks to protect one of their own. I knew I was potentially starting a war between not only the firefighters and the investigation division, but by asking Detective West to investigate him, it could be pitting cop against firefighter. It was a dangerous situation and it had to be handled very carefully.

"For the past ten years, including the two most recent fires. I believe he has a mentor who is responsible for the earlier fires. We have Taye on security footage purchasing, with cash, over a hundred of those cameras. I just spoke to his brother, my Captain, and he said that Taye has always had issues. That he started fires when he was six and has been unstable his whole life. Their father had been killed in a storage fire ten years ago. My Captain believes it's possible that could have been the first fire that Taye started. I'm going to pull the case file and review it. He didn't know of anyone who could have been a mentor, but he recommended that I speak with Captain Clarke, they were in the same firehouse at the time," I said as I climbed into my car.

"All right, I will start looking into Taye, quietly. You speak with Captain Clarke and let me know if he has someone in mind. I'll see if I can find someone on my end. I'll speak with ADA Barba about a search warrant for Taye's home."

That's what I loved about the detective. He didn't care if he was stepping foot into a war, he would do it in a heartbeat because it was the right thing to do. He never shied away from a tough case, even when it would have been in his best interest to. He was a good man and the reason why I always relied on him.

"Thanks, West. I know this puts you in a hard position."

"People are dead, kids are dead. That's the only thing that matters. Keep me posted."

"Will do," I said, before I ended the call.

Letting out a sigh, I cranked the ignition, shifted the car into gear and started to head toward firehouse Twenty-One. The only good thing about the impromptu visit was that I would get to see Hawke. That thought instantly warmed my heart and turned up the corners of my mouth, putting a smile on my face.

CHAPTER FOURTEEN

Hawke

I STROLLED INTO the Station House and immediately started toward where the bathroom was. I had been working on a rundown fire truck that Cap was hoping we could get started again. I wasn't the one who had experience with engines but I told him I would give it my best shot. I wasn't confident I could get it working again, but I was hopeful.

It had been a pretty slow day today, so far, thank fuck, but I also knew how quickly that could change. I had been hoping for a lighter day. I was feeling the fatigue of the past few days with pulling a lot of late nights working on the case with Tristan. I didn't regret it for a single second, but getting to sit for a little bit today would be nice. Hell, I was hoping to sneak a nap in later.

I couldn't stop the huge smile that spread over my face as I made my way into the main area and saw Tristan standing there. He looked very sexy wearing his suit, and what made it even better was knowing exactly how sexy he looked underneath it.

"Well, this is a nice surprise. What brings you by, Darlin'?"

"I spoke with my Captain and he recommended that I speak to your Captain. Apparently Captain Clarke and Taye worked in the same firehouse at the time of Taye's father's death."

"How did it go?" I asked, with a nod toward the hallway as I started to walk toward the bathroom.

"As well as could be expected. He was angry at first, but he came around. According to him, Taye started making fires at six and he's always been disturbing. Their father didn't want to see it, but apparently his mother did. I truly don't believe he knew what Taye was doing. He has barely seen him in ten years, since their father's funeral. I called Detective West and he's going to look into Taye. My Captain also wants me to look into the storage facility fire that killed their father. He is now wondering if Taye started the fire. I'll look into it, but I might not be able to find anything to pinpoint it to Taye."

"That might be impossible, unless he wants to admit to it, but even if he does there's no way to know if he's being honest. That might be something your Captain has to live without knowing for certain. Hopefully, Cap might know someone you can speak to."

"Where is everyone? It's pretty quiet in here."

"Cap is actually out meeting with someone and he won't be back for about forty minutes or so. The rest of the guys are outside running drills. I was working on an old engine that Cap is hoping I can get started," I said as I walked into the bathroom. "Care to shower with me?" I asked over my shoulder, flashing him a sexy smirk.

I really hoped he would say yes. I would have loved to be able to get my hands on him again, but there was no pressure. It was completely his call to make.

"What if someone walks in?"

"No one will. They just started a drill, so they'll be busy for an hour, easily. It's completely up to you," I said as I reached to pull my t-shirt over my head.

"He says, as he gets naked," he teased with a grin plastered on his face.

"What? I need a shower," I said with a wink and a playful smile.

"We're gonna get in trouble."

"That's part of the fun," I said, with a chuckle before I stepped into the shower, turning the water on so it was nice and hot.

It was only a minute later when the door opened and a very naked Tristan stepped in. The second he was inside with me, I pulled him in for a kiss. He effortlessly pressed his lips right back on mine and I deepened the kiss. He moaned and ran his calloused hands over my chest as he felt my tongue tangle with his.

I moved my hands down the curves of his back and over his ass. He had a great ass. I pulled him closer to me until both of our hard dicks rubbed against each other, causing us both to moan into the kiss. We started to grind against each other as the pleasure overtook our bodies.

He was like gasoline to the fire that was spreading through my body and it was one fire I never wanted to put out.

Tristan was the first one to break away from the kiss. He pressed open-mouthed kisses over my skin, making his way down my chest and over my stomach as he got down onto his knees. I watched, my breath hitching in my chest as he ran his tongue along my hard shaft from my balls to the slit. I couldn't contain the rush of air that left my lips as I watched him open his luscious lips and suck my tip into his hot mouth.

We didn't get to do this last time. Last time, I was much more interested in exploring his body. This time, it seemed like he wanted to discover more of mine and I was more than happy to let him explore away.

Tristan hummed his appreciation as he sucked on the head of my cock and I throbbed in his mouth. I couldn't help but thread my fingers through his hair, gripping it tight as electricity and heat washed trough me when he tongued my slit. I placed my hand on the back of his head, holding him in place as he wrapped his fist around the base of my dick and moved his mouth down to take in more of my hardness.

I knew that I was a very good size and it wasn't simple for someone to take all of me in their mouth so I really didn't expect it from Tristan. I couldn't take my gaze off of him as he worked my dick in his mouth, taking more and more with each pass. As he opened his throat and sucked me down, I couldn't help but lightly thrust my hips toward his mouth. It was a knee jerk reaction to the pleasure that was creeping up my spine and the feel of his throat closing over my hard shaft. I was pleasantly rewarded with a deep, rumbling sound that came from Tristan's chest and sent all kinds of new feelings racing through me. I knew it was safe for me to do it again, that he would welcome my taking control.

I *needed* to hear that sound again.

I started to lightly thrust into Tristan's willing mouth and I moaned right along with him, the pleasure building in my stomach.

"Tris," I hissed out, as he again pulled up toward the tip and then hollowed his cheeks as he sucked me all the way down to my base, his other hand fingering my balls as they pulled up tight.

The sounds of intense enjoyment kept coming from Tristan, groans and growls, humming and whimpering, and they were driving me insane, ramping up the pleasure thrice fold. That he could appear to take such amazing pleasure in giving oral sex as much as I was enjoying receiving it blew my mind.

I felt his hands moving around to cup my ass and he pulled me closer, making sure that I stayed deep in his mouth as I continued to shuttle in and out of his throat even faster now. It didn't take long before I let loose a deep groan as I snapped my hips forward and buried myself completely in his mouth, coming down his throat.

Tristan moaned and greedily swallowed every last drop that I had for him, moving up to suck my sensitive tip clean.

I quickly pulled him off my cock and yanked him onto his feet, capturing his mouth with mine all over again. Instantly, his tongue was tangling with mine and I could taste myself as our tongues danced once again.

The contact was nowhere near enough for either one of us. I moved my hands to cup the bottom of his ass and picked him up. Tristan wrapped his legs around my hips as I moved us so his back was against the wall of the shower. I held him up as I reached for the shampoo and poured some on my already hard dick and three fingers before I slipped two fingers into Tristan's waiting hole. He let out a deep grunt into the kiss at the rapid invasion and started to rock his hips back and forth, fucking himself on my fingers as heady whimpers escaped his throat.

I could feel how urgent and needy he was so I worked my fingers in and out of him quickly as I focused on stretching him enough so we could have sex without causing him any pain. I quickly slipped in a third finger and searched out that bundle of nerves that would make Tristan scream. He broke from the kiss and let out a hoarse cry, arching his back from the pleasure as I swiped over his sweet spot.

I smirked as I pressed my mouth along his neck, licking the salty taste from his skin as I hit the same spot again.

Tristan wrapped his arms around my shoulders and rocked against my fingers inside of him.

"Oh god, Hawke. Make me yours. Please." He whimpered, moving his hips back and forth rapidly, grinding his ass down on my digits.

"You want to be mine?" I lightly teased as I sucked gently on his neck, being careful to not leave a mark.

"Oh fuck yes, please, fill me now," he begged.

That was all I needed to hear. I removed my fingers from his hole and quickly notched the tip of my dick into place, hesitating only briefly. I knew that I should be wearing a condom, we both did, but right now that wasn't important. We both wanted this. I knew he wanted it when he asked me to make him mine. Firefighters had regular testing as part of the health and wellness program, so I knew I was clean and I had no doubt that he was as well.

I started to gently push myself into his sweet ass. Tristan let out a soft moan as I breached his tight ring of muscles. We had just had sex last night, but he felt just as amazing as he did the first time.

Maybe even more.

I pressed inside of him until I was balls deep in his tight, hot ass. His walls felt glorious around my dick and I never wanted to leave. I would have been happy to spend all day and night buried deep inside of him. Without the barrier of the condom, the sensation was even more intense.

"Oh, you feel so good," I said, my voice betraying me as I fought to control myself.

"Move, and don't hold back," Tristan begged.

I did not need to be told twice. I was happy to know that Tristan felt just as much in need as I was. I pulled back almost all the way before I slammed back in, causing Tristan to let out a whimper as he moved his hips to try and get the right angle.

I knew I hit his sweet spot on the next thrust when Tristan tossed his head back and let loose a small scream from the pleasure scorching through his body.

"Your delicious pleasure sounds are driving me crazy," I growled out, my voice breathy and gravelly as I rocketed my hips back and forth, pounding even harder into him. I moved my mouth over his skin, the salty taste of him flooding over my tongue and adding to the building euphoria.

I had never felt this good before. I couldn't even describe how remarkable it felt with my bare cock buried deep inside him. There were no words. I knew sex felt great, but I had no idea it could ever feel like this.

Sex with Tristan was earth shattering and I never wanted it to end.

I knew we were only going to have time to do this once, but I would have loved to do this a hundred times. Hell, a thousand times.

We were going at his pace, but I knew I was never going to be satisfied with having just a casual fling with Tristan. My body would want more, just like my heart would.

I made sure that my dick hit Tristan's

sweet spot dead on with each thrust. I could feel his legs trembling with need. I could feel his ass getting tighter, his walls squeezing my dick and ramping up my pleasure to a whole new level.

"Fuck, I'm close, don't stop," he begged, as he clenched his hands on my shoulders, his nails embedded in my skin. They were going to leave marks but I didn't care. In fact, the light pain as they broke the skin sent my mind soaring.

I picked up my pace even more, giving him everything that I had to offer. I was close as well and I wanted—no, I *needed* to feel him come. I needed to feel his walls tightening around my dick without a condom to dull the pleasure.

I moved my mouth along his neck, my tracing the shell of his ear with my tongue before I whispered. "Come for me, Darlin'."

Tristan whined, bucking back against my thrusts as his orgasm inched closer. I could feel his ass tightening around my dick and after two more direct hits against his prostate, Tristan let out a loud moan as he started to come, his hot seed spreading between us, coating my belly and his.

I loved knowing that I could push him over the edge without even touching his dick. The knowledge sent a heady spike of pleasure through my brain and the tightening of his muscles around my dick only pushed me over the edge.

I slammed my hips forward and buried my cock inside of Tristan as I erupted with a long, throaty moan.

Tristan let out a soft moan as I continued to paint his walls with my heat. I had never come inside of someone before, never had sex without a condom, and I knew in that moment I was addicted to the sensation.

We were both breathing heavily as we continued to pulse. I lightly began to kiss Tristan as we both tried to catch our breath. We kissed for a few moments before I started to feel Tristan's lips not pressing as hard against my own. I could feel his body getting weaker and I knew we needed to get out of the shower. The water was hot and the heat was clearly getting to him.

I pulled back from the kiss and placed my hand on the side of his face as I spoke.

"You okay, Darlin'?"

"Ah... yeah. Just starting to get light headed. I think the heat and exertion is getting to me," he said with a warm goofy smile covering his features.

I let him gradually slide down my body until his feet touched the floor, but I kept my arm wrapped tightly around his waist as I reached over and turned the water off. I carefully helped him climb out of the shower stall and wrapped a towel around him before sitting him down on one of the benches.

"Thanks. I haven't eaten since breakfast and I didn't eat yesterday. My blood sugar level is likely quite mad at me."

"You do that often?" I asked, worried about his physical health. It wasn't safe to be skipping meals.

"Sometimes, more often than I should, if I'm being honest. I can get lost in the cases that I'm working on and next thing I know it's been sixteen hours and I haven't moved from my desk. I'm trying to get better with it. Sometimes I remember to set an alarm on my phone so I come up for air," he said with a small shrug and a light chuckle.

"You have to be careful. You need to eat more than once a day, Darlin'," I chastised as I tugged on my clothes.

"I know. It's a work in progress," he said, as he started rub the towel over his flushed skin.

I kept my gaze on him as he got

dressed. I wanted to make sure he didn't fall over or get dizzy. I knew we should be talking about the fact that I didn't wear a condom, but I doubted here and now was the best place or time for it. Still, it was a conversation that we really should have.

"Real quick, I know I didn't wear a condom. I'm clean and I know I should have asked," I started, but Tristan cut me off.

"You didn't have to ask, I said it first. You knew what I meant and I'm clean, too. I might not know your favorite food or color, but I do know that you would never put me at risk like that if you weren't clean as well."

The fact that he could say that so confidently told me that he knew me better than most people. He knew that I would never put anyone in that kind of danger or position.

The way our bodies connected, the way it seemed like we knew one another so well, it was cosmic. We *had* to have known each other before this life. I was convinced of it.

With us both dressed, I went over to him and pulled him in for a quick kiss. I didn't get to kiss him anywhere near the length of time that I wanted to, but I knew we couldn't get caught in the bathroom together. It wasn't a big deal for us to be seen together or to be seen kissing. But I didn't want the guys to meet Tristan in the bathroom with me for the first time as the announcement of our relationship. I also didn't want to rush Tristan. He was out, but he wasn't screaming from a rooftop about it. I had to take things slow and wait until he was comfortable. Unlike the other guys that I'd dated who wanted to live in their carefully constructed closets, I knew that Tristan would be okay with going public one day.

I just knew it in my heart.

I pulled back after a moment and flashed him a warm smile.

"Come on, Cap might be back now."

I guided him out of the bathroom and I went and poked my head around the corner to see if Cap was back in. I wasn't sure he would be, but sure enough he was back in his office. A brief thought flickered through my mind that he might have heard us in the bathroom, but I dismissed it. If he had heard anyone having sex, he would have been standing outside the bathroom door waiting to see who walked out.

"He's back. And no, he wouldn't have heard us," I said with a smirk, already knowing what he was going to say.

"You sure?" he asked, his face slightly flushed.

"Yes, trust me. Come on, let's see if we can get you that mentor's name." The sooner we wrapped this case up, the sooner I could try and help Tristan move on from his childhood trauma.

We headed over to Captain Clarke's office. He had the door open and he looked up when he heard us approach.

"Hey Cap, do you have a minute?" I asked, but I knew he would say he did. He was always like that. Even if he was drowning in work, if one of his guys came up to him and asked to talk, he always said yes.

"Always. Close the door," he said as he went and sat down in his seat.

I closed the door as I spoke. "You remember Investigator Cole."

"Of course. How are you, Cole?"

"I'm doing well, Sir. I'm hoping you will be able to help with the investigation into the Rollins' fire as well as the Lewis' fire from yesterday."

"I'm always happy to help, though, I don't know how much help I'll be."

"One of the cameras from the Lewis' fire, we were able to get a serial number off of it. We traced it back to Spy Guy, a store that caters to private detectives and spy enthusiasts. We were able to get a warrant for the security footage and customer transaction lists. We were able to find the suspect that purchased a bulk order of the cameras, Lieutenant Taye Amaro."

I kept my eyes on Cap. I had to see what his reaction would be. I hadn't known he worked with Taye in the past until my Captain mentioned it and I had no idea what his stance on him was. Tristan had already had to argue with one Captain today; I was really hoping he wouldn't have to battle with another one.

"You think he's an arsonist. Have you spoken with his brother yet?" Captain Clarke said. I couldn't get a read on his emotions, though. His tone stayed the same, his facial features betraying nothing.

"I just came from there. He's my Captain and it was a shock, but at the same time it wasn't. He recommended that I speak with you. I think Taye is the apprentice. I believe his mentor is responsible for over two dozen fires over the past twenty-five years. Including the fire that killed my parents and almost killed me."

"I'm sorry to hear that. I had no idea," Cap piped up, sympathy lacing his voice.

"It's not something I broadcast. We think the death of his father ten years ago was the stressor that pushed his desire as a firebug into an active status. Captain Amaro is also having me look into the fire that killed his father, he is now wondering if it was Taye's first arson attempt. I was hoping though, that you might remember someone older that was around Taye. Someone who could have been a mentor to him."

"I never liked Taye. I always got a bad vibe off of him. He didn't have much in the way of friends. Some of the guys would hang around him because he was a legacy and they hoped to get some of that rubbed off on them. There was one guy though, Wilson Stan. He used to come around a couple times a week. It wasn't to just see Taye, though. He hung around all the time. He used to work at the firehouse, but about twenty-six, twenty-seven years ago he was injured really badly in a factory fire. Both of his legs sustained third degree burns and were broken from a steel shelving unit falling on him. He was medically released, placed on long-term disability. He was twenty-eight at that point, I believe. He's about fifty-five, now."

"He would have been thirty at the time

of the apartment fire. More than old enough to start setting fires. It would have been a year, maybe two years, since the fire he was injured in. Plenty of time for his legs to heal. And they were around each other often?" I asked.

Wilson sounded like our guy. He would have the experience and knowledge of starting fires. He was around Taye and could have easily spoken to him after his father's death. Not to mention these guys knew each other. Arsonists have a way of sniffing out other arsonists like their lives depended on it. Wilson could have easily discovered Taye's desires and started to groom him.

"A few times a week, and that is just what I know of. They could have easily met outside of the firehouse. Whenever people came around and saw Taye, he was stoic, as if being normal took every ounce of strength he had. But with Wilson, he came alive. They would go off and talk to each other for hours and Taye hung on Wilson's every word. Taye was practically obsessed with him."

"That sounds like our guy. I'll give Detective West a call and let him know. Thank you, Captain," Tristan said, flashing the other man a friendly smile.

"You're welcome. I hope you get the

evidence that you need to put them both behind bars. If there is anything you need from me, please don't hesitate to ask," Captain Clarke said.

"I will, thank you," Tristan responded.

"I'll walk you out," I offered.

He gave me a nod and we both headed out of the Captain's office. I was starting to feel excited knowing that we now had both of our suspects figured out. However, I was also worried because now Tristan was going to have to hunt them down and that could be very dangerous.

I walked him outside before I decided to speak. I knew his mind would be going a mile a minute and he might appreciate the quiet couple of minutes.

"You won't be going after them alone, right?" I inquired.

"No. I'll give Detective West a call and he'll look into Wilson. I'll be there when they go after them, but I won't be in any danger. We've done this before. I let the strong men with the guns handle things," he quipped with a teasing smirk.

"You joke, but I'm glad that there are strong men with guns when you are around arsonists. Please let me know when you go in and come out so I know you are safe."

I had no right to ask that of him, but I

hoped he would give me a break for asking. We weren't official, we were friends and even that was new. Still, I was going to worry about him until I knew that he was safe.

"I will. I'll be fine, don't worry. Am I going to see you after work tonight, or do you need to get some real sleep for a change?"

"Who says I can't get sleep with you?" I countered.

"The two hours of sleep we got last night would dictate otherwise."

"Well, I'm willing to try again if you are."

I knew he usually had a hard time sleeping anyway, but I hoped that with finding his suspects it might be a bit easier on him. And if not, I had no problem holding him all night long even if we didn't get much sleep.

"Okay, text me after your shift."

"I will. Be safe."

"You, too," he said, before he turned and strolled off to his car.

I had no choice but to watch as he walked away. I had no choice but to hope and pray that when I saw him tonight that he would be okay. One thing I did know, if Taye or Wilson tried to hurt him, it would be them getting burned up in a fire next.

CHAPTER FIFTEEN

Tristan

I PULLED UP to Taye's house and parked across from it. I had called Detective West before I left the firehouse and he was able to easily find Taye's address. He was registered with the Fire Department and Human Resources needed updated addresses and contact information for everyone who was being paid by the city, so finding that information was a breeze.

I had hoped he would be able to locate Wilson as well, but with the older man no longer being with the department, it was going to be harder to track him down. He was getting disability, but he could have it set up as an automatic deposit and email updates so he didn't have to have mail going to a physical address. Any address on file with the disability office could be a decade old.

I knew we would find him eventually, it was only a matter of time, but that didn't change the fact that I didn't want him to go out and find someone new to mentor and we'd then have this whole process to start all over again.

I climbed out of my car and made my way over to Detective West. He had arrived not too long before me and he was waiting for me so we could question Taye together. This was going to be a touchy conversation. We had enough to arrest Taye on. We might not be able to charge him, yet, but we could hold him for forty-eight hours while we cleared the warrants and grabbed solid evidence. It would also give us the chance to interrogate him, and if he was like other arsonists, he'd talk.

"Any luck finding Wilson Stan?" I asked, once I was close enough.

"Not yet. No address on file and his cell phone isn't in service any longer. It's going to take some work to track him down, but we might be able to get something from Taye."

"Assuming he is feeling chatty."

"Let's hope. I don't want to kick the door down, so it would be better if he felt like we were going to him for help on a case. It should get us in the door without any confrontation. I got the arrest warrant, but it would be easier if he played ball, though. The last thing I want to do is start a war between the PD and FD."

That I could understand fully. We were walking a very dangerous fine line right now and the last thing we needed was a war between our two departments. We had to tread carefully and the best way to prevent World War Three would be to get Taye to come in on his own accord.

I gave him a nod and we made our way over to the front door. Detective West knocked and we waited a moment before it finally opened. Taye stood on the other side of the door and I could tell he wasn't surprised to see us, but he faked it. He had to have known it was coming at some point. Somewhere along the way, he had to have known that he would get caught, either him or Wilson. It was hard enough to stay going for long periods of time as an arsonist; it was even harder to keep two arsonists working together under wraps.

"Lieutenant Amaro, my name is Detective West and this is Investigator Cole. We would like to come in and speak with you for a moment about a case we are currently investigating."

"Of course, I am always happy to help,"

Taye said with a forced smile.

I knew he was trying to play a game. It was the only thing he could do. He couldn't turn us away. It would look suspicious. He would also want to know what we knew. We weren't the only ones walking a fine line. All I could do was hope that we knew how to walk it better than he did.

He stepped back and allowed us to enter. I didn't see anything that stood out as dangerous. One could never tell when they went to a suspect's home what they would find. I had walked into places that were filled with explosives and bomb making materials completely left out in the open. It was like people believed that we wouldn't arrest them for things in plain sight.

We made our way into the living room, but before I could even sit down on the couch, Detective West let out a grunt before he collapsed to the floor. I snapped my eyes up to see Wilson standing behind where Detective West was with a gun in his hand.

I held my hands up slightly as I risked a quick glance down at Detective West. He was out cold. There was some blood on the back of his head and given that I hadn't heard a gunshot, I assumed that

Wilson had pistol-whipped him. I hoped he would be okay. I knew head injuries were hard to gauge and something as simple as getting hit on the back of the head could cause swelling and bleeding, both of which could kill him if I didn't get us out of this soon.

"Tie him up," Wilson snapped to Taye, and it was clear he was furious that we were here.

I couldn't blame him, he had gone for twenty-five years, a quarter of a century undetected, and now he was going to be arrested along with Taye, because Taye had screwed up with the new cameras.

Wilson kept the gun pointed at me as Taye approached me. I could fight, sort of, but there was no way I would be able to take on Taye and Wilson together, especially when Wilson had a gun. I didn't doubt for a single second that the man wouldn't be afraid to fire it.

Taye grabbed my right arm and pulled me over to the kitchen that was in plain view of the front door. He grabbed one of the wooden chairs from under the dining room table and forced me down into it.

I watched helplessly as Wilson grabbed Detective West by the back of his shirt and dragged him over so he was closer to me, but not close enough so I could reach out with my foot and touch him. I knew he had done it so it was easier to keep an eye on both of us.

Taye quickly zip-tied my wrists to the arms of the chair before he stepped back, appearing to be satisfied with himself.

This was not how I had imagined my day going. I didn't know what I had expected, but it wasn't this when we came here to speak and arrest Taye. With Detective West now out of commission, it was on me to try and get Taye and Wilson to come in peacefully.

I knew they wouldn't, though.

Trying to talk them down would be like trying to walk an unstable homemade bomb across a rickety bridge with missing planks.

One wrong step and everything went boom.

"How the hell did you let this happen?" Wilson snapped at Taye.

He wasn't happy about the situation and it made sense. He had gone for so long not being caught and now his carefully constructed world was falling down around him and there was nothing he could do about it. The situation was out of his control and for an arsonist that was a major issue. They hated not having control.

"I didn't do anything wrong," Taye instantly denied.

"If you didn't do anything wrong, then they wouldn't be here. They clearly have figured this out. You screwed up somewhere. Over twenty years I have never been suspected by a single cop," Wilson seethed.

"It was the cameras," I stated. I didn't really want to listen to them arguing back and forth about whose fault it was. It was one thing to try and buy time, but no one was going to come for us. It wasn't like someone would be checking up on Detective West if he didn't check in within the hour.

"What about the cameras?" Wilson asked, looking right at Taye.

"Nothing. They were perfect."

"They were new. The switch between the old cameras that were untraceable to the new ones led me right to you. They didn't burn up in the fire, leaving a serial number behind that I traced back to the store where they were purchased. I got the security footage and found Taye. Then it was just a matter of talking to people who knew Taye to find you," I explained.

I wasn't sure how this was going to end, but all I could hope for was that I could make them turn against each other and then somehow figure out how to get out of there. The chair I was restrained in was wood, so I could break it if I got the chance to. The trick was getting the chance. They were both unstable, no matter how well they had been able to fake it; they were unstable and unpredictable. The new intel only pissed Wilson off. He pistol whipped Taye across the face as he spoke.

"You stupid son of a bitch. I told you to never use new cameras. You were supposed to only use the one brand. They were untraceable."

"They were garbage cameras. They didn't last long enough from the heat. The new cameras stay intact longer, letting me watch them die longer."

"And I told you new cameras last longer in the heat making them easier to trace. How could you be this stupid? Now we have no way of knowing how many people know about us. I taught you better than this. I taught you to be smarter than this. I thought you had what it took to be one of the best, but I was clearly wrong. You're a disgrace and disappointment."

"I'm a disappointment? You're the old man who couldn't start a fire anymore. You have to rely on me to give you the footage just so you can jerk off to it.

You're the disgrace," Taye seethed.

I knew what was going to happen before it even did. Wilson was the first to make a move. He went to raise his gun, but Taye punched him and pushed the gun out of his hands. It didn't take long at all before Wilson recovered and charged toward Taye, wrapping his arms around his waist and pushing him down to the ground.

While they were busy fighting each other, I turned my attention to trying to get out of this chair. I pulled against the zip ties to try and break them. They were tight and they were already cutting into my skin. The chair was stronger than I had expected. I thought it would be easy to break, but with the zip ties being so tight, I wasn't able to get enough slack to pull my wrists back far enough to hit the chair with any real force.

The echo of a gunshot pulled my attention back over to Wilson and Taye. Wilson was on top of Taye and they were both on the floor. I couldn't see the gun, so I had no idea who had been shot or where they were shot. I kept my eyes locked on them, waiting to see which one of them would move.

After a second, Wilson's body moved, but he wasn't the one controlling it.

Taye pushed Wilson's body off of him and I was able to see the large blood stain growing on Wilson's chest. He wasn't moving and his eyes were open, but they were blank. He was dead and I couldn't feel upset about it. I was upset that I wouldn't be able to question him, but I knew in my gut that he was responsible for my parents' death.

Taye stood and he didn't even appear shaken by the fact that he'd just killed a man. His mentor. He had the man's blood all down the front of him and yet, he looked at Wilson as if he was just some bug he had stepped on.

I knew there was only one way this was going to go.

Taye was going to do what every arsonist did.

He was going to start a fire.

I could see the gears turning in his mind, deciding on how he wanted to do it. He was angry at the situation that he was in. I knew he wasn't able to feel emotions, so losing his mentor wouldn't affect him the same way it would for a normal person.

For Taye, it was just another body.

He had outgrown his mentor, surpassed him, and improved on the techniques that he had been taught. It had only been a matter of time before they'd butted heads and one of them died anyway. This was why arsonists don't work in pairs. They didn't like to compromise on their processes and they didn't like sharing the pleasure that they got from the fires they started. It was honestly a miracle that Willson and Taye had managed to get along for the ten years they had.

"Taye, listen to me," I started. I had to try and get him to see reason, or at least some self-preservation.

"Shut up. You have nothing that I want to hear," Taye snapped before he turned on his heel and strode quickly out of the room.

The second I was alone, I resumed my struggles against the zip ties. I had to get us out of here. Detective West hadn't even so much as twitched since he went down. The only reason I knew he was still alive was the subtle movement of his chest. I took comfort in seeing his chest rising and falling, but it would have been more comforting if he was awake and talking. At least then he would be able to help me get out of here. Instead, it was up to me and so far, I couldn't even get out of the damn chair.

Taye came back into the room far

sooner than I would have liked. He clearly knew what he wanted to do, so it hadn't taken him long to grab the gas can from his garage.

I continued my struggles against the zip ties. No amount of talking was going to change what he was about to do. Taye was ready to die there today and he was going to take us all with him.

When I heard the liquid splashing the floor, I snuck a quick glance his way. He was pouring the gas all over Wilson's body and around the kitchen. He was going to make sure that Wilson burned up first, but it wasn't out of respect for the man. This was his way of giving his dead mentor one last *fuck you* by killing him a second time.

My gaze went to Taye as he pulled out a zippo lighter. With a flick of his thumb the flame came to life.

CHAPTER SIXTEEN

Hawke

WE HAD MANAGED to make it through most of the day before we got a call. It was better than getting calls back to back and if it was a slow day, at least that meant less people were being hurt. This was another residential fire and I couldn't help but wonder if the fire would be connected to Taye and Wilson, or if this one was a true accident.

Before this case, I'd never wondered how the fire got started. I was always focused on making sure anyone who was trapped inside got out and that we got the fire out before there was nothing left of the house. Now, my thoughts immediately went to arson and I knew it was going to take some time before my mind went back to normal.

"Here we go, boys!" Gage called out from the front seat as we pulled up to the fire.

I put my gloves on and got ready to climb out of the truck. The second we stopped, we all tumbled out of the truck and took in the scene. The flames were starting to come out of the windows on both floors and I knew right away by the smoke color that an accelerant had been used. I scanned the area to make sure everyone who was outside was far enough away to remain safe. A couple of cop cars were already there and they had started to evacuate the homes that were around the fire. My heart dropped to the pit of my stomach as my gaze landed on a car that I knew.

Tristan was here.

If Tristan was here, that meant that this house had to belong to either Taye or Wilson, and that meant he was in the house.

"Hey, we got a detective's squad car over here!" Zander called out.

"It's gotta be Detective West's car. He was working with Investigator Cole in an arson case. Cole's car is here, too. They have to be in the house," I informed them as I ran over to join the rest of them.

Everything in me was screaming for

me to run into the house and save him. I didn't care if I had a hose or not, I needed to get to him. I had to make sure he was safe. He was trapped in another fire and he had to be scared.

I couldn't believe this was happening. I didn't even think it would happen when he went to speak with Taye or Wilson. I'd foolishly believed that he would be safe, because Detective West would be with him.

I should have known better.

I should have told him to wait and go with a fire engine on standby just in case either one of them started a fire to get out of being arrested. I should have done more and now Tristan might be paying for my mistakes.

Before anymore could be said, we saw a man running out of the house and I instantly knew it was Taye. I was not about to let him get away with this.

"Grab him!" I yelled.

I didn't know who would listen to me, but with enough firefighters and cops there, I figured someone would. Two local patrol officers that I didn't know grabbed him and tackled him to the ground, and all that mattered to me at that moment was that he had been caught.

"He's a firefighter," Gabe instantly

said, shock filling his voice. But he had no idea what type of firefighter Taye really was. Thankfully, before I had to be the one to say it, Cap did.

"Arrest him. He's suspected in multiple arson investigations, including this house."

I could see the shock on all of the guys' faces, minus Zander's. I knew it was going to be shocking and I knew most wouldn't want to believe it, but it was the reality that we faced. Taye was an arsonist who was responsible for multiple deaths and he was not about to get away with it.

"Get the hose lines going, we've got two men in there!" Cap yelled and got everyone to snap back into focus.

I watched as the cops took Taye, struggling and running his mouth about it being a lie, over to their patrol car. They would have to take him to the hospital to get checked out, but right now he was being handled. With Taye under control for the time being, I didn't even waste a second before I threw on my oxygen mask and ran toward the house.

Zander came right behind me.

I ignored the shout from Captain Clarke demanding I had to go in with a hose. I was not about to let Tristan stay in the house a moment longer. He was already in danger and any delay, even just a second, could be fatal and that was not something I was willing to accept.

The moment we were in the house I was scanning every room. I had to find him. Tristan was here and he had to be terrified. It was bad enough he had already been trapped in a fire as a child, but to have to experience it again. He wasn't mentally recovered from the first fire and now he would have more trauma to pile on top of the already existing trauma.

The fire was burning hot and flames licked at my suit, the heat almost overwhelming as thick black smoke billowed throughout the room. Taye had obviously used some type of accelerant.

That was the problem when you confronted an arsonist, they always preferred to go down in their own fire. They didn't like being kept in a cell or locked up unable to indulge in their compulsion. We had Taye, but I had no idea if Wilson would be there as well. We also had to try and find Detective West.

I was trying to ignore the likelihood that Detective West and Tristan were already dead, either from the heat or the smoke. With Tristan already having been in a fire where there was smoke inhalation, I was worried about what it could do to his lungs a second time around. I knew from other firefighters who'd had to go in without a mask, breathing in the toxic fumes, it had a way of eating at your lungs. The more often it happened, the longer the recovery time took.

Keeping low, I walked into the kitchen area and instantly my heart went up to my throat. I vaguely picked up Detective West's body where it lay unmoving on the floor. All I could see in that moment was Tristan tied to a chair, unconscious. There were flames all around him and quickly approaching his chair. If we had been another minute longer and he would have been on fire.

I hastily crossed the distance between us and though it violated protocol, I pulled off my mask and placed it over his face. I grabbed my clippers and cut the zip ties that kept him bound to the chair. I briefly caught sight of Zander grabbing Detective West and carrying him out. I hoped the man would be okay.

I knew Tristan would blame himself if the detective didn't make it. It wouldn't be his fault, but that wouldn't matter to Tristan. It was his case and that would be enough for him to place all the blame on his own shoulders. I couldn't think about that right now. All that mattered was getting Tristan out of there safe.

I picked him up in my arms and ran as quickly as I could out of the house. The smoke was already burning my lungs and I had only been without my mask for less than two minutes.

The second I was out of the house and able to take a breath of fresh air, I couldn't help but cough. The smoke had been so thick in the house it didn't take long before it restricted my breathing. I carried Tristan over to the first stretcher and Newt instantly removed my mask from Tristan's face and replaced it with an oxygen mask. I faintly registered that the paramedic was speaking to me.

"You need to get checked out. That smoke is thick."

"I'm fine. He was in a fire twenty-one years ago. His lungs might be weakened from it."

"I got him," Newt promised.

Newt was one of our more recent paramedics, he had been with us for two weeks now and he seemed like a good guy. He was a bit different, nerdy and not what one would expect for a paramedic. He was thin, but he ate all the time. He was never far from a package of M&Ms. I didn't know much about him, none of us really did. He liked comic books, he was always reading one. Outside of that, I knew nothing about him. That wasn't unusual with paramedics. They came and went so many times it was hard to keep track. According to Zander, we used to have the same paramedics for years, but the city wanted them to float so they could constantly have enough in each firehouse. Most were also female and the city was constantly worried about relationships occurring between the paramedics and the firefighters and sexual harassment suits becoming a problem. Apparently, the city felt it was easier to make them rotate than to expect for the men who worked around them to behave themselves.

I had no choice but to watch as Newt had to intubate Tristan. I had no alternative but to stand by and do nothing as Newt, a man I hardly knew, worked to help the man that I was falling in love with. I had to trust that Tristan would be okay.

I had never felt so helpless before in my entire life and there had been plenty of times in my life where I couldn't help someone. I'd never expected to be put in the position to feel powerless when it came to someone that I cared about. I'd foolishly believed that nothing bad would ever happen to someone I cared for. It was childish and naive, but it helped me to feel better to believe that I would never have to be the one sitting next to a hospital bed. I would never have to be the one in the waiting room pacing around and hoping someone in a set of scrubs told me something good.

I saw horrible things every day. I saw people on the worst day of their lives frequently. Sometimes it was from a fire and sometimes from a horrible accident. And yet, I'd never expected for any of that to happen to me, to someone I knew. I had managed to convince myself that it couldn't possibly to happen to me or someone I loved.

I had just gotten one hell of a dose of reality and I didn't like it.

"Is he going to be okay?" I tried to make sure my voice didn't shake as I spoke, but I could tell by the flash of concern that moved across Newt's eyes that I hadn't succeeded.

"It's hard to say with smoke inhalation. Doctors at Mercy will have a better guess for you. We gotta move," Newt answered as he pushed the stretcher into the back of the ambulance.

I looked back over at the house, at the guys as they were still fighting to put the fire out. I should be back over there helping them, but my whole body was screaming for me to get into the back of that ambulance and never leave Tristan's side. I was on duty and it wouldn't be appropriate for me to just up and leave in the middle of a call, in the middle of my shift. The guys all knew that I was gay, but they didn't know about Tristan. He wasn't hiding, but he didn't broadcast it and right now was not the ideal time to do so.

At the same time though, how could I leave him alone?

What if he didn't make it?

I couldn't leave him to take his last breaths around a bunch of strangers that barely knew his name. He deserved better than that.

"Hawke!"

I looked over at Captain Clarke. I knew what he was going to say, that I needed to get back to work, that I needed to focus. I knew what I had to do, but I couldn't seem to get my body to do it.

"Yes, Sir," I said, forcing my mind to function.

"Go with Investigator Cole. We have this."

That was not what I had expected. I thought for sure he was going to lecture me about getting distracted while on a scene. The look on his face though, told me he knew exactly what I was feeling. He knew himself how it felt to have a loved one injured and being taken to the hospital.

I didn't think anyone had noticed the difference between Tristan and I. I thought we had covered up our budding relationship pretty well. Apparently, the one conversation we shared with Captain Clarke had given him more insight into our connection than I had expected.

I really shouldn't have been so surprised that he had noticed something, though. The Captain had always been observant. He had always been able to notice the smallest details. It was what made him so talented out in the field. Of course he would have noticed something in his office earlier. It could have been something simple like a lingering glance that I sent Tristan's way and that was all he needed to know. Still, I wasn't about to look a gift horse in the mouth with this one.

"Thank you, Sir," I promptly shouted back as I climbed into the back of the ambulance just before Newt's partner closed the back doors.

I sat off to the side, doing my best to not get in Newt's way as he worked on Tristan and got his vitals. I watched as he cut up the middle of Tristan's shirt and I was pleased to see there weren't any bruises or burns to his torso. I didn't see any injuries anywhere, so hopefully that meant Taye didn't hurt him before he tied him to that chair. I suspected that Taye might have used Detective West against Tristan to keep him compliant.

What wasn't clear was where Wilson was. If he was still out there, he could be a danger to Tristan. Hopefully, Detective West would be okay and he would be able to find Wilson and get him in cuffs before he decided to go after Tristan. I had no idea if he would come for Tristan, but I had to imagine the man would be upset that his apprentice was now going to prison.

There was no way Taye would be able to talk his way out of it, thankfully. He was going to prison and that meant that Wilson would no longer be able to get his fire jollies out through Taye. He was going to need a new apprentice and it would take time to find one and train them. What I did know for certain was I was not leaving Tristan's side until I knew he would be all right.

The second we arrived at the hospital the back doors of the ambulance were flung open and two doctors were standing there ready and waiting for us. I knew Newt or his partner would have radioed in that they were bringing in a first responder. Even though Tristan was a fire investigator, that still made him a first responder. He was still out on the street every day helping people.

They pulled the stretcher out and started to head inside at a rapid pace. The words started to blur together as Newt spoke what sounded like a different language to give the doctors Tristan's vitals and stats. I didn't really understand most of it, but the doctors' faces didn't change drastically and I took that as a good sign that his vitals weren't too bad. They wheeled him into an exam room, and I started to follow but that was when a nurse stood in front of me to block me from entering the room.

"I'm sorry, Sir, but you have to wait in the waiting room," she said with a warm, but firm smile.

I'd known it was coming, but I hadn't been ready for it. I wanted to be in there with him. I wanted to keep my eyes on him and make sure he was going to be okay. I didn't want to let him out of my sight for a moment but I knew I had to. I had to let the doctors do their job and trust everything would be okay.

"He was in a fire twenty-one years ago. I don't know if that will affect his lungs this time around."

"I will let the doctors know. Do you know if he has asthma or any lasting effects from the first fire?"

"No, he's never said anything and he doesn't have asthma." I was confident on the asthma. In order to be in the Fire Department, to go through the Fire Academy, you couldn't have asthma. The smoke would constantly cause the asthma to act up.

"Thank you, please go and wait in the waiting room. We have your friend."

I had no choice. I gave the nurse a distracted nod and moved away from the room that held Tristan. I had to walk away from the man I was falling in love with as he lay, still unconscious and now hooked up to all kinds of lines and wires, on the stretcher, and with each step that I took away from him I felt a knife stabbing me in my heart. I didn't want to be away from him and now I was going to be stuck in a waiting room for who knew how long.

With a sigh, I stared down at the black

plastic chair, but I couldn't bring myself to sit in it. Another ambulance pulled in and I watched as multiple cop cars came with it. I kept my gaze on the ambulance to see if it was Detective West or Taye. I was relieved when they rolled out Detective West and immediately took him into an exam room.

I didn't want it to be Taye, because then he might die from the smoke he'd inhaled and that was too quick of a death for him. He deserved to be trapped in a cell for the rest of his natural life. Based on the look of the cops' faces, they felt the same way. They all piled into the room and flopped into chairs, knowing that it might take a bit before they got any information.

I knew soon enough the waiting room was going to be filled with police and fire fighters as we all showed our support and waited to hear that our men were going to be okay. I just prayed that they both would be.

***

Three hours. It had been three hours and we still didn't know anything about either of them. I knew that wasn't a good sign. Tests could take a while, but it was never good when no one came out to update us.

Everyone in the ER knew that there were cops and firefighters flooding the waiting room and the hallways waiting for news on our men.

Captain Amaro was there, but he was keeping further away from everyone. I could see the guilt set on his face. He clearly blamed himself for what his brother had done and I knew it was going to take him a very long time to overcome that feeling of responsibility.

I could also see the looks that some of the other firefighters were giving him. By now, word had spread about Taye and what he had done. They were going to judge Captain Amaro for it, even if that wasn't fair.

The fire department was like high school when it came to gossip and juicy news. It was going to spread faster than an inferno with an accelerant and I wasn't certain that the Captain would survive the blaze. I hoped he would, though. I didn't really know him, but he seemed like a good man. He was obviously brave and cared about his men for him to risk the stares and potential conflict from both firefighters and cops by coming here. The whole situation was a mess and I really had no idea how it was all going to play out. All I could do was be there for Tristan and help get him through it.

"Hawke Colton?" A male voice said off to my left, startling me out of my musing.

I glanced up and saw a man that I did not recognize. He gave me a small, polite smile as he helped himself to the hard plastic chair next to me. I wasn't certain who he was, but I suspected he was a cop. Maybe he had news about Wilson or Taye.

"That's me. Who are you?"

"Mason Wright. I'm a Federal Agent with the Federal Protection Agency."

Now I knew who he was. He was in charge of the FPA, an agency that focused on crimes against children all over the country. They were very popular there in town and I knew that they had helped hundreds of children. They were as close to superheroes as you could get.

"Agent Wright, it's a pleasure to meet you. What can I do for you?" I didn't know why he was here, but I was more than happy to help him.

"Detective West works very closely with us. He's helped us on multiple cases over the years. When I heard that he was in the fire, I started to pull his file to see what he was working on. I went down to the scene and the body of Wilson Stan has been identified. He was in the fire, and based on what your Captain discovered, it looks like Taye shot him and then used him to start the fire. I had my men search Mr. Stan's home and they discovered he had a storage locker. They searched it and they found extensive evidence of the many fires he had started over several years, including proof that he was the one to start the fire twenty-one years ago that killed Investigator Cole's parents. It looks like he started fifty-three fires over the past twenty-five years. He also had a list of potential mentees that he was going to use to start more fires."

Oh my God.

I let out a deep breath I hadn't even realized I'd been holding. I was relieved to hear that Wilson was dead, that was one less threat against Tristan. But to hear that he had started fifty-three fires, that surprised me. We didn't know about that many. We'd thought it was thirty-seven over the past twenty-five years.

And if Wilson had that many fires under his belt, how many did Taye start that we didn't know about?

The whole situation was a mess already and the information Agent Wright had just imparted made things even worse than I'd ever expected. The Investigation Unit would have to go through multiple cases that had been closed as accidental and re-open, re-investigate them and/or change them to arson. They might have to inform surviving victims that they were, in fact, victims to arson. Definitely a mess they would have to wade through, and that was just for Wilson's fires and not Taye's. They would also have to investigate to make sure that Wilson didn't have another mentee out there.

"That's more fires than we thought. I appreciate your help on the case. I'm sorry about Detective West."

"It's not your fault. He was doing his job and Jonah is far too stubborn to die. He'll be okay. Our tech specialist, Cooper, is going through the federal database to make sure that the electrical device hasn't been used elsewhere. I don't suspect it will have been, but he's going to double check. He's the man with the laptop over there. Him and Jonah are engaged," he said with a nod at a blond haired man who sat in the corner huddled over a laptop and typing furiously.

I had no idea that Detective West was even with someone. Now I felt terrible, because the man who was in love with Detective West was sitting in a hospital waiting room hoping to hear that he wouldn't have to bury the man that he loved. And yet, he sat there working away on his laptop like he was sitting in a coffee shop.

I wasn't judging. If I could be working right now I would be. It would at least give me something to be distracted by. It hated waiting. I was usually pretty tolerant, but waiting in a hospital to hear about the welfare of people I cared about, there was no amount of patience in the world to get me through that.

Before I could say anything else, a doctor finally came out from behind the double doors to the ER bays. I didn't get up. I held my breath and waited to see if he was here for Detective West or for Tristan. Before he even spoke he had everyone's attention by just walking into the room.

"Good evening, everyone. I have an update on both of your men brought in today," the doctor started and now I stood up. We all made our way over to the doctor so we could hear everything the man said.

"Detective West was given oxygen and taken for a CT-Scan for his head. He has a concussion, but he has regained consciousness and is currently on oxygen to help with the smoke inhalation. He will make a full recovery and he can leave in a few days. We need to monitor his lungs and his concussion, but we suspect that no additional problems will arise. He should be able to be back on the street within two months."

Everyone clapped and I saw some of the police officers give Cooper a hug or a pat on his shoulder. I could see the relief on his face and I couldn't blame the man. I wanted that relief, too, and I prayed that the doctor wasn't giving us the good news first and saving the bad news for last.

"Investigator Cole didn't sustain any physical injuries outside of some bruising and abrasions to his wrists. He sustained more smoke inhalation than Detective West, but that was to be expected with him being higher than Detective West. He is on a ventilator currently and he will need to be on it for a few days to help his lungs heal. We suspect that he, too, will make a full recovery and he should be able to go home in seven days, assuming his lungs start to heal properly, which I believe they will. He will have to take it slow for the next three to six months, and he will have to go through breathing treatments and exercises, but I am confident that his lungs will mend and he will be able to return to work."

I closed my eyes and felt a rush at the pure relief that flooded my body. Tristan was going to be okay. I hated that he was hooked up to a ventilator, of course, but I understood the need to give his lungs a break. The only thing that mattered was that he would recover. It might be a bit of a long journey, but I would be there for him through it all.

"Can I see him?" I asked.

"Yes, of course. One person at a time right now, both Investigator Cole and Detective West need to rest. Investigator Cole is in room four-ten and Detective West is in room two-fifteen."

"Thank you so much, Doctor," I said, flashing him a warm smile.

The doctor gave a nod and then he headed off, getting patted on the shoulder by both cops and firefighters.

I didn't even wait around for anyone to say anything to me. I had to get to Tristan and see him with my own eyes. He didn't have family and he didn't really have any friends. All he had was me and I would make damn sure he didn't wake up alone this time. This time around, when he woke up I would be sitting there with him. He was going to wake up knowing that he wasn't alone and someone was there who cared about him.

As I walked into his hospital room though, I was not prepared to see him lying so still. I was not prepared to see him with the ventilator pumping air into his lungs and helping him breathe. I knew he was hooked up to it, and I knew it was giving his lungs the break they needed so they could heal, but that didn't make the sight any easier to handle.

I slowly made my way over to the bed, watching Tristan's eyes for any movement, though I really didn't expect any. I bent forward and placed a gentle kiss on his forehead. I pulled the chair over so it was closer to the side of the bed before I sat down. I threaded my fingers through his on the one hand closest to me and then moved my right hand his head and ran my fingertips through his hair.

I had to fight to keep my anger down at the sight of the black and blue of bruises that wrapped around both of his wrists. I would have loved five minutes alone with Taye for everything he had done to Tristan. I would have loved to make sure he knew exactly what pain was. I couldn't, though, and I would have no choice but to wait for the day he was sentenced to life in prison.

I knew the investigation into Taye was only just beginning. It wouldn't surprise me if another agency took over the case with the close connection to Captain Amaro. Tristan wouldn't want to let it go, but he might not have much of a choice with having to be on medical leave for the next few months. Regardless, we would get through it. He wasn't alone in this world anymore and I would do everything to make sure he knew it.

"I'm right here, Darlin', for when you are ready to wake up." And that was a promise I would always keep.

EPILOGUE

Three Months Later...
Tristan

LEANING AGAINST THE railing, I enjoyed the view as the sun almost completely disappeared off in the distance, leaving behind shades of crimson, burnt orange, and butter yellow. I still couldn't believe this was my view. I couldn't believe I'd managed to accomplish it. It might not seem like much to most people, but to me it was everything.

I had bought a house, *a real house*, that I was planning on turning into a home. The first home that I'd had since my parents were killed. It was a huge step for me and I was terrified to make it. I had gone to look at close to a hundred houses for sale over the last three months. None of them had felt *right* and the ones that did feel good, I had been too afraid to make the jump.

Hawke had been amazing with me. He came and looked at every single house with me. He didn't judge me when I turned them all down. He didn't get annoyed when I refused to pick a house. He just reassured me that I would know which one was my home when I walked into it. I thought he was crazy, but then we saw this house and I felt it.

I truly *felt it.*

The place instantly felt like home and I knew before even seeing the whole house that I had to have it.

It was a three bedroom home, not that I needed more than one bedroom, but I was open to fostering and the extra bedrooms would be nice for that. It had all been renovated recently so I didn't have to do anything to it. It was an open concept home and I liked that I could see the kitchen and living room completely. The kitchen was beautiful with clean with white cabinets and countertops. There was an island that faced the living room with enough room for four bar stools. I knew right away that island was a place that I would be spending a lot of time at for meals and working.

One of the best features of the house

was the working fireplace that required real wood. We had one growing up at my parents' house and I'd loved it. We used to cook hotdogs on it or make s'mores and drink hot chocolate. I had a lot of great memories from the hours we'd spent in front of the fire and I wanted to that continue tradition again. I wanted to be able to share that with the children that I would eventually bring into my home.

The backyard was also very impressive. I had two acres of property and it would be perfect for a garden, having a little playground, and I was thinking of having an above ground pool. I was also thinking about getting a dog. I'd never had one growing up because my mom was allergic to pet hair. I'd never had one when I was with my grandparents, because they always wanted everything spotless. I knew this would be a perfect chance to have the dog I'd always dreamed of having.

I looked forward to having a real life again. To make this house a home and go back to living.

A smile instantly turned up the corners of my mouth as I felt strong arms wrap around my waist. Hawke pressed his warm lips on my cheek before he spoke.

"How are you feeling? Lungs tight?"

I had to fight not to roll my eyes. It had been a very common recurring question from Hawke for months. I understood why he was worried. I did. He had found me barely alive in the middle of a fire. This time around I had been lucky to avoid getting burned, but only because he had arrived in time to save my ass and Detective West's.

I did, however, inhale a nasty amount of smoke, resulting in me being hooked up to a ventilator for a week and in the hospital for two more weeks after that.

Hawke had been amazing through it all. He spent every day and night with me the whole time I was there. Captain Clarke had allowed him to take the time off without a single complaint. The man was very generous and he understood what was going on without Hawke needing to say anything.

When I did finally get to leave the hospital, they'd discharged me with a prescription for an inhaler for when my chest got tight or I just couldn't catch my breath quite right. I didn't have asthma, but with the smoke inhalation, I was still going to have moments where I needed the inhaler until my lungs were fully healed. Right after I'd left the hospital, I'd had to use it a few times a day, but in the past couple of weeks I hadn't needed it at all. That still didn't change the fact that Hawke worried about me.

"I'm fine. It's been two weeks since I've used the inhaler. I have even been able to go for runs again. I'm good, Babe."

"Good. Why don't we test that fireplace out? We can sit on a blanket and enjoy a drink with the fire going," he suggested.

"Sounds perfect."

"All right, I'll get the fire started. Why don't you grab us a blanket and we can relax."

"Sounds good. Do you want wine or whiskey?"

"Whichever you're feeling. I'm not picky," he said with a small shrug before he pulled away from me and strolled over to where the wood was kept. There wasn't too much left from the previous owner and I knew I would have to get some before the winter months hit. It didn't get very cold there, but the nights could be chilly and it would be nice to warm up the house with a fire.

I made my way inside and upstairs to grab a blanket. I had moved in yesterday, but I hadn't done much in the way of unpacking outside of the kitchen. I didn't have much to unpack. I had to order furniture and have it delivered to even have much in my house. I did order a new bed though, and I was very happy about that. I hadn't realized how uncomfortable my bed had been until I'd slept on my new one last night. I hadn't slept that well in decades, though it definitely helped that Hawke held me all night long.

I grabbed a thick blanket and made my way back down the stairs. I spread it out on the floor, tossing down a couple of couch cushions, too, as Hawke worked away at getting the fire going. I went over and poured us both two fingers of whiskey over ice in crystal glasses. I didn't mind wine, but I wasn't feeling like it tonight.

I placed the glasses down on the side table just as Hawke stood from where he kneeled by the fireplace. With a grin, he went and sat down with his back against the fat cushions and I plopped down in front of him with my back pressed against his chest. His arms wrapped around me, pulling me into his body heat, and just like that I felt relaxed and at home.

"You know, I love what we do in the bedroom, but I love this part too," I admitted.

The time we spent in the bedroom was incredible; it was earth shattering and eye opening, no doubt about it, but I did love these moments, too. The moments where it was just us and we could relax and enjoy each other's company. We didn't need to talk or even have to watch anything. We could just curl up with each other and enjoy having the other near. I felt him press his lips the side of my head before he spoke, echoing exactly what I had been thinking.

"It's these moments, the lazy days in bed, waking up in each other's arms, those are the moments that make a relationship for me. It's more than just sex, even though the sex is definitely very good and important, too."

"Oh, it's very good," I said, with a flirty smile plastered on my face as I turned my head to look at him. I leisurely ran my hand up Hawke's inner thigh to his already half-hard dick. "Very good, indeed."

Hawke let out a soft moan before he grabbed me and turned me around so I was straddling his lap. He slowly closed the gap between us and gently pressed his lips against my own. The kiss was soft and slow, but it was filled with passion. Hawke had a way of taking even the most simplest of kisses and making me feel loved and wanted. The passion and desire he could put into a kiss was remarkable and I never wanted to stop kissing him.

I felt his tongue lightly licking at my bottom lip, requesting permission, and I happily opened my mouth and welcomed the addition of his tongue. I couldn't help the whimper that slipped from my lips at the feel of his tongue dancing with mine as he deepened the kiss.

He placed one of his hands on the back of my neck and ran the other down my back to cup my ass. He squeezed a cheek and the movement caused my hips to rock forward, rubbing our hard, cloth-covered dicks against each other. We both began to pant, little moans and groans escaping us as I continued to rock my hips and grind myself against him.

It amazed me how strong my desire was for him, and his for me. We had been having sex for months now, and I figured our desire for each other, our *need* for each other, would have cooled off by now. Only it hadn't. No matter how many times we'd had sex, we'd never lost that uncontrollable need for the other person. Our desire continued to rage, soaring to levels I'd never experienced before in my life with any other man. Our cravings for one another were just as scorching hot and exhilarating as the first time we'd been intimate and I highly doubt that would ever change.

When the need to breathe became too much, Hawke pulled back and started to pepper kisses down my neck as I continued to rock our hips together. My own hands instinctively went to the hem of Hawke's shirt and I started to pull it up his chest.

I needed to feel his delicious bare skin against mine in the worst way.

Tugging it off over his head, I quickly divested him of his shirt and Hawke did the same with mine. With our shirts out of the way, I could run my hands down his chest and enjoy the feel of his toned abs, play with the fine hair on his happy trail, but it was nowhere near enough for either of us. The pleasure was blazing through us and we had yet to even truly touch.

Getting the rest of our clothes off would be tricky; neither one of us wanted to break contact with the other and I definitely did not want to get up. I worked swiftly on undoing his pants as his hands fumbled with my belt. I sat up slightly so Hawke could lift his hips and I was able to slide his pants and boxers off of him.

Once we had him naked, I sat up on my knees and removed one leg of my pants at a time. With my pants and boxers removed, I dropped back down onto his lap and rocked my hips against his. The second the bare skin of our hard cocks touched directly, we both let out a deep moan in unison.

"Hawke..."

"That's it, Darlin', just feel," he whispered into my ear before he gently nibbled on the lobe.

I moaned as I continued to rock my hips slowly, letting our pleasure build. Hawke's lips were back on mine, his kiss deep as his hands moved up and down my back and over my ass. I took the time to run my own hands over his chest and stomach, exploring every inch of his body, feeling every bump and groove as my fingers danced over his skin. Our need was increasing slowly, building up the volcano within us.

It was Hawke who broke first, needing more contact than the slow rhythmic rocking that I had been doing. He placed his hand on my lower back and gently rolled us over, pulling me underneath him on the soft, thick blanket. I opened my legs so he could fit between them as he pressed his hand down my body to my ass and ground himself against me. He kissed all along my neck and over my chest, nibbling one hard nipple and then the other as he continued to grind his cock against mine, frotting and fueling the inferno inside of me.

"I need to be inside of you," Hawke whispered against the hollow at the base of my neck, scraping his five o'clock shadow over my collarbone. I knew the delectable marks he left there would be a scrumptious reminder in the morning.

"Fuck, yes, please," I whined as a shockwave of electrical pleasure shot up my spine and I arched my back.

Hawke sat up on his knees and I immediately followed, wrapping my mouth around his swollen tip. Hawke hissed at the unexpected pleasure. I knew he had intended to reach for the lube, but I wasn't about to let him get away from me that easily.

I took him down to his base with a deep moan as his dick slid along my tongue and his flavor exploded in my mouth. Hawke started to lightly thrust in my mouth, his hand going to my hair to hold my head in place, and I couldn't stop moaning my appreciation. The small submissive part of me loved it when he did that.

I loved knowing that I could push him to the edge of bliss, to drive him wild with his need to feel more. He never went too far or too hard. He made sure he didn't cause me to choke or hurt me. He was always in control, even at the height of his pleasure.

I could feel him getting harder and I knew he was close. I moaned again, long and low, knowing it would send vibrations straight down his dick.

Hawke let out a cry, shouting my name as he snapped his hips forward and came hard down my throat. I greedily sucked and swallowed everything he had for me as his breaths shuttled from his chest.

He was still half-hard and I continued to suck on him until I felt his dick grow once again. With a final suck to his tip, I popped my mouth off his cock and lifted my head and at once his mouth crashed down over mine, his lips capturing mine. His tongue invaded my welcoming mouth as he carefully pushed me back down onto the blanket.

He effortlessly slipped between my legs as I heard him opening the lube bottle that he had managed to reach. His mouth never left mine as he teased my pucker for a moment, just long enough to make me buck my hips with need, before he inserted his fingers inside of my hole. I whimpered into the kiss and I couldn't help but rock my hips to get more friction and encourage him deeper.

Our mutual need was reaching a peak and once Hawke felt that I was stretched enough, he removed his fingers from inside me and once again switched our positions so I was straddling his lap, the balls of my feet perched on the thick blanket, heels in the air, as he sat back against the couch.

"Go slow, let it build up, Darlin'."

The last thing I wanted to do was to go slow, but I understood what he wanted. He didn't want to rush this one, like so many times before. He wanted both of us to experience new heights of pleasure and I was all for it.

I lowered myself down onto the tip of his dick. I went slow, and bit by bit, took all of his girthy hardness until he was balls deep and I sat on his hips, both of us breathing heavily. It was glorious to be able to feel him inside of me once again. I was never going to get tired of feeling his dick buried inside of me.

"You feel so good. Your body was meant for me and mine was meant for you." He kissed all along my neck as he spoke, his whiskey-scented breath feathering over my skin in little puffs of cool air, and I could feel goosebumps rise over my hot skin in his wake.

I couldn't argue with that at all. I knew we had both felt it before, that familiarity to the other. As if we had loved each other for several past life times and once again our bodies were reconnecting, our souls were reconnecting, merging as we came together once more as one.

I let out a breathy moan as I leisurely slid myself upward until I was almost at his tip before I slowly moved back down with a hiss, enjoying the stretch and burn in my channel as his thick cock filled me in all the right ways. I continued to go agonizingly slow just like he wanted. The pace was driving me insane but his pleasure was my top priority and I knew it would be worth it in the end.

He placed his hands on my hips, grasping them to force me to keep the unhurried pace. He already knew once I hit my sweet spot it would be hard for me to keep the pace slow.

I angled my hips so I could hit my sweet spot and I let out a loud cry the second his dick hit it dead on.

Hawke held onto my hips tighter, his fingers digging into my skin as my need to go faster increased. I knew I'd have bruises there tomorrow but I didn't care.

"Go slow, Darlin'. I want to watch as

you come all over my belly without me even touching your dick."

I moaned as I put my head back and arched slightly so the angle would be even better. Hawke kissed and nipped at my neck, lightly thrusting into me to make himself go even deeper inside of me. We were both moaning, our bodies trembling with need, but we continued to move leisurely as one.

I wrapped my arms around Hawke's neck as he held me close against his chest. We kissed slowly and gently, just as our movements were. We allowed our bodies to feel everything that the other was giving to it without the need to chase our pleasure. It built slowly and I truly felt amazing. I had no idea that sex could ever feel this wonderful. It was always amazing with Hawke, but this felt on a whole other level. This wasn't sex, this was tender love making, as if our souls were physically connecting to the other. It was overwhelming and remarkable all at the same time.

Time held no meaning. I couldn't tell if it had been ten minutes or ten hours that we had been pleasuring each other in slow motion. I just knew it was excruciating and incredible all at once, my pleasure centers were firing at top speed, I felt almost high from the endorphins flooding my system, and I never wanted this moment to end.

I felt the heat in the pit of my stomach turn into an inferno and my balls pulled up tight. My panting and moans had picked up and I felt like I was about to explode. I could feel Hawke getting even harder within me and I knew he was close, too. I couldn't stop moaning as my walls tightened around his cock and my body detonated.

The tightening of my walls was enough to push Hawke over the edge and he erupted fiercely inside of me. I couldn't contain the deep moan at the heat from his jizz filling the inside of me, scorching my walls.

"Hawke," I moaned as it felt like my whole body became consumed with his heat. I felt complete at the very simple sensation. As if there was a piece of Hawke within me, a part of his soul that would forever belong to me now.

Once I finally stopped pulsing, I placed my forehead against his as we both tried to catch our breath. I felt lightheaded and my body was weak and trembling from the pleasure and exertion. At the same time, I felt a bit like I would never again catch my breath, like I floated, a bit stoned. I knew it was from all of the panting and lack of oxygen, but I didn't care. I loved the heavenly euphoric feeling and I never wanted to come back down to earth.

Hawke pulled me in for a gentle kiss before he pulled back. He too was breathing heavily and seemed like he barely had enough oxygen himself. Still, he placed a hand on the side of my face, cupping my cheek in his meaty palm as he spoke with so much love and emotion lacing his voice that it nearly brought tears to my eyes.

"I love you."

Those were three words I never thought I would ever hear again. I never expected to ever fall in love with someone, nor had I wanted to. I had been fully prepared to handle life completely alone, baggage and all, and I had been good with that. And then Hawke came into my life and completely destroyed my world. He blew it up without a single care or concern for the consequences as he tore down all my carefully built up walls and I should probably hate him for it, but I loved him. He had saved me, even when I didn't know I needed saving. He was my soulmate and I was his.

"I love you, too."

Hawke pulled me to him once more, his mouth capturing mine in a tender but passionate kiss. He kept it slow, but I could feel exactly how much he loved me through that single kiss.

I let out a soft moan and melted into his arms. After a moment, Hawke placed his hand on the small of my back and flipped us once again so I was lying back down on the blanket with Hawke now above me. Hawke slowly moved his hips back and forth as he softly began to fuck me once more.

I broke the kiss first as I couldn't help but pant heavily, my heart tripping at the pleasure already slowly building inside of me yet again.

"I'm going to make love to you all night, Darlin'."

I could hear the promise in his voice and it was one I knew I was going to thoroughly enjoy. Suddenly, I was no longer tired and in need of a breather. I felt energized and ready for Hawke to fulfill his pledge.

This night was going to be special and I knew I would always remember it for the rest of my life. Just like I knew that tonight was only one of the many nights that Hawke and I would share together. For the first time in decades, I couldn't wait to see what the future had in store for me.

Thank you for reading!
Continue the series with <u>Cyrus</u>, Book Two in Smokejumpers.

CYRUS

SMOKEJUMPERS

BOOK TWO

BY EVIE RILEY

CHAPTER ONE

Damon

THE LITTLE LIGHT changed from red to green and I strolled into the hotel room. This wasn't the first time I'd done this in the past three months. It wasn't even the tenth. I wasn't one for one-night stands. I didn't tend to do this. There was too much risk involved.

As a Captain in the Investigations Unit of the Fire Department, I was supposed to live up to a level of reputation and ethics. I couldn't have questionable morals or make questionable decisions, and up until three months ago I never had.

Up until three months ago, I'd always made sure that none of my actions would be questionable. I never got drunk on a weekday. Hell, I'd never gotten drunk on weekends. I'd never smoked, done drugs, or engaged in reckless sex. I'd never allowed myself to take risks, to ever be in a compromising position.

The past three months, though, I'd been reckless. I'd been spiraling and I knew I shouldn't be, but it was hard to stop now. I'd been getting drunk multiple times a week, even on weekdays. I'd gone to sex parties, actual sex parties in an underground secret club with drugs. I'd done ecstasy and cocaine, something I never thought I would do, but I did them. I enjoyed doing them. It was wrong and I shouldn't have done it, but I couldn't seem to stop.

It was as if I had spent my whole life living in a box and having to do everything perfect, everything right. And for the first time in thirty-eight years, I'd broken out of that box and now I was struggling to get back inside.

The trick was, I didn't know if I truly wanted to go back inside that box. My whole life I'd had to be perfect. I'd had to uphold the reputation of my family, my family name, multiple generations of firefighters.

People often thought being a legacy meant we had it easier. That we got instant respect and had a golden road paved ahead of us. What they didn't realize is that everyone looked at us like we were supposed to be amazing. Like we came into the world capable of extinguishing the most deadly of fires without breaking a sweat. The reality was, though, that wasn't me.

I'd never wanted to be a firefighter. I'd never had any interest in running into a burning building. I'd had a great deal of respect for every firefighter, for every man and woman who were brave and courageous enough to run into an inferno to save lives. But that just wasn't me. It wasn't because I wasn't brave or courageous; it was because I didn't like fire.

I grew up with my father and grandfather both going through horrific days. Days where they drank themselves into oblivion just so they didn't have to deal with the emotions and trauma they felt. I'd watched as my father slowly faded away. As his smile started to appear less and less. As the drinking increased, as the anger increased, as the fighting increased. I'd had a front row seat to all of it, and the very last thing I'd wanted to do was put my future husband or myself in that position.

I can still remember clear as day what my father's face looked like when I told him that I didn't want to sign up for the fire academy. I was seventeen and I thought he would be okay with me not wanting to be a firefighter because my older brother, Taye, was already one.

Taye was older by a few years and he had always wanted to be a firefighter. He had always been interested in fire and he signed up right when he turned eighteen without hesitation. I thought I would be okay to chase after my own dreams. I thought my father would allow me to have my own life.

As it turned out, I was wrong.

To my father, both of his sons had to be in the fire department. Otherwise it would be a disgrace to the family name. I'd never told anyone that I didn't want to be a firefighter, only my father knew. I knew most people would have told me to do whatever I wanted. That I was an adult and my father couldn't force me to join the fire department.

It wasn't that simple, though.

My father had a way of making sure you did whatever he wanted. He never raised a hand to us, but he didn't have to. He knew how to keep us in line, how to pile on the pressure and make clear his disappointment if we didn't do as we were told. After eighteen years of it, I knew the only way I wasn't going into the fire academy would be with his permission.

I was never going to get his permission, so I settled for trying to make a life in the fire department that I could live with. Once I graduated from the academy, I immediately took the route of an officer and became a fire investigator. It kept me out of the burning buildings and I naively believed I would be protected from the horrors that took place every day on this job. I'd thought if I investigated fires to determine what caused them, I wouldn't have to experience the trauma that normal firefighters did when they arrived on scene. I never expected that I would have to see the burnt up bodies, the ones so horribly burned, suffering and fighting for their life in the burn unit. I thought it would be just burned out buildings.

I was so very wrong.

Still, I'd dealt with it like I was supposed to. I buried it and pushed through the trauma and pain to do my job. I had a reputation to live up to and that meant I couldn't show any weakness. I had to be perfect and work my way up through the ranks. Now twenty years later, I was a Captain in the Investigation Unit and I was responsible for three dozen men and women with hundreds of open cases.

I had a lot to lose. I had a lot of reasons why I needed to go back into my perfectly created box. I knew logically I needed to get myself back into that box so I wouldn't drag my family's name and reputation through the mud more than it already had been.

I had always been responsible. I had always been the dependable one. The one who made sure our family name was kept in good standing. And then three months ago one of my best investigators blew up my world.

Tristan Cole had been one of my best guys and I relied on him and his instincts to help close some of the most difficult cases. On top of that, he had an amazing conviction rating. The evidence he found was always exactly what our Assistant District Attorney needed to convince a jury that we had our arsonist. He was a huge asset to the department and I often relied on him to work cases that were left cold.

I just never expected him to change everything in one single shot.

Three months ago, Tristan informed me that my older brother was a suspected arsonist. I didn't want to believe it at first, but it got increasingly hard to ignore all of the signs from growing up and the damming evidence.

Tristan had been working on cold cases since the first day he'd started in the unit. I knew he had been trying to find the arsonist who had started the fire in his family home that killed his parents and left his arm severely burned.

To be honest, I never expected for him to find his arsonist. I had hoped he would, for his own sake, of course, so he could heal and recover from the tragedy. I just never expected for him to discover multiple fires all connected to not one, but two arsonists. I thought he was crazy. I told him as much. I thought he was trying to see a pattern where there wasn't one, only for him to have been right the whole time.

I should have listened to him years ago. Maybe if I had, Taye wouldn't have had the chance to kill anyone yet. But I didn't listen and fifteen years had gone by with Taye and his mentor setting fires and killing people. Taye himself had been starting fires for ten years, ever since our father had been killed in a storage facility fire.

I still wasn't certain Taye hadn't started that fire.

I knew he wouldn't have wanted to kill our father, but he wouldn't have known that would have been the result. I had asked Tristan to look into it, but so far he hadn't been able to find anything definitive.

Taye was now in prison awaiting trial for multiple homicides, including two young children. His mentor, Wilson Stan, was dead, killed by Taye himself when their relationship reached its boiling point.

I knew from my career that arsonists didn't usually work in pairs. It was very rare for an arsonist to want to work with someone, to teach someone his hands on methods, and I suspected that Wilson had a more complex psyche than the average arsonist. Unfortunately, we would never truly know now that he was dead.

What it did mean was that for the past ten years every fire that we could connect to Wilson or Taye, Taye could be charged with the fire and any injuries or deaths associated with it. It didn't matter if Taye lit the fuse, all that mattered legally was that it could be connected to any fire that Taye had been part of.

So far, Taye was refusing to speak to anyone, he wasn't going to confess, so it was up to Assistant District Attorney

Barba to get a conviction. I knew he would, though. He might not get a conviction on every fire, but he would on the murder of Wilson Stan and the attempted murder of Detective West and Tristan. Both Detective West and Tristan had survived the nightmare and they were both set to testify. Taye would be going to prison for the rest of his life.

Along with my family's name and legacy.

A knock at my door dragged me out of my thoughts. Tonight I was meeting up with a guy that I'd messaged on Grinder named Cy. That was all his profile had for a name, along with a very nice picture of his bare chest and a sexy face. He was younger, but I didn't care. I wasn't looking to date or marry anyone. This was just about having some fun, hooking up and letting off some steam.

Cy's profile didn't reveal anything about him personally. I had no idea what his job was or if he went to school or not. I didn't care about any of that shit anyway, and the profiles that came across as someone looking for something more or ongoing, I skipped over them.

Nope. Not my deal.

I strolled over and opened the door and was instantly relieved to see that he matched his profile picture. There had been a couple of times where a profile picture wasn't exactly a match to what the hookup looked like in person. They weren't a completely different person, but it had been clear the photo was an old one.

I didn't let him in right away, though, because there were rules that I needed to hear him agree to. If he didn't, then I would find another guy for the night.

"No questions, no small talk, just sex and then you leave. Deal?"

He smirked before he spoke. "Aye, works for me."

Holy shit, he was Scottish! He didn't have a thick accent, but he had one and it was the sexiest thing I had ever heard.

I stepped back and allowed him to enter. The second the door was closed, I pushed him back against it and captured his lips. He knew from my profile that I was a top so we didn't need to have the discussion of who was driving or not. Cy easily gave up control and allowed me to dominate the kiss without any fight.

He had a red beard, just a bit more than a five o'clock shadow, and it felt rough against my hand, but that didn't bother me. I was so used to guys being clean-shaven, that the feel of the roughness was a pleasant new sensation against my skin.

As our tongues danced with each other, we both turned our attention to the other's clothes. He was wearing just a t-shirt and jeans so it didn't take me long to get him naked. The second his shirt was off, I ran my hands over his chest and down his chiseled abs. He felt amazing against me and my body was already ready for him.

I pulled him away from the door and brought him over to the bed. He easily lay down and opened his legs for me to fit in between. The second our bodies connected, we both gave a soft moan as our dicks pressed against each other.

I broke the kiss, not wanting to draw this out. We were both here for one thing and one thing only. We didn't need to make out for hours first.

I made my way down his neck, kissing and nibbling his skin as I ground my hips against his. The added friction, the real skin on skin friction this time, caused us both to let out a deep moan. I hadn't gotten to see his dick yet, but he felt big. Something I'd discovered I enjoyed.

I only topped, I held no interest in bottoming. There had been a few guys who'd wanted me to try, but I always turned them down. Even before I'd started to do this, the Grinder hookups, I'd had a few secret boyfriends and I'd never allowed them to top with me. I never wanted a finger inside of me, much less a dick; that just didn't interest me, nor did it make me all tingly at the thought.

What did make me excited was the prospect of a large dick in my mouth. I liked the feeling of it and I liked the control, the power, of knowing I could drive another man wild with need. To make him so desperate for a release that he was willing to do anything for it. I liked being in control. I'd also discovered I liked being a bit rough. Especially recently.

I continued to kiss and lick my way down Cy's chest and made sure to nibble and suck on each of his nipples as I slid further down in search of his hard dick. He was already dripping precome from his slit and my gut instinct told me he was going to be vocal. Some guys found it annoying when their partner was vocal, but not me. I loved it. I could tell how wound up a man was getting by the different sounds they made.

I sucked on his tip, humming my appreciation as the sweet musky taste of him finally hit my tongue. I only gave him a quick suck before I took him all the way down to his base in one go. He was a good size, easily ten inches, but I stopped having gag reflexes long ago.

"Damon," he moaned as he moved his right hand to rest on the top of my head.

I grabbed his hand and placed it back down onto the bed, making sure to grab his other hand to do the same. I didn't like it when someone tried to control me. I was in control and Cy was going to know it. Respect it.

I felt his hands fist in the sheets and I knew he understood that he wasn't allowed to take control. Still, I put my hands on his hips, holding him tightly, my fingers pressing into his skin to make sure he didn't try thrusting into my mouth. He was at my mercy and that was too bad for him if he didn't like it. He'd have bruises there the next day but that wasn't my problem or something I cared about. He'd known what he was getting into.

I worked all up and down his dick, teasing him and not putting too much pressure on his dick. I wasn't about to allow him to come yet. I wasn't ready for this part to end yet and based on the throaty moans he was giving me, he wasn't ready for it to end either.

I slid my right hand down his hips and

around to cup his ass and I was surprised when I felt something brush against my fingers. I pulled my mouth off his dick, Cy letting out a whimper at the loss of contact as I turned my attention to what I felt against my fingers.

"My, my, what do we have here?" I asked as I pushed the end of the plug, forcing it deeper inside of him.

This wasn't the first time I'd hooked up with a guy who was already stretched or wearing a butt plug. More often than not, when I was in the gay clubs and hooking up in the bathroom or back alley the guy would already be stretched so he wouldn't have to deal with that part of things. It worked for me. It was convenient and made for a quicker fuck. This was the first time a guy had shown up for a booty call with one in, though. Cy moaned as I continued to move the plug in and out of his hole.

"I asked you a question," I demanded.

"My plug," he managed to get out as he started to wiggle his hips and grind himself down against my hand.

I moved my hand back to his hips and pressed them down as I spoke. "I didn't say you could move." He gave a shiver, but he stopped moving.

I moved my hand back down to his ass

and once more started to slowly pull the plug out before pushing it back in as I spoke.

"Good boy. How long has it been in?"

"Six hours."

That shocked me. I was expecting him to say maybe an hour at most.

Now that was exciting.

"Six hours. Well aren't you a naughty whore. You've just been sitting around with this plug inside of your ass all day waiting for when you could get a real dick inside of you?"

"Aye. I like the feeling. Please, fuck me," he begged, and I could tell he was struggling not to wriggle his hips to get better friction. I was purposely missing his sweet spot, just skimming it to wind him up, but nowhere near enough to let him explode.

I moved my mouth down to the crease of his leg and inhaled his manly scent, relishing in the sweaty smell before I moved on to suck on his inner thigh, right by his hip. He let out a long moan as I continued to suck hard at his sensitive skin there and when I pulled back I knew he would have a hickey for the next few days.

A reminder to anyone who fucked him next that I had been there first.

"I'm nowhere near done with you yet."

I would fuck him and I would let him come, but only when I was ready for it. Only when I deemed him worthy of it.

I continued to fuck him with the plug as I took his cock back in my mouth. He gave another deep, throaty moan and I knew the pleasure was building up within him, but he wasn't going to be getting a release just yet. This was my favorite part, the torment and the teasing, and I was not about to let it slip me by.

As time went on, I could tell that he was growing desperate by the change of his sounds. They were more whimpering and whining now as his need grew to the next level. He was trying to stay still, he was trying to be good, but his body cried out with need and it was getting harder for him to keep his body from instinctively thrusting and wiggling to get more friction. To finally give him what he needed for his release. His dick was rock hard in my mouth and I had no doubt that he was hurting slightly from the hardness. I wasn't going to stop until he broke, though, until he begged, and only then would I give him the release he desperately needed.

"Fuck, please. I need to come, please. Please, let me come, I'm beggin' ye."

There it was.

That's what I needed to hear.

The next time I moved the plug back in, I made sure to hit his prostate dead on, causing him to let out a small scream of pleasure. I sucked on his dick harder, hollowing my cheeks as I continued to hit his sweet spot and after only a moment, he let out a long roar as his cum shot out of him and down my throat. I moaned my appreciation as I swallowed and sucked him for every last drop that his body had for me.

Once he finished pulsing, I carefully pulled the plug out of him and removed my mouth from his dick, giving him one last lick on his tip to catch a few last drops of the tasty treat. I tossed the plug down beside the bed as I reached over to the bedside table and grabbed the condom and lube that I had left there.

Cy was breathing heavily and he had his eyes closed as he tried to calm his body down from the roller coaster ride I had just taken him on. I slipped on the condom and added some lube, coating my latex-covered cock just in case the lube inside of him from the plug wasn't enough.

Cy opened his eyes as I grabbed his legs and hauled them up onto my shoulders, exposing his winking pucker to me. I lined the tip of my dick up with his stretched and needy hole, then I slowly pushed in. I wasn't small and I knew I was thicker than the plug he had been using. He gave a lengthy, sharp cry as I pushed inside of him, his walls welcoming me within their tight grip.

He was so responsive and I loved it.

The second I was buried deep inside of him, I pulled out and slammed right back inside of him. Hard. Fuck, he felt good. He was tight and hot and slick.

Perfect.

I hit his sweet spot dead on and he let out a scream as pleasure shot through him.

"That's it, you naughty whore, let it out," I growled.

"Oh fuck, don't stop," he panted as he reached up and gripped the headboard behind him.

I reached my right hand up and ran the tip of my finger over his swollen lips. He opened his mouth so I took the invitation and shoved my finger inside of it. He moaned as he sucked on my digit, his gaze locked with mine, his hips bucking up against each thrust inside him. I could see the heat in his heavy-lidded gaze and it drove me wild.

He loved this just as much as I did.

He was young, early twenties, so I had to imagine he didn't have much experience with sex. At least not as much as I did. I didn't mind that, though. It meant he'd likely be more into learning and enjoying experimenting, finding out what worked for him, than someone who'd already done it all before.

"Such a good boy," I praised, and he let loose another loud moan at my words.

It would appear Cy had a praise kink.

Nice.

I pulled my hand away from his mouth and he let out a soft whine at the loss of my finger in his mouth. I wrapped my hand around his throat, applying a small amount of pressure, and he whimpered, his gaze glazing over.

He wrapped one hand around my wrist, grasping it tight, but I knew it wasn't so he could pull my hand away or indicating I should stop. I allowed him to keep his hand there as I picked up my pace and pounded hard and deep inside of him. I made sure to hit his sweet spot each time I thrust, and he arched his back in encouragement as skin slapped against skin and my hips punished his ass.

I could feel the walls of his hole getting

tighter, gripping my dick, and I knew he was close. I was close too, but I didn't believe in coming before my lover.

"Touch yourself. I want to watch as you come," I ordered.

He sucked in a hissing breath and instantly, his hand went to his hard dick, fisting his length, and he started to jerk himself off furiously. I moved forward so he was more folded into himself, and I knew I was trapping his hand between us, making it hard for him to complete the previous instruction, but it brought me closer to his mouth. I placed my lips close to his, not allowing his lips to touch mine yet but just hovering a hair's breadth over his mouth.

"You like it when I call you a good boy, don't you?" I asked softly, allowing my lips to lightly skim over his. He went to press his against mine, but I pulled back just enough so he couldn't touch me.

"Aye," he panted.

"I want to feel you come. I want to feel your tight ass milking my dick for every last drop. Now, be my good boy and come for me," I said, as I slammed hard against his sweet spot once more.

That was all Cy needed before he gave a long scream as he came hard and shot his cum all over his stomach. The tightening of his walls around my dick was just the push I needed for my own orgasm to hit. I snapped my hips forward and buried myself deep inside of him as I exploded into the condom. We were both breathing heavily as our dicks pulsed and the wash of our climaxes rolled over us repeatedly.

Once my body calmed down enough, and my breathing had returned to more normal, I moved back and removed my hand from his throat. I slowly pulled out, grasping the edge of the condom, as Cy's legs collapsed down onto the bed. I could see that he was spent, but I didn't believe in cuddling afterward. This was just sex, which meant it was time for him to get going. I climbed off the bed as I spoke.

"I gotta shower. You know where the door is."

I didn't look at him to see what his reaction was, it wasn't important. I headed into the bathroom and closed the door without another word or glance in his direction. It was what we'd both agreed to, so if he had a problem with it, that was on him and not on me. This wasn't going to turn into a relationship from a one-night stand. That wasn't what I was looking for. That wasn't what anyone was looking for off Grinder. We'd had a good time, it was just that simple.

After tossing the condom in the garbage can beside the sink, I turned the shower on and stepped under the hot spray. The night was just getting started and I was looking forward to the rest of it.

CHAPTER TWO

Cyrus

I PULLED OFF to the side of the road as I approached Station Twenty-One. Today was my first shift with them and I should've been excited about it, but all I felt was dirty.

I had brought it on myself. I knew better than to use Grinder for anything meaningful, but last night I wanted to celebrate getting selected to be a Probee at a firehouse. Not everyone who made it through the fire academy actually got chosen by a firehouse. There was not always a position available or the funding for another firefighter and then everyone had to wait in a queue. I was lucky enough to have graduated closer to the top of the list so I was chosen.

I was even luckier to have been picked

up by house Twenty-One. I didn't know much about the guys there, but I did know that Captain Clarke was a gay man and he was out and proud. That meant that his firehouse had a zero tolerance for intolerance. It was the type of firehouse a guy like me needed. I was gay, but I wasn't necessarily out. I wasn't in the closet either, though. I lived in this gray area where I was proud to be a gay man, but I wasn't exactly screaming it from a rooftop. If someone asked, then I would tell them the truth, just like if someone asked if I was seeing anyone. But I didn't feel the need to tell everyone that I was gay right from the start.

If no one asked and relationships never came up, then why should I have to tell people?

Straight men and women didn't go around telling everyone they were straight so why should I?

I knew this station was going to be a good one. I knew I wouldn't have to worry about little snide comments or jokes when the guys eventually did discover that I was gay.

My issue was last night and my extreme error in judgment.

I didn't often go on Grinder. I was only on it because every now and then a man got an itch that he needed scratched and sometimes it was just easier to have a quick hook up than to build a relationship. There was a reason why my generation had so many dating and hook up apps.

I had been focused on being in the fire department since I was a kid. When I turned eighteen, I was crushed to discover they weren't taking on any new recruits just yet. They had to live by the budget set out by the city and they were already pushing it, so they couldn't take on any more firefighters. Even with that setback, I didn't let it stop me.

I had gone to work full-time in a shitty, meaningless job and during my free time I spent it working out and running different drills so I would be ready for the academy when it opened up again.

That finally happened this year, just before my twenty-first birthday.

I was down at the recruitment office bright and early on the morning registration opened. I was first in line with all of my paperwork in order, including a full medical exam report that I had gotten the week prior.

When I'd gotten that acceptance letter, I had never felt excitement like that in my entire life. I had worked hard for it and I was finally on the road to living my dream. I pushed myself as hard as I could in the academy so I would stand out. So I could be at the top of my graduating class and so hopefully, I could guarantee a position in a firehouse. And it was all worth every all-nighter and every sore muscle.

So last night I wanted to celebrate.

I wanted to have one last fling before I would need to put all of my time and attention into my new position. I had almost given up hope, but then I came across Damon's profile and I couldn't resist sending him a message. He was sexy and I'd always had a thing for older guys as well. I didn't have much experience in the bedroom, but I did know that the few guys I had slept with who were older than me, they were a hell of a lot better than the guys my age. Older men knew things in the bedroom. They had the experience to truly take a lover on a roller coaster ride of pleasure that left their legs weak for hours afterward and that was exactly what I'd wanted last night.

When Damon rhymed off the rules at his hotel, I didn't think anything of it. I'd heard the same things plenty of times. Hell, I'd said them. But I knew they were never true, at least not fully. Yes, most of the time there wasn't any talking, but afterward there was usually a few minutes of civility, at least. We would normally lie there as our bodies started to come back down to Earth. During those moments there was small talk, there was politeness and the other person eventually saw the other one off at the door with a goodbye kiss. That's what I had expected from Damon.

Only I essentially got a polite *fuck you*.

I felt dirty, used, like I was a prostitute who had given it away for free because a cute guy winked at me. I had never done a walk of shame before, but I did last night and it didn't feel good.

What made it worse, was last night had been the best night of my life.

The sex was incredible. I hadn't even known it was possible to feel that good, to feel that level of pleasure, and now just thinking about it made me feel dirty and cheap. Maybe it was my age or maybe it was inexperience, but I'd never expected to feel that way after sex and I never wanted to feel that way again.

I let out a sigh and shook my head slightly to try and clear my thoughts and emotions. Today was supposed to be a good day, a happy day, and I couldn't let what happened between Damon and I taint this day. I had waited a long time for it and I wasn't going to let anything destroy it.

I reached over and grabbed my bag before I climbed out of my car and walked the short distance to the firehouse. I was really hoping today went well. I knew I would have to pay my dues. I would have to do the smaller tasks that no one would want to do, but I was ready for it. I was ready to cook and clean and grab equipment. I was ready for it all because once the probation period was over, I would be a real firefighter. It would take a year before my probation period was over, but the guys wouldn't be riding me hard the whole time. I just had to prove to them that I was capable and also a team player.

I had this.

Walking inside, I was instantly looking around. Each firehouse was a bit different in how they had everything setup. Some were older than others as well, but Twenty-One appeared to be one of the station houses that were renovated within the past five years. It looked great and it looked like a lot that I would need to clean. I knew cleaning was going to be one of my daily tasks, but that was fine. It would keep me busy, at least during our downtime.

I made my way toward where the voices were coming from. I walked into a kitchen and living room area. There were five guys, one of which I recognized as Captain Clarke. I didn't really know the others. It didn't take two seconds before they all noticed me. I gave a friendly smile as I spoke.

"Hey, I'm Cyrus MacMillan, your new Probee."

"And we bagged a Scot," the one man said from his position behind the kitchen counter.

"Great, now Zander will be multilingual with swearing," another guy said and the guys all laughed.

"About fucking time." I was going to assume that was Zander.

Captain Clarke walked over to me as he held his hand out and spoke. "It's a pleasure to have you here. From what I have heard you were top in your graduating class and a real joy to have around. I'm Captain Clarke. This is Zander, Gage, Hawke, and Newt. Newt is our paramedic who has somehow managed to stick around for longer than two weeks."

"Do they normally not?" I asked,

slightly confused.

"The city tends to have paramedics floating from one firehouse to the next. They feel it is the best way to handle having females around the neanderthals who are firefighters." Newt answered, but that did nothing to ease my confusion.

"We are not all Neanderthals," Hawke instantly defended.

"I'm not saying you guys are. The firefighters in this house are all amazing. Everyone tries to get shifts here. Captain Clarke has made this house a safe place for men and women, straight or gay. We all know that we can work here without any harassment. That's not true at most of the other houses, though. I've seen about a dozen female paramedics walk off the job because they couldn't handle the male firefighters' bullshit. It's a serious problem, one that the city doesn't seem all that interested in correcting," Newt fully explained.

"That's terrible. I'm sorry they've had to go through that."

I couldn't believe that paramedics would have to float around because there were too many problems with staying in one firehouse for any length of time. No one should have to go through that and no one should feel like they needed to quit because the job wasn't going to get better. That wasn't fair to any of them.

"So, were you born in Scotland?" Gage asked.

"No, I was born here. My parents were and they came over when my Ma was up th' duff with me. They were visiting some family friends in New York, but a snowstorm grounded their flight. Ma went into labor and a wee bairn was born one month early. By the time they could fly with me, they had decided they didn't want to leave."

"*Up th' duff.* Love it! You are going to be my new best friend," Zander said, flashing me a big smile.

"Hey," Hawke said, clearly insulted.

"What? You know I love you, but he gives me new fun words," Zander said with a playful wink.

"How are your parents with you being a firefighter? You don't look much older than twenty, I have to imagine they are worried," Gage commented.

"My parents are dead. They died when I was sixteen."

It wasn't anywhere near that simple, though.

My parents had been amazing growing up. I didn't ever remember a time where we went hungry or we didn't have a place to live. They never hurt me, they never hit me, they barely yelled at me or each other. It was a happy home. A home filled with love.

I didn't discover that it was also a home filled with lies until I was sixteen.

I had been in school when my principal pulled me out in the middle of class. I got out into the hallway and saw a detective and the guidance counselor standing there. They took me into the principal's office where they then informed me that my mother was dead and my father had been arrested for her murder. As it turned out my father, Jamie McDougal, was a prolific arsonist who had been responsible for setting over a hundred fires and killing eighty-three people in them.

The last person he killed was my mother.

He had started setting fires not long after they were married in Scotland. Apparently, that was the reason why my father didn't argue with my mother about staying here after I was born. The Scottish police and fire investigators were already getting too close to identifying him over there.

It took the police and fire investigators sixteen years and eighty-three victims before they finally discovered that my father was responsible. They had caught a lucky break via a bird watching camera that caught him starting the fire. The signature was the same as the previous fires and the police had everything they needed to make the arrest. Only somehow my father caught wind of it and he ran with my mother to the Couturie Forest where he doused her with gasoline before setting her on fire. His plan had been to take advantage of the dry weather to start a forest fire that would either kill him or give him the perfect opportunity to escape. Still to this day I was not really sure which outcome my father was rooting for. Either way, he had been captured and convicted. He was sentenced to a hundred and eighteen years. One year for each fire he'd set. Apparently the judge felt like it was poetic justice.

With my mother dead and my father in prison, I didn't have any family over here and I wasn't about to be shipped off to Scotland to live in a country that I had never even been to either. As a minor, I had been placed in a group home where I'd lived for two years before aging out of the system.

Growing up in the group home was

horrible for the two years I had to endure being there. I was often bullied or beaten up by the other guys there. Word spread very quickly who my father was and I was bullied and hated at school. Like somehow it was my fault for the sins of my father. Those two years were the hardest years of my life.

The second I turned eighteen, I changed my last name to my mother's maiden name with the hope that I could go under the radar and no one would recognize the similarities in our facial features. So far it had been working, but I was always worried it would come out.

"We're sorry to hear that. It couldn't have been easy for you. Did you live with family afterward?" Captain Clarke asked, and I was relieved that he didn't ask me how they died.

"Group home. My family was all back in Scotland and I had never been. I was an American citizen as well and not a Scot. I spent two years in a group home before aging out."

"I grew up in the foster care system so I know it wasn't easy on you. If you ever want to talk, I'm always willing to listen," Hawke said with an understanding smile.

That was something that I had noticed, a lot of first responders were foster kid survivors. I never referred to anyone that went through the foster care as a victim. We all survived the experience, we all survived our own experiences, and sometimes those experiences could have ended us, but we came out stronger. To me, even the ones who didn't come out stronger, the ones who came out with demons they needed to work through, they were still survivors. That didn't mean it was easy to adapt to the real world. I was lucky, because I had only been in the foster care system for two years. I couldn't imagine having to grow up in it. Before anymore could be said the alarm was going off.

"Engine Fifty-Seven, Ambulance Sixty-One, multiple motor vehicle accident on Freeway Eighteen by Vine Street off ramp."

"All right, let's go, Probee," Zander chirped, flashing me a smile as the guys all started to head out.

I dropped my bag and headed out with them. They all grabbed their gear and I could see my own firefighter's jacket with my name on it hanging up. I grabbed it and tossed on my boots before I ran over to the truck. I climbed into the back with the rest of the guys while Newt headed to the ambulance with his partner.

"That's Jackson driving and this is Sinclair," Zander said with a nod to the other guy who was in the back with us.

"Cyrus MacMillan," I said, flashing them a friendly smile.

"Nice to meet you," Jackson called out from behind the wheel.

"You'll be with Sinclair, he's the Lieutenant," Captain Clarke informed me.

"I look forward to learning from all of you," I said.

I knew this was going to be a crazy experience and I had no idea how well I would do outside of the academy. The academy prepared recruits to have the skills to be able to handle surviving through their probation year, but they didn't tell them exactly what to expect. It was one thing to be able to handle a controlled fire in a training house and quite another to be involved in a fire that was unpredictable with real lives in the line. To see real people being put in danger and being hurt, killed. There were going to be a lot of rocky days and nights ahead of me, but I was really looking forward to experiencing all of the good that came with it.

The second we pulled up to the accident scene, the guys were jumping out of the truck before it even came to a full stop. I quickly jumped out after them and ran to catch up with the Lieutenant.

"Probee, what do you see?" he asked as the guys started to pull equipment from the truck.

I took a moment to look around and take in the scene as I spoke. "Three cars involved in the accident. Lots of additional cars are still driving. Police are trying to get the lanes shut down, multiple tow trucks waiting for their turn. Skid marks on the ground... so they tried to stop. Three people injured and sitting on hoods of the different cop cars. Two people still trapped in their vehicles, a male and a female."

"What is the most dangerous threat to an accident scene?"

"The gasoline. One spark could make it explode."

"Exactly. In a freeway accident we have to watch out for passing cars. Until the police can get the lanes closed down everyone is in danger. Most cars will go slowly as they pass by, but others will barrel right through and not care if they hit someone. You have to keep your head on a swivel and be aware of your surroundings."

"Aye, Sir."

"When you arrive at an accident scene,

you have to have fire extinguishers ready to go in case one of the cars starts to burn. Your priority is to quickly evaluate which victim is the main concern and how to get them out of the car as fast but safely as possible. Every accident victim gets a c-collar, whether you or they think they need it. It's protocol and only a doctor can clear their c-spine. Once a c-collar is on a victim, you never take it off no matter what. If there was damage done to their c-spine, you could have aggravated it and permanently paralyze them. Do I make myself clear?"

"Crystal."

I was more than happy to listen to his instructions and to watch the guys work, but I also wanted to be out there working with them. I wanted to get my hands on the equipment and to help save a life.

"We run things a bit differently. When we can, we like to make sure our Probees get to watch as a real life rescue goes down, then the next time you will be doing it with them. We will also be running multiple drills back at the house. We don't just do fire drills, but accident drills as well. We get old crushed up cars from the tow yard and recreate different scenarios. Today you will be learning how to use the equipment back at the house.

We will have you extracting different dummies so you can get a feel for the equipment and best practices. I know it's different to other firehouses, but Captain Clarke and I believe it's important for a Probee to be able to make mistakes without someone's life on the line. Doing complex drills allows you to make those mistakes so when you have to do it in a real life situation, you won't make them and someone won't die."

I could understand that and it seemed like the Captain and Lieutenant had thought their training process through. It was different compared to what I had heard about other firehouses, but I did like the safety net that it provided me. Generally, you had no safety net. You get a call and you do it and just hope that your training is enough. The way they were doing things though, it allowed me to get practice in. It allowed me to learn how the guys do it and the best practices. It allowed me to build muscle memory so when I arrived on scene it would be instinctual and I wouldn't have to think and analyze everything.

"I understand. I look forward to learning everything I can from you and the guys."

And I meant that.

Watching as the other guys worked, I realized quickly that they were a well-oiled machine. They easily worked together, knowing what their partner needed without them having to say anything. It was a fluid dance and in no time they had both of the pinned victims out of their vehicles and on a stretcher. I knew if I was going to be able to stay in their family, I would need to learn how to intermix into their process. It would be a delicate process, but I was hoping that we would all click and I could just become another piece of their machine. I had a lot of work ahead of me, but I was determined to make it happen. I would prove to them that I was the right choice and that I belonged in their family, on their team.

Today was the first day of the rest of my life and I just knew that it was going to be one of the best days of my life.

CHAPTER THREE

Damon

I QUICKLY MADE my way through the building to reach my office.

Before Taye had been arrested, I would walk with my head held high and I would speak with my investigators as I walked by. I would check in with them and ask them how their cases were going and offer any support that I could. Now though, I pulled out my phone and kept my head down and made it look like I was too busy to stop and talk. I didn't want to hear any of their sympathy or false claims of hope.

When the news first broke, everyone looked at me like I was the victim and I hated it. I wasn't a victim. Taye didn't hurt me. He'd hurt and killed other people. They were the real victims and I didn't need sympathetic and sad looks being thrown my way. I needed them to focus on their work, on the cases that were left open on their desks. That was what I needed.

Some days, I wanted to scream at everyone to stop looking at me like I was an abused dog. To leave me the hell alone and focus on their work. That I was their Captain and they needed to remember that. I didn't though, because I knew that if I yelled at anyone, I would only be making myself appear unstable. I had to keep up appearances. I couldn't let anyone suspect that I was struggling or not one hundred percent.

The second I was in my office, I let out a sigh. I was safe in here, but I knew eventually someone would be knocking at my door looking for approval on something. I would have to interact with someone soon enough. I knew I needed to get my head back in the game. I knew I needed to get my life back in order and stop being stupid and reckless.

The problem was, I didn't want to yet.

I didn't want to stop drinking and partying. I didn't want to stop having random hookups. I knew what the Shrink would say: I was denied the freedom to be rebellious and to express and explore my own sexuality through normal societal actions of a young adult. Now that my father was dead and the family's reputation destroyed by Taye, I was seizing the opportunity to live out the actions and decisions I never got to have growing up. Which basically translated to me being a drunken manwhore now, because I couldn't do it growing up with all of the other young adults free from their parent's house and control.

I suppose that could be true. I didn't get to be a normal teenager or twenty-something years old. I didn't get to party or go to the bars. Even when I was old enough to drink, I still didn't get to go out and party. My father always told me, told us, that we had to uphold the family name. We couldn't be drunk and sloppy. We couldn't have meaningless hookups that would bring forth unwanted attention and make people question our focus and dedication to the job.

My father refused to accept that I was gay. I had told him, my whole family, when I was fourteen, and he made sure to tell me that I wasn't and never would be. I was never allowed to be around a guy and never allowed to be alone with one. He would even set up dates for me. He would invite a girl over who he felt was suitable for the family name and would be able to handle the life of a firefighter. I would get asked to come over for family dinner and there she would be. Always attractive, always polite, submissive, and completely stupid. I didn't mean stupid in a social sense, no. I meant it in the literal sense. They were always airheads. The type who believed as long as they were attractive everything would be fine. They all only wanted to have a man who would take care of them so they didn't have to work. Their only job was to cook, clean, and be good looking. They were empty of any personality or self-respect.

Even if I was interested in women, I would never have dated them. I wanted someone real. Someone who didn't always need me to be the strong one. I didn't want to have to constantly take care of someone. I wanted someone who I could support and be there for, but someone who could also do the same with me. Someone who could be the strong one when I needed the time to be vulnerable and uncertain. I wanted someone who could have shared interests with me. Someone who was proud of who they were and confident in themselves. I wanted a real person, one that could click with me and we could complete each other. I wanted an equal partner.

CYRUS

I used to think it was possible, but after all of these years, I now know that it was just a fairytale. I was never going to be able to have that with someone, because I was never going to be able to be open and honest about who I was. I was very much in the closet; I was so far in the closet that I could see Narnia. I spent most of my time hanging out with the lion, Aslan.

At first, I had kept my sexual orientation to myself, because I knew as long as my father was alive I was never going to be free to be myself. He was never going to allow or tolerate my coming out publicly. To him, I was a disgrace to the family name and if people knew I was gay, then I would be disrespecting and shitting on our family's legacy and that was something he would never allow.

After his death, I was technically free to be myself, but I had spent so many years too afraid to be honest with people. Coming out seemed terrifying, too terrifying, so I stayed quiet and kept living my life just as I had with him alive.

Like I said, he never laid a hand on us, but he didn't have to in order to keep us in line. He was never short to call me a name for being gay. Every chance he got, he threw it in my face, calling me a faggot or homo. If I didn't get top grades in the academy, it was because I was a fag and needed to screw a woman to be a man. It didn't matter how many times I told him that I was born this way, he refused to believe it. All he cared about was the legacy. *His legacy.* Nothing was more important than honoring that.

It was a good thing he was dead now, so he wouldn't have to deal with Taye. At the same time though, there was a small part of me that wished he was alive so he would have this thrown in his face. He thought it would be me and my sexual deviance that would ruin the family name. I would have loved to see his face when instead it was Taye on the front of every newspaper for multiple counts of arson, homicide, and attempted homicide. To watch as he had to sit in that courthouse and listen to people testifying about the damage Taye had done. To watch as he had no choice but to listen to Tristan's testimony, a gay man's testimony, about his eldest son trying to kill him and a cop. It was petty of me, but I was allowed to think it. It was natural after everything he put me through, that I would want to wipe that smugness off his face.

I strolled over and slid into the chair behind my desk and quickly reviewed at what needed to be done today. I had a bunch of paperwork that needed to be completed and filed before the cases went to court. I also knew that Assistant District Attorney Barba had some documents that he needed me to go over to sign off for him. I had a lot of work that needed to be done and I knew I had to get started, but like every morning, I was finding it hard to get motivated enough to care about any of it.

This morning, I was also nursing a hangover.

After Cy left last night, I had two more guys come over for a party and the three of us enjoyed each other for a good chunk of the night. We drank and the one guy, Jay, brought some cocaine with him. I knew I shouldn't be doing it, but again, I didn't care. It wasn't like I was going to be randomly drug tested, that was only for active firefighters in the field.

Sure, I had a reputation to uphold, not just my family's name, but that of a Fire Captain. I wasn't in the field, but I was still a Captain and was expected not to be doing anything illegal. So if it ever came out that I was using cocaine recreationally, it wasn't going to go well. I was risking my career, my livelihood, but again, I couldn't care enough. It was the weirdest thing, because I knew I had to care. I knew I had to straighten back up and stop drinking so often, stop the drug use and random sex. I knew all of that and if it was one of my guys telling me about the shit that I had done, I would be suspending them and sending them to the Shrink. I was a hypocrite, and I needed to stop, but I couldn't bring myself to do it. I didn't understand why and it wasn't like I could talk to anyone about it.

The few friends I had in the department, they weren't in any position to offer advice and really, I knew what they would say. It would be the same thing I would say to them if they approached me. I knew I could talk to my best friend, Will, but I also didn't want to put him in a compromising position. He was a Captain himself out of the Twenty-First and it wasn't fair to put him in a position where legally he was required to report me to the Upper Brass. I knew he wouldn't, but he couldn't have plausible deniability if he was ever questioned down the line. By not telling him, I was protecting him. At least that was how I was rationalizing it in my mind. Again a Shrink would call bullshit on me, but that was precisely why I was refusing to speak to a Shrink. I had survived this long on my ability to lie to myself and to believe those lies as truths. The last thing I needed, the last thing my psyche could handle, was someone telling me I was a liar and blowing up my whole coping method.

I booted my computer and pulled up my email. I usually had it on my phone, but I'd deleted it once emails started to come in about Taye. After his arrest, the Upper Brass, rightly so, had to release memos and newsletters about the arrest and charges. They had to show their support for Taye, while also being sympathetic to the victims as well as Tristan and Detective West. It was a deadly tightrope that they were walking, because they couldn't outcast Taye without him being officially convicted of these crimes.

If he was found acquitted, never going to happen, but if it did, then technically, he could still come back to work. The Upper Brass couldn't show they were biased one way or the other. By showing support to every party, they were covering their asses while protecting them at the same time. It was a dance that the Upper Brass were very good at, and just another reason why I didn't want to be promoted again. Thankfully, with Taye's arrest there was a very good chance that I would never be looked at for a promotion ever again.

"Fuck off," I said, as I saw the email for a mandatory therapy session with Dr. Keaton Raitt.

I knew it was coming. My boss had told me I should speak with him to be cleared officially for duty. I was never taken off duty, but as ADA Barba pointed out, any defense attorney could call into question my judgment. If I saw the Shrink, then everyone's ass was covered that I was mentally cleared for work and mentally competent, therefore any case I signed off on couldn't be done with ill intentions.

I tried to tell my boss, to convince him that I didn't need to be cleared by a Shrink, that I was fine. My work hasn't diminished. I made sure I got everything done that needed to be done. I never handed anything in late and I had never been late for work or missed a shift. I was always here doing what needed to be done. I didn't need some Shrink poking around in my head, because he would.

It wouldn't be just about Taye being arrested, it was going to be about how I felt about my brother, about my father, about my job, my childhood. He was going to turn it into some bullshit session only to tell me I had deep-rooted childhood issues that needed to be worked on before I could be cleared for work.

Part of me couldn't help but wonder if my boss was trying to push me out. To force me to quit or give the Upper Brass a reason to let me go. That legacy that worked in my favor was now working against me, because now they needed to save face and the best way to do that would be to eliminate the name Amaro. With me being the last one, they didn't have much work ahead of them to get me out. The best way would be to have the Shrink come up with some psychological reason for me to not be fit for duty. From there it was just a short hop, skip, and a jump to my walking papers and the department could save face.

I wasn't going to go that easily, though. I wasn't about to let them push me out. I might not have chosen this career, nor wanted it, but it was mine now and I was not about to start all over again. I was living with this career and doing my best to make it work.

I was too old to start a brand new career and I was not old enough for some midlife crisis. I had no choice but to go. It was mandatory and it would look worse if I didn't show up for it. I was going to have to play this smart, give the Shrink enough insight, but not too much. I could also lie my ass off if he brought up my father or my childhood. Show the Shrink that I was competent and capable of still working. If I did that, then he wouldn't be able to tell my boss that I needed some time off or that I wasn't suitable to work anymore.

I knew the Upper Brass would be coming after me at some point. Taye was a huge black spot on the fire department's record. They needed to cover their asses and clean house. I expected it from them. I just never expected for my own boss to be coming for my job. I thought we were on good terms and that I had his loyalty, but apparently I was wrong. I wasn't about to make that mistake again. I was on my own in this and I wasn't going to forget it.

My phone rang and I looked over to see the name of Taye's lawyer flash across my screen. I hit ignore and sent the call to voicemail. I knew he would leave a message and he knew I wasn't listening to them or I would have called back. He wanted to talk to me, he needed to talk to me, but I wasn't about to do that. I wasn't going to be supporting Taye in court or through the trial. I wasn't even going to go. I wanted no part of that circus and I wasn't going to sit there and listen to Taye trying to reason and excuse his actions or for his defense lawyer to tear apart any of the witnesses.

Not my pig, not my farm, not my problem.

Barba could handle the trial and I would be spending the day getting as drunk as possible. My brother's lawyer would just have to give up and take the hint for the hundredth time. I didn't care what he wanted, but I suspected he was hoping I would testify on my brother's behalf.

But that was never happening.

Even if I believed he was innocent, which I didn't, I still wouldn't be getting up on that stand to testify for him. He was cruel to me growing up and I didn't doubt for a single second that my father had known what he was. He knew and he didn't care about what it could do to everyone else. All he cared about was making sure the family legacy continued. That the family name stayed in good standing.

And now here we were.

All of the good that my grandfather and father did was all in vain now. It was all for nothing because whenever someone Googled the name Amaro they were only going to find the news articles about Taye. All the future firefighters would know was Taye's crimes. They were both rolling in their graves and it served them right, especially my father. He thought his gay son would be the one to bring dishonor to the family, only for it to be the golden boy. It was almost laughable, really.

My grandfather and father were dead, and now Taye was going to prison for the rest of his life. I was finally free of all of them and I was not about to let my newfound freedom go to waste. I just had to get through the trial and the months afterward. Once things calmed back down, then I would be able to focus on myself and not some name on a plaque. Within a year it would all be a horrible nightmare. I just had to last that long.

Thank God for whiskey.

CHAPTER FOUR

Cyrus

TODAY HAD BEEN amazing. It was truly a surreal experience. I was tired, my body was tired, but my mind was wired. I didn't think I could sleep even if my life depended on it. My body was sore from running drills all day and then going on calls.

We didn't have a single fire, but we had a lot of rescues. The guys said that wasn't uncommon, that some days all they did was go from one fire to the next and some days it was accidents. It was common when it was bad weather for car accidents to pick up, too.

I wasn't upset that there wasn't a fire today. It was a good thing that no one was trapped and dying in our sector, but it would have been nice to get some real life experience using a fire hose. The guys all had a system in place and they were fluid. I knew it would take me some time to work my way into their system, but I couldn't get started if we didn't get to work beside each other in the field.

We did run drills, a lot of drills, but wasn't the same. There wasn't an urgency that was present during a real accident or fire. In a real emergency, everyone has their adrenaline pumping and lives are on the line, real lives and not just dummies. There was a difference and I wouldn't get used to it until I got to experience it enough times. I was hoping tomorrow that I could experience my first fire and get my cherry popped.

I headed into the bar with Newt, Zander, and Gage. They wanted to take me out to the Fire Bar, a bar for first responders. I had never been here before. I didn't even know there was a bar where first responders would all go to. I liked the idea, though. I liked knowing that I could go to a bar and have a drink with guys that I knew, with people who understood the life. I could go and not have to deal with being hit on just because I was a firefighter. It was a place where everyone could just be themselves and if you'd had a bad day, there were people around you who understood how you felt. It was a place where you could celebrate your accomplishments, but also a place where you could mourn the losses and hardships from the day. It was a safe zone and it was something we all needed.

The bar was pretty busy considering it was Monday night. At the same time, it also made sense. It wasn't like we were all working nine to five, Monday through Friday. To some of the guys, today *was* their Friday.

It was a decent size bar; one that could easily fit two hundred people in it. It wasn't fancy and I liked that. Patrons could get beer and shots here. It was a neighborhood friendly bar. It was comfortable, inviting, and it didn't make anyone feel like they couldn't afford to drink here. It was really nice.

I followed the guys over to the bar even as Newt moved off to speak with a group of guys perched around a high-top table. I figured he had worked with them in the past now that I knew that paramedics were floaters.

I still couldn't believe they had to float around and all because it was easier than having to make sure the guys that the female paramedics were around acted appropriately. That blew my mind. It seemed like the Upper Brass just wanted to do what was easier for them and screw everyone else.

I knew I really shouldn't have been too surprised. I had heard enough horror stories about the Upper Brass. Most weren't very open-minded about female firefighters and gay firefighters.

I had been very lucky to get into Captain Clarke's firehouse. I knew no one there would care that I was gay. I still wasn't screaming it from a rooftop, but it was nice to know that I could have a conversation about a guy I was seeing without it turning into a whole social debate.

"What do you think, Probee?" Zander asked.

"It's a nice place. I like it a lot. I can see why it would be your favorite watering hole. Are most people firefighters here?" I asked as I took in the crowd.

"Um..." Zander started as he looked around before he continued. "Mostly tonight, yeah."

His voice was a bit tight, but I didn't press. If there was a story there, it wasn't any of my business. I grabbed my beer and took a sip before I let my gaze wander around the crowd. I doubted I was going to see someone that I knew, but it was possible that I might see some of the guys from the fire academy. When my gaze landed someone that I did know, it was the last person I ever expected to see there.

The guy from the hotel last night was sitting at the other end of the bar. He was by himself and seemed to be drinking a good amount, if the empty glasses in front of him were any indication.

He looked just as sexy as he had last night and I couldn't help thinking about how amazing he had made me feel. The sex with Damon had been the best sex I had ever had, but it also made me feel like a cheap whore with the way he ended things. I knew that was what he wanted. He had told me as much, but it still stung with how I was dismissed.

Even though I was still hurt by it, I couldn't help but ignore the excitement that ran down my spine and ended right at my cock at the sight of him. My body didn't care that my mind and heart might still be hurt by our interaction; all it cared about was how he'd made me feel.

I had to give it to him, too. He could make a guy feel like he was on cloud nine. It was like his body knew mine, like we had done this dance before. He instinctively knew I got off on the praise of being called a *good boy*. I had no idea why I had always had a praise kink but nonetheless it was what floated my boat. I was sure there was some therapist out there who would love to dig into my childhood and obvious daddy issues.

Still, the way he made me feel, I hadn't felt like that with anyone. I wasn't some innocent flower, either. I may only be twenty-one, but I'd been having sex since I was fourteen. I'd always been attracted to older men, too. I don't know why, but I was always more interested in them than someone my own age. I think it was because they were usually more stable and they knew what they wanted in life. There were typically no games with older men.

When I was sixteen, I had tried to date guys my own age, but they were inexperienced and just looking to play head games. That wasn't what I wanted and I went back to dating older guys, guys in their thirties.

The first time I had sex, I was fourteen and it was with my Freshman Science teacher. It was my first year in high school and Science was nowhere near my best subject. It was just after midterms and I had barely passed with a fifty-five percent. I knew I wasn't going to pass the final exam. Mr. Deacon had offered me tutoring sessions after school and on weekends. I had been so happy to have the extra help that I had agreed right away. My parents were thrilled because they weren't any better at science.

We didn't think anything of it, why would we?

Teachers were supposed to help their students when they were struggling. That first tutoring session, he had placed his hand on my thigh and we ended up making out. Afterward, he had told me I was a *good boy* and I remember it made me feel proud and warm on the inside. I wanted to hear it again so during my next tutoring session when he kissed me and wanted to take it further, I didn't tell him no. Within a week we were having sex and a whole new world had opened up to me.

We lasted until the start of the new school year. During that summer though, he took me to all sorts of private parties where I met other older men. So when Mr. Deacon moved on, I just found one of those guys and began having fuck buddies. Sometimes, I would have threesomes with them all weekend long.

That was my life and it got worse after I was in foster care. I've always had a high sex drive. I've always loved the feeling of having a dick inside of me. I can't explain it, I wouldn't want to even if I could, because it was just a piece of who I was and I wasn't about to change it for anyone.

Damon though, he made me feel the way Mr. Deacon had and it'd been years since anyone had ever made me feel that good. It was only natural that my body was suddenly craving his touch.

"Who's that guy at the end of the bar sittin' all alone?" I asked, trying my best to not sound too interested. I didn't know if Damon was out or not and the last thing I wanted to do was out someone.

Zander looked over real quick before turning his attention back to me. "That's Captain Damon Amaro. He's the Captain for the Investigation Unit."

Captain?

Fuck.

How was this even possible?

The best sex I'd had since I was bloody fourteen and the man was a Captain within the Fire Department. It didn't matter that he ran the Investigation Unit, a Captain was a Captain, they all had the power to end your career and I had gone and slept with one.

The other oddity that hit me was that Captains worked Monday to Friday, so why the hell was he getting plastered on a Monday night?

He wasn't around anyone; he had purposely kept to himself in the corner at the bar. He didn't want company, clearly, but he didn't seem to want to sit at home and drink alone either. As if being at home drinking oneself into oblivion on a Monday night was somehow better than doing it at a bar.

"He doesn't seem like he is in a good mood," I commented, trying to calm my racing heart.

Damon had yet to look my way and I was hoping I might be able to avoid eye contact with him for the rest of the night. My dick didn't like that idea though, as it was already starting to swell behind my zipper. The monster was hungry, but that was too bad for it, because I was not about to go over to a Captain who had fucked my brains out and chat him up with the guys from the firehouse here. I had no idea if the Captain would even acknowledge my existence, but I wasn't about to find out.

"He's been going through some stuff. It's best to keep a wide berth from him. Cap is best friends with him so we see him at the firehouse at times, but not too often, especially recently. You ignore him, he'll pretty much ignore you as long as you don't give him a reason to look your way."

That did nothing to ease my concerns about the drinking. Not that I was anyone to be lecturing on drinking or reckless decisions. I was twenty-one and could finally legally drink, but I had started when I was young too, just like every other teenager.

Especially a teenager in foster care.

Just like drugs. Some of the parties I had gone to with whatever guy I was with at the time, it wasn't uncommon to see bowls of ecstasy and cocaine on different tables. I could understand better than anyone the desire to forget. I wasn't judging Damon and I wished I could say that it made him less attractive, but the exact opposite happened.

I had a thing for damaged men. Also closeted married men that were completely emotionally unavailable. I was a sucker for punishment and I never learned my lesson.

"Duly noted," I said with a nod.

Zander picked up his beer and gave a nod toward the opposite side of the room, even further away from Damon's eye line.

I was torn between hoping he wouldn't see me and hoping that he would. I knew the likelihood of him acknowledging me was slim to none. He was most likely going to dismiss me like some common street whore, but I wanted his eyes to catch mine. I wanted to see if he would recognize me or if he had already forgotten about our time together.

Just the thought of him not remembering me, it cut deep. It shouldn't bother me, I knew that. I was sure there were plenty of one-night stands that I'd had with guys who wouldn't remember me. There had been ample hook-up nights where me and whatever partner I'd picked up for the night had both been very drunk and I could barely remember anything the next day. It shouldn't bother me if Damon didn't remember me, but it did.

For the next couple of hours, my gaze kept trailing back over to Damon. He was still at the bar, still drinking. I thought at one point he had left, but he only went to the bathroom before returning to his stool and resuming his drinking, staring off into space.

It was just after midnight when Zander finally called it a night. I hadn't meant to stay that long. I'd only wanted to come out for a couple of beers before heading home. The guys wanted to show me the bar and it was vital for me to get to know them outside of work. Still, I should've already been home and in my bed. I had just worked a twelve-hour shift and I had another one in the morning.

With Zander gone and Damon still here, I decided to stop being a chicken and mentally torturing myself. He was either going to remember me or not. He was either going to be pleased to see me or not. Either way, I wasn't going to get an answer until I manned up and went over to see him.

Letting out a deep breath, I made my way across the bar, which was drastically less crowded now, and over to Damon. Once I was there, I leaned my back against the bar and kept my eyes on the wall across from me. I was too afraid to look him in the eye right now, not until I knew what he was feeling.

"Of all the bars, in all of the towns," I started.

"I was wondering if you would get the balls to come over and say hello. You've been looking my way since you walked in," he said in a slightly harsh tone, but I didn't take it personally. He did have a lot to drink so far.

"I wasn't certain you would want me to come say hello."

"What house?" he asked.

"Twenty-One with Captain Clarke, but I guess you already know that part. Zander, one of the guys, told me who you were. I swear, I didn't know before last night." The last thing I wanted was for him to think I had targeted him in some way.

"You're the new Probee. No one can know."

Not surprising.

"I would never tell anyone. What happens in my personal life is no one's business. I'm not in the closet, but I don't scream it from every rooftop either. I don't think it's anyone's business if I'm gay. No one straight has to tell people they are straight, why should I?"

He took a drink from his whiskey before he spoke. "You're gonna walk out the front door, turn right, walk three blocks, take another right, and go into the abandoned factory. I'll be there in five minutes," he said with a slight demand to his voice.

"Is that an order, Captain?" I asked, as a tingle ran down my spine.

"Not professionally. If you decide not to, no hard feelings. Choice is yours."

His husky, whiskey-soaked voice did things to my insides that I couldn't even describe. It might have technically been my choice, but there really was no choice to make. My body was already screaming yes.

I made my way out of the bar, the heavy wooden door closing behind me and cutting off the sound of the music and laughter. I paused for a moment in the sudden quiet and then turned right. I knew it was crazy, going to meet up with a Captain in an abandoned factory to have sex, but it honestly wasn't the craziest thing I'd done. I knew it could be dangerous and come back to bite me in the ass, but I was also a strong believer that the best fun in life tended to be the riskiest.

A part of me also knew how stupid the idea was going to be on a mental level. I doubted Damon was going to get all warm and fuzzy on me, which meant I would be feeling like a cheap whore again. A very satisfied whore, but a whore nonetheless. I should care, but all I could think about was the pleasure that Damon was going to be giving me.

When I arrived at the abandoned factory, I didn't have to wait long before Damon arrived. He was clearly drunk, but he was still able to function. The man could certainly hold his liquor and I couldn't help but wonder if he had some Scottish in him.

"Strip," he ordered.

I kicked my boots off and started to remove my clothes, but he didn't strip. Apparently, I was going to be fully naked for this. I was hoping he would get naked as well, but I couldn't be certain that he would. He stood there and watched as I stripped, never taking his eyes off of me, and I suddenly felt like I was his prey. It should have bothered me, but it only made my dick pulse with need.

"On your knees," he ordered in that husky, spine-tingling voice once I was naked.

I got down on my knees as he pulled his shirt off. Leaning against a post roughly twenty feet from me, he unzipped the front of his jeans and pulled out his hard dick. His oh-so-glorious dick. He was the biggest man I had ever been with before and I instantly recalled how he felt wonderful inside of me.

My mouth watered at the thought of getting to feel that huge cock sliding along my tongue, pushing against the back of my throat. That was something I missed out on last time and I was really hoping I would get to this time around.

"Crawl over here and suck my dick,

whore," he ordered in a dark tone.

He seemed to really like that word, *whore*. It should have pissed me off. Hell, I'd punched guys in the mouth for calling me a whore or a slut before. Yet, when he said it electricity overtook my body and all I wanted to do was please him.

Without allowing myself to think too deeply on it, I let a groan slip from my lips as I started to crawl toward him. I could see the arousal heating up in his gaze as I got closer.

He loved this part.

He loved the control and dominance.

It made sense with him being a Captain. He would be telling people all day long what to do.

The second I was close enough to him, I took his cock in my grip and brought his tip to my mouth, moaning as the sweet taste of him hit my tongue. He threaded his fingers through my hair, grabbing a fistful in a tight grip. He started to push my head down his shaft as he spoke.

"You're gonna be my good whore and take it all."

I couldn't help but moan, a shiver running though me and straight to my balls at his words. It should terrify me that he wanted me to take him down to his base. This man was not small and I had never deep throated before, which I would essentially have to do in order to get his size in my mouth.

He pushed my head down inch by inch and didn't allow me to pull back to try and catch my breath. I should have been scared, but I wasn't. My dick kept pulsing knowing that this man had complete control over me. He was giving my body everything it had been craving.

"Good boy. Relax your throat. That's it, you can take all of Daddy's dick. It's going to slide right down that pretty, tight throat of yours."

The moan that escaped me was not human. Never, not once, had anyone ever referred to themselves as Daddy with me before. It shouldn't have elicited that much of a reaction out of me, but it did. Fuck, I'm sure a Shrink would love to dissect that one. Just chalk it up to more unresolved daddy issues.

Fuck it; those issues would still be there tomorrow.

I did as I was told and relaxed my throat and if I didn't think about it, it was easier to take him deeper. The second he bottomed out, he let out a deep moan and I could tell he was very pleased with me.

"Such a good whore you are. You have no idea how beautiful you look with my dick down your throat," he growled, fisting my hair even tighter.

He started to lightly thrust his hips and I knew he was going to fuck my throat. I couldn't stop moaning at the sensation of his dick sliding up and down my throat. It shouldn't have felt this good, but the faster his hips went, the more I was moaning and silently begging for more.

I gave a start, whining as I felt myself come in my pants. He had made me come without even touching me. I had never come like that before. I didn't even think it was possible to come from a blowjob and yet this man had done the impossible.

"Naughty whore, Daddy didn't give you permission to come. Now I have to punish you," he said with a slight edge to his voice and it only caused me to whimper again as need rushed through me.

Fuck, this man should not be this sexy. The control he had over me should not be this strong. It was like he knew exactly what my body needed, what it craved, even though I didn't even know it.

"You want Daddy to punish you. All dirty whores do. Don't worry, I'm going to punish you just as soon as I come down your throat."

His thrusts started to become faster, harder. I could tell he was close, that his body was on edge just as much as mine was. Even though I had just come, I was already rock hard again and in desperate need for more.

After a few more thrusts, Damon snapped his hips forward and buried his dick fully down my throat. I had felt a guy come before plenty of times in my mouth, but I had never felt a guy's dick pulsing in my throat. The sensation should have been weird, but it only made me moan and writhe even more.

I already knew I was addicted to this, addicted to this man. It was like he was made for me or I was made for him. God, this couldn't be the last time we did this. I needed more from him and I seriously doubted I would ever get tired of this man.

I greedily swallowed every single drop he had for me before he was pulling out. I whimpered at the loss, but he didn't care. His hand left my hair and wrapped around my throat and he pulled me up and in for a rough kiss.

I easily gave up control to him and melted against his tongue. I was vaguely aware that he was moving backward toward some large wooden crates that had been left in the factory. When my back hit the rough wood, he pulled back from the kiss and roughly turned me around.

He used one end of his belt and cinched it around my neck before he pulled my arms back behind me and wrapped the rest of the thick leather around both of my wrists, making it impossible for me to move my hands. He then roughly pushed me down, bending me over the crates and kicking my legs out, spreading them as far apart as possible before he spoke.

"Naughty whores get punished. You're not allowed to come, do I make myself clear, whore?" he growled in my ear.

"Aye."

The sharp slap to my ass was unexpected and I couldn't help the small scream of surprise. "It's yes, *Daddy*."

"I'm sorry. Aye, Daddy," I moaned, my accent more pronounced now that I wasn't as focused on keeping the lilt from my voice.

Fuck, this shouldn't be this hot, what the hell was wrong with me?

I heard the foil of a condom being torn open and I felt my excitement and arousal increase. I needed him badly and I was desperate to feel him inside of me again. I expected to feel his finger against my hole, but to my surprise and pleasure, it was his tip. Apparently stretching was overrated tonight. That was fine with me, I liked the slight burn and I had slept all night with a plug in, so it wasn't like I hadn't had sex in a few months.

He was slow at first as he entered me and I couldn't help the needy moans that poured out of my mouth as I felt his girth stretch the tight ring of muscle. He pushed in until I felt his balls against my ass, seating himself inside me fully. I was breathing heavily as my body adjusted to his size.

He placed his left hand on my hip and then wrapped his right hand around the middle part of the belt that was slung along my back before it reached my wrists. I didn't even have a chance to adjust to his size before he was pulling back on the belt, forcing my throat to constrict, cutting off the air. I arched my back quickly as he pulled almost all the way out and slammed right back in.

His pace was hard, deep, and fast. He wasn't holding back at all as he chased his pleasure, his cock just skimming past my sweet spot each time. Enough to make me hard and throbbing, but not enough to get me off. He was doing it on purpose, he knew exactly where my sweet spot was and he was avoiding it to punish me for coming without his permission. That should infuriate me, but instead it had me in even more of a desperate state.

"Fuck, Daddy," I moaned as I neared yet another climax.

As if he sensed my approaching release, the hand that was on my hip slid around and suddenly squeezed the base of my dick as hard as he could, effectively killing the orgasm that had been building.

"Naughty whores who don't listen to their Daddy don't get to come."

"I'm sorry, Daddy," I whined, feeling the loss intensely for only a moment before the feeling again began to build in my balls.

He moved his hand back to my hip and continued his brutal pace, grasping my hips tightly and pulling me roughly backward toward him with each thrust. I knew I would likely have bruises there tomorrow but I didn't care.

My legs were trembling from the need coursing through me and I was desperate to come. Every time I got close, and my balls pulled up tight against my body, that special tingle beginning to rush through my spine, he would wrap his hand around my dick and squeeze like his life depended on it.

I was going insane with need, almost delirious now as the intensity of the edging and orgasm denial rushed through me continuously. My moans and whines were echoing off the factory walls and I was certain someone three blocks away could hear me.

"Please, Daddy, I need to come, please let me come," I begged when he stopped me for the fourth time.

"Shut up and take your punishment like a good boy," he growled and I knew I wasn't going to get to come until he was ready to come as well. Hell, maybe even after.

His thrusts started to become more erratic and frantic. I knew he was getting close and I foolishly hoped that meant I would get to as well. With a loud groan, he snapped his hips forward and I could feel his dick pulsing inside of me, the heat from inside the condom filling me and sending chills rushing through me.

I suddenly had this uncontrollable urge to feel him coming without the condom. It was surprising, because I'd never had sex without one. I was always careful about that. And yet, there was this urge to be owned by him. As if him coming inside of me would somehow make me belong to him. It was ridiculous and yet that need only grew with each pulse I felt.

When he finished, he pulled out and I thought for sure that it would be my turn. I heard him pulling his pants back up and then he was removing his belt from me. I was hoping that I wouldn't have any bruises around my neck and wrists tomorrow. That wasn't something I would be able to explain away very easily. With myself free, I stood up and turned to face him. He had walked away and was putting his shirt back on.

"Get dressed," he ordered.

"What?" Surely he was joking. I was standing here rock hard, dripping with need. There was no way I was getting dressed without coming first.

Damon walked back over to me and placed his hand around my throat. The grip wasn't tight, but it was possessive.

"Did you think me fucking you was your punishment? You came without my permission and now you will get dressed and you will go home. What you won't do is touch yourself. You don't get to come again, not until I allow it. Either you play by my rules or we don't play, *whore.*"

A shiver ran right down my spine and I knew I had never wanted someone so badly before in my life. This man should be all wrong for me. I should be telling him off like a good Scot does, but instead, I wanted to drop to my knees and await my next order.

Fuck, how could one man have such a strong influence on me?

How could he have this type of power over me and all we'd done was have sex twice?

I'd been with guys for a year or more and if they ordered me to do something I would laugh at them.

What made Damon so different?

"Aye, Daddy," I said in a whisper of a voice.

He pulled back and pulled out his cell phone and spoke before handing it to me. "Put your number in."

I easily took the phone and entered my number in the contact screen that he pulled up. Normally, I would call or text myself, but apparently he didn't want me to have his number. It was another way he could control the situation. Control was obviously very important to Damon and I couldn't help but wonder if he was always like this or if something had made him change.

After I entered my number, I handed the phone back to him. He ran his index finger along my hard shaft and I hissed at the pleasure.

"You're going to get dressed and go home. And if you want to be Daddy's good whore, you won't touch yourself, you won't come. And maybe next time, if you are my good boy, I'll reward you by sucking your dick and swallowing every last drop that you have for me."

I let out a deep moan as his finger ran over my tip, gathering the pearl of wetness there, and he brought his digit up to suck on for a moment to get the precum off of it. Before I could even form words, he was leaving.

I stood there watching as he walked out of the factory, unable to move to even get dressed. This night had been very intense and I didn't want for it to end. I wanted to come, but I knew I wasn't supposed to. I also couldn't stand here all night long. With no other choice, I got dressed and strolled out. Tonight was one for the record books and I was truly hoping there would be another round.

CHAPTER FIVE

Damon

THIS WAS BULLSHIT. I shouldn't be sitting here. I shouldn't have to go through this. It wasn't me who started the fires, that was Taye. I shouldn't have to be forced to see a Shrink. I didn't need it. I didn't need to talk about what Taye had done. I didn't need to talk about my father or the legacy that was associated with my name. And I sure as shit didn't need to talk about the drinking or recreational drug use. More than anything, I didn't need to talk about the astonishing sex that I had last night with Cy.

I still can't believe he's a firefighter, a rookie firefighter. He is twenty-one, which I suspected, but I didn't expect for his Captain to be my best friend. The only true friend that I had within the department. Multiple red flags had been raised and I knew I had to walk it back.

We could never hook up again. Not that I had been planning on it and yet, by the end of the night my dick was down his throat and buried in his ass. I knew I was pushing his limits. I had always enjoyed taking control in the bedroom. I had always enjoyed being the boss and I had always found guys who were good with it.

The way Cy responded to my touch and demands though, thrilled me to no end. He was begging for it and more. He loved being dominated and submissive. He loved having a dick in him, whether that was his mouth or his ass. The man was the perfect sex partner and my body was already craving him. I could go for days straight and never get bored of being inside of him.

Addiction much?

I had no idea if he had listened to my order. He could have easily gone home and jerked off. It wasn't like I would know if he did. I was hoping he didn't, though. I was hoping that he had spent the night laying there with a raging hard on for hours until he fell into a restless sleep. I wanted him to be going crazy for my touch. To be in so much need that if I decided to text him for another round, he would drop everything and come over.

I hadn't thought I would want to have an ongoing relationship with anyone, but with Cy it was certainly appealing to me. I just knew we were only scraping the surface of what we could be like with each other. The lengths we could go, the lengths that *I* could go. He was a wet dream and I wanted to explore more with him.

I didn't tend to use Daddy in the bedroom, at least not as a rule. I had in the past, but usually it was Captain, Sir, or Master on the rare occasion. For some reason though, Daddy just flowed right off my lips with Cy and I could tell he didn't have a problem with it. The way he moaned *Daddy* every time he said it, I could tell he loved it and I somehow knew I wasn't the first older man he had been with.

Some guys preferred older men because they were more experienced in the bedroom. I was going to assume Cy did as well. But I could definitely tell he had a daddy kink, along with his praise kink. They did go hand in hand in most instances, and I was sure a Shrink would tell me it was because the guy had some daddy issues to work through.

I didn't care what his issues were as

long as he wanted to play by my rules, and Cy seemed very open to my rules.

I had done some pretty reckless things in my lifetime, but sleeping with Cy again might actually top the list. I was not out of the closet and I had no interest in coming out of it. Not even Will knew I was gay. I was putting myself in the position to not only be outed, but to potentially lose my job.

We weren't in the same department, so it wouldn't be wrong for us to date, wouldn't be a direct conflict that way, but the age difference was an issue, not to mention the ranking. I was a Captain and he was a Probee, it would be like an attending doctor sleeping with an intern. It was unethical and career suicide.

Even though I knew all of that, my body was still craving him. I had to jerk off this morning just to be able to get my pants done up. My sex drive felt like it was in overdrive and all I wanted to do was be buried inside of him. I had told myself it wouldn't happen again, but I knew that was a lie. I was going to be having sex with Cy again, many times. I just had to make him wait a bit longer. I wanted his need, his desire for me to explode out of him when I finally did touch him.

I took a drink from my coffee. I was feeling the hangover this morning and I was really hoping that Dr. Raitt wouldn't notice, or he'd at least have the common courtesy to not call me out on it. I doubted he would offer me that courtesy, but I could hope.

There was nothing worse than a psychiatrist appointment first thing in the morning. It was a great way to ruin your entire day. I'd never actually had to speak with Dr. Raitt in a professional capacity before. I'd had to refer to officers under my command to him many times, though.

I almost sent Tristan his way before he solved the arson cases that implemented Taye. I did send him to Dr. Raitt after he had almost died and before he could be cleared for active duty again.

Dr. Raitt had cleared Tristan and he was going to be back to work within the next week or so. He was cleared medically and I was relieved to hear that his lungs were back to one hundred percent. I was thankful that Tristan was going to be okay.

I had never been in a fire myself, but I did know that smoke inhalation was extremely dangerous, especially if you have a history of being in a fire unprotected like Tristan had been. It was going to be good to have Tristan back. He really was my best investigator and I needed him back to work.

The door opened to Dr. Raitt's private office and he stood there in the doorway with a warm and friendly smile plastered on his face. I had a strong urge to punch him right across his stupid face. I couldn't help but wonder how many times he'd actually been hit.

Dr. Raitt wasn't a very large man. He was around five foot eight, but only a hundred and forty pounds, at most. I knew that he was a runner, so that accounted for his lithe, compact form. He was active, but he didn't have any bulk to him. He often volunteered to do the charity runs and marathons for the department fundraising, which was admirable. He was always clean-shaven and kept his hair mostly short, but it had a bit of length to it. Enough that you could run your fingers through his hair and mess it up. He was attractive and I knew he was gay. I'd seen him with his fiancé out at the bars or charity events. From what I'd heard, he was an all around decent guy and most people weren't bothered by his position as the firehouse therapist. Apparently he was super easy to talk to.

Under normal circumstances, I would be happy to have a chat with him, just not about my issues or myself. I was a firm believer that therapy was good for some people, but I didn't believe I was one of those people. I didn't need to talk something to death. I didn't need old issues brought up and examined, dissected. What I needed was a stiff drink and to push through. Erase and override. It worked for me and I was not about to let a pretty face change that.

"Captain Amaro, please come in."

I pushed up out of my seat and made my way over to him. He closed the door behind me and spoke as he made his way over to one of the chairs that were set up in the room.

"Late night?" he asked, with a nod to my to-go cup.

"You don't drink coffee in the morning, Doc?" I countered, not even bothering with sitting down.

"I do. But when you have that large of a to-go cup and you look like you've barely slept three hours, that tends to make me think it was a late night. Do you often drink on a Monday night?"

Fuck this.

I was not going to be doing this dance with him. I knew why I was here. The

Upper Brass wanted a reason to push me out. To force me to leave so they could pretend like the Amaro name didn't exist. I was not going to play this game with any of them. If they wanted me out, they could grow some balls and come say it to my face. I didn't have the time or patience for this shit.

"I'm not doing this with you," I said with an icy edge to my voice.

"Doing what, Captain?" he asked patiently, his voice completely calm and controlled, and that only pissed me off more.

"You think I don't know what this is really about? I know the Upper Brass wants me out and they are doing it through you. This is all just a show, a formality so they can fire me with an iron clad defense. Once the Shrink says you are unstable, out the door you go. If they want to take my shield, then they can come down to my office and do it themselves instead of sending a puppet to do it."

Dr. Raitt held his hands up in a mock surrender before he spoke. "Okay, I have no idea what is going on right now. I don't know what the Upper Brass wants or about anyone coming after your shield. What I do know, is that I was asked to speak to you to make sure you were doing okay with the bombshell that was dropped on you. I'm not reporting back to anyone if I think you are suitable to continue working. We're just here to talk. I hear your worry and concern though, and if it eases those worries then I will let you know that with you being a desk jockey, it is extremely difficult for the Upper Brass to push you out. Any psychological issues that you have or are trying to work through, as long as I don't believe you are a harm to yourself or others, there is no reason why you can't keep working."

It sounded good and I wanted to believe him, but it wasn't that simple. I didn't know him well enough to trust him. I didn't know him well enough to know where his loyalties lay. I had looked through the department's policies and bi-laws and I wasn't able to find anything that would give the Upper Brass grounds for terminating my employment with the fire department. However, I also knew that loopholes could be found and political connections could be used. He was saying all of the right words, but that didn't mean I could believe them. I knew that made me sound paranoid and it wasn't a good look to have when you were trying to convince a Shrink that you didn't need therapy.

"You really expect for me to believe we're on the same side?"

"We don't know each other on a personal level, Captain, but you have worked with me before with your other investigators. When was the last time you received a recommendation from me that dictated you remove one of your investigators from the field or their position? I don't believe in taking someone's career and purpose away. I believe in helping my patients to heal and become stronger. To not allow their trauma to have full control over them. I'm not your enemy. I'm here to make sure you can keep doing your job without being destroyed by it. Please, Captain, will you just sit down and we can talk about anything."

Every fiber in my being was telling me this was a trap. That he was trying to get me into a false sense of safety before he would pounce. Like a lioness that leaves one gazelle alone only to come up behind it and rip its throat out. Standing there, refusing to sit and listen, it wasn't helping my case. I had to keep my composure. I had to keep myself in control and calm, otherwise he would think I was too unstable to work.

Resigned to at least try it his way, I sighed and strode over to sit on the couch, keeping my eyes on him. I did my best to school my features so he couldn't read into my emotions.

"What do you want to talk about?" I asked, trying to keep my voice even.

"It's not about what I want to talk about, Captain, it's about what you want to talk about. We can talk about your family, any cases that you are having problems solving with your guys. We can talk about the weather, your favorite coffee or drink. I don't care what we talk about, as long as we talk."

He was trying to build trust, to build a rapport. He wanted me to let my guard down and that was when he would strike, but I wasn't going to let it happen. I would placate him, but I wasn't going to fall for his tricks.

Once again, I knew that line of thinking made me sound crazy, but I knew people were gunning to have me removed from my job. I had made enemies before this. Having the title of a legacy worked in my favor but it also worked against me. There were people who resented my grandfather and father and would have loved nothing more than to destroy the reputation they had built. Myself and Taye had always been told by our father to not trust anyone and to always watch our backs. It had been drilled into us that you never knew when the knife was coming for you, so stay aware. I couldn't exactly be blamed for waiting for that knife to finally come my way.

"My coffee order is pretty boring," I said, lifting my shoulder in a small shrug.

"Mine as well. My favorite drink though, is scotch. A nice glass of scotch at night after a long hard day at work can always help me relax. What about you? I bet you are a whiskey man."

I used to be just a whiskey man, but now I was more of a liquor man. If it had alcohol in it, I was drinking it. It didn't matter if it was vodka, whiskey, gin, tequila, or even that flavored shit that most women drink. If it had the power to get me drunk, I was all for it.

"I like whiskey," I simply said.

"How often do you drink?" he asked gently, as if it was some horrible thing to do.

"Never on shift, so why does it matter?" I countered.

"I'm not saying it does matter. I was just asking. You look a bit hungover today. I was just curious how often you drink during the week. Look, I'm not asking for you to reveal your deep dark secrets to me here. I just want to talk so I know how you are handling the bombshell that got dropped in your lap. This is our first session and realistically, we are going to be seeing each other two times a week for the next couple of months."

"Hold up, what?" I snapped.

Months?

Like fuck.

I wasn't going to be doing this for months. I thought I would just have to come here once and then I'd be done. I wasn't going to be talking to a Shrink for months. I wasn't unstable. I didn't need therapy. It wasn't me who set fire to those houses. It wasn't me who killed all of those people. I didn't deserve to be punished like this.

This was so much bullshit.

"Whether you wish to admit it or not, either out loud or to yourself, you have experienced a trauma. The arrest of your brother, what he was arrested for, that is a trauma and you need to work through it. I can tell you haven't been sleeping properly. I can tell that you have been drinking more often. We might not have known each other very well before all of this, Damon, but I do know you were not a man who drank during the week. You've always had control over yourself and how you presented yourself. You have been hiding it well, but I'm trained to see when someone is struggling. It's okay for you to not be okay right now. That doesn't mean you can't still work. I'm not recommending that you take a leave of absence. All I'm asking is that you are open and honest with me so we can work through the trauma and get you back to being fully healthy. As long as you can do that, I will go to the mat for you should the Upper Brass ever try and take your shield."

Slowly, I let out a deep breath. I had to try and think about this rationally, even though everything inside of me was screaming to run out of here and give Dr. Raitt the middle finger. I knew I couldn't do that, though.

Currently, he was looking to do these sessions while allowing me to work. If I fought him on it, that was likely to change and I would be trapped in my condo staring at the walls. That was the last thing I wanted. The last thing I could handle right now. I had no choice but to play ball right now. To bide my time and do the minimum needed so I could keep working.

"I don't drink every night. It doesn't affect my work, so what does it matter if I drink at night?" I challenged.

"I'm not saying it does matter. I think after what you have been through it's only natural that you are struggling. It's natural that you would be drinking more frequently right now while your mind tries to process the trauma you are going through."

"You keep saying that, *trauma*. I'm not going through trauma. The people my brother burned alive, they have trauma. Their loved ones have trauma. Nothing bad happened to me."

I wasn't a victim in this and I was not about to let anyone call me a victim. I wasn't hurt by Taye's actions. I got caught in the crosshairs, but I didn't experience any trauma.

"People don't like that word, especially men. It's even worse when you add in an alpha male in a male dominated career, such as a Captain in the Fire Department. The truth is though, Captain, you did experience a trauma by what your brother has done. You weren't in the fires. You weren't hurt physically, but you were still hurt emotionally and most definitely mentally. Just because Taye is your brother, doesn't change that it has affected you negatively and that is called trauma. If it didn't affect you, if it hadn't traumatized you, then you wouldn't be spending your nights getting drunk. And I think it's safe to assume that you are also participating in other risky behavior and being promiscuous. There's nothing wrong with that. It's perfectly natural for you to be acting out. For you to be letting off some steam and taking a break from being yourself. I want you to know though, eventually, you will have to find your way back to your true self, and I'll be here to help you," he said, flashing me a small warm smile.

There was no judgment in his voice. He didn't look disappointed or disgusted with me. I didn't tell him anything and yet he was able to figure out that I was different. That I had been acting differently and feeling lost. I wasn't certain how I felt about him knowing me so well after only spending ten minutes with me. We had never spoken like this before. Nothing more than just a polite hello in the hallway as we passed each other. I couldn't help but wonder if he had been watching me these past three months.

If he had, then were others watching

me?

Could other people tell that I wasn't fully myself?

That thought was unnerving, because I was supposed to be stable, strong. The people who worked underneath me needed to be able to trust me and rely on me. They couldn't rely on someone if they thought they were unstable.

I had to always be the strong one. I needed to pay more attention to my appearance. I needed to pay more attention to how I was presenting myself and interacting with others. I couldn't let people think I was going weak, that wouldn't be good for anyone's cases.

"I'm fine," I instantly denied.

He gave me that warm smile once again before he spoke, "No, you're not. But you will be."

He sounded so confident that I would be able to be fine one day. That I would be able to stuff myself back into that box that I had broken out of three months ago. It seemed impossible, and truth be told, I still didn't know if I wanted to be in that box ever again. For now though, I would let him think that was my goal. For now, I would let him think that he was helping and I was doing what I was supposed to be doing. What he didn't know, it wouldn't hurt him.

And if it hurt me, well, that was my business, too.

CHAPTER SIX

Cyrus

"YOU LOOK GOOD," Zander said, flashing me a smirk as he walked into the main area of the firehouse.

I was currently trying to stay awake while sitting on the couch. I shouldn't have stayed out that late, but it was well worth it. I had spent the rest of the night trying to get some sleep. My dick had stayed hard even after I got home and what little sleep I did get was filled with naughty, delicious dreams of Damon.

I didn't jerk off. I could have and I knew I could have. There was no way for Damon to know if I had jerked off or not. As long as I didn't tell him, then he wouldn't have known. Not to mention I didn't know if we would ever get to hook up again. The ball was in his court and that was exactly what he wanted. I was fine with it, though. There was a serious excitement within me at the prospect of getting a text from him to go and meet him.

I wanted to meet him again. I wanted to have sex with him again. More than anything, I wanted for him to tell me I could come. My balls were heavy and swollen from the serious case of blue balls I had. I had no idea if Damon and I were now fuck buddies or if it was just a two-night stand, but I was really hoping we would get to hook up again. The man might not be all warm and fuzzy, but he sure knew how to make a man purr.

It also helped that I could tell he was going through something. Everyone at the bar seemed to avoid him and it wasn't because he was a Captain. Something else was going on that everyone seemed to know about, everyone *but* me. I knew I shouldn't be asking, that it was none of my business and I had no place in asking, but at the same time, I needed to know. If I was going to be having sex with Damon again, I had to know exactly what I was getting into. It would no longer be a one-night or two-night stand. We would be fuck buddies or even friends with benefits. I had to have a rough idea of what I was stepping into.

"Can I ask ye a question?"

"Generally," Zander said as he flopped down on the other end of the couch.

"When you spoke about Captain Amaro, you seemed to be holdin' back. There seems to be a story there and I was just curious as to what it was."

"It's not really my story to tell," he started, looking down at his lap, and I could tell he was hesitant to let me in. I was getting the feeling though, that it was more public knowledge than something he was trying to keep secret.

"I know and I wouldn't be askin' if I didn't think I needed to know. At the bar, folks seemed to be more interested in keepin' away from him. I'm not lookin' to step on any toes, lad, but I'm also not lookin' to shoot myself in the foot either."

I was really hoping he would tell me. I didn't want to have to go and ask someone else. I didn't want it getting back to Damon that I was asking around about him. I usually wouldn't care, but I couldn't get over this nagging feeling in the pit of my stomach that I needed to know this piece of information. I just needed someone to tell me.

I knew I could have just asked Damon directly, but I seriously doubted he would tell me. He wasn't into sharing, and he had no reason to share with me. I was a twenty-one year old Probee and he was in his late thirties and a Captain. There clearly was a chain of command and my ass was all the way down on the bottom. Professionally and personally, he had no reason to tell me.

Zander let out a soft sigh before he looked around to make sure we were still alone before he spoke. "Captain Amaro has an older brother. Taye. He was a lieutenant with the Fire Department. I didn't know him personally, but Cap had worked with him before he was promoted and transferred here. From what I've heard from different guys, Taye was always weird. There was just something about him that made a lot of people not like him and prefer to avoid him whenever possible. They respected him though, because they are legacies. Their father and grandfather were firefighters and had impressive, records and saves, to say the least. They were legends, so when Taye and Captain Amaro were eighteen, it was assumed they too, would be enrolled in the Fire Academy. Captain Amaro went into investigations straight from the academy and Taye became a Probee."

I didn't know that Damon was a

legacy.

I should have heard about that in the fire academy, so why didn't I?

I had heard the story of other legacies and legendary firefighters; there was a whole class on it, on the history of firefighters. Damon should have been mentioned, or at least his family name. He also should have had his name on the plaques that were at the main entrance to the academy. And I knew it wasn't. I had read every name on those plaques every single morning as I walked through those doors. It was my way of staying motivated and to remind myself what I was fighting for. I wanted to be on one of those plaques one day. The name Amaro never appeared.

"Three months ago, there was an investigation into a series of arsons. They went back twenty-five years and Investigator Tristan Cole, he's the guy that Hawke is dating, discovered that it was the work of two arsonists, a mentor and an apprentice. The mentor found his apprentice ten years ago, roughly, and started to teach him his best practices. Once the apprentice was ready, the mentor stood back and watched the apprentice start the fires. They used cameras to record the whole thing and they would watch them, it's how the mentor was able to get his rocks off still. The investigation revealed that the mentor was an old firefighter who was injured on duty and given a disability pension. Wilson Stan. The apprentice though, was Taye. When Tristan and Detective West went to speak with him, Wilson was there and knocked Detective West out. Taye then tied Tristan to a chair, killed Wilson, and started a fire. We were able to get there in time to save Taye, Tristan, and Detective West. Taye was fine and Detective West and Tristan had some recovering to do, but they are fine now. Now, Taye's kill count is up to forty-eight and he's been connected to twenty-seven fires and that's just so far."

Holy shit.

I was expecting something bad, but I wasn't expecting anything like that. I thought maybe he had done something questionable to someone in the Upper Brass, had a disagreement about something. I wasn't expecting for his older brother to be an arsonist.

A rather brutal one at that, based on the kill count.

Plus he tried to kill someone who worked underneath Damon.

Shit.

No wonder his family's name wasn't on the plaques, they must have removed them. The Upper Brass would have had to do damage control and the best way to do that would be to erase any traces of the Amaro name. I couldn't help but wonder if they were gunning for Damon next. If he was the last Amaro in the department, they get him out and then they could pretend that the name Amaro never existed.

They had already removed his name from the curriculum at the academy, obviously. They were teaching the next generation nothing about them and eventually, once the old timers were gone, all that would be left were the young guys who had never heard of the name Amaro. It wasn't fair, but the Upper Brass rarely was.

"I don't even know what to say to that. Do people blame him?" I really hoped not, it wasn't his fault. He shouldn't be held accountable for the actions of his brother.

"Naw. Things are a bit tense between the fire department and the police. Detective West did the right thing by arresting Taye, but that doesn't change that he was a brother and the firefighter brotherhood is pretty strong. Things have also been tense for Tristan. He was investigating not one, but two firefighters and now one has been arrested and the other killed. It's a mess on all fronts. The trial will be starting soon and hopefully, once all of the evidence comes out, people will see that Tristan and Detective West did the right thing. With any luck, they will give Captain Amaro a break. We all know that he didn't have anything to do with it. He had no idea that Taye was even an arsonist. They hadn't spoken in almost a decade. Still, people are doubting it and I'm sure he's getting shit from the Upper Brass about it."

"That explains why everyone was avoidin' him. Still, it's not his fault his own brother did those things. It's not fair to punish a whole family for the actions of one."

The information I'd just learned, and the fact Damon was pretty much being punished for guilt by association to his brother, was making me even more worried about my own family heritage getting out.

Would they want to kick me out if they discovered my father was one of the most prolific arsonists in Louisiana?

How would they treat me when they discovered that my father was responsible for the death of thirteen firefighters who were killed trying to put out the fires he started?

The information had only solidified what I suspected all along, no one could know my heritage or anything about my past or everything I had worked for would be ruined.

Our conversation was interrupted by the alarm going off. A house fire roughly ten blocks away, according to the dispatch announcement. We both climbed to our feet and trotted off to grab our gear and suit up.

It was going to be my first official fire and I was bouncing with excitement. At least internally. It was wrong to be excited about a house fire, I knew that. There could be people trapped in the house and in danger. I had no business being excited. However, I was only keyed up about getting to help put out a real fire. It was different when it was happening for real and it wasn't just a drill in a burn house.

It didn't take long before we arrived at the scene of the call. I could just make out the house from the window and it didn't look too bad. There weren't any flames coming from the windows and the roof was still intact. It looked like we might have arrived in time to save the house. We climbed out of the truck and Cap instantly started to call out orders.

"Sinclair, take a hose with the rookie and do the primary line inside."

"Sure thing, Cap. Let's go Probee!" Sinclair called out to me.

I was actually getting to be on the primary line, this was awesome! Based on how I was kept off to the side as an observer for the accidents, I'd had a feeling I would be on the fire hydrant or something. I didn't think I would actually get to be in the house and working the hose.

I ran over to help Sinclair with pulling the hose out and we made out way into the house while Gage hooked it up to the hydrant. The second we walked in, I could see where the fire was coming from. The kitchen. It hadn't overtaken the house, but the whole kitchen was on fire and it was spreading across the floor, rapidly making its way to the living room. We had arrived just in time. Another five minutes and the first floor would have been a goner.

Fire didn't take nearly as long as people suspected to spread, especially in a house filled with furniture and curtains. A lot of household furniture and objects could be accelerants if it was hot enough.

Manufacturers could only make fabric fire resistant to a certain level and it was never enough to protect it from a hot burning fire. This fire was burning hot from the stove. I could make out a pot on the stove and I was willing to bet the homeowner had been cooking something and grease dropped down into the open fire from the gas burner. It happened more times than people thought and it was often the cause for the majority of kitchen fires.

"All right, Probee, you're taking the nozzle. You're gonna hold it tight, just like in the academy. You aim it low to cut off the fuel to the fire."

"Aye, Lieutenant," I said as I took the hose from him.

Sinclair went behind me and held onto the hose to help me control the flow. The power that flooded through the hose was always immense and it took a lot of physical strength to be able to keep control of the hose and where the water was hitting the fire.

I made sure I had a strong grip on it before I pulled the release valve on the nozzle and the water came shooting out of it. I aimed it low. Most would assume you aim it high so the water sprays down onto the fire. However, you have to aim the water low because that is where all of the fuel and oxygen for the fire comes from. The water chokes off that fuel and oxygen and it kills the fire from the base, eliminating the flames that are attached to it.

Getting to put out a real fire for the first time felt indescribable. I was getting to be a real firefighter and I felt like I was on the moon. The adrenaline high was likely to last me hours.

It took a good ten minutes before the flames had died down and I was able to put the fire out. I couldn't get the smile off of my face. I had put out an actual fire. I had saved someone's house. Today had just started and it was already one of the best days of my life. This was why I had chosen to become a firefighter over anything else. To be able to help people, to save lives, and to save homes. Today was only going to get better. I just knew it.

CHAPTER SEVEN

Damon

IT HAD BEEN a week since I had last seen Cy. I hadn't texted him, because I wanted the anticipation to build up. I wanted him to wonder if I was going to text him. I wanted him to have to wait longer before he could come, assuming he listened to my order. I wouldn't know until I saw him again in person and asked. I would know if he was lying to me based on his facial expression when he answered the question.

I was hoping he had listened, that he was willing to play along. He seemed more than willing that night at the factory. There was no doubt in my mind that he had Daddy issues and that should have been a red flag for me. That meant he had emotional issues and baggage and wouldn't be someone who would be able to handle a no-strings attached relationship like the one I would be interested in.

I didn't want a relationship with emotions and obligations. I didn't want strings. I wanted to be free to come and go whenever I wanted and had control of everything. It wasn't easy for a man to give up control to a complete stranger. They wanted to know the other guy first and build up trust. It was that very reason why I didn't have relationships. I didn't want anyone to get to know me.

Once they got to know you, they thought they had a say in your life. They started to make demands like meeting my family or my friends. They demanded that I come out of the closet and when I told them no, they assumed it was because I didn't care about them. It was just easier to avoid all of that and I was really hoping that Cy would follow the rules and be a good boy. If not, then I would forget about him and move on to someone who would.

There was a knock at my door and I let out a sigh. I wasn't in the mood to deal with people. That's why I kept my door shut, after all, so I wouldn't have to be bothered. Apparently, whoever was on the other side didn't get the memo.

I needed to get out of here. I needed a stiff drink and some fun. I had already been thinking about texting Cy and having him come over tonight. I didn't need to get a hotel room, not if I was going to be having an ongoing fling with him.

I didn't tend to bring anyone back to my condo, but I didn't know where Cy lived and it was safer to have him come to me than for me to go to him. If he lived in a highly populated area, I couldn't risk being seen by someone who might recognize me going into his place. I also didn't know if he lived alone.

When there was another knock, I knew whoever was on the other side wasn't going away, which meant they knew I was in here. Forcing myself to sit up straight in my chair and pick up a pen so it looked like I was busy doing paperwork, I called out.

"Enter."

My door opened and on the other side was a man I didn't recognize. He wasn't dressed like anyone from the Upper Brass in his suit and I knew the suit was too expensive for him to be a fire investigator that I hadn't met personally. I didn't know what he wanted, but the briefcase in his hand told me he was here on business and I suspected I wasn't going to like the business he had with me.

"Can I help you?" I asked, doing my best to keep the annoyance out of my voice. Some days though, were harder than others.

"My name is Kevin Fox and I am your brother's defense attorney. I have been trying to get a hold of you for months now."

Fuck.

This man was one of the last people I wanted to speak with. The only one above him would be my brother. He had been calling me for months, since the morning he received my brother's case, in fact.

I had no idea why he had agreed to be my brother's lawyer. I knew Taye didn't have money, for one, not with the cops freezing his accounts after he tried to kill one of their own. Cops were generally good people, but if you tried to harm one of their own, if you killed or almost killed one of their own, they were relentless and they would destroy you. They had frozen every asset and bank account that Taye had before dawn the following day. They had destroyed what was left of his house and they investigated for evidence. They went to his locker at the firehouse and took everything from it. They impounded his car and even reached out to the insurance company that had his 401K and made sure no funds were allowed to leave it.

Taye was going to be stuck with a legal aid lawyer who worked for a salary and not by the hour. The result was a bunch of overworked attorneys that didn't really care if they got you out of prison or not.

I had been happy that Taye would get a shitty lawyer because I was hoping that meant he would be forced to take a plea deal. I didn't want to have to go through a trial. I didn't want Tristan to have to go through a trial. It was bad enough that he had been through something traumatic; he shouldn't have to relive it all over again with the hope that a jury would find Taye guilty.

I had no doubt though, that they would find him guilty. There was no way he was getting off from any of it. Even if they couldn't convict him for the fires, he had killed Wilson in front of Tristan and then proceeded to try and kill him and Detective West. He was done. He was going to prison for life just off of that one incident.

"I have nothing to say to you about Taye. I don't care about whatever message he is trying to get you to relay. If that's all, you can leave."

Kevin pulled out a folded up piece of paper from his inside suit pocket and handed it over to me. I took it as he spoke.

"I am calling you as a witness on your brother's behalf. This is a subpoena to appear in court once the trial starts in thirty days. Have a good day, Captain," he said, before he turned and headed out, closing the door behind him.

"What the fuck?"

I opened the subpoena and saw that he wanted me to testify on Taye's behalf, but it didn't specify what exactly I would be testifying to. I wasn't there during the attack, so I couldn't speak to what happened. I could only talk about what Tristan had told me while he was working the case.

Barba had said that there was a chance he would have to call me, but I would just be testifying to the case itself and what I had recommended for Tristan to do. And that was only if he needed that deep of a background history on the case, something he doubted he needed.

This subpoena, the demand to show up in court and testify on behalf of my brother, was confusing and shocking. I wasn't certain how I felt about it outside of confusion.

I was also surprised that the trial was going to start in thirty days. I thought for sure Taye would take a plea deal to get less prison time. I didn't think he would want to drag it all out through a trial.

I picked up my desk phone and called Barba. I had to find out what was going on. I hadn't spoken to him except that one time when he told me I might have to testify. I hadn't asked about the case; I didn't want to know. I didn't want to get involved. I wanted to forget that any of it was going on and be kept in the background of it all.

After four rings, Barba answered and he sounded exhausted and overworked.

"ADA Barba."

"Joseph, It's Damon Amaro. You got a minute to talk?"

I knew he was busy and I didn't know if he was about to head into court. I was hoping he would have a minute so I could get to the bottom of this shit without having to wonder about it for the rest of the day.

"I'm assuming this is about the subpoena you just got from Taye's lawyer."

"You knew it was coming? I would have appreciated a heads up."

"Just found out this morning. Fox has

been working on trying to get your brother's name cleared. He has filed a plea of not guilty due to mental impairment."

"What? He's not mentally impaired." I rolled my eyes at that news. I seriously couldn't believe Taye was trying to get off with that bullshit excuse for what he had done. Of course he wasn't going to be a man and take his punishment like he deserved. Of course he wasn't going to do what was right and make things easier for everyone. Nope, he wanted to drag our family's name through the mud even more with a public trial and now he wanted to make it seem like it wasn't his fault.

This was so much bullshit.

"Fox is trying to show that the emotional and mental abuse he suffered as a child has permanently altered his mind and has given him PTSD that was made worse by being a firefighter. He wants to make it appear that Stan manipulated him during a vulnerable time when his father was killed in a fire that Stan started. He's going to attempt to make it appear that Taye had been abused his whole life and is a victim and shouldn't be held accountable for the fires that Stan forced him to start."

Unbelievable.

It was all a load of shit. He didn't have PTSD. He wasn't affected by our father growing up. They spent the most of their time together. He had been a firebug since he was a young child. He was born that way. He wasn't made into a monster by how he grew up.

"That's complete shit. He started a fire when he was a kid. He's always been like this. He kept a scrapbook of the worst fires he had come across in his career and he used to look at them before he went to sleep at night. He loved the gruesome fires. He's not scarred, he's just fucked up."

"I agree and I think Fox looking to call you to the stand is going to destroy his case completely. That doesn't mean he's not going to turn it into a complete circus first. He took Taye's case pro bono. He is already working the press. He wants to make this into a huge show. With the number of fires that Taye started and the deaths and injuries connected to them, it's huge news. Stan and Taye are the first partner arsonists in decades and the press is chomping at the bit to get coverage on it."

"Great, so Fox is just looking to build his own exposure. Tell me this isn't going to work."

The last thing I was going to be able to handle was Taye getting off on all of it. I knew if he was found not guilty due to mental impairment, he still wouldn't be able to be a firefighter, but that wouldn't stop him from starting fires again. It wouldn't put him in a mental institution. He would be a free man to do whatever he wanted.

"Not a chance. It's going to blow up in his face. You are not a mess. You are not starting fires just to deal with the pressure your father put on you. He can't claim that the home you both grew up in permanently damaged Taye when you are perfectly fine. If he was an only child or if you were in prison for starting fires or killing people, then he might have had a chance, but you aren't so he doesn't have one. It's just a reason for him to drag it all out. I have offered a plea deal, but Fox refuses to allow Taye to accept it. He's got Taye believing he can get away with it all. Realistically, with the number of homicides through the fires, he's looking at the death penalty. A plea deal would take that off the table, and Taye knows that, but he's refusing to cooperate."

I could hear that Barba was frustrated by the entire situation, too. He had probably figured that this case would be easy enough to plead out. Most criminals would take a plea deal if it meant they wouldn't get the death penalty, but of course Taye wasn't going to do things the easy way. Arsonists loved the limelight and he was thriving on the thought of all the attention he would be getting from a public trial.

"And someone who almost killed a cop is treated like a God in prison. It's not like he has any motivation on the inside to get a deal. He's probably got prisoners kissing his feet. What if I don't testify?"

"You've been served, you don't have a choice. If you don't show up, you can be arrested for contempt of court, and then still have to testify but Fox will treat you like a hostile witness. He'll get you on that stand one way or the other, so it would be better for you to testify and not have to spend two days in lock up for contempt of court. The best thing you can do is show up and tell the truth. He will get to question you first and then I will, so if there is something that is a little gray, we can clear it up on my cross."

"Yeah, all right." I rubbed my hand over my face, still shaking my head over the whole situation.

I wasn't happy about it, but there was nothing that I could do about, it either. I was going to be testifying whether I wanted to or not. I might as well do it the easy way.

We said our goodbyes and I debated for a moment before I gave in and pulled my cell phone out. I knew that it was going to be a terrible idea, but I needed something to put me in a better mood. I needed some type of a release and I might as well make it good. I hit Will's contact number and put it to my ear and listened to the rings. After three of them he finally answered.

"Hey, D, how the hell are ya?"

"I'm fine, just busy over here. I need you to send over your new Probee to my office."

"Is something wrong?" he asked, and I could hear his concern that Cy had screwed something up or was being investigated for something.

"Naw, the Upper Brass has us walking all of the new Probees through the division and offer tips on how they can better identify arson. I just need him for a few minutes, then he'll be back with you."

"Yeah, okay. I'll let him know and send him your way. I'm sure the Upper Brass are looking to cover their asses with everything that is going on. You want to talk about it yet?"

I could hear the concern in his voice and I didn't blame him for it. Will knew I was struggling, but doing so silently. I wasn't ready to open up to anyone right now about all of this shit with Taye. What I wanted was for Cy to get over here and suck my dick. Talking could come later.

"Nope. I'll see you later. Be safe."

"You, too."

I ended the call and tossed my cell phone down onto my desk before I sat back in my chair. Soon, Cy would be here and he would be able to take the edge off. I wasn't going to let him come, not yet. That would be tonight. I was going to make sure he was craving my touch all day long. Now, I just needed him here and the fun could start.

CHAPTER EIGHT

Cyrus

I KNOCKED ON Damon's office door and waited until I was told I could enter. I was surprised when Cap told me that Damon had asked for me to go down. Apparently, the Upper Brass wanted all of the new guys to see early and obvious signs of arson. I wasn't sure I believed that was why I was being asked to come down here, though. At least, I was hoping that wasn't why.

I highly doubted that Damon brought me down here so we could have sex in his office, either. That would be very bold, especially for a man who I suspected wasn't out of the closet yet.

Still, a man can dream right?

"Enter," Damon called out.

I could tell by the tone in his voice that

he was stressed and not happy. I couldn't help but wonder if it had something to do with his brother. It still blew my mind about all of it. To know that his own brother had done something like that, most people wouldn't understand how he was feeling, but I did. I went through the very same emotions with my father and I could completely understand what he was feeling. It made sense why he was taking a stronger control in the bedroom. Why he would be drinking and getting drunk during the week. He didn't start those fires. He didn't kill those people, but he would feel the guilt all the same.

I knew that Taye wouldn't be capable of feeling guilt, my father sure as shit doesn't. But I did. I felt the guilt of every life that my father took. Damon would be feeling that same guilt and there was nothing that anyone could do or say that would make it magically disappear. I was still dealing with it and what my father had done happened years ago. All of this was still fresh for Damon and it truly made sense for him to be spiraling slightly.

I strolled into his office and saw that he was sitting at his desk with a bunch of paperwork scattered around it. He glanced up for a moment before he leaned back in his chair and looked me up and down. A shiver of excitement ran down my spine with the way he looked at me. There was just something about this man.

"Close the door," he ordered.

I closed the door behind me and waited to see what he wanted to talk about. I didn't care what it was that he wanted, I was more than happy to spend the rest of my day here just looking at him.

This past week had been brutal. I'd spent it fighting with my dick to not get hard while at work and fighting to get my dick soft while I was out of work. I'd spent all night long hard just thinking about sex with Damon.

I knew I could have touched myself, but he had told me not to and I couldn't bring myself to go against him. Every night, I went to sleep my dick was hard. Every morning, I woke up to a hard and aching dick, but I never touched myself. I never allowed myself to come, just like I had been told. I was in a constant state of blue balls at this point, but I would be lying if I said I didn't enjoy this game we were playing.

"Get down on your knees and crawl over here to suck Daddy's cock," he ordered, and my dick instantly went hard.

Holy fuck.

We were actually going to do this right here in his office. Anyone could come in; anyone could hear us. I thought he was in the closet, but apparently that closet door wasn't as tightly nailed shut as I thought it was.

This was insane.

We could get caught.

This could ruin my career as a firefighter and yet, I slid down on my hands and knees and started to crawl toward him. I went around his desk as he turned in his chair and opened his pants, pulling out his hard cock for me. My mouth watered at the sight of the already engorged flesh, his tip glistening with precum.

My own cock was hard and already pulsing with need. I was praying that after getting him off he was going to finally let me come. The second I was close enough, his hand went into my hair, pulling on it tight as he pushed my head down on his cock. I relaxed my throat as he pushed my head all the way down to his base.

I moaned as I felt his cock sliding down my throat. I'd missed him. I'd missed his dick and how it could make me feel, how good it felt in my mouth and down my throat.

"Rub your cock on the outside of your

pants, but stop when you are going to come. You are not allowed to come yet, my slut."

A deep moan escaped my mouth at his words. I instantly did as I was told and started slowly rubbing my cock along its length through my pants. I was insanely hard and all I wanted to do was to come. I was going to be a good boy though, and then he should allow me to come. I knew I was still being punished for coming without permission from last time and I was not about to make that same mistake twice.

I couldn't stop moaning and humming my appreciation as he started to fuck my mouth. I knew I had to be careful, I didn't want anyone to overhear us, but with his cock in my mouth my moans were muffled.

He was more aggressive this time with his thrusts, but I suspected he was in just as much of a need to orgasm as I was. I also suspected that something had pissed him off enough to bring me here. The man was in the closet and this was a very bold move for him to be making. He was clearly in desperate need of a release, but he wasn't the only one. I had to stop my hand and squeeze my cock through my pants to stop myself from coming.

With my pleasure denied, my balls got even heavier.

"Good boy. That's my good slut," he praised, and it only turned me on even more.

He picked up his pace and I knew he was chasing his own release. I suspected that my throat was going to be a bit sore after this, but I didn't care, it was well worth it.

His grunts were soft and I knew if I looked up he would be biting his lip to keep his groans inside. I knew he was close, I could feel his cock getting harder, swelling against my tongue.

After a few more thrusts of his hips, he pushed my head down fully on his cock as he shoved his hips up, forcing his cock as deep as possible down my throat as he came with a deep groan, his grip tightening in my hair and sending shivers down my spine. I greedily swallowed his cum as he continued to pulse in my throat. I would never get tired of this feeling. I could have done this all day without a single complaint.

He pulled my head back once I finished swallowing everything he had for me. He placed his right hand underneath my jawline and pulled me in for a rough kiss. I easily melted against him and opened my mouth when I felt his tongue seeking entrance. I moaned at the roughness, as he took control over me. He knew how to make me writhe and whimper beneath him and I relished every moment of his control.

All too soon he was pulling back, but he kept his hand on my throat. He stood, pulling me up with him, and then he quickly turned me around so I was facing his desk.

"Drop your pants and bend over, my slut."

"Aye, Daddy."

I was more than happy to drop my pants. I was painfully hard and desperately needed to come. I needed to feel his cock buried deep inside of my ass. I didn't care anymore that we were still in his office and anyone could overhear us or walk in on us. The need to come, the need to feel him inside of me, was stronger than any logic running through my mind.

He placed his hand on my back and pushed me forward. I laid my chest flat against his cool desk without complaint or resistance as he spoke.

"Spread your ass. Show your Daddy that sweet hole."

I moaned as I reached behind me and

spread my ass cheeks apart for him. My dick pulsed and I knew if he touched me, I was going to explode. My balls were heavy and aching with the need for release.

"Daddy has something for his little slut," he growled into my ear. He was so close I could feel his hard cock pressing against my needy hole.

"Oh fuck. Aye, Daddy," I whined.

I heard him opening his desk drawer and I was praying it was for lube. I didn't want to know why he had it in his office, and I didn't care right now. All that mattered at that moment was him pounding into me.

When I finally felt something against my hole, it wasn't a lubed up finger. It wasn't even his tip; this wasn't flesh against my hole, it was silicone. I knew that feeling all too well.

I had to bite my lip to keep the deep groan from echoing off the walls as he pushed in the butt plug. It wasn't too big, but it was big enough to sting as it was slowly pushed inside of me. I had no idea how long it was, but it was longer than the last one I had in me. When I felt the blunt end rub up against my prostate before he finally bottomed out, I couldn't help but shudder. It was long enough that it would constantly rub up against my sweet spot with every step I took. If I sat down, I was going to be feeling it.

I was not shy when it came to sex toys. I had used plenty of butt plugs and dildos in my life. I had a healthy sex drive and when I couldn't hook up with a guy I had no problem pleasuring myself.

"Get dressed," he demanded.

"What?" I asked, shocked.

He didn't just tell me get dressed, that didn't happen.

That can't happen.

I can't get dressed.

I had a raging hard-on, and I had this toy up my ass. I needed to *come*. I needed him to let me come or make me come. I did not need my pants back on.

"Get dressed, slut. Don't make me repeat myself," he said with a deadly edge to his voice.

"Sorry, Daddy," I instantly said. The last thing I wanted was for him to not let me come again.

I stood up and pulled my boxers and pants back up. It was not easy with the plug inside of me. I could handle a larger one, but usually I wasn't going to be walking around with it.

Once I was dressed, he turned me around and started to rub his hand along my hard cock through my pants as he spoke.

"There are rules you will have to follow if you want to keep doing this."

"What rules, Daddy?" I knew there would be, but I wasn't certain what all of them would be. To be honest though, at that point, I so didn't fucking care what they were as long as it ended up with me coming.

"I am in control of everything sexual between us. You come only when I give you permission to. This never gets talked about with anyone. I am not out and I do not plan on ever being out. As far as anyone will ever know, you're just another Rookie and I'm a highly respected Captain. Are you negative?"

"Aye." I didn't need him to elaborate more on what he meant.

"Good, so am I. Moving forward there won't be condoms. When I am fucking you, I will be coming deep inside of your needy ass and I will own you. Your body will belong to me. Neither one of us will be with anyone else. There won't be any dates, going out. When we are in public, I won't even acknowledge you unless it is for professional reasons. You are nothing more than a dirty needy slut for me to put my cock into. Now, is that something that you can agree to?"

The answer should be, no. No, I didn't agree to be a living sex doll for him to use whenever he felt like it. But I also knew that human beings were stupid.

I was stupid.

If I was smart and made smart choices, I never would have slept with my teacher. I never would have gone to sex parties as an underage kid. I am not that smart, not when it came to sex and my body. I knew all of that. I knew I should say no. He was essentially telling me I was going to be his personal prostitute, only I wouldn't get paid for anything he did to me. I was also going to have to go through it knowing that there was a chance he wouldn't let me come every time, meaning I got nothing out of our time together. Even though I knew all of that, every ounce, every fiber in my being, was screaming at me to say *yes*.

I was clearly a glutton for punishment. I really needed to consider speaking to a Shrink about my issues and obvious lack of self-esteem if I was even considering agreeing to his demands. Even knowing exactly what he wanted from me. Even knowing that I was never going to be anything more than a dirty secret—shit, a dirty secret would be a step up to what this would be. Still, even knowing all of that, there really was only one answer I could give.

"I can agree to your terms, Daddy."

Maybe I would live to regret it, but that was my choice to make. I could also live to regret not agreeing to it and allowing this opportunity to pass me by. If I was going to regret something, I would rather regret doing something then not doing anything.

"That's my good slut. I will text you my address. When you are done work tonight, you will drive there. When you arrive, you will text me and then wait until I text you back to give you permission to come up. Do you understand?"

"Aye, Daddy. I'll be your good slut and do as I'm told."

"Good, now get out of my office," he said as he moved back.

"Aye," I said as I started to move away.

With every step I took, I noticed the toy up my ass. It was going to take some getting used to and it was going to be hard when a call came in. I was only just two hours into my shift and I had ten more to go.

This was going to be a long ass day.

Just as I opened the door, I was thrown through another shock. There was a man standing on the other side of it and he was clearly about to knock on the door. The second his gaze landed on me, he instantly registered who I was and disgust quickly grew upon his face. Before he had a chance to say anything, I was moving and quickly making my escape.

Ronnie Mack.

Fire Investigator Ronnie Mack. The man who had been responsible for discovering my father was a serial arsonist.

I can still remember clearly the night he stormed into our home and dragged my father out in cuffs. He didn't even care that I was there. That I was mourning the loss of my mother. He just threw my father down and cuffed him, going on and on about all the people he'd killed, including my mother.

Then, he tossed me into another police car and dragged me down to the station and put me in an interrogation room. I was in there for over twelve hours, not being spoken to, never checked on, no food, no water, not even a bathroom break.

When he finally did come in, it was to interrogate me to make sure I wasn't starting fires with my old man. They held me for a total of forty-eight hours before they let me go. Twenty in that interrogation room with no food, water or a bathroom break, even when I did ask. I spent the rest of it in a holding cell with other adult males, some of which gave me extra special attention when I finally did get to use the toilet in the cell. Only to be let go two days later and into the custody of social services. By then, my mother had been buried and no one knew where. It took six months before my lazy ass worker finally told me where she was.

I understood that Mack had a job. I understood that my father was a criminal, a murderer, a mass murderer by all accounts. I got that. What I didn't understand still to this day was how anyone could treat me like he did. I was just a kid. I didn't deserve to be treated like a killer. I didn't deserve to be treated like I was worthless and some criminal that they could do whatever they wanted with.

I'd had no idea he was even still working. I figured he would have retired by now. He was older to begin with back then, in his early sixties. After that arrest, he should have retired and gone out on an epic high note. If he was still working that meant that Damon was his Captain. There was no way Mack wasn't going to be telling Damon all about me and my father.

A deep sadness overtook me at the knowledge that Mack was going to tell Damon. That Damon was going to hear about how my father was a prolific serial arsonist and I was hauled in for questioning on the crimes. That he always suspected I'd helped, but he could never prove it. Mack had taken something from me growing up when he arrested me and now he was going to take my career and someone that could possibly be a long-time lover.

Someone who I could possibly fall in love with one day.

He was going to ruin my life and once again, there was nothing that I could do to stop it. He had made me powerless again.

I got into my car and started to head back to the firehouse for what very well could be my last shift as a firefighter.

CHAPTER NINE

Damon

IT WAS CLOSER to eleven when I finally decided to text Cy and let him know he was allowed to come up. I knew I was being more controlling than I usually would and I knew there was only so long it would be fun and exciting for Cy before he got sick of it and wanted some control and equality in this arrangement.

It was only logical and rational for Cy to grow tired of being treated like a piece of meat. At first it was always fun and exciting, but it took a toll on a person's mind and I knew he wouldn't last for very long. He was young and had his whole life ahead of him. The world wasn't all darkness and horror to him yet. He could still see the sunlight, something I used to be able to see before everything went to shit. I couldn't let this go on for very long. I didn't want my darkness to taint his light. He was still young, he had a lot of years left to live, and the last thing I wanted to do was for him to see the world as nothing but shades of darkness. That wouldn't be fair to him. We could have some fun for a bit and then I had to let him go, no matter what.

I was pulled out of my thoughts at the knock on my door. I knew it was Cy and I knew he was going to be in serious need of coming. I might have been taking things too far with him. Normally, I would never have him wearing a plug that size for that long and never at work. I had gotten too excited and let my lust cloud my thinking. It was something I would be more cautious with in the future and I would be speaking to him about it and letting him know I was crossing a line. That would come after, though.

Sex first and then talking.

I opened the door and I could see how desperate he was, it was written all over his face. I felt a wave of pride hit me at knowing how crazy I could drive this young twenty-one year old man. He was well on his way to craving my touch and it was only going to get worse after tonight.

"Follow," I ordered, before turning

around. I heard his quick and eager footsteps behind me as he closed my front door. Tonight was going to be exactly what we both needed and I couldn't wait.

We walked into my bedroom and I could see the surprise and excitement mixed within his eyes. I had four restraints already set up on my bed and he didn't need me to tell him that they were for him. I was going to have him tied down and at my complete mercy. Tonight, he was going to finally get to come and I was going to make sure I milked him for every last drop he had been building up over the past week.

***

With the last restraint removed from Cy, his body instantly collapsed down onto my bed. I could see him struggling to catch his breath and I knew he was thoroughly pleased. He had come six times and I was surprised he even had any left after the first five of them. I knew I had made up for the wait though, and it pleased me to see him so sated he was practically jelly.

"You all right?" I asked, flashing him a knowing smirk.

"Aye," he said in a dreamy voice, and I knew he was well up on cloud nine right now.

"Look, I'm sorry about earlier with the plug. I was out of line having that in you while you were going to work. I got a bit carried away and I'm sorry if it distracted you while you were at work or made the guys look at you like something was wrong."

It really wasn't fair of me to do that to him. I knew better, but I had been so blinded by my own lust that I unintentionally put him in harm's way while he was working. I also put him in a position for the guys he works with to think something was going on with him.

"The guys didn't notice and you have nothing to be sorry for. That was fun. Maybe not with one that long again, bit awkward to sit down for very long, other than that it was good. I enjoy using toys and having a plug in me during the day or at night. I like the feeling. I like feeling like I'm connected to someone and not alone. I enjoyed today and I'm hoping to do it again, Daddy," he said, flashing me a sexy smirk and a wink. It sent a heatwave all through my body.

Fuck, this man just might be perfect.

Too bad I was not interested in having a relationship.

Even if I was, could I really have one

with a twenty-one year old?

We were at two completely different points in our lives, in our careers. He would want to go out and party at his age and I was past the club-hopping phase. There was also a maturity level difference. Most twenty-one year olds were irresponsible and immature. It wasn't their fault, they were still growing up and learning who they were. We'd all done it. I was just past that stage in my life.

Now I was in a new stage of my life, my early mid-life crisis where I drank, did drugs, and had random sex with strangers.

Shit, maybe we were at the same maturity level.

He pushed himself up and started to get dressed. I knew we weren't going to be going around again, we were both spent and it was getting late. He had to be at work tomorrow morning at eight.

"The man who went into your office when I left, did he say anything about me?" he asked, carefully, and I was surprised by the wave of jealousy that hit me.

"I was serious about the rule 'you don't fuck with anyone else,'" I responded with a slight growl to my voice.

"Don't make me yak. He's old enough

to be my Grandda."

"And I'm old enough to be your father if I started young. He didn't say anything about you, why?"

If he wasn't interested in hooking up with Mack, then why would he want to know if Mack said something about him?

That would lead me to believe that he knew Mack; that they knew each other. Where they would have met I had no idea, perhaps the Fire Academy, but to my knowledge Mack had never volunteered his time there.

Mack was one of my oldest investigators. The man was sixty-seven and should have long retired by now. It wasn't because he loved his job that he was still working. It also wasn't because he needed the money. It had everything to do with he didn't know what else to do. It was not uncommon for firefighters, or first responders in general, to stay well past their retirement age. For most, it was the only life they'd known, the only career they had ever done. They had no wives, only ex-wives, and the ones that did have children, their children hated them or their ex-wives were keeping them apart. They had nothing but the job so they stayed, even when they should have left long ago.

Mack was a good investigator, but he was getting sloppy. He was getting caught up on doing things the old fashioned way. It was becoming difficult to trust him with any high profile case or a serial arsonist case. ADA Barba also cringes whenever he has to try and prosecute Mack's cases now. He has the lowest close rating out of all of my investigators, including my rookies. The Upper Brass liked him, so they were letting him stay on, but pretty soon I was going to have no choice but to let him go. I had been thinking about doing it soon while I was still hated by the Upper Brass. After all, it wasn't like they could hate me more than they already did.

"Nothin'," Cy said, trying to dismiss the conversation as he finished dressing. I wasn't about to let him get away with that, though.

"People don't bring up some random guy after sex for no reason. We can do this one of two ways, Cy. You can either be honest with me and tell me why you want to know if Mack was asking about you, or you don't get to come again until you do tell me, and if I find out from him first, which I will come morning, then I'll make it so that you don't come for the next six months. Which road would you like to take, my slut?"

I knew it was wrong for me to order him to tell me something that had nothing to do with sex. I was crossing a line by doing it, but it seemed like something that was important. He wouldn't have asked unless there was an issue and if there was an issue between one of my investigators and a firefighter, then I had to know about it.

There are investigators and firefighters that I couldn't put together because they didn't get along. It might seem childish, but certain personalities just can't work together and sometimes there's a history there. I had a dozen or more female investigators who had dated a firefighter before and when things went south, I had to keep them apart. It wasn't just for professional or personal reasons, but also legal reasons. A defense lawyer would tear the entire case apart and if they got a whiff of a bad break up it turned into a shit show.

Cy let out a sigh as he rubbed his face before he sat down on the end of my bed next to me.

"My father is Jamie McDougal."

"*The* Jamie McDougal?" I asked, trying to keep the shock from my voice.

Everyone in the fire department knew

who Jamie McDougal was. It didn't matter if you were an investigator or an active firefighter, we all knew about him. His name went nationwide. He would be going down in history as the most deadly arsonist. He'd been connected to a hundred and ten fires, that we could prove, and had killed eighty-three people. That didn't include all of the other victims who would forever be scarred by the fires he'd started.

I had still been a rookie Captain when McDougal came across my desk. Mack had been working it. I had assigned it to him with being my most senior investigator. I had trusted him to look through the cases and find the arsonist who was responsible.

At the time five years ago, there were over a dozen fires that could be connected to one arsonist from his signature. We didn't know how many fires were connected to him at the time. We didn't find out until after the arrest was made just how many fires he had started. I was confident there were more, but he was no longer disclosing any. Arsonists liked to talk. They liked to relive their fires. However, there were also fires they liked to keep to themselves. Generally, their favorite ones; the ones that were most significant to them. They kept the information on those to themselves for only them to enjoy. We'd never know how many fires he'd truly started.

"Aye," he said softly.

"I didn't know he had a child. Mack never said anything about him having a son. I know your mother was killed in his last fire. I'm sorry, Cy. I had no idea."

There was nothing anywhere that stated McDougal had a son. It should have been in his case file, but for whatever reason Mack had left that out. I also had more questions about why Cy was a firefighter.

His father was a historic arsonist, why would he pick this career out of all of the possibilities?

"Doesn't surprise me. I changed my last name to my Ma's given name when I turned eighteen. Spent the morning on my eighteenth birthday at the Government office. Mack never told you?" he asked, appearing slightly surprised and confused.

"No. Did he know?" If Mack knew about Cy it should have been in the files. There should have been a report about his interview and the Social Worker's report on him and his placement. That was standard for any investigation where children were left behind.

"Aye, he all but arrested me."

"Hold up, what?" I demanded.

Mack would have had no reason to arrest a sixteen year old kid. If he had brought him in, he should have had a child and youth advocate present for any questioning. He would have had to call in Barba to help with the interview in case there was a reason to press charges. That was standard procedure and it was done that way to protect everyone's asses.

"When he stormed in to arrest my father, he brought me in as well. Put me in the back of a cop car and took me down to the station. He left me alone in an interrogation room for twelve hours before he came in. Then spent the next eight drilling me with questions. He kept tellin' me to admit to helpin' my father. It didn't matter how many times I told him that I had nothin' to do with it. He kept me in that room for twenty hours. No food, no water, wouldn't let me go to the bathroom, he just drilled me with questions. Then he tossed me in a holdin' cell with all of these other blokes until the forty-eight hours were up. I spent twenty-eight hours curled up in the far corner tryin' to keep the perverts from touchin' me. When I finally got to leave, he told me we would be seein' each other again. That he knew I was a firebug and he would prove it. I missed my Ma's funeral while I was in that cell. I didn't even know where she was buried for six months."

The hurt within his voice was still raw and it fueled my rage. What happened to him never should have happened. He was a sixteen year old kid. Even if Mack suspected he was involved it never should have been handled like that. He should have had a lawyer and a child advocate present for any questioning. He should have been kept in a holding cell alone or with other juveniles. He never should have been placed in a holding cell with grown men and he never should have been kept for forty-eight hours without a shred of evidence, for fuck's sake.

Yes, we can hold suspects for forty-eight hours without charging them, but we do so only when we have some scrap of evidence that tells us he is our guy. We hold them so we have the time to find more evidence and build a solid case before charging. Keeping them those two days keeps people safe, it is why we do it. We don't do it because we have nothing and just feel like being assholes, which is exactly what Mack obviously did. I would be talking to him about this tomorrow and he would be reprimanded. I wasn't going to be putting up with this shit from anyone, past or present.

"I'm sorry, that never should have happened to you. I'm assuming no one knows about your connection to McDougal."

Thirteen dead firefighters.

It wouldn't go well for Cy if people discovered who his father was. It wouldn't matter that he was just a kid at the time, or that he didn't have a hand in the fires. They wouldn't care. All they would see was his father and they would ice him out. I didn't know if the guys at the Twenty-First would. Will didn't tolerate bullying of any kind for any reason. I also knew that Will wouldn't hold Cy's father's actions against him. However, the second shift Captain lost his son in one of those fires and that would put a serious strain between the two shifts.

"No, I've kept my mouth shut about it. Though, now I suppose it's only a matter of time before it gets out. I didn't expect for Mack to still be workin'. I thought no one would recognize me so there was no need to disclose."

"Mack has no interest in retiring. Why pick this job? You had to have known it wouldn't have gone over well if people discovered your connection to McDougal."

I mean, was he a glutton for punishment?

It wasn't like his father started only a couple of fires. He was a huge deal. His name wasn't going to go quietly into the night and be forgotten about. Cy had to know this was potential career suicide.

"I didn't know what I wanted to be when I grew up, not like most kids. I didn't have dreams of being anything. Nothin' interested me. And then I started to hear about my father's fires and all of the people he killed and hurt. I thought maybe I could try and make it right. That I could help people and try and make up for all the pain and destruction that my old man put out into the world. I wanted to be a firefighter and help people. To save lives and to stop people like my father from hurting anyone else. And I'm good at it. Maybe his DNA lets me see things differently, I don't know, but I feel like I can read a fire, know what it's thinkin'. That sounds daft, I know, but being a firefighter feels *right*. It feels like this is what I was born to do and I don't want to lose that."

He was a good man, I had to give him that. Most in his position would have done the opposite. They would have avoided the fire department all together. He had every reason to hate the fire department after what he had been put through. And yet, he wanted to keep helping people. He wanted to help save lives and prevent future arsonists from adding to their tally. It was honorable work and it really showed a level of maturity and what type of man he was. He certainly had more depth and layers to him than I was expecting. Than I judged.

"Will, Captain Clarke, he's a good man and he won't let anyone treat you differently because of your father. That isn't to say that other firefighters won't have an issue, but Will won't kick you out. He won't let anyone push you out. He'll protect you and so will his guys. You can still be a firefighter, you just won't be the most popular kid in school."

"I didn't join to be popular. Even if no one likes me, I'm not goin' nowhere. I got my own reasons for joinin' and if no one likes it, that's too bad for them. I'd appreciate you keepin' this between us. I don't need no sympathy or people lookin' at me funny. They don't need to know what I've been through."

"Of course. If anyone gives you a hard time though, when this eventually comes out, let me know. I can't promise anything, but I will look into it and I know your Captain will as well."

I couldn't make him tell me if someone gave him a hard time, but I was hoping he would tell me anyway. This was going to hit eventually, and my money was on sooner rather than later. I just hoped that the guys at the Twenty-First were there for him and didn't turn their backs on him. I knew Will wouldn't allow it, but that didn't mean they had to talk to him and be friendly. There was being professional and then there was being friends. Tomorrow though, I would be speaking with Mack and getting to the bottom of things. I wasn't going to tolerate that kind behavior from anyone, especially someone who had been here longer than dirt. He knew better and he deliberately went against all of our rules and protocols. There was no excuse for any of it and tomorrow he was going to have to answer to me and he better pray that I liked his answers otherwise his ass was out the door. I wasn't going to stand by and let anyone treat Cy like garbage. As a Captain it was my professional responsibility and obligation to make sure everyone was treated fairly. Even if the situation was in the past. Shit like that didn't fly in my house, ever. Not when I could do something about it. Even if I couldn't make it right for Cy, I could at least make sure Mack got what was coming to him and prevent it from happening to anyone else.

I knew my anger over the situation, how Cy had been treated, might be a little over the top at the moment but it was because I took pride in my team and we worked on the straight and narrow, never deviating into behavior like Mack had displayed. If nothing else, I had an image to maintain and uphold for my team.

It had nothing to do with any personal connection that I had with Cy. At least, that's what I was telling myself.

CHAPTER TEN

Cyrus

I WAS FEELING really good today. Last night with Damon had been amazing and I was really hoping we could keep it up. He seemed to be interested in making it a more ongoing thing and I was excited to see where it would take us. I knew there were plenty of obstacles standing in our way and chances were we weren't going to last very long. But, even though I knew all of that, I still wanted to give what we had a shot. Odds were our attraction would burn hot and flame out pretty quickly, but I was going to enjoy every second that I had with him.

After parking, I made my way into the firehouse through the roll up for the trucks. More often than not there were a few guys that were here in the truck bays, but they weren't outside today. I figured they must be in sitting around the kitchen and living area. Generally, when the shift started, they were always there talking and seeing how everyone's time off was. It was a lot like school in that way. When you first get to school you always check in with your friends, even though you just saw them.

I headed into the main area of the firehouse and my heart instantly dropped down to my stomach.

Investigator Mack stood in the middle of the living area and everyone was surrounding him as they listened to what he had to say. I didn't need to know that I had interrupted his speech, nor did I need to be here from the start to know what he was talking about.

No one even recognized or acknowledged me as I made my way quietly into the room. I knew today was going to go downhill with him being here and there would be nothing I could do about any of it now. All I could do was wait until he finished telling my deepest, darkest secret before he waltzed out of here and left me with the destruction.

"He's been going by his mother's maiden name, but his real last name is McDougal. His father was *Jamie*

McDougal, something he must not have disclosed on his application, otherwise they never would have taken him. I had arrested him and I have always believed he was involved in the fires, but there wasn't enough evidence for it to stick. The Department already has a black mark smearing its reputation with Taye Amaro up on multiple murder and arson charges. The last thing we need is another arsonist within our ranks. I have already reported him to the Upper Brass and they will be looking into him, but while that happens, I felt like you all should know."

This arsehole was making me look like an accomplice to multiple counts of arson and murder when I had nothing to do with any of it. I was just a sixteen year old kid and he came into my life and destroyed it. He treated me like I was a murderer, like I had helped to plan those fires and purchased the gasoline myself.

I was just a kid, for god's sake, and as far as I knew my parents had a healthy and happy marriage. I thought my father was a normal and loving father just like everyone else. I saw no signs. I wasn't old enough to know what the signs even were supposed to be. And Investigator Mack was looking to make a bigger name for himself by trying to intimidate and arrest a kid for the crimes of his father.

It made me wonder what his relationship was like with his own father. Maybe that was why he was so bound and bet on ruining my life and reputation. I was just starting my career as a firefighter and I wasn't going to let him destroy it, not while it was within my power.

I didn't have to declare the name change or my connection to my father. They never asked if I had any criminals in my family tree. All they cared about was my own criminal background check and it came back clean. If the Upper Brass had a problem with my genetic connection to my father, then that was too bad. They had no legal reason to terminate me and if they tried, they would be in for the fight of their lives. I was not going to go quietly into the night.

"I appreciate you coming down, Mack, and giving us the head's up," Captain Clarke said, his face stoic and unreadable.

I didn't know him well enough to know if he was being polite or he genuinely was going to have a problem with me now. Damon had said he wouldn't stand for it, that he would be on my side. I wanted to believe him, but it was hard when I didn't know the Captain all that well just yet.

"It was the least I could do. I would hate to see any of your men being hurt because of him," Investigator Mack said, as he held his hand out to Captain Clarke.

The Captain shook the offered hand with a small smile in return. It was then that Investigator Mack turned around and his gaze finally landed on me.

I had stayed back by the entrance to the kitchen from the roll up, everyone had been so focused on Mack's words that they hadn't even noticed me coming into the room.

Mack gave me a smirk, and it took everything in me not to punch him right across the jaw as he walked right by me. He knew what he had done and I was praying that he had failed. That the men I had been working beside, even for a short time, knew me better than to think I was an arsonist, especially at the young age of sixteen.

The second we were alone, Captain Clarke spoke first. I was thankful that he had said something, because I wasn't certain I would be able to form any words right now.

"I'm assuming you heard most of that."

"Aye, Captain," I said with a small nod. I had no idea where he was going to go with it, but I was hoping Damon was right and the Captain wouldn't tell me to pack my gear and get out.

"Mack has always been an asshole. The Upper Brass have been trying to figure out a way to get him to retire, but they can't force him and he hasn't done anything worthy of being forced into retirement. I know Damon would love to get rid of him. Is there anything you would like to address about what Mack said?" Captain Clarke finished.

I breathed a sigh of relief at his words. I felt better knowing that the Captain didn't like Mack. I was hoping that meant that he was on my side with all of this. I was going to need all of the support that I could get and it would help to have support from someone with a Captain ranking. I knew I had Damon on my side as well, but I had no idea what was going to happen with our personal relationship and I didn't think it would be wise to assume that if we stopped seeing each other that he would be on my side.

"I didn't know what my father was doing. I didn't have anything to do with it," I started, but Zander cut me off before I could get much further.

"We might not be mathletics, but we can do basic math and know that you would have been sixteen at the time."

"We know you didn't have anything to do with the fires. That's not even up for debate," Sinclair added.

It made me feel good to know that these men knew, without me even having to say it, that I wasn't an arsonist. That I didn't have anything to do with what my father had done. I felt a weight being lifted from my shoulders and I was getting to see a bit of the light at the end of the tunnel just knowing that they believed me.

"I'm assume Mack didn't feel the same though, based on what he just said," Newt said.

"Naw, he didn't. He treated me like a suspect, including putting me with adult males in a holding cell for twenty-eight hours until someone finally came and got me out. My Da killed my Ma in his last fire, that was his mistake. When I got out of that holdin' cell, I was placed in foster care. I didn't even get to go to her funeral," I said.

"He had no right to do that to you. You were just a kid. I'm assuming you didn't disclose the connection on your Fire Academy application," Captain Clarke asked, understanding in his voice.

"Naw. They didn't ask about any

connection to a criminal or arsonist. I had changed my name on my eighteenth birthday to my Ma's maiden name. I didn't see the need to mention who my father was. I think part of me was scared they would turn me away and all I wanted to be was a firefighter."

"Why? Out of all of the things that you could have been, why a firefighter?" Gage asked, obviously not understanding why I would choose to put myself in the situation at all.

"I know it doesn't make sense, that I should want to be anything else. But I wanted to be a firefighter so I could help people. To save lives that might have otherwise been taken by a fire. The lives my father took, those are not on me and I have no business taking on that guilt, but the guilt is there anyway. If I can help people and try and save more lives than the lives he took, that's a peace I can live with."

I wasn't certain how well they would take my answer. I knew that some could argue that my intentions were misguided and I shouldn't be a firefighter with the desire to try and even out the scale left behind by my father. It was the truth though, and it was part of the reason why my desire to be a firefighter was so strong.

But I also wanted to be a firefighter because I enjoyed the work. My intentions were pure and hopefully they would see that; if not today then in the near future when I had earned their full trust and respect.

"It's not your guilt to carry, Kid," Sinclair instantly said, his hand going to my shoulder in comfort.

"Aye, I know, but the guilt lives there all the same. I had wanted to be a firefighter for years, so the second I was able to apply, I was first in line. I want this career, I want this life, and I am not about to let anyone keep me from it," I said with strength in my voice.

"And you shouldn't. Mack is an asshole, and he can tell the Upper Brass whatever he wants, at the end of the day you were never arrested or charged and you were a juvenile. It holds no weight over your employment. Even if someone within the Upper Brass wants to make a thing out of this, you can meet them with your Union Rep and tell them your side of the story. Mack is going to have a hard time finding anyone who will believe at sixteen you were helping your father plan and start fires," Captain Clarke said.

"Captain Rouke is probably going to be an issue though," Hawke commented.

Captain Bastian Rouke was the Captain for Second Shift here at the Twenty-First house. I didn't know he had lost his son in one of the fires that my father started. I had discovered that after I got here, and so far, I had been lucky enough not to come across him on my shifts. I knew he wouldn't recognize me. He had never seen me before, and my face had never been in any of the newspapers about my father. Still, there was a small fear inside me that he would know who I was just by looking at me. I knew if he discovered who I was that it could be a problem. Even though I wasn't the reason his son was dead, I was still the son to the man who was that very reason. He might not handle it well and it would be best for me to not be alone with him until I knew for certain how he would feel toward me.

"I will speak with him. It would be best for him to discover this piece of information from a friend as opposed to the grapevine. It will be hard for him to hear, but he will come to see and understand that Cyrus is not his father and cannot, *should not,* be held accountable for his actions. Just like the rest of us are not to be held accountable for the actions of our parents," Captain

Clarke said, his eyes hard.

I would definitely be allowing him to speak to Captain Rouke on my behalf, but only because I felt like it would be best coming from a third party that Captain Rouke trusted. All I could do though, was hope that he would be able to handle the truth. I had to trust that he would be able to handle that I was working in the same house as him.

I knew we didn't work the same shift and the odds of me ever working under him were slim, but even being in the same firehouse as him could be a quandary. He was a superior and if he wanted to he could have me transferred to a different house. To a house that might have a serious problem with my DNA and with me being gay. It wasn't a situation I wanted to be in, but it was out of my hands. All I could do was hope that things would work out and that Investigator Mack would find someone else to play around with.

Our conversation was cut short by the alarm going off. The shift was just starting and with some luck, things would go well today. If I was really lucky, maybe tonight I would be able to see Damon again.

CHAPTER ELEVEN

Damon

THE SECOND I walked into my office, I noticed the brown envelope sitting on my desk. It hadn't been there when I left last night and considering it was just after nine in the morning, there was only one thing that could be in that envelope. Something bad. It was either going to be from the Upper Brass or it was going to be from Taye's lawyer trying to get me to testify in Taye's defense. Both of which had to power to put me in a shitty mood for the rest of the day.

I had been in a half-decent mood this morning. Last night with Cy had been amazing and I was enjoying the time I was getting to spend with him. I had no idea where our relationship would go and I had learned long ago to not try and put a label on anything, or a clock. It was better to let life take its course and see how it would all play out naturally. Still, I was hoping to be able to see him again in a few days. When I was with him I didn't feel like a Captain or the older brother of the serial arsonist. I was just myself. I could be just myself and not have to worry about how I felt or what I did. I could be me and I desperately needed that in my life.

I knew the clock was ticking on my behavior. I couldn't keep acting the way that I was. I couldn't keep drinking and using drugs. I had to get my life back on track. I had to smarten up, be responsible, and get back to who I was. I knew it wasn't going to be easy, but it was something I had to do or I risked my career and that was something I couldn't stand for.

I also knew that I could be risking my career by being with Cyrus. I should never have done it. The second I discovered he was a Probee, I should have ended things. I never should have slept with him again, much less multiple times since.

Even though I knew I could lose my job by being with Cy, I couldn't bring myself to stop seeing him. I didn't want to lose my career, it was all I had, but I also didn't want to stop seeing Cy. Being with him made me feel so good and not just in a sexual manner. He made me feel like I used to feel before this whole mess started with Taye.

I felt alive around him.

When I was with him, I didn't want to drink or do drugs just to escape from the stress or horror of my life. I couldn't lose him, not right now. We would just have to be extra careful to ensure no one discovered about us just yet. Eventually, it could come out, but it would have to be after his probation period.

It wasn't just for me, but for him as well. He deserved the chance to make a name for himself, to build respect and a reputation as a firefighter without it being connected to his relationship to me. The last thing I wanted for Cy was for people to think he only made it because he was sleeping with a Captain. That wouldn't be fair to him and he didn't deserve to have that following him around.

Letting out a sigh, I closed my door and made my way over to my desk. I picked up the envelope and saw that there was no return address on it. I turned it over and opened it before pulling out the letter. I immediately knew that it wasn't from the Upper Brass by the lack of the Fire Department insignia at the top of the page. I was starting to think getting a letter from the Upper Brass would have been better than what I got, because what I got was a subpoena and a notice that Taye's court date had been moved up to next week.

Five days from now.

I collapsed down into my chair as I read the letter again. I thought I had a month before the trial to prepare myself for it. I thought I would have a month for Barba to try and convince Taye to take a deal. Now I was only getting five days before I would have to be in court. And I would have to be there to testify against my own brother.

I knew Taye's lawyer was going to try and make me testify for Taye, to prove that our childhood was the cause for his actions, but it wasn't going to work for him. I couldn't understand why his lawyer would ever want me to testify, because I didn't turn to criminal activity to cope with our childhood. I wasn't an arsonist and nothing he had to say would ever change that Taye was born broken and hadn't been made broken by his childhood.

I reached for my cell phone and pulled

it out of my pocket. I looked first to see if I had gotten any texts from anyone, mostly Cy, but there was nothing new. I then pulled up Barba's number and hit the call button.

I didn't even hesitate to call him at this hour. I knew he would have been awake already and going over casework. There was no way he didn't know that the trial had been moved up to five days. I could picture Barba now, sitting in his office freaking out as he tried to prepare for a trial that he was supposed to have another month to prepare for. He was also going to have to get ready to cross-examine me in court. We had both believed that I wouldn't have to testify and that Taye's lawyer truly wouldn't want me to testify for Taye. Now that had gone out the window and Barba was going to have to prepare for my cross. I highly doubted anything Taye's lawyer had to say would sway the jury, but you never knew how someone would vote. All Taye needed was one jury member to be on his side and he would be acquitted of all charges. We had to get all twelve on our side, and that in and of itself was stressful as hell.

"Barba," he barked into the phone as he picked it up, the stress very clear in his voice.

"I take it you got the news," I said, without introducing myself. I knew he would know me based on my voice.

"Fuck. Fox is hoping that he can catch us off guard by pushing the trial date up. He wants us to miss something or screw something up so he can twist it all around to get Taye off. It's not going to work. I will be ready for the trial. No matter what."

I could hear how determined he was and that was something about Barba, he thrived under pressure. He wouldn't let this throw him off, it was going to do the opposite, and Taye's lawyer was not going to be prepared for the storm that was coming his way.

"I got a subpoena to testify for Taye. It looks like Fox is going to try and use our childhood to get him off."

"It's the only play he has to make. Taye has been through psychological evaluations and nothing came back that would work to get him off on non-compos mentis. He has to attack his childhood and he will have a Shrink that will back him up. It's a smart move, because there isn't anything that could say definitively that his childhood didn't alter his mind. Even when I prove that your childhood didn't turn you into an arsonist, a Shrink could counter that everyone's mind reacts differently to childhood trauma. It's a Hail Mary and it's not going to work, I don't care what I have to do. His victims will be getting justice."

"What do you need me to do?" I was more than willing to help out in any way that I could.

"Keep your head down and stay out of trouble. Anything could be used against us to justify Fox's defense. I need you to be completely honest with me, is there anything that Fox could have on you that would help with his defense?"

There was a loaded question. I highly doubted that Fox would have anything that could be used against me. I knew he could use my drinking, drug use, and promiscuity from the past few months, if he found out about them, but I highly doubted he had anything that would show my actions. I had been careful to keep everything that I had done completely discreet to ensure that no one discovered what I had been doing. My career could be in jeopardy if anyone discovered what I had been doing. With that said, I wasn't about to tell Barba about it. He didn't need more stress about the case and I wasn't in the mood for a lecture.

"No, there isn't anything. He could try and bring up how my parents were with us, but they weren't any different than millions of other parents in the world. He doesn't have anything."

I was confident on that. It would be insane for anyone to believe that our parents were to blame for Taye's actions. He had always been broken. Ever since I could remember, he had been different. There was nothing that our parents had done to make Taye that way. No, our father shouldn't have gotten him so involved in the Fire Department, but it wasn't like he knew this would be the result. Taye was just looking to lay the blame on people who couldn't defend themselves and I wasn't going to allow it. He deserved to be in prison for the rest of his life, it was just that simple.

"Good. Keep it that way. I have to go, but I will reach out before the trial so we can prep."

"I'll make sure I'm available. I appreciate it, Barba."

"I'll be in touch," Barba said, before he ended the call.

I gently tossed my cell phone down to my desk as I let out a sigh. This whole mess was turning into a circus and I really wasn't in the mood for it, but I was going to have to find the strength to get me through it. If I had to get up onto the stand and talk about my childhood, then I would do it, because Taye's victims deserve to get justice.

Tristan deserved to have justice.

I couldn't let my mind focus on all of that right now though. I had a shit load of paperwork to get through and I still had Mack to deal with. I would be speaking with him today about Cy. I wasn't going to tolerate him attacking Cy. He had handled his father's case wrong. He never should have interrogated Cy or kept him in a holding cell with grown ass adults. He put his life in danger by doing so and there was no excuse for it. I was going to be squashing that shit today before it went to the next level.

***

It was just after eleven in the morning when there was a knock at my door. I knew it was going to be Mack. I had reached out to him and told him to come in right away. I thought he would be here an hour or so ago, but apparently he decided to take his sweet ass time to come in. That was something else with Mack, he had been here for so long he forgot that he wasn't in charge, he wasn't a superior to anyone. He had experience over most of the other investigators, yes, but that meant nothing when it came to rank. He was getting to be more loose with the chain of command and that was also something he needed to be corrected on.

"Enter," I called out, and I started to gather some of the papers that were all over my desk and get them in order. He didn't need to see what I was working on.

The door opened and Mack walked in, closed the door, and then plopped down in one of the chairs across from me. It added to my annoyance that he felt like he didn't need to stand and show respect while waiting for permission to sit, like he was supposed to do. Most days, I would have let it go, but not today. Today, it was time for Mack to learn his place once again, and if he didn't like it, then he could finally quit and I would be free of him. I knew Barba would be all too happy to get rid of him working cases.

"I didn't give you permission to sit. This isn't your office and you will not treat it as such, nor disrespect me," I started with a clear edge to my voice as I sat up straight.

"Sorry, I didn't mean any disrespect, Sir," Mack said as he slowly stood up. I could tell he wasn't happy, but I didn't give a damn. I outranked him and he was going to have to suck it the fuck up.

"It has been brought to my attention that you have an issue with Probee MacMillan."

"I investigated him when he was sixteen. His father is Jamie McDougal, and I had a strong feeling that he was helping his father to plan the fires and help him start them."

"I read the file and your investigation into him. Your so-called *feeling* resulted in you arresting a sixteen year old who just lost his mother. You kept him in an interrogation room for twenty-eight hours, no food, no water, no bathroom breaks, no child advocate, nothing that followed his rights. Then you placed him in an adult holding cell for the remainder of the forty-eight hours without food and water and had adult criminals in there with him. Once again violating his rights. And you did all of that on a feeling. Does that sum it up?" I asked in a growl.

"It's more complicated than that, Sir," Mack said with a tightness to his voice.

"It's more complicated than you violating a sixteen year old boy's rights? Because from where I'm sitting it looks like you had a vendetta against him and were looking to use him to make a bigger name for yourself. *You violated his rights.*

You went against multiple protocols and now you are trying to ruin his career. I'm going to need you to give me a really good reason why I shouldn't suspend you pending an investigation."

Oh, I had heard all about Mack's visit to Station House Twenty-One this morning. He was down there talking shit about Cy when he was supposed to be in my office speaking with me, like I had ordered him.

"He was involved, Sir. I *know* he was involved. He shouldn't be a firefighter. We already have one firefighter up on arson and murder charges, we don't need to create another arsonist, another black spot to this department. People need to be aware that he lied on his application and of his connection to one of the most deadliest arsonists that the State has seen."

"All I'm hearing is that you have a vendetta against him. You had no proof, because there is none. He was a sixteen year old kid. He didn't know his father was an arsonist. He didn't help plan anything outside of a school dance. You are blinded, I don't know why, but you are blinded by his family, and I'm done. He didn't have to report his connection to McDougal to the Upper Brass. He only has to report on his own criminal background, which he doesn't have. What you have done, it is unacceptable, both past and present. You are officially suspended, pending an investigation."

"You can't do that," Mack instantly said, jumping to his feet, and I could hear the barely controlled rage in his voice.

"I most certainly can suspend you and I have every right and grounds to do it. You violated a child's rights. You went against protocols. You could have compromised that case's integrity if McDougal's lawyer had gotten wind of what you had done. And this isn't the first time you've compromised a case with your lack of professionalism. You're suspended and I honestly don't know if you will ever be allowed back. Clear out your desk. I will be in contact with your F.O.P Rep and they will let you know how the investigation is going."

I was done with Mack. I had more than enough proof to show that his competence in his work had been decreasing and it was time for him to retire. I also had multiple people who would be willing to vouch that Mack needed to be put out to pasture. It was time, and how he'd handled McDougal's case was more than enough proof. Fuck, Cy could still sue the department for his actions if he wanted and he would win. Mack was putting us all in a difficult and vulnerable position and I was not going to tolerate it any longer. It was time for a change and the Upper Brass were just going to have to jump on the bandwagon with this one.

Mack gave me one very dirty look, but he didn't comment, before he turned and headed out. I knew it was going to be a long process with him. I highly doubted he was going to take retirement with grace, but he would see soon enough that he had no choice but to take retirement or he risked being disgraced and fired without his pension.

Once I was alone, another sigh escaped me and I couldn't help but think I was starting to sound old. Mack had been handled for now. Now it was time for me to turn my full attention to Taye's trial and with any luck, we would win and I could put that behind me as well.

CHAPTER TWELVE

Cyrus

TO SAY THE past few days had been shit wouldn't even come close to it. I knew that it would get around that my father was Jamie McDougal, but I had underestimated the power and speed of the gossip mill within the Fire Department. Within forty-eight hours everyone knew about my connection and everyone had an opinion about it. Most were nice enough to only talk about it behind my back. There were some though, who felt it was appropriate to tell me exactly what they thought right to my face and while on a call. Every time we pulled up to an accident scene or a fire and another company was there, I would get looks, there would be whispers, and then there would be the ones who came right up to me to inform me that I shouldn't be there and was a disgrace to the department.

I normally would ignore shit like that, but most of the guys would jump to my defense before I could even think about walking away and focusing on the job. It helped to know that all of the guys had my back. That no matter how rocky things might get, I was going to have a safe place with Station Twenty-One. That didn't change that today still fucking sucked.

Damon had texted me, asking if I wanted to come by tonight and I had quickly replied yes. The only light in my life right now, the only thing that was simple and just fun was my time with Damon. I knew it wouldn't always stay simple and fun, there was going to come a time when shit between us got real and problems would show up, but I didn't care, because right now it was fun and freeing. He always knew how to make me feel good and he always knew what I needed. It was as if our bodies had known each other for life times and they were enjoying reconnecting with each other.

I grabbed my coat from my locker and made my way out of the firehouse. Most of the guys had already left for the night and

I was the last one. I had decided to take a shower before heading out so I didn't smell like smoke. I knew Damon wouldn't care, he would be used to it, but I still didn't like the smell of smoke seeping from my skin where I could smell it all night.

I exited the building and just as I reached the parking lot I saw Captain Rouke making his way across the parking lot toward me.

Fuck.

I had yet to see the man, even before all this shit about my father came out. I had never met him and it wasn't because I had been avoiding him since I got there. I didn't even know that my father had killed his son. It was just because I was always gone before he arrived. This was not how I wanted to be meeting him for the first time and I had no idea what was going to happen. What he was going to say.

I knew Captain Clarke had spoken with him the day that Mack had shown up and spilled the beans about my father. Captain Clarke had pulled me aside the next day and told me that he had spoken with Captain Rouke and explained the situation. Apparently, Captain Rouke was upset, but he didn't appear to be upset with *me*. I was hoping that meant that he would be okay with me being in the same Station House.

"Probee MacMillan, a word," Captain Rouke said, once I was close enough to him.

"Aye, Captain," I said, because really what else could I say.

"I wanted to speak with you for a moment and clear the air between us. I know we haven't met before, but I am aware that your father is Jamie McDougal. I want you to know that my son was killed in a fire your father started, but I suspect you are aware of that fact."

"Aye, I am now, Captain. I'm sorry about your son. I didn't know until Captain Clarke informed me."

That wasn't fully true, I'd learned about it from Damon first, but he didn't need to know that part.

"My son, he was just twenty-two when he was killed in that fire. He never got married or had children. He was my only child and he had a bright future ahead of him. He was very proud to be a firefighter and he was a natural at it."

I could hear the pain in his voice and I could see that it was a wound that would never scar over. Not that I would ever expect it to. To lose a child was bad enough, but he had lost a child to someone else's actions. Because my father had a compulsion that he couldn't control, Captain Rouke's son was dead.

I could feel the guilt building within me again and it made my chest ache.

I had tried to not feel guilty over the lives my father took and destroyed with his own actions, but it wasn't an easy thing. My mind naturally told me that I should have seen the signs. That I should have noticed what he was doing so I could have stopped it sooner. I knew logically that none of this was my fault. I was just a child and I had no training or knowledge to be able to see the signs of an arsonist. As far as I knew, my father was boring and as average as they come. Still, knowing something and believing it were two very different things.

"I really am sorry, Sir," I said. If I had been a bigger man, a better man, I would have told him I would transfer to another Station House, but I didn't. I didn't want to leave Twenty-One, it was the only place that I knew I would be safe to be myself. That wasn't something I wanted to lose.

"I'm not telling you this so you will feel guilty, son. I am telling you this so you understand that the firefighters your father killed, they were good men and I know they would be proud and honored that you have decided to become a firefighter."

I wasn't expecting his words, at all.

I was expecting for him to yell, demand that I leave, threaten me even. I definitely wasn't expecting to be complimented.

"Sir?" I managed to ask and thankfully, he understood what I meant, because I didn't know if I could get more words out at that moment.

"Every firefighter knows when they respond to a call that there is a chance they could die that day, but they run into burning buildings to save people anyway, because that's who we are. They died in the fires that your father started, but with you becoming a firefighter, they didn't die in vain. My son didn't die in vain, because now every life you save is a life they save with you. You have nothing to apologize for, Cyrus. You didn't start those fires, your father did. You didn't know what he was doing. You were a sixteen year old kid and if you were anything like my son at that age, you were too busy playing video games and talking about girls with your friends. Of course you didn't know what he was doing. Of course you didn't help, and of course you can't be held accountable for the actions of your father. Just like I would hope that no one held my son accountable for the questionable actions that I have made in my life." He flashed me a warm smile, before he moved closer to me and placed his hand on my shoulder as he continued.

"You could have buried your head in the sand. You could have left town and gone on to do something else. But you didn't. You enrolled into the Fire Academy, you decided to become a firefighter, and that right there shows what type of man you are. I am honored and proud to share this fire house with you."

Well, shit.

If that didn't make a man misty-eyed, I didn't know what would. I didn't expect this to be happening. I thought he was going to lose his shit with me, but instead, he pulled some fatherly knowledge and got me all emotional. He understood. He got it without me having to explain or say a single word to him. He understood why I had to become a firefighter, why it was so important to me. He had every right to hate me and try to force me to leave, but instead he was welcoming me with open arms, and that cut deep.

"Thank you, Cap. It really means a lot to me. And I will do my best to honor your son's memory and every firefighter who lost their lives because of my father."

That was a promise that I could easily keep. I was going to make sure that I honored their memory and made them all proud. Captain Rouke was right, every life I saved was a life that they got to continue to live. When I go through those doors, I am doing it with all of them watching my back and hopefully, my fire brothers would help to protect me and keep me alive, so I could keep saving lives for all of us.

"I know you will do them all proud, that you will do *me* proud. Don't carry the guilt around though, Cyrus. It's too heavy and it's not your weight to carry. That weight belongs on the shoulders of your father and only his. Stop making his job easier. He doesn't deserve it."

"I'll try," I promised. But I knew that promise was going to take some work to accomplish. I was just hoping that one day I would be able to achieve it.

"If you ever need to talk, I'm always here for you. Same as the guys on my shift. I have already explained the situation fully and they have your back. You don't have to worry about anyone in this house giving you any sort of problems."

"I truly appreciate that, Sir. And if I need to talk, I will reach out."

"Good. Now, go. Get out of here and have some fun. I have a desk full of paperwork waiting for me." He said it with a groan and I couldn't blame him. The paperwork was insane and not something they talked about in the academy.

I gave him a nod and flashed a warm smile before he headed off. I made my way to my truck and climbed in. I sat there in the driver's seat for a moment, thinking over the conversation I'd just had with Captain Rouke. I was still shocked by his acceptance of the situation, by his lack of blame on me for my father's actions. I honestly had no idea how I was supposed to feel about it.

I felt a lot of things, but mostly just stunned. Never in a million years had I thought the conversation with Captain Rouke would go that way. I was very surprised but also very relieved that it had. I had to admire the fact that he was an understanding man and was able to separate me being my father's son and my father's actions as not being two side of the same coin like so many others did. I hated that he'd had to bury his son because of my father, but it did bring closure and comfort to me to know that he didn't hate me for it.

A ding from my phone snapped me out of my thoughts and I picked it up to see a text from Damon

You on your way?

Just leaving now. Be there soon, Daddy.

I quickly texted him back before I dropped my phone into the cup holder. I knew he was waiting for me and I didn't want to keep him waiting any longer. My own excitement began to build, too.

Letting out a long, slow breath to calm myself down, I pushed my thoughts and feelings about my conversation with Captain Rouke away and focused on getting to Damon's place. I was going to be seeing him and I knew he would make all of my troubles melt away and right now, I needed that more than anything.

CHAPTER THIRTEEN

Damon

I WAS CONFIDENT that I was going to throw up at any minute. I was stuck in one of the stairwells within the courthouse as I waited for my turn to testify. It had been five days since I had been told that Taye's trial date was pushed up and today was the day I was set to testify in open court about our childhood. I knew Taye's lawyer was counting on me to tear my parents apart, but that wasn't going to happen. I wasn't going to let him get away with what he had done.

The past five days had been a rollercoaster. I was enjoying the time I got to spend with Cy. He was so easy to be around and there was a certain kind of peace when I was with him. We had seen each other three times in the past five days and each night was perfect and amazing.

I was becoming addicted to him and I knew it. Not just to his body, but to his personality and presence. He had a way of calming down the anxiety and stress inside me. A way to bring the peace to the storm within me.

I'd never expected to feel that way about anyone, especially someone who was so much younger than me. I knew it was crazy and the chances of us lasting was so slim it was almost impossible, but even knowing that, I couldn't bring myself to stop seeing him.

I wanted him all the time.

Just seeing him and I had to fight with my cock to stay down. He was perfect, as if he was made for me and me alone. Our bodies fit perfectly together and I doubted I would ever get tired of having him around me.

The door to the stairwell opened and my stomach flipped thinking it was going to be the Bailiff to tell me it was my turn. I instantly relaxed when I saw it was Cy coming in. He had come today to provide me with some moral and emotional support. I knew people couldn't see us interacting with each other, at least not more than colleagues would, but I appreciated him being here with me. Just knowing that I would be able to look out into that courtroom and see him sitting there was enough to allow me to breathe again.

He flashed me a warm smile as he closed the door. He was dressed in an all black suit and he looked very good. If we weren't in a courthouse, I would have been tempted to press him up against the wall and fuck him right here.

"How are you holding up?" Cy asked, gently.

I had told him last night that I was worried about testifying. It had been years since I had to testify in court for a case and never for my own flesh and blood.

"I feel like I am going to throw up. This isn't a position I ever expected to be in. Even after Taye was arrested I didn't think I would have to testify. I wasn't even planning on attending the trial, let along being in it. How is it going?"

Because I had to testify, I couldn't be in the courtroom until I had testified. It was standard procedure to ensure that a witness wasn't influenced by what either lawyer said or things other witnesses might disclose. I was stuck here in purgatory until it was finally my turn.

"I have no idea. This is my first time in court. I didn't even go to my father's trial. The jury members, they have no expression on their faces. I can't get a read on 'em. Barba doesn't look worried, though, and it sounds like a solid case."

"What about Tristan, did he testify yet?"

"Aye, he did really good. He didn't shake at all when Fox was questioning him. There are a lot of firefighters sitting behind Taye, showing their support to him. I don't know why, but I didn't expect that," Cy said, shaking his head as he sat down beside me on the stair.

I didn't surprise me at all that there would be firefighters here, most of which would be Taye's fake friends. The ones who needed him to be innocent so they could try and use their friendship with him to get ahead in their careers. There would also be an Upper Brass or two that would grapevine the information on the trial to others. Grown ass men and at the end of the day, we were nothing but a bunch of gossiping fourteen year old girls.

"They have to be here in case he is acquitted. They need to show support without showing the city that the Fire Department is supporting him. You have to remember this isn't just about arson cases or murder cases. This is a firefighter. A *legacy* firefighter. The Fire Department can be sued by every survivor and loved one who lost someone in a fire that Taye or Wilson started. If Taye loses, the Fire Department will be out hundreds of millions of dollars, which means the city will be out that amount. As horrible as his crimes are, the city is hoping he doesn't lose today because then any class action suit loses all hope of being granted."

"So the city would rather have someone as dangerous as Taye back on the street than pay people what they are owed?" he asked, disgust lacing his voice, and I knew that information was a shock to him.

He was new to all of it, but this wasn't my first rodeo with the city and payouts. We weren't talking about a couple of million, we were talking about easily a hundred million between all of the surviving victims and loved ones of those who didn't make it. It would be a nightmare for the city if Taye lost.

"It's a lot of money and you have to remember, Cy, that the city is run by politicians and they don't like giving up their money. He's not going to get away with it, everyone knows that, shit, even he has to know that, but that doesn't change that the Fire Department has to show some type of support for Taye."

"They won't let him back in though, right? I mean, even if by some miracle he is able to get acquitted, the Fire Department won't just give him his job back, right?"

"It's not that simple. Legally, if he is cleared of all charges, he has every right to return to work. But, the Upper Brass can delay his return to work with a bunch of procedures that they would need to take to get him re-instated. They would also be looking for a way to force him to take very early retirement or to place him into a position that would force him to quit. Such as putting him in as a file clerk. Taye could also fight to get his position back with his union rep and a lawyer. He could easily argue he was wrongfully terminated. He could make it appear like Tristan had a vendetta against him and made up all of those lies. That he was there to try and get Wilson to turn himself in and Tristan misunderstood or some other bullshit."

"So, if he gets acquitted it would be a shit show," Cy simply stated, and I nodded. That summed up everything perfectly.

"It'll be fine, that's not going to happen. All the jury will need to see are the two dead kids and hear Tristan's testimony. That's all they need to convict him. The other fires might be circumstantial, but even if we only get a conviction on the homicide of Wilson and attempted homicide of Tristan and Detective West, Taye will go to jail for life."

That was the only reason I was so confident that we would get a conviction on Taye. Arson cases were hard to prove, even when you had a shitload of evidence. If the fire didn't destroy the evidence, the firefighters did when they put the fire out. But homicide and attempted homicide, that had real evidence. There were fibers, shell casings, witnesses, real evidence that ADA Barba could present to the jury and the jury could actually see it. We also had Tristan and Detective West who survived Taye trying to kill them. They were the perfect witnesses, trained to pay attention to even the smallest details and to be able to remember what happened to them with perfect recall. There was nothing that Taye's lawyer could do to discredit them.

The only hope that Taye had was if his lawyer could convince the jury that he couldn't be held accountable for his actions due to a mental deficiency. In this case, he was using our childhood as that defect. It wasn't going to work, because I wasn't going to allow it. It was time for Taye to finally take responsibility for his actions.

Before any more could be said between us, the door opened once again and a Bailiff stood on the other side. I knew without him even having to say anything that it was my turn. The court recess was over and it was showtime again.

"Captain Amaro, they are ready for you," the Bailiff droned in a calm voice, but I could hear the edge to his voice. He most likely wasn't too happy about Taye trying to kill a cop. Court officer or not, he was still law enforcement and he wouldn't be happy about someone trying to kill a fellow brother.

I gave a nod and both Cy and I stood up. I had him walk ahead of me, mostly so I could get a look at his ass one last time before I had to testify. It was a great ass and it looked amazing in the trousers he was wearing.

Fuck, I could not wait until this was over and I could fuck him.

I had planned to wait until we got back to my place, but now I was thinking about pulling off to some deserted area on the way home and pounding into him with him lying across the hood of my car. I had to quickly push that image to the side as I could feel my cock getting hard. The very last thing I needed was going into court with a raging hard cock for everyone to see.

As we approached the door, I let out a long and slow breath, calming my nerves one last time before the door opened and I walked into the courtroom. It was as busy as I had expected it would be. The whole place was packed on both sides. I knew that the one side would be all cops, but there were also some firefighters here to show their support of Detective West and for Tristan.

Detective West may have begun the investigation into Taye and was planning on arresting him, but he had done it with good intentions and fellow firefighters had come around once they heard all of the evidence against Taye and what he was suspected of doing. It also helped to know that Tristan had witnessed Taye killing Wilson and tried to kill him. Going against the brotherhood was not easy, but they also defended and stood by their own even against a fellow brother once it was clear that one was in the right and one was in the wrong.

Cy left me as he went to go and take his seat next to Captain Clarke. His whole team was here to show support for their fellow brother and I appreciated it, but at the same time, I didn't like that others would be hearing about some of the things I'd had to deal with growing up. I didn't doubt for a single second that Taye hadn't told his lawyer about some of the more violent incidents within our home growing up. Just like I knew he would have left out him starting fires and killing animals when he was a child.

I made my way over to the stand and after being sworn in, I sat down and waited for the circus to start.

Fox, Taye's attorney, stood and spoke as he walked over to me. "Captain Amaro, you are the Defendant's younger brother, correct?"

"I am."

"And how would you describe your childhood?"

"It was fine, pretty average," I said with a small shrug. I wasn't going to be giving him anything until I saw what he had.

"Average? According to the Defendant, your father was a mean and violent drunk and your mother was checked out for the most part. Is that how you think everyone's childhood was like?" Fox asked, gently, but I knew it was a bullshit tone. He didn't care about hurting anyone's feelings. He just wanted to win and rake in the money.

"Was our mother checked out most of the time, yes. Did out father drink after work, yes. And yes, at times he got violent and he threw things or yelled. But he never raised a hand to either of us, same as my mother. Our father, as you know, was a firefighter and with that came some problems, but he was loving toward us. Taye had problems his whole life and none of them were because of our parents."

"You were not here to hear Dr. Hamilton's testimony, but after doing a deep evaluation of your brother, it is his professional opinion that the neglect, emotional, and mental abuse has caused irrevocable damage to your brother's mind. You yourself are also seeing a therapist, a Dr. Raitt," Fox started, but Barba cut him off.

"Objection Your Honor. The Defense has no access to the witness' medical file."

"Your Honor, it goes to the Defendant's defense that their childhood has caused irrevocable damage, and therefore, he cannot be held accountable for his actions. The witness' mental stability is completely within the realm of questioning," Fox easily countered and I knew he was going to win. It was fine though, because I was seeing a Shrink *because* of Taye's actions.

"Overruled," the Judge snapped.

"Answer the question, Captain Amaro," Fox said, his voice laced with a smug tone that made me want to punch him.

"After Taye's arrest and him trying to kill one of my subordinates, the Upper Brass in the Department felt it would be best for me to speak with the departmental Shrink to express my feelings and thoughts on the matter. I am still on full active duty. I am not medicated or being requested to take time off. It's just procedure," I simply said in a calm voice.

"*Allegedly* tried to kill Investigator Cole," Fox corrected.

"You can't really claim it's *alleged* when the person he tried to kill still lives," I easily countered.

"Your commentary is not needed, Captain Amaro. Stick to just answering the questions," Fox said and it was clear he wasn't pleased with my comment.

I simply gave him a shrug before he turned and picked up a piece of paper from the table. "It is your claim that you have no mental demons from your childhood?

"That is correct."

He spoke as he turned the paper around to reveal a photo. "Then how do you explain your homosexuality, Captain?"

My blood ran cold as I saw the photo. It was of me and another man kissing outside of the hotel room that I frequently rented. I had no idea that they would be going to hotels and getting security footage.

How the fuck did he even get the warrant for the footage?

And how would he have known to look for it?

He must have had someone following me and I didn't notice. Taye didn't know I was gay. I had kept it hidden my whole life from everyone in my family. I could hear the whispers within the courtroom. This was a shock to everyone and I had no idea how I was going to explain this.

"Objection, Your Honor, the witness' sexual orientation has nothing to do with this case," Barba said, as he popped right up.

"I have to tell you, Counselor, I am agreeing with ADA Barba. You better have a good reason for this display," the Judge said to Fox.

"The witness has claimed that his childhood hasn't left any negative marks on who he is as a man today. This photo is just one of many that would suggest he is lying," Fox said.

"Last time I checked, sexual orientation wasn't a mental defect," Barba countered.

"Some would argue it is. Dr. Hamilton is fully prepared to retake the stand to speak on how some children, especially males, who grow up in a violent and abusive home will turn to homosexuality in order to escape the abuse," Fox argued.

"Not in the eyes of the law," Barba said, annoyed by Fox and what he was trying to pull.

I was still trying to figure out how to breathe. This wasn't what I was expecting and I had no idea what I was going to say. How could I deny it, when he had a photo of me, apparently multiple photos of me.

But could I really say I was gay right here in this courtroom, in front of people that barely knew me?

"And under the law, I have the right to question a witness about his career, personality, sexual orientation, and any addiction if it could be relevant to the Defendant's case, which this is. It has already been proven within the law that a person's sexual orientation can be altered from traumatic experiences," Fox stated.

The Judge took a breath and I could see that he was debating. It was a fine line and he wasn't sure how to walk it. After a moment he spoke. "I am going to allow this, but tread very lightly, Counselor," the Judge warned.

"Captain Amaro, that is you in the photo, correct?" Fox asked as he brought it over to me.

I could see that it was one of the random men I had hooked up with off Grinder. I didn't even remember his name. I knew what he wanted me to say, I knew what I had to say, I just didn't know if I could say it.

I looked out and saw Cy looking back at me. He flashed me a warm smile and gave a small nod. I could feel his support being sent to me. I moved my gaze over to Will, my best friend and a gay Captain within the Fire Department.

"It's okay," he mouthed at me before he gave me a strong smile.

I knew there was going to be a conversation about the news with him later. He was going to understand why I kept it quiet with everyone else, but he was going to be upset that I didn't tell him. He was gay and had come out himself not that long ago, so he knew what this felt like. Well, not like this exactly, but he knew how it felt to come out at our age. I never thought I would come out, but Fox was giving me no other choice.

Letting out a small sigh, I made sure I sat up straight and held my head up high. If I was going to be coming out about my sexuality, then I was going to be confident about it. I had nothing to be ashamed of.

"Yes, that is me in the photo. And to answer your next question, yes, I am gay."

Holy fuck.

That actually felt good.

CHAPTER FOURTEEN

Cyrus

MY HEART SANK as I could do nothing but sit there and listen to Taye's lawyer trying to force Damon to admit to being gay. It disgusted me to begin with that he was trying to use Damon's sexuality as a way to justify Taye's defense. Being gay had nothing to do with a mental deficiency and it wasn't an excuse to justify starting fires and killing people. I wanted to scream at Fox to shut the fuck up and leave Damon alone, but I couldn't. I couldn't do anything but sit there and watch while Damon fought with his thoughts and emotions.

"Yes, that is me in the photo. And to answer your next question, yes, I am gay," Damon said with pure confidence.

I couldn't help the smile that spread

across my face. Damon had been forced to come out of the closet, but he was doing it with grace and confidence and I was very proud of him. I could see Captain Clarke giving Damon a warm smile and I knew that the Captain was very proud of his best friend. I also knew there was going to be one hell of a conversation between them later.

"I have a lot of photos, over fifty of them, with you and different men, some of the photos are you with multiple men going into a hotel room. Some of the photos show the men carrying alcohol and drugs. You can clearly see that there are ecstasy pills and cocaine in at least a dozen photos. Have you ever done drugs, Captain?"

I knew that Damon had been with other men—shit, we met on Grinder—but the drugs were new. I didn't know he had been with other men who were drug users or that he might have done some. I wasn't a prude. I wasn't a stranger to party drugs. I had never partaken in them, but I had been to a few parties where they were being passed around. I didn't expect for Damon to be the type of person to be using drugs, so that accusation came way out of left field.

"Within the past three months I have

done ecstasy and cocaine on multiple occasions, but always while I am off duty."

"So, to clarify, promiscuous sexual activity, drug use, and drinking. It sounds to me like your childhood left its own scars on you, Captain," Fox said with a smirk before he continued. "No further questions, Your Honor."

Fox went back over to his seat as Barba stood up and I was really hoping he was ready to do damage control, because there was no way he saw any of this coming.

"Captain, let's get the giant elephant out of the room first, shall we? When was the first time you did drugs?" Barba started.

"Three months ago. I've never done any drugs, not even marijuana, before that. I used to drink only on Friday or Saturday nights, and even then it didn't happen often. I also never used to have random hook ups. It all changed three months ago."

My heart went out to him. He had everything figured out and then three months ago his older brother went off the deep end and tried to kill someone he worked with. He discovered that his own brother was an arsonist who could give my own father a good run for his money. I still remember how I felt when the rug got pulled out from under me when I was sixteen. I didn't handle it well either, so I could understand Damon's need for an escape, in any form that he could get it in.

"What prompted the change in you?" Barba asked gently.

"Taye's arrest. I felt guilty. I still feel guilty about not seeing it. Two innocent children were killed, a good Detective was almost killed, and one of my best investigators was almost killed. I just needed to not feel the guilt or anger for a little while. I admit, it was wrong of me to do it. It's not who I am, nor who I wish to be."

I could hear the guilt and remorse in his tone. I knew that Damon had been struggling with Taye's case and everything that it meant for him. I hated that I couldn't hug him right now and tell him it would be okay. I wished I could make it all better for him, but I was going to have to wait until we left to make that possible.

"What were your parents like?" Barba asked.

Damon let out a small huff before he spoke. "Our mother was a good woman. She was great with us growing up until Taye was about twelve. Then, she started to feel overwhelmed with everything. Our father had been going through some hard fires, he lost a few men and he almost died three times. She was overwhelmed with having to be there for our father and his trauma. Our father, he never used to drink, but as the fires got worse, he started to drink more. He used to yell and throw things, but like I said, he never raised a hand to any of us. On his days off though, he would spend the time with Taye. They would go to the firehouse and use the burn house to run drills. Our father taught Taye how to start a fire and to control it."

God, I couldn't imagine why a parent would think that would be a good idea. I get that he was a firefighter and he wanted to share his job, something that took up the majority of his time with his children, but that didn't sound like good parenting to me.

"And what was Taye like?" Barba asked next.

"Objection, Your Honor, the witness is not a professional. He can't speak on my client's behavior," Fox tried.

"He doesn't have to be a professional to speak on his own memories. He grew up with the Defendant. He can speak on his own memories of his brother," Barba said, annoyed that Fox would even try and block his line of questioning.

"Agreed. The objection is overruled. The witness may answer the question," the Judge decided.

Nice try, Fox.

"He had always been different. There had been a few times where I overheard our parents talking about him. Our mother was worried about Taye spending so much time with our father at the firehouse. He had been starting fires since he was six. That's what made our father bring him around the firehouse. He thought Taye was just interested in what he did. It helped to control his urges for a bit, but then he began to start fires on his own, bigger ones. He had been killing small animals. One day when he was fifteen, I came home from school and he had taken our neighbor's cat, put it in a storage bin and set it on fire. He watched as it burned to death. I told our parents and Taye had to go and speak with someone. After that, our father's drinking got worse and I wasn't allowed to be left alone with Taye. I would sleep in the couch in the living room so I wouldn't be alone in the bedroom at night with him."

Fuck all mighty, how the hell did Taye ever pass the mental evaluation for the

Fire Department?

There were so many red flags and everyone seemed to ignore them because of his last name. He never should have been allowed to be in the Department. Yes, even if he hadn't been allowed to be a firefighter, he still would have been an arsonist, but maybe he would have been caught sooner.

"I'm sorry you had to see that, Captain. In your opinion only, do you think your brother knew what he was doing when he started those fires? When he tried to kill Investigator Cole and Detective West?"

"He knew. From a professional viewpoint, those fires were meticulously planned. Each home was chosen and surveillance was done. The smoke detectors were removed; the cameras were installed and hidden. For a decade, Taye had been able to plan those fires all the while working for the Fire Department. He was able to balance both lives without anyone even suspecting it. In my opinion, Taye doesn't have a mental deficiency. In fact, he's a criminal genius to be able to live in both worlds so perfectly."

Wasn't that the truth right there. No one suspected that Taye was an arsonist. Having to hide a huge part of yourself like that, it couldn't be done by someone who wasn't playing with a full deck. He was a genius and it wouldn't surprise me at all if he was a psychopath.

"Thank you, Captain Amaro. No further questions, Your Honor," Barba said with a polite smile before he turned and went back to his spot.

"The witness is dismissed. We will recess for ten minutes as the next witness is brought in," the Judge said, before he banged his gavel.

I watched as Damon got up and started to make his way toward me. He was heading for the door and I was not surprised at all when he kept going. I knew he needed air. That had been a lot and he had expected none of it. There was simply no preparing for that.

I made my way out after him and when I reached him I simply walked beside him, allowing him to guide the way. We headed out of the courthouse and he walked until we got to his vehicle. I didn't even think twice about climbing into the passenger seat as he got into the driver's side.

He turned the key in the ignition as he let out an audible sigh. He shifted the vehicle into gear without a word and then we were heading out of the parking lot.

I sat there in silence, knowing he

needed some time to get his thoughts and feelings in order. The fact that he didn't tell me to go away indicated that he wanted me to be around him. That he wanted to talk about what I had just learned about him. I was more than happy to talk about it, once he was ready.

We drove to the waterfront and once there, he parked and climbed out of the car. I climbed out after him, making my way around to the front of the car at the same time he did. We walked down to the water and he sat down on top of one of the picnic tables. I climbed up beside him and just enjoyed the heat of the sun against my face for a beat.

"I'm sorry you had to find out that way," Damon started after a few moments of silence.

"You don't owe me an apology, D. We've only known each other less than a month. We're still learning plenty about each other. There's a lot you don't know about me, too. After everything you've been through with your brother's case, it's only natural that you would be looking for an escape from reality for a little while. What is going to happen when it gets back to the Upper Brass?"

I was worried that he might be losing his career all so he could make sure Taye was in prison where he belonged. That wouldn't be fair to him and it wasn't like he was a drug addict or in active field duty. He sat behind a desk all day. I was hoping that meant he wouldn't be fired.

"Random drug testing and I will be seeing Dr. Raitt for a lot more than I would like, but maybe it's a good thing. Be able to talk about all of this with someone that is a professional and can help me deal with the guilt in a healthier manner. I didn't want to say anything in court, but growing up wasn't peachy. There are moments that still bother me. Some memories from Taye, but also my father and the pressure he put on me, the times where he just barely controlled himself from hitting me. Maybe it's time that I finally fixed my head."

I hated that he had been through something that still lingered inside him. I could understand what he was feeling, though. My life had been pretty perfect up until my father was arrested. After that, it went to shit for two years and I did some things I shouldn't have. Like having sex with my teacher and older men before I was even of legal age. Him speaking with a Shrink, it would be good for him. It would be a way that he could talk about what has been bothering him and he could get some tips on how to cope and work through it. And I was very relieved to hear that he wouldn't lose his job over it. He didn't deserve that.

"I think that's a great idea. If you feel like it could help, then you should do it and I completely support you. I know I'm not a professional, but I'll always be there if you ever feel like you need to talk about something," I said, flashing him a warm smile.

"I appreciate that. You need to know that even though I just came out, and by tomorrow everyone in the department will know I'm gay, it doesn't mean people can know about us. And that has nothing to do with me being ashamed or trying to put a genie back in a bottle. You're on probation and the last thing you or your career needs is people thinking you passed your probation period because you're sleeping with me. You need to establish a reputation and respect within the department before we drop that bomb into the water."

I was actually really relieved to hear him say that. I didn't want to hide our relationship, but I also didn't want it to come out just yet. I completely agreed with him. I needed to be able to build a reputation off of my skills and not because people thought I was that good at sucking cock. I was that good, of course, but it wasn't what I wanted people to talk about. I was also still dealing with the fallout of practically everyone knowing I was Jamie McDougal's son. I had to let the waters calm back down before something else came out.

"Aye, I completely agree. It actually makes me happy to hear that you think that as well. I was worried you would be upset that I wanted to keep this, us, a secret for a bit longer."

"Not at all. Besides, sneaking around can be a lot of fun," he said with a sexy smirk and it had my cock pulsing. This man was sex on a stick and just as deadly.

"Aye, that it can. We headin' back to the courthouse?"

Fuck, I hope not.

"I wasn't planning on it. I had other ideas on how to spend the rest of the day," he said, flashing me a cheshire grin as he looked me up and down and I knew exactly what he was thinking.

"I was really hoping you would say that. I'm wearing the new toy you got me," I said, flashing him with what I hoped was a sultry smile.

Damon gave a groan before he stood

up. "We have to go," he said in a hurried tone and I couldn't help but chuckle at the reaction.

We practically ran back to his car and climbed in. I buckled up mere seconds before he cranked the engine and reversed out of the lot. His excitement was damn near palpable, and quite contagious.

I knew everything between us was still so fresh and it would most likely simmer down, but until that happened I was going to enjoy every single second that I could with him.

EPILOGUE

Three Months Later...
Damon

IT WAS CRAZY what a difference three months could make.

Six months ago, my brother was being arrested for multiple arson and murder charges. My whole world had been destroyed and I spiraled almost out of control. For three months after that, I spent my time when I wasn't working fucking every guy that I wanted, getting drunk, and even doing drugs. Then just three months ago, Cy walked into my life and everything since has changed.

The pain, the anger, the guilt, the storm that had been raging inside of me started to disappear.

I was able to find my way back to myself and it was all because of him. The trial for Taye had been hard. Everyone discovered that I was not only gay, but I had been using drugs recreationally and screwing random men. It resulted in a very long conversation with Will, but I'd expected that. It also resulted in me being pulled into my boss' office first thing in the morning to discuss my future with the Fire Department. It wasn't anything extreme; it was exactly what I had expected. Random drug testing and mandatory therapy sessions with Dr. Raitt for the next six months.

I was fine with it and I was enjoying the therapy sessions with Dr. Raitt. He was helping me to resolve my guilt over Taye's actions. He was helping me to accept who I am and how to deal with some of the things that happened growing up. It had been good to speak to someone where I didn't have to worry about him judging me or trying to bring up things and throw them in my face later. I could tell him anything and he would listen and offer his thoughts or he would help to come to a realization on my own.

I had told him about Cy roughly a month ago and it had been very good to be able to talk about it with someone. I hadn't even been able to tell Will about him because he was Cy's Captain and I didn't want to make things awkward or weird for either of them, especially Cy.

He had also been doing really good for himself at the firehouse. He was building a reputation and I couldn't be more proud of him. Things were finally starting to cool off with him and other firefighters. He was finally making progress with all of that. It terrified the hell out of me knowing that he was running into burning buildings every day, but it was also something I was working through. The very last thing I wanted was to become my father or my mother. I had to be able to handle Cy being an active firefighter or our relationship was going to be doomed like theirs had been.

As for Taye, he was currently serving three consecutive life sentences in a maximum federal prison. He had been found guilty on all charges, including the arson cases. The only reason he didn't get the death penalty was because his surviving victims got together and decided that being trapped in prison for the rest of his natural life was a worse punishment then getting to go to sleep.

I have to say, I agree with them. At least while he is in prison, he will know what it feels like to be trapped in a place that you want nothing more than to escape from. As his brother, I should be horrified at the idea of him being trapped there, but knowing that he can't ever hurt another innocent person again is a huge relief.

I hadn't visited him and I have no plans to. I knew he would never give me a straight answer about anything and I would just be feeding into his control. I was done with him having the control and trying to manipulate me into doing his bidding. It was time I got to live my life the way I wanted to live it, and that was exactly what I was doing.

I glanced over and saw Cy wiggle once again in his seat. We were currently heading to a restaurant in a nearby town. It was something we had started doing three months ago so we could have normal date nights and not have to worry about someone seeing us together. It was a compromise that we had come to.

We both knew we had to keep our relationship a secret for now. Cy deserved the time to build his skills and his reputation before we made our relationship public. However, we both wanted to try actual dating with each other and that meant going on real dates and not just fucking each other at one of our places. Going to a nearby town was the best solution that we could come up with. It would allow us to hold hands and kiss in public without having to worry about being recognized.

Tonight was date night and I was taking us to an Italian restaurant for dinner. Tonight was a bit different though, because tonight I had made sure that Cy wore tight pants, but also a vibrating dildo was currently in his ass to keep him nice and hard for me. To top it all off, there was nothing to stop him from coming except his own willpower. He was currently trying to handle the dildo on the middle setting and I could tell it was driving him crazy, but that was exactly what I wanted. I wanted his body so sensitive tonight when I fucked him that he couldn't stop screaming and begging for more.

"You okay there, Baby?" I asked, flashing him a smirk.

"Oh fuck, Daddy," he half moaned and whined.

I knew it was going to be a first for him and it was going to be difficult for him to get used to, but I knew he would love it and I was going to love watching him try to eat and have a conversation while he sat hard as a rock at the table in a room full of people for an hour or more.

The sex over the past three months had become very intense and remarkable. Cy was very open to try anything and his body was so responsive to me. It was as if we were both made for the other and only the other's body could bring true pleasure to each of us. There was a great deal of trust that went into what we had. He had to trust that I knew what his body wanted and would find pleasure in, and I had to trust that he would tell me when he needed me to slow down or stop. So far, we had been on the same wavelength and it felt amazing. I knew there was going to come a time when one of us had to say no or pump the brakes, but I was okay with that. It happened in every relationship and I would never push Cy to try something that I knew he wasn't ready for or something he wouldn't find pleasure in. What we were currently doing was new to him, but I knew he was going to love it because he had shown me that he would from our time together.

I pulled into the parking lot for the restaurant, and after turning my car off, I looked over at Cy. I could see the pleasure all over his face, but I could also see some nerves starting to build as well. I knew he had worn a plug in public, but this was taking things to the next level and I wasn't certain he was ready for it now that we were here. I reached over and placed my hand on his knee, making sure I had his attention before I spoke.

"Tonight can go one of two ways and how we spend it is completely up to you. The first way, I can turn the device off and we can go inside and have a nice dinner before heading back to my place. Or way number two, the device stays on and we go inside and have a nice dinner before going back to my place. I don't care what option we do. Both will result in a great night and us having amazing sex. The choice is completely up to you and what you are comfortable with."

I meant it, too. I didn't care what we did. All I cared about was getting to spend time with him. Being able to go out on a date like a normal couple. If the devices were on for it, then great, but if not then that didn't change how I felt. There would be no disappointment. I didn't want him doing something he didn't feel comfortable with, because then the fun was taken out of it and that wasn't the point in what we were doing.

I could see him thinking about it for a moment, but after a second he gave me a warm smile. He moved in and pressed his lips against mine. I placed my hand on the side of his neck, pulling him into me and deepening the kiss.

I loved kissing him.

I usually didn't care for kissing much, but with Cy I could do it all day and night and never get tired of it. All too soon, he was pulling back and flashing me that sexy smirk of his before he spoke.

"Let's go."

Option two it was, and I would be lying if I said my own cock didn't get hard at hearing which one he had chosen.

We both got out of my truck and I placed my hand on the small of Cy's back, guiding him over to the entrance and inside. The place was pretty packed, not surprising considering I had to make a reservation just to get us a table. The hostess gave us a warm smile and I gave her my name for the reservation.

"Um... yes, right. Um, right this way," she said.

She guided us over to our table, which just so happened to be in the middle of the room. I guided Cy through the room and held his chair out for him. Cy slid into the seat and I sat across from him in my seat. I could see other patrons looking over at us and I could see a slight blush creep up Cy's cheeks, but I could also see the arousal in his eyes. He was enjoying this, just like I suspected he would.

"This place is nice," Cy managed to say as he looked around.

"It is nice. I've never been here, but everything that I read online said it was a great place with really good food. Do you have a favorite pasta dish?"

"Not really," he said with a small shrug.

He didn't even bother with looking at the menu; he knew I would order for him. It was something that we did. Cy was very easy going and he didn't mind being told what to wear or me ordering his food for him. He was pretty used to it from his past relationships and I liked that he trusted me with making these small decisions for him.

The waiter came over and I placed our drinks and food order. Once he left, I reached into my pocket and turned the device up a bit higher. Cy let out a whispered moan as the pleasure within him started to peak. I knew it wouldn't be long before he was coming for the first time tonight, the first of many.

"You okay?" I asked with a knowing smirk.

"Don't suppose we could just skip to dessert, huh?" Cy countered with a small smile as he tried not to wiggle too much in his chair.

"Now where would the fun be in that, Baby?" I said with a playful wink.

"How, um... how was work?" he asked, and I could tell he was trying to focus on a conversation and not the pleasure that was currently overtaking him.

"It was good. Busy with paperwork. We also have been going through Investigators. Ever since the Upper Brass discovered what Mack did to you on your father's case, all of the old timers have been getting looked over. The Upper Brass want me to go through their files and make sure they didn't compromise anyone's rights or take things too far. I have to go through their conviction rates as well. It would appear the Upper Brass are looking to tighten things up."

"That's not a bad thing, though."

It wasn't. It just meant I had a lot more work because even though the Upper Brass had finally figured out that some of the firefighters and investigators were too old school and they were getting lazy in their old age, not everyone wanted to retire. I understood that and there was no problem with having older people on staff. The problem came when they got too comfortable with their bad habits and laziness. Conviction rates were important and getting the right arsonist meant we would prevent future fires. It was time for the Investigation Division to get a complete overhaul and I was very happy with it finally happening.

"It's not. It just means more work for me, and some pissed off investigators, but they will simply have to deal with it. If they have done their job properly and to the best of their abilities, then they have nothing to worry about. What about you? How was your day?"

Things had gotten better for Cy with the other firefighters that he was frequently around outside of Twenty-One. There were still plenty of people who didn't believe he should be in the Fire Department but thankfully, they were fewer than they were three months ago when the news broke out about Cy's father. It also helped that people started to hear about how Mack treated him the night he arrested his father. That gained him some sympathy votes and even though I knew Cy wasn't happy about them, I was relieved to have less people to worry about.

"It was," Cy started, but then he stopped as he had to bite down on his lip to cover the moan that was threatening to escape.

I was still able to hear it though, and a quick look around told me the few tables around us could hear him. I kept my eyes locked onto him as he rode each wave as he came right there at the table. I knew his cum would be soaking into his boxers and then it would soak through his jeans and I couldn't wait until we left and everyone saw the wet spot on his pants.

Fuck, this man was perfect and one day, if everything worked out, I was going to marry him.

After a moment Cy let out a shaky breath as he tried to calm his body down, not something that was easy to do considering the device was still going.

"I'm sorry, I didn't quite get that, how was work?" I asked, flashing him a smirk.

"Um... it was, um, it was fine. We didn't have many calls today, so it was a good day in that sense."

"Good, I'm glad you had a good day. How's your night going?"

"Fucking awesome," Cy said with a shaky breath as the waiter brought over our drinks.

Once he left, I picked up my whiskey and held my glass up as I spoke. "Tonight is all about you, Baby. You came into my life a little bit over three months ago and you were only supposed to be a quick fling and that was all. But then you changed my whole world and now I can't imagine not having you in my life. You are a wonderful human being and I'm madly in love with you."

I could see the slight surprise flicker through his eyes. I hadn't told him I loved him yet, just like he had never said it to me, but we both knew the other felt it. We both knew we were in love, but we had no reason to say it with words.

Tonight, I was saying it and I had every intention of saying it every night after this.

"I love you, too," he said warmly as he gave me the most radiant smile I had ever seen.

We clinked our glasses together and I knew that tonight was going to be the night that changed everything. He had already changed my world when I opened that hotel door to see him standing on the other side.

And he continued to change my world every day after that.

It had only been three months, but I was looking for thirty more years with him and I knew I would get it. Whether we were soul mates in another life or not, it didn't matter, because in this life he was my soul mate and I couldn't wait for whatever else the world had in store for us.

Thank you for reading Cyrus and
Damon's story.
Continue the series with Jase, book 3
in Smokejumpers!

JASE

SMOKEJUMPERS

BOOK THREE

BY EVIE RILEY

DEAR READER

While many readers say my books are often dark and gritty, and that may be true, I also think they contain realistic themes that plague us in every day life. Which is why I would like to mention that *Jase* may contain some scenes that could be a trigger or very uncomfortable for some readers. **If you need to skip those memories, please do.**

The descriptions of some historical incidents in this book are graphic and detailed. This is necessary to ensure readers understand the effect bullying can have on a person's psyche, often leading them to make less than positive life choices, and the consequences of those actions can last a lifetime.

In this story and in real life, both main characters spent several years in therapy to overcome their respective issues, even though I have skipped those formative years in the book. I contemplated starting from their teen years, but when I began writing I found the traumatic and horrible ruminations of such a childhood too much. I can only imagine how hard it was to actually live through it, so my utmost kudos go out to these men and the many more like them.

Could I have crafted this story without the details I did include, the memories of Jase and Quinn both? Probably. But the impact wouldn't have been the same, in my humble opinion, and the person for whom the memories were written for deserves to have his story told, even if it is in a fictional manner.

I would like to take the opportunity to encourage anyone who is being bullied, or suffering suicidal ideations, or for *any* reason whatsoever is in need, to seek out help. Someone does care.

Support is available 24 hours a day, 7 days a week through 9-8-8: Suicide Crisis Helpline.

Help is also available through Kids Help Phone (1-800-668-6868) and the Hope for Wellness Help Line (1-855-242-3310).

ACKNOWLEDGEMENTS

I'd like to give a nod and shoutout to Justin Menard, the owner of Bolt, the hottest and only LGBTQIA+ bar/dance club in Lafayette, which is mentioned in this book.

Also, Mary Gresham, thank you for being so awesome. Keep on reading! <3

Readers, if you are ever in the Lafayette, Louisiana vicinity, make sure you drop in and tell them Author Evie Riley sent you. ;)

CHAPTER ONE

Quinn

I STOOD THERE, the deafening roar of the flames drowning out everything else. The older warehouse loomed above us, a monstrous entity swallowing the night. My fellow firefighters, a band of brothers and sisters, geared up beside me. We exchanged nods, words stolen by the crackling inferno before us.

"Sanders, you ready for this?" Captain Hagan shouted, his voice muffled by the mask that obscured his face. I nodded, the weight of my gear comforting in its familiarity.

We charged into the heat, a relentless wall of fire waiting to consume us. Smoke stung my eyes as we pushed forward, our hoses spitting defiance against the red fury. My helmet shielded my face from the intense heat, but sweat soaked my clothes as we advanced through the orange haze. The embers danced like fireflies, and the air was thick with the acrid scent of burning wood, a reminder of the unforgiving challenge ahead.

I swallowed the harsh taste of fear, a veritable lump in my throat as we trudged through the powerful flames toward the center. Black smoke clung to the air like a shroud as we pushed forward, the red fury rolling through the room feeling even hotter now. Adrenaline surged through my veins, pushing back the almost all consuming panic that threatened to take my knees out from under me with each step.

I could do this. Had done so more times than I could count. I breathed the warm oxygen through the mask. In, out, in... the repetitive motions calming my thudding heart, centering me, if only a little.

The building groaned and shifted, its walls creaking in protest. My radio suddenly crackled to life, the voices echoing, overlapping with urgency.

"We need backup on the west side! It's spreading too fast!" I heard the voice of my teammate, Irving Jessop, crackle through the airwaves.

"Roger that! Hold if you can, Jessop!" Captain Hagen shouted into his radio, his silhouette a beacon in the darkness mere steps in front of me.

We fought, not only against the fire but against time itself. My heart raced, adrenaline coursing through my veins as I swung my axe, smashing through obstacles and punching through fire-brittle walls in our path. The heat was relentless, a punishing force that tested the limits of our ability.

"Sanders, watch your back!" shouted Jakes, one of the newer recruits. I turned just in time to see a flaming beam hurtling toward us. Instinct kicked in, and I pushed Jakes out of harm's way, the beam crashing down with a shower of sparks behind me, the rush of sound, almost a physical force, overwhelming my eardrums.

The warehouse seemed to breathe, a living entity with a desire to consume us. The walls shuddered, and panic gripped the air.

"We gotta get out, now!" Captain Hagan's order cut through the chaos.

Retreating was a battle in itself. Smoke thickened, visibility reduced to shadows dancing in the haze. My lungs burned, each breath a reminder of the peril we faced. The sound of creaking beams overhead sent a chill down my spine.

"Move, move, move!" Captain Hagan screamed into the darkness, the creaks and groans of the beams now reaching a fever pitch that made my ears ring.

We stumbled back, racing to retrace our earlier path toward the door, toward freedom, the fire chasing us like a relentless predator. The world became a blur of orange and black, and I felt the building shudder beneath my feet.

Then it happened—the deafening roar, the ground trembling and then heaving beneath my boots, everything around me became a moving maze of broken footings and charred obstructions.

I turned, horror gripping my chest as the warehouse crumbled, a cascade of fiery chaos sucking the very breath from my lungs. The flames licked at my heels as I sprinted for the flashing lights visible just through door, a desperate escape from the collapsing nightmare.

The air was thick with ash, and my heart pounded in my ears. I emerged from the inferno, coughing and gasping for air. I turned back to witness the once-mighty structure reduced to a smoldering ruin. The guttural roar of the fire had silenced, replaced by the crackling of embers.

JASE

The realization hit me like a physical blow—my comrades, my brothers and sisters, gone. A lump formed in my throat, and my hands trembled as I surveyed the devastation. The weight of my survival pressed heavy on my shoulders, a guilt that threatened to consume me.

CHAPTER TWO

Quinn

THE FLICKERING GLOW of the television illuminated the dim room, casting shadows that danced along the walls. The remote felt heavy in my hand as I hesitated to press play. I punched the button and the news anchor's voice filled the stony silence, a voice that seemed too cheery for the story it carried.

"Breaking news in New Orleans tonight. A devastating warehouse fire claimed the lives of several firefighters. The blaze erupted late last night, turning the structure into an inferno that raged for hours. The cause of the fire is still under investigation."

The images on the screen painted a vivid picture of the chaos I had left behind. The orange glow of the flames, the billowing smoke, the silhouettes of firefighters battling an enemy that cared nothing for mercy. My comrades, my brothers, their faces frozen in time on the screen.

I felt the lump in my throat grow, an ache that mirrored the pain in my chest. The news report continued, listing the names of the fallen, of the men and women in my company, on my shift—people who had become friends in my time at the firehouse—each mention like a hammer striking my heart. Hagen, Jakes, Jessop, MacDonald, Ramirez, Kramer. Their images flashed on the screen—faces etched with determination, smiles that echoed in the recesses of my memory.

Survivor's guilt clawed at me, an invisible weight that threatened to crush my spirit. A tear slipped down my cheek, and I wiped it away angrily, as if the physical act could erase the emotional turmoil within me.

The newscast moved on to interviews with grieving families, the raw pain evident in their eyes. I watched, a silent spectator to the aftermath of a tragedy I had somehow escaped. The remorse weighed heavier with each passing moment, my breaths becoming shallow, my chest constricting, the pressure building as I grappled with the harsh reality.

I reached out to the screen, fingers grazing the faces frozen in time. "I'm so sorry," the words slipped from my lips, a whisper lost in the stillness of the room. The ache in my chest intensified, overwhelming me and stealing my breath from my lungs just as the heat and flames had right before the world had crumpled around me, and I opened my mouth in a silent scream that echoed inside my head.

The room seemed to close in around me, the walls pressing in as if trying to suffocate the responsibility and sorrow that clung to my soul. I punched the remote, shutting off the television and plunging the room into darkness once more. The silence was deafening, broken only by the distant wail of a siren, a haunting reminder of the world outside.

I sat amidst the shadows, my mind a storm of emotions—grief, guilt, and a profound sense of loss. The weight of my survival bore down on me like a heavy cloak, and the faces on the screen lingered in the shadows, with accusing eyes that only I could see.

In that moment, the room felt colder than the night of the inferno. The flames may have taken the warehouse, but the fire within me continued to burn, fueled by the memories of those who would never return.

The days that followed the blaze were a blur of debriefings and condolences. Sleep came fitfully, haunted by the screams and the inferno's roar. Each face, each laugh, now a ghost that danced in the shadows of my mind.

CHAPTER THREE

Quinn

A WEEK LATER, my livingroom remained shrouded in darkness, the blackout curtains closed tightly over the large windows, a silent sanctuary where my thoughts echoed over and over in my mind, louder than any spoken words would be. The faces of my fallen coworkers lingered behind my eyelids, flashing back at me on repeat, their spirits cast as shadows on the walls, tormenting me each time I opened my eyes. I could almost hear their voices in the stillness, their laughter and camaraderie haunting the air.

The weight of the guilt bore down on me, an oppressive force that threatened to break me. I couldn't escape the relentless questions that echoed in my mind on repeat.

Why me?

Why was I the one who walked away while they became memories etched in the ashes?

I reclined on the couch in my unwashed state, my hair and skin greasy and a foul stench emanating from my skin, the remains of beer bottles and empty food containers littering nearly every square inch in the filth that was now my apartment.

The silence of the room was broken by the distant wail of another passing siren, a reminder that life still continued outside my dark cocoon. I sucked in a deep breath, the air feeling thick and heavy in my lungs. The room seemed to close in around me, and I stood, needing to escape the suffocating stillness.

I paced the room, running a hand through my hair as if trying to grasp hold of something tangible. The images from the news report replayed in my mind—as they had a dozen times or more each day since—the flames, the collapsing structure, the faces of my brothers and sisters frozen in a moment of despair. The guilt twisted in my gut, a relentless knot that refused to loosen its grip.

A framed photograph caught my eye,

nestled among the clutter on a shelf. It was a picture of us, the firefighting crew, taken on a day when the sun shone bright, and laughter echoed in the air. I traced the contours of each face with my fingertips, a bittersweet connection to the past.

"I'm sorry," I whispered again, the words barely audible in the murky room. The stark and silent walls seemed to absorb the confession, offering no solace in return. The photograph became a relic, a portal to a time when we were invincible, untouchable by the harsh reality that had unfolded.

As I gazed at the faces frozen in the frame, anger and determination sparked within me. I couldn't change the past, couldn't undo the choices that led to the tragic outcome, but I could honor their memory. The guilt remained, a scar etched on my tortured soul, but perhaps, in honoring their legacy, I could find a way to carry the weight.

A sudden beep pierced the silence, pulling me from my reverie. I glanced at my phone, and an email notification flashed on the screen. The subject line caught my attention like an icy cold slap, cutting through the haze of my grief.

"Transfer Notice: Firehouse 21."

The words stared back at me, and a bitter taste settled in my mouth.

With a heavy sigh, I opened the email. The words unfolded before me, a new chapter waiting to be written. Firehouse 21, a fresh start in a city that held both memories and a potential prospects. The dark room, once suffocating, now seemed to expand, to lighten just a little as a gentle breeze rippled the edge of curtain open just a sliver, allowing the bright sunlight from outside to pierce the gloom, offering a glimpse of a future yet to be defined.

A fresh start, it said.

A chance to heal.

Firehouse 21.

A new chapter, a new team.

Hope bloomed in my chest for a brief moment.

But could returning to Baton Rouge, my hometown, truly be a new start for me?

I'd fled the city years ago in an attempt to escape from the life I'd led there, and I'd succeeded. I'd started anew in New Orleans already.

Was there even another chance for me to get it right this time?

Did I even deserve another chance?

Doubt dampened the optimism that

had only moments ago raced through my veins like a light in a pitch-black tunnel.

I sighed, staring at the screen, the cursor blinking like a relentless reminder of the past. I wasn't even entirely sure I was ready for this, to return to work, but the mandated psychiatrist had cleared me for duty after only three appointments, so what did I know. Maybe I was as good at fooling him as I was at fooling myself into believing I was okay.

My outlook on so many things had changed recently, the reflection of what could have happened to me in that fire bringing clarity to my mind for the first time in my entire life. Clarity and so much regret. I needed to do better from here on in, *be* better. Maybe I wouldn't make up for all the transgressions of my past, for surviving where all my peers had perished, but I would sure as hell try to make my future something I could be proud of.

I pocketed the phone, the glow of its screen a beacon in the darkness. The shadows of the fallen firefighters lingered, but in that moment, a spark of resilience ignited within me. I had to try. The guilt would remain, but I would carry it forward, a silent tribute to those who could no longer walk beside me.

As I stepped into the bathroom to wash away the filth on my body, to prepare for the tentative future, the shadows in the dark seemed to recede, replaced by a flicker of hope that refused to be extinguished. Firehouse Twenty-One awaited, a new canvas where the echoes of the past and a strong desire to become a better man might just bring redemption and the possibility of a future.

Little did I know, that transfer to Firehouse Twenty-One would thrust me into a world of facing more of my past and thus, future challenges far beyond the flames I had left behind.

CHAPTER FOUR

Jase

"YO, TURNER! YOU actually going to drink that or just stare at it until you fall in it?"

The deep voice pulled me out of the vacant void I stared into without realizing it. I looked up at the guy who was only a year or two younger than me with shaved blond hair, which he could keep up with at home, blue eyes, and a smile that was much too bright for me right now.

My name is actually Jase, but my coworker, Mark, insists on calling people by their last names. Mark Rollins was an interesting guy. Although he never joined any of the out-of-work socials, he was recognized as a good man with a good sense of humor. He was fun to work with and was always the first to make something into a game when the atmosphere got too heavy around the fire station or out on the trucks.

But not even his chirpy attitude could lift my spirits after the three weeks of night shifts. I hated them. Not only did you never see the sun apart from when you went home and tried to sleep, but there were only two extremes of events that occurred even in a city as large and as busy as Baton Rouge. Either everything happened, and there was barely any time to have a breather, or nothing happened, and the minutes just dragged. We were the most central station, so we often got called for most of the events in the city, but there were still plenty of quiet nights where nothing really happened. Sure, on those nights, it was possible to catch some sleep in the bunks, but they weren't comfortable, and the sounds of the station around you would keep everyone awake.

"How the hell do you still have the energy right now?" I asked incredulously. Part of me almost thought he was magic for his energy levels.

Night shifts were usually twelve hours, and it was always four days on, three days off. But at the end of the fourth day, everybody's spirits were always low, and I was constantly irritable. I knew I shouldn't be, or at least I should mask it enough so my colleagues didn't bear the brunt of it, but I couldn't help it. I had never been one to deal well with a lack of sleep.

Still, not even the crappy night shifts every few months could make me think about quitting. I loved my job. It kept me fit and alert, and there was a real feeling of pride when I got back to the station after a fire or during the day when people smiled a little brighter when I told them my occupation. I am slightly more slender than the average firefighter, but that means I get to be an inspiration for all the smaller kids out there who might like the idea of this. I found it was a job where you were admired for the masculinity of it without having to be toxic in the way you portray yourself.

Mark laughed brightly and let his shoulders roll in a shrug. "I have a newborn at home. I'm a pro at functioning on no sleep!"

"What was your excuse before the baby?" Johnson called across the room.

"I got loads of sex!" Mark barked a laugh.

Everyone else laughed aloud at that statement. "Yeah, right," I laughed. "She blue balled you so often, even Captain Rouke got more than you, and he's getting divorced."

Laughter rippled through the crew as Mark shrugged without argument. I decided not to point out that, like everybody else here, Mark had been one to fall asleep in every nook and cranny of the station. It was impossible to do four twelve-hour shifts in a row at night and not doze off when it was lacking in excitement. So long as you did your grunt work and kept your equipment clean and ready, none of the team gave each other hassle for it.

Still, he must be doing something right as Mark was the only one not sitting cradling a coffee like a lifeline as the clock ticked closer and closer to the nine o'clock point, which would allow him to go home and crash.

That was all I could think about. My fresh double bed, still in shadow from blackout curtains, and maybe if I was lucky, the cat who visited from time to time would come in for a snooze.

Unfortunately, it seemed like we would need more time to be able to vanish as soon as the clock struck nine that day. At ten to the hour, the station's Captain walked into the room, and immediately everyone went quiet, hoping there wouldn't be some situation that kept us all here on overtime.

"Morning, everyone," Captain Clarke spoke with a deep voice and an energy he would not be getting returned at this time of the day. He didn't take any notice of the tired mumbles he received in return before continuing. "We've got a new recruit to introduce who will be working your shift patterns. Figured the extra set of young hands would be very helpful since Trevor recently retired. He's been part of the team over in New Orleans, so he knows what he is doing and should be a wonderful asset."

A ripple of relief washed through the team. I could feel it in waves from my closest friends here. Trevor had been a good worker even with his older age, and losing him had left everyone feeling a little spread thin during their hours here. If they had found someone who was already good at the job in general, it would take off a lot of pressure.

A man walked in behind the Captain, and frankly, I had to be very careful to control my expression. At this stage of my life, I was an expert at hiding my attraction to other men, but this man was stunning. He must have stood at nearly six foot three, a good three inches taller than myself; I had always liked a man who was taller than me, and the idea of being able to curl into someone's arms was always my biggest secret. His shirt did nothing to hide the firmness of the muscles that molded his shoulders and chest into something that was difficult not to stare at.

It was his face that really drew me in, though. He had a solid, strong jawline with a very slight dusting of stubble where he hadn't quite gotten close enough with a wet shave earlier that morning. Short, near-black hair was styled into a messy shag toward the front, just long enough to bury fingers into and get a slight grip of. Plump lips with a healthy pink hue to them and deep green eyes sitting under severe brows.

Fuck me.

The man's gaze met mine, and I froze. A dash of brown over his right eye, and though small, the birthmark was unmistakable and something I recognized immediately. Dread, anxiety, and anger pooled in my stomach as I vaguely listened to the Captain's introduction.

"This is Quinn Sanders. He's joining me today to learn the ropes of this place specifically compared to his last station, then it's up to you lot to make sure he settles enough to be good as he was before."

Shit.

It was really *him.*

Quinn Sanders was one of my biggest bullies back in high school. He made my life a living hell... and now here he was, tall, handsome, charming smile.

Fucking dick.

Sure, I wasn't a shabby deal myself. But that didn't stop me from immediately becoming self-conscious as I compared myself to him. It wasn't fair that someone who was such an asshole as a kid could grow up to look like that.

I could not help but scowl a little as I watched Quinn move around the room and introduce himself to the team. Johnson gave me a raised eyebrow when he noticed my expression, but with a shake of my head, I knew he understood that I would explain another time.

"Word of warning, don't drink the coffee. It tastes like shit," I said as he stepped over to shake my hand, placing my half-empty coffee in his extended hand and walking past him without another word. I needed sleep or alcohol right now, probably both if the memories of a young Quinn surfacing had anything to say about it.

CHAPTER FIVE

Jase

THE MEMORIES ASSAULTED me like it hadn't been over fifteen years, reminding me of the horrors of my days in high school and sucking the breath from my lungs.

The school hallway buzzed with the chaotic energy of passing students. Lockers slammed shut, laughter echoed, and the air was thick with anticipation. I navigated through the crowd, trying to stay inconspicuous, but I could feel Quinn's predatory gaze following my every move.

"Look who's here, guys! It's Jase the loser!" Quinn's voice cut through the clamor, drawing the attention of the onlookers. He approached, flanked by his loyal followers, a menacing grin etched

across his face.

"What's up, Jase? Still thinking you belong here?" Quinn taunted, his words dripping with disdain. The hallway became a narrow alley with no escape, and the air grew heavy with tension.

I kept my head down, trying to ignore him, but Quinn wasn't one to be ignored. He shoved me, and I stumbled against the lockers, the metal biting into my back. The metallic taste of fear surged in my mouth, and I bit down on my bottom lip to suppress it. I knew if I showed him my fear it would only spur him on, make things worse than they already were.

"Pathetic," Quinn spat, his cronies snickering behind him. "You're always in the way, Jase. Can't you take a hint and disappear? Like, die already, dude. You're nothing but a waste of space and you know it."

The hallway seemed to close in around me as Quinn's aggression escalated. He grabbed the collar of my shirt, yanking me forward until our faces were inches apart. The stench of his overpowering cologne mingled with the metallic tang of my own blood. I focused in on the small brown birthmark over his right eye, determined to keep my mouth shut, trying desperately to avoid speaking or any sudden movements, anything that might set him off more.

"You think you're tough, huh? You're nothing but a fucking queer," Quinn sneered, punctuating each word with a cruel shove that sent me staggering backward. The taste of copper intensified, and I wiped my mouth, trying to hide the evidence of his attack.

Emotion swirled within me—a toxic blend of shame, anger, and helplessness. Quinn's belittling remarks echoed in my ears, each insult carving a deeper wound inside me as if he had taken a knife and twisted it in my gut. The physical pain mirrored the emotional turmoil that filled my chest, heavy and debilitating, making me wonder if what he said was true.

I was a waste of space, wasn't I?

No one liked me. I could never do anything right so why would they?

I had no friends, no one I could go to who would understand how I felt and take me seriously. So why did I continue to bother?

My parents, as good of parents as they may be, or at least tried to be, just didn't understand me. They were convinced it was just a phase and I would outgrow it soon.

The bell rang, signaling the end of the torment, this time anyway. Quinn and his cronies dispersed, leaving me leaning against the lockers, battered and bruised. The hallway returned to its frenetic pace, but the echoes of Quinn's cruelty lingered, a painful melody that refused to fade. I sucked in a deep breath, swallowing the blood-tinged taste of defeat.

CHAPTER SIX

Quinn

MY FIRST DAY on the job in my hometown had not started the way I had hoped. I watched the light brown-haired man walk away before looking down at the cup he had left in my hand. The liquid inside was black and thick, like tar. A shiver ran up my spine when his eyes met mine from across the room before he turned and walked from the room.

What the hell?

What kind of greeting was that?

"That's Jase Turner, don't mind him. He can get pretty grouchy by the end of a three week stint on nights," the Captain said to me.

But I knew that wasn't what I had just witnessed.

His name was all the explanation I

needed.

He had grown up for sure. Jase had been a weedy little kid at school whose life I had made a living hell. He wasn't the only one, but I had picked on him enough to remember him vividly. I hated myself for who I used to be, I wanted to make things right, but I suspected that wouldn't be so easy having to work with Jase. He clearly had not forgotten me or forgiven my actions.

Deciding to keep that to myself for now, I forced a smile onto my face and nodded along with the Captain's brief description of the team I would be working on. It sounded like they were a close-knit group of guys who trusted each other, there was only one female, Carmen Diaz, but she could run rings around every other person there. Still, if they were all so close, it could pose some problems fitting in.

The station was more significant than the one I was used to in New Orleans, but it was self-explanatory. Everything was generally kept in similar places that I would logically look at when searching for that specific item or piece of equipment. At least that made it easier for me to ponder what I was going to do about the Jase situation.

JASE

If I hadn't known him in the past, he was precisely the type of man I would ask out on a date. His jaw was softly rounded, and his brown eyes were gentle and kind. He had a slight mop of styled hair on his head, which I would have adored to make a mess out of. His nose was straight, but not too long or wide. And he had dimples.

Dimples!

He had the kind of face that most girls dreamed about; one that made their stomachs flutter when they saw him. Of course, I was no girl... but that didn't make him any less gorgeous.

I shook those thoughts out of my head pretty quickly. I would be lucky if Jase didn't hate me enough to convince the Captain to move me to another team, let alone appreciate me checking him out and damn near drooling.

The day didn't take as long as I feared it might after the revelation of who I would be working with.

The fire station was central to a lot of Baton Rouge, so even as I walked out of the front doors that evening, the streets were bustling with students, commuters, and groups of people meeting for a social life I had not yet experienced in this town. It wasn't as lit up and as mystical as New Orleans had sometimes been as the sun began to set, but there was still a sense of pride in the town. There was little graffiti to be found, and a lot of the shops on the walk back to where I was staying were independent and quirky, reminiscent of old-time family businesses that most cities were in the process of destroying with their chain stores.

On the way home, I stopped at the small eccentric coffee shop just around the corner from home. Ordering a large, unhealthy frappe and a double espresso, I couldn't help but chuckle to myself that Jase had been right. The coffee available at the station was utterly god awful and should be illegal.

I sipped at my espresso as I entered the apartment I was staying in. As my parents were still highly God-fearing and I was openly out as a gay man, when I moved back to town, I had figured that it would be easier for all of us if I weren't around constantly. Thankfully, an old friend had come to my aid.

Jared Linwood was someone I knew from school, not one of my peer group, and therefore someone who also ended up bullying alongside me, but an older student who actually kept me from becoming worse than I was. He kept me away from the temptation of drugs and smoking when my peers had started to turn to them. He was like an older brother, and since coming back to town, I was crashing with him.

I would forever be glad for Jared in my life, though I often wished I had been smart enough to listen to all his advice, like now. If I had listened more back then, perhaps I wouldn't have bullied others so much in order to cover my own fears and insecurities... And then maybe I wouldn't be facing the predicament I was in.

But I'd learned and accepted a long time ago that you couldn't change the past. Hell, you couldn't even change other people. The only thing I had any control over was myself and how I lived my life.

"Hey! Awesome!" Jared chirped up as he saw the frappe I held out to him. "What did I do to deserve this? Or do you want something?" He raised an eyebrow at me and laughed.

In the past, I had had a major crush on him for his free attitude, but that had faded over time... and with the knowledge that he was straight and his high school sweetheart would always be the love of his life even if she was always traveling abroad with her work.

"Why do you assume I want something?" I laughed.

"Because I know you."

I shook my head with a slight chuckle as I plopped down on the sofa beside Jared. "I just wanted to ask for some advice," I admitted after a moment.

"See. I know you." Jared laughed, taking a long sip of his frappe before leaning into the back of the sofa and looking at me through his floppy blond fringe. "Go on then, what's up? Bad first day?"

"Not exactly. The Captain was cool, and the team seemed like a close-knit group," I started.

"So... what's the problem?" Jared asked.

"Do you remember a kid at school called Jase Turner?"

"Should I?" Jared raised an eyebrow at me.

Shrugging softly, I leaned back and took a couple more gulps of my espresso. "I suppose not." I sighed. "He was one of the kids I gave hell to..."

"Ah... He's a fireman now?" Jared hadn't taken long to figure that out.

I nodded slowly.

"Yeah. And on my new team. And, by the look of it, he remembers me and is not pleased about my arrival," I explained.

"He said that?"

"Didn't need to. I grew up in a highly religious environment and came out as gay. I know what revulsion looks like." Though his disgust was much more understandable and something I didn't know how to work with.

"Well, there's not a lot you can do about what happened," Jared started, mulling over a mouthful of frappe.

"I could apologize to him," I suggested.

"Is that to make him feel better, or you?"

"Huh?"

"Well, he might not want to acknowledge it. He might still need to be angry to heal from it," Jared mused.

I understood what he meant. It wasn't that anger needed to be out loud, but the anger that could be felt after being mistreated was the part of yourself that knew you deserved better, and learning to accept and deal with that anger in a healthy way was a big step in healing.

I had learned that in the first couple of years away from home.

"What you can do is just show him that you have changed." Jared smiled, though he quickly laughed when I looked at him with confusion. "You know, be a good guy. Work hard. Show you respect him. All that jazz. And if he ever brings up the topic of school, you let him say his piece before you say yours. He's the one who was tormented by you. It ain't his fault you were internally tormented by family and religion."

I let my head flop back onto the back of the sofa, looking up at the magnolia-colored ceiling. "Yeah, I suppose you're right."

I would have much preferred to make things right immediately, but there was also an excellent chance that Jase was expecting me to still be as horrible as I used to be. If there was any chance of forgiveness, he would need to believe I was no longer a danger to his physical or mental health.

"So, what about the rest of the place? Think you'll be cool there?" Jared asked, turning the conversation to the job itself.

"Oh yeah. Bigger than my last station, but that should mean it's better stocked and has the proper manpower." I smiled lightly before glancing at him as Jared clapped me on the shoulder.

"I'm proud of you for getting back to it," he said almost cryptically, knowing the reason I left New Orleans wasn't my favorite topic. "You're doing good, kid."

"Dude. I'm a year younger than you," I protested with a laugh, shoving his hand away.

"And don't you ever forget that that makes me the wise old sage here."

"Senile, more like it."

With the atmosphere much lighter and my head not buried in concerns and regrets, it was easy to let myself relax properly for the evening.

By the time I headed to bed, three beers and a good healthy amount of meat lovers pizza later, I at least had an idea of how to present myself at work after the first few introduction shifts.

CHAPTER SEVEN

Jase

"COME ON, CAP. Can't you just stick him on another team?" I pleaded as my first port of call the moment I walked into the station a few days later.

I had spent the last few days stewing on the fact that Quinn Sanders was joining my team at work. The mere idea of it had me drinking extra and gave me anxiety-like jitters.

Back in school, he had been one of the tall good-looking guys from a good respectable family. His father was a preacher, and so he always turned the other way whenever Quinn's victims were what he deemed as sinners. Quinn had always claimed that I was gay, and that was why he would torment me. He would call me slurs and laugh about how the bible claimed that a man who lay with another man should be stoned while throwing stones at me.

Even though I had never come out and still kept my sexuality a deep secret, his words and actions cut me deep. I wasn't manly enough back then to avoid such torture. I knew the present would be different, though. I had a masculine job, a larger and more manly body frame, my parents approved, and I could get any girl I wanted… but if Quinn was back, I was petrified that he would start back with the old comments. Comments that would make people realize that perhaps I wasn't as straight as I portrayed myself to be.

"I'm sorry, Jase, but you need the manpower more than any other team." Captain Clarke sighed. He didn't really understand; I couldn't share everything without outing myself either.

Fuck.

Imagine being in a job with very fit men and then them all suddenly discovering you were gay and hid it from them. I knew the Captain had come out as gay last year, as had Hawke and a couple others on both our shift and the second shift, but they were different. Cap wasn't on the line like I was but rather sat up in his office most of the time, Hawke had been super-popular since I'd started at the station so even though he'd never hidden that part of himself, no one was going to look down on him for it. Even if they did, it wasn't something Cap would tolerate in his house. I knew that, I did, but I was still convinced they would all get weird around me. They might think I perved on them when we got back from jobs and changed out of smoke-ridden clothes or might hit on them in the showers. I felt sick thinking about how they would look at me with judgment and disgust.

No. Keeping my secret was more important than getting the Captain to understand.

Leaving his office, I headed back to the main room, where we would wait for a call. It had some scruffy old sofas to sit on and a pool table. It also had a little gym area where the staff had pooled money together to get some weights and a treadmill. It wasn't much, but on quiet days, it was nice to do a little bit to keep active.

"Hey, man," Mark stepped over to me and held out a coffee bought from the shop across the road. I took it with a grumble about him being some kind of angel sent from above. Even with a newborn and lack of sleep, Mark was still thoughtful, and he knew how much I hated starting my day with the swill the coffee machine here served... and how I always woke up too late to stop off at a shop myself.

"Where have you been?" he asked, following me to the sofas and plonking himself down.

"Captain's office."

"Shit. Everything good?"

His immediate concern made me chuckle. I suspected that Mark would be one of the few here who I could tell everything, and he wouldn't judge, but I never had the guts to do it.

"Yeah. I just don't want that Sanders guy on the team."

"Why not?"

"Because he's a jackass that I went to school with who bullied people until they tried to kill themselves," I explained, leaving out the fact that one of those people was me. Though, the way Mark looked at me suggested I didn't need to say that part.

"You serious?" he asked.

"Yep. Never made any attempt to change, and being the son of the preacher who taught at the stupidly religious school, he got away with everything." I shook my head.

"Fuck. Yeah, that's not good. If he was like that, he might even end up triggering people that we are trying to help," Mark mused, anger simmering in his eyes. He was a fairly righteous man. He often got into arguments with people who were discriminating, even without realizing it.

"Exactly. And this is the local area to that school... a lot of people will have known him," I said.

"There might even be people here who he tormented. There's a few from your school in the other teams, right?"

I nodded as he looked at me for confirmation.

The door opened across the room, and the man in question walked in. Mark let a small hum leave his throat as we watched Quinn quietly greet Johnson, who was closest to the door.

"We'll keep an eye on him. Leave the rest to me," Mark commented, ignoring my raised eyebrow as he pushed himself to his feet and smiled.

"Quinn, just the man. Got a job for you and your giant height!" he chirped, seemingly as friendly as ever.

"Of course." Quinn nodded with a small smile on his lips, obviously put there to seem polite. A smile that somehow managed to stay there as Mark explained that the tops of all the lockers needed a good cleaning, but no one else was tall enough to do it.

I had been at the station for nearly ten years now, and I had never seen the top of the lockers cleaned. The cleaner who worked here was a tiny little lady who would have had no chance, so everyone had told her not to worry about them. The dust, dirt, spiders, and god knows what else, was something we just ignored. I almost laughed as Mark handed Quinn a pair of gloves and a bucket of hot water for the job.

I didn't expect Quinn to take to the job so easily or to actually do a full and excellent job without so much as a complaint.

The son of a preacher doing cleaning work happily?

Seemed unlikely. I suspected he was just putting on a front for the beginning of the job. At least by lunch, word had gotten around about what kind of man he was.

"Gotta ask, man..." Johnson nudged my shoulder as we cleaned up the equipment on truck fifty-seven. "Were you one of them?"

"What you talking about?"

"I saw the way you froze up when the Captain introduced him. You were one of the kids he bullied, right?"

I raised an eyebrow at the man who was still fresh-faced out of college but a damn good addition to the team. "Was I that obvious?"

"Nah, but me and my twin were bullied in school too, so I know the haunted look it can give you." He shrugged as though we weren't talking about something potentially very painful.

"Huh. Well, yeah, I was," I admitted. "I was a scrawny kid, and I still have a scar from one of those days." And some from the attempt I made to make all the pain end, but that would remain unsaid.

"I get it. If I had to work with my bully, I'd be all over the place. Puts the whole team at risk to be on edge like that." Johnson sighed.

I hadn't thought about it like that.

Damn.

That would have been a much better argument to take to the Captain. There was no way that I was about to trust Quinn with my life out in the field, and sometimes that was a level that was required. It could put my life in danger or someone else's.

I pushed myself up to stand at my full

height, planning on going back to the Captain's office, when the alarm went off.

"Small stove fire on Fern Avenue. Get your asses there quick before it becomes a house fire!" the dispatcher called over the tannoy system as everyone on the team dropped what they were doing and ran for the gear.

Having a another member jump onto the trucks should have been a relief, but frankly, as Quinn slid into the passenger seat next to Johnson with Mark sliding in on the back bench, I immediately jumped into the other truck with Hawke, Carmen, Gage, and Zander. I couldn't help but feel on edge with the man around, even for a routine job like this.

CHAPTER EIGHT

Jase

THE SUN HUNG low in the sky, casting long shadows across the courtyard. I trudged over the blacktop with my head down, backpack pulled tight against my shoulders, trying to make myself smaller, invisible. But high school had a way of amplifying everything, and I could feel his eyes on me before I even saw him.

A towering figure with a twisted grin, Quinn led his entourage straight toward me. Their laughter sliced through the air like a knife, and the scent of impending humiliation filled my nostrils. I tightened my grip on the straps of my backpack, bracing for impact.

"Well, well, look who we have here," Quinn sneered, his voice dripping with contempt. "Jase, the eternal loser. How's it

going, loser?"

The acrid taste of bile rose in my throat as I tried to ignore the jabs, but Quinn wasn't one to be easily brushed off. He shoved me, sending my backpack sprawling across the concrete. Papers scattered like confetti, and the laughter around us intensified.

"Oops, clumsy Jase," Quinn mocked, his lackeys chuckling in agreement. "Maybe you should stick to something you're good at, like being a total failure. Mommy's little gay boy, can't even be a man. More like a girl than anything else, eh, Jase? You like other boys, Jase? "

I clenched my jaw, feeling the sting of embarrassment burning on my cheeks. The metallic tang of blood filled my mouth as I bit down hard on my tongue.

"What's the matter, Jase? Cat got your tongue?" Quinn jeered, a wicked glint in his eyes. "Or maybe you're just too dumb to come up with a comeback."

The bell echoed through the courtyard, a cruel reminder that the torture would have to be cut short. But Quinn wasn't finished. He grabbed my backpack, dangling it high above his head like a trophy, while his lackeys closed in, forming a circle.

"Come on, Jase, reach for it," Quinn

taunted, holding my belongings just out of reach. "Unless you're too much of a wimp even for that."

I could feel the frustration boiling within me, the desire to fight back clawing at my insides. But I held back, not wanting to give them the satisfaction.

"Look at him, guys! Jase is about to cry!" Quinn announced, his buddies erupting in laughter.

The scent of asphalt mixed with the bitter taste of defeat as I stood there, surrounded. Quinn finally dropped my backpack, but not before shoving me one last time. I stumbled backward, crashing into the chain-link fence. The metallic clang echoed in my ears, drowning out the laughter that followed me like a haunting melody.

As the bullies sauntered away, triumphant in their cruel victory, I collected my scattered belongings. The courtyard lay silent after the storm of humiliation, the laughter of Quinn and his cronies lingering like a persistent echo. Everything around me seemed colder, the world a little darker.

I sat alone against the cold, unforgiving bricks, shoulders slumped, backpack abandoned beside me. Blood pulsed in my temples, my body a canvas of pain from

Quinn's relentless assaults. A bruised spirit, aching bones—a testament to my perpetual status as Quinn Sanders' punching bag.

The tinny tang of blood clung to the back of my throat, and I could feel the weight of hopelessness pressing down on me.

Why did I have to endure this day after day?

What had I done to deserve the constant torment?

As the darkness threatened to swallow me whole, a thought emerged, insidious and tempting. The idea of escaping it all, of finding solace in oblivion, crept into the corners of my mind. A desperate plea for an end to the suffering.

An idea formed as I climbed to my feet, hot tears tracking down my cheeks.

The sun dipped lower on the horizon, casting long shadows across the deserted courtyard as I made my way toward the path that led home.

I was so done.

CHAPTER NINE

Quinn

I WASN'T EXPECTING too much from my first day at work, but I wasn't sure I was expecting quite so much hazing. At least, it could have been seen as hazing. I suspected it was more than that, though. Usually, hazing was something that brought a few laughs and made the newcomer feel like an idiot for a brief moment, like asking them to go and find a skirting board ladder or ask the Captain for a long weight. They were small and daft tasks and it usually didn't take long for the newcomer to catch on.

What I received were jobs that clearly no one had needed to do previously.

Cleaning on top of the lockers was, frankly, disgusting. There was muck and dead insects and mold up there, which had obviously been left to grow for a while. The gap between the ceiling and the lockers was slim, and I managed to hit my head five times at least before I stopped trying to stretch my back out and just accepted the cramps around my lower spine.

By the time the alarm went off, I was grateful to do something that was actually part of my job. Jase jumping into the truck with Hawke, Zander, Gage, and Carmen seemed almost too obvious. Given they were all bulky men and even though Carmen was a more slender body, there still would have been more room in the truck with Johnson, Mark, and me. But given that he had avoided me all morning and specifically left smaller rooms when I entered made it pretty clear he didn't want anything to do with me.

"I don't like conflict in the team, but I would suggest you avoid Jase," Johnson piped up as we drove. "He's got you pegged as an asshole, and the team is family, so you gotta prove yourself before they'll do anything except have his back."

"He's already said something?" I asked, a sinking feeling in my stomach.

"He said something to Mark, and Mark has decided to take it upon himself to see if you really are still as bad."

"Ah, I see." I sighed. "So I've got a world of hard work and patience-testing coming my way?"

"Pretty much. I can talk to them if you want?" Johnson offered.

Smiling slightly, I shook my head. "Thanks, but I'm all right. I know I'm not a good memory for Jase. I was hoping to be able to prove I've changed, so this might actually work for me." I laughed softly.

Johnson glanced my way while he paused at a red light. "You really are odd, but if you can look at it that way, you will probably be fine."

"Thanks for the heads up, though."

"Just don't want my job to become a warzone." He shrugged.

At the site of the fire, even though the blaze had grown to take over the kitchen, I was instructed to stay outside and keep anyone from entering. It was a shitty task to be given and usually reserved for a Probee, not a seasoned firefighter. After all, civilians never really ran into a burning building—that only happened in rare cases and movies.

There was a little girl, however, who was crying loudly.

"Hey, kid," I crouched down in front of her and her mother. "It's okay. It'll all be done in a bit."

"B-but..." She whimpered.

"She's worried our cat is still inside," her mother explained.

I glanced at the girl with tears trailing down her cheeks and fear etched all over her face. "Hey, sweetie. Is your cat clever?"

Sniffing in the disgustingly loud way only a child can, she rubbed her nose on the sleeve of her shirt. "Uh-huh. He's super clever. He even knows how to get into my room when mom shuts my door at night."

A small chuckle left my lips at the childlike innocence in that piece of information. Worked in my favor, though. "So, if he's that clever. Do you really think he would still be inside? And if he is, don't you think he's found a safe place away from the fire?" I raised an eyebrow with a small smile as I watched the little girl think about it.

"That's true..." she finally mumbled before nodding quickly.

"See. Clever kitties are usually just fine." I gave her a small wink before nodding to her mother, who mouthed a word of thanks at me.

"Oi, Sanders. Quit slacking off. We need an extra oil fire kit!" Jase yelled across to me from the door. Resisting the urge to roll my eyes at his words, I turned and jogged back to the truck I had arrived in and dug out the foam required to douse the fire inside. Once mixed with their powder hose, it would be just fine. Tossing it over to Jase, I watched him race back inside, not missing the irritating look on his face he had just from having to interact with me.

This was going to be a long road to getting Jase to understand I wasn't going to make his life hell just because I still existed.

The fire was easily brought back under control by the team. We hadn't really needed two trucks on site, but with an oil fire, you could never be sure how it was going to turn out. Some members of the public knew how to deal with them, while others made it a million times worse in their panic.

"So, what caused the fire? And why did it take the authorities so long to arrive that it was able to spread?" A voice followed me up and down the perimeter that I was making sure stayed clear of civilians. I turned my gaze onto the female with blonde hair pulled back in a bun and a notepad in her hands.

Journalists.

God, I hated them.

I wouldn't mind them so much if they ever wanted to put a positive spin on everything, but these days the media tended to give more grief and cause more doubt and fear.

"Please, stay back. This is still a live fire scene," I replied without acknowledging any of the questions. It was people like her that meant tax money had to fund PR teams for something that should have been left at fighting fires and saving lives.

"People are saying you all took a long time to respond. Too busy playing on the pole?" She smirked, making me realize she wasn't even a news journalist. She likely had a conspiracy blog or worked for a tabloid that truly just fuelled chaos and mistrust.

"Any questions you have can be answered by the station," Carmen called to the woman as she stepped over to me and handed me a new hose head. "Run that inside, will you?" She raised an eyebrow, and I realized that she was saving me from the overly nosey woman.

Nodding my thanks, I took the chance to jog over to the house and head inside. There was less smoke damage than I expected, and I quickly found Johnson holding the hose, which had malfunctioned.

"Here's the new one!" I called, swiftly moving around to the front of him while he choked off the flow of foam so I could remove the old head and replace it with the new one.

"Where's Carmen?" he asked.

"Saving me from a journalist," I laughed honestly.

"Didn't fancy fifteen minutes of fame?"

"I just want to do my job. I don't need a tabloid painting me in any light." I shook my head and backed up so Johnson could get back to work. Through his visor, I could see him level me with a curious look before getting back to it.

Perhaps I would have some chance of proving myself. From then on I delved into anything else that needed doing to help the crew inside doing most of the fight.

"I thought you'd done this job before," Jase grumbled as we got out of the over layers of our uniform once back at the station.

"I have," I replied with a raised eyebrow, wondering what part of my day he had a problem with. Everything had gone well, there were no casualties, and the fire was out with only damage done to the kitchen itself.

"Then why the hell were you off flirting with some mother and child while there was a fire to be fought?" Mark stood with his arms folded, leaning against his locker with a judgmental eyebrow raised, waiting for the answer.

I took in a slow breath to keep my tone even and my aura patient. I couldn't let my annoyance at the way they thought I would fob off my job take this into an emotional argument that would only isolate me further.

"You told me to keep the public back," I started. "That little girl was scared because she thought her cat was still inside the building, and I wanted to ensure we weren't at risk of her running in to find the creature."

Later on, she had spotted the cat in the neighbor's front garden and immediately shot out from her mother's arms and climbed the fence to grab the little white kitten.

"I was doing the job that was given to me with as much observation of the environment and situation as I could," I continued calmly. "If you would like me to act differently to meld with the team better, I would welcome the advice."

"You're such an arrogant sonofabitch," Jase grunted at me before stalking off, throwing his uniform at his locker without bothering to close it.

"But. I..." I glanced at Mark, who did nothing more than roll his eyes and walk away as well.

What was I supposed to have done?

Apologized and said I wouldn't do it again. That would have been bullshit, as I knew in the exact same scenario, I would try to calm the child again to stop her from possibly harming herself.

Swallowing my frustration, I shook my head and tried to push it out of my mind. Unfortunately, it wasn't the only time in the first couple of months that Jase took issue with how I acted when out on jobs.

"I'm doing the jobs I'm given! What is your problem?" I eventually snapped at him after another snide comment slipped from his lips. I knew where this had come from, and I knew I shouldn't bite and argue back, but I couldn't stand having my attitude toward my job questioned. This was a job I loved, a job I took originally as a way to level my cosmic karma, but I fell in love with the variation it could bring, the different people you could meet, and the energy of a team that worked together.

God, I missed my old team.

"You know exactly what my problem

is," Jase spat back.

"Oh, get over yourself. You fucking child," I growled angrily. How dare he be so petty as to take some bullying from childhood and turn it into actions that could potentially fuck with my career? "I'm good at what I do."

"You're an arrogant prick."

"Better than a sniveling coward who needs the rest of his team to give me the shitty jobs and crap attitudes so you can remain on the high ground," I snarled, pushing myself away from the truck I had been told to clean. Throwing the sponge with force onto the ground at Jase's feet, splattering him with dirty soapy water, I glared at him. I was officially done trying to prove I was a good person by just smiling politely. If he couldn't find it in him to have a simple conversation with me after two months of working together... Well, fuck him.

"Clean your own fucking truck," I spat out before storming out of the room and heading for the Captain's office. If Jase wanted me off the team so badly, he was getting his way. I wanted to be away from him and on another one as soon as humanly possible. I wasn't going to take *no* for an answer.

Captain Clarke was on a phone call

when I arrived, which at least allowed me a little time waiting outside to calm down from the sheer frustration I had been feeling. At least, that was what I hoped the time would allow. Instead, I just found myself pacing up and down outside of the office door, getting more and more frustrated.

By the time I was welcomed inside, I was practically seething.

"How can I help you, Sanders?" Captain Clarke asked as he motioned for me to take a seat across from him.

"I want to be transferred to another team," I said without hesitation, obviously attempting to keep my voice at a steady level.

Captain Clarke raised his eyebrow in my direction. "And why is that?"

I fell into an explanation of what had been happening over the last few months. The extra work, which wasn't exactly kosher, the criticism of my work, the past that Jase and I had, and how I felt he was discriminating against me because of it.

"I just want to be able to do my job," I continued, having calmed down a little from my rant.

The Captain sighed softly. "I have no spaces in the other teams to move you into. I know you are good at your job. The fact you are is the main reason you even survived what happened in New Orleans. But I need you to mesh with this team, or I have nothing else to offer you here."

I growled softly in frustration.

"So what am I supposed to do?" I asked.

"I'll think of something." The Captain sighed before waving me out with his hand when his phone rang again.

Damn it.

So much for getting any solutions from him. Heading back to the central room, I punched some numbers into the vending machine to get some solid sweets to chew on as I went back to my uniforms that I had yet to clean.

Ignoring the dirty looks I got from Jase and the rest of the team, I spent the rest of the day scrubbing out burn marks and scuffs from my uniform and the truck Johnson drove. He hadn't been the most friendly per se, but he had also been the only one other than Carmen who also actually treated me like a colleague, and when I jumped onto his truck during callouts, I actually felt like I was doing my job rather than being some rookie that just got in the way.

A few hours later, the Captain came back in with his solution.

"Right, I've had enough of this whole tension and bickering within the team," he announced gruffly, looking around and settling his gaze for longer on everyone but Carmen. He obviously knew she was the only one here not making anything worse.

Captain Clarke raised a hand as Jase opened his mouth to speak. "Don't start. I don't have any resources to change the teams around. Therefore, my only choice is to force you two to work together properly."

What did that mean?

"Quinn, you and Johnson will be swapping trucks. Jase, you and Quinn will work together on the two-man calls instead," he said.

"What?" Jase protested.

"Johnson?" The Captain turned to raise an eyebrow at him. "That okay with you."

"I'll work wherever, Captain." He nodded, glancing between Jase and me as though wondering if either of us would survive working with just the two of us. Somehow... I doubted it if the way Jase stormed out of the doors at the end of the day was anything to go by.

CHAPTER TEN

Jase

A PIERCING RINGING in my ears hammered at my skull. I couldn't be forced to work with Quinn.

How could Cap even think to insist on that?

Didn't I get any fucking say in the matter?

Anger bubbled in my chest, fueled me as I hastily stomped to my car, slamming the door and throwing my head back, howling my frustration into the silence of the stifling, lung-burning air.

The sharp blade rested on the edge of the tub, its brushed metal finish glinting in the flickering lights from above the sink.

The water in the tub sloshed toward the edges as I slipped inside its over-heated depths, the temperature of the clear liquid turning the skin on my legs and abdomen crimson almost instantly. I reveled in the pain, tears tracking down my cheeks, the taste of salt forming on my lips, finally freed from the heat that had gathered behind my eyes since that moment in the courtyard only mere hours ago. I wouldn't let them see me cry then, I couldn't let them know how much they hurt me, but now I could let every single ounce of that torment free to reign, reminding me of the bitterness of humiliation, the sting of embarrassment on my skin, the sour taste of defeat as the world seemed to close in and choke off the breath from my lungs.

I wished for a moment that the pain of the scalding bathwater was enough, that it would give me some sort of relief from the internal crushing pain of the sentiment that I didn't belong, I was a 'waste of space', as Quinn had repeatedly told me so many times this year, but that respite was not granted. I had to assume I didn't deserve that kind of reprieve.

I sobbed, my breath hitching in my chest as I strained to hear anything outside the bathroom door. A creak of the floorboards, the phone ringing, the sound of a car in the driveway. Anything to tell me that I was no longer alone. Nothing came. Not even the chipper bark of a dog from the neighbor's yard or the trill of a bird playing its blissful notes broke through the oppressive silence surrounding me.

I was truly and utterly alone.

Steam covered the mirror, the gathered condensation marking jagged tracks down the reflective glass much in the way I would assume the tears spoiled the smoothness of my skin.

My heartbeat thudded behind my breastbone, the need to make it stop, to end the daily torment of my life a palpable living being that lodged itself inside my very soul. This was the only way to cease the suffering. I couldn't take it anymore.

The bite of the silver-colored rectangle sliding effortlessly over the delicate, soft skin of my wrist felt so much more soothing than being slammed into the unforgiving metal of the lockers at school. More pleasing than the inevitable tear of my teeth through my lips as I fought to hold on, not to respond or react to Quinn and his buddies' incessant torture and repeated assaults. Somehow, the razor slicing through my skin was easier, simpler to bear, and for a heartbeat or two I watched, a small smile gracing my lips, pleased as the scarlet blood welled up at the site of the neatly parted skin.

EVIE RILEY

As the scent of copper reached my nose, I marveled at the unique and diverse patterns each drop made in the water, swirling around, becoming heavier than the water from the tap, pausing in suspended animation for a moment, and then finally falling, melting through the glassy surface to coat the bottom of the tub beside my leg in dotted splendor.

As my pulse began to thrum slower, an electric kind of buzz taking up residence in my ears and spreading over my skin, the pressure in my chest eased and I sucked in a deep, shuddering breath.

With that single breath I suddenly felt so clean, so relieved, so free...

A stuttered sigh slipped from my lips as my head lolled to the side, the panic receding, all thoughts fleeing my mind and letting me sink into the numbness. All the torment ended, every single trickle of my humiliation ceased as I watched the bathtub water turn a pretty brilliant ruby red.

Only two insignificant beats later, thunder rolled and the resonance of the community of dogs yipping, the unmistakable quick chirpy squeal of tires on hot pavement, that creak of the wood enveloping footsteps in the hallway that I'd so longed to hear finally reached my fuzzy mind. The echo of my name slipping from my mother's lips reaching in and tugging, even as harsh movements reverberated in the bathwater as someone viscously banged their fists on the door.

The crack of wood splintering filled the room with a roar as the door suddenly imploded and broken screaming reached through my muddled brain to stain my psyche much in the way my blood now covered and pigmented every inch of my pale, tattered skin.

I stared into the water, my eyes unseeing, the piercing pitch of a jacked up feminine tone making my ears hurt, pulling me from my newfound comfort and peace, the intrusion burrowing uninvited through my tranquility like an axe slicing through wood.

Letting my eyes fall shut, I gave into the darkness that now surrounded me, the voices fading like they might as if I'd reached the other end of a long tunnel.

Sweet blissful relief finally overtook me and I breathed out that last shred of excruciating tension.

CHAPTER ELEVEN

Jase

"I CAN'T BELIEVE he actually wants me to work with that bastard!" I exclaimed over a pint that evening down at the local steakhouse bar, which Johnson and I frequented every other week. It was a quaint place run by a mother and daughter pair who somehow kept the food top quality while keeping the atmosphere chilled. From inside, it was almost like it was a joint you'd found on the side of a highway or in a smaller town where everyone knew each other.

"You'll be fine, just do your job as you usually do, and it'll quickly show up how he gets in the way." Johnson chuckled, waving over the daughter with a small awkward grin. It was hilarious to watch him attempt to flirt with her and fail every time.

Ruth was a badass redhead who rocked tight leather trousers and crop tops. She kept her hair in a fishtail braid, and she was the queen of pool around these parts. So many had tried to win against her with her phone number as the winning prize, and she had wiped the floor with every single one. Johnson had it bad. Even though he was a masculine being, he became flustered whenever she came over.

"All right, boys. What can I get you?" she chimed, flashing a wink in our direction and smirking knowingly when Johnson stumbled over his order.

Rolling my eyes at him, I laughed softly. "Double cheeseburger with bacon."

"Thought firefighters were meant to be healthy?" She laughed.

"Well, it's been a shit day." I sighed. "We'll have a couple more rounds too."

"Damn. What happened?"

"Jase has his panties in a bunch over having to work with the new guy." Johnson chuckled.

I scowled at him both for making me sound childish but also pushing out the idea that I might be wearing panties. God, the image that went through my mind was enough to make me recoil.

Who the fuck would want a man in panties?

"I don't have my *panties* in a bunch," I growled.

"Fine. Your tighty whities then." Johnson rolled his eyes.

"I prefer the image of panties." Ruth laughed with a wink sent my way. Okay, apparently, Ruth wouldn't mind a man in panties. Johnson had clearly had the same thought as he spluttered around his beer while she walked away cackling.

"You've gotta know she's messing with you every time you come in, right?" I asked Johnson with a laugh.

"I know. She prefers older men too, so you're more her type anyway." Johnson sighed.

Glancing over at the bar Ruth had ventured behind to fetch our drinks, I briefly wondered for the billionth time in my life how much easier it would be if I was attracted to women. I could have found someone like her who could give banter as well as she took it, who could drink with the men and laugh with the women. My parents would have been happy, and they wouldn't ask every other weekend when I was going to find myself a 'nice girl to settle down with'.

If only it was that simple. I was about

as likely to do that as I was to get on well with Quinn at work.

The thought of the man annoyed me to no end. Especially because—and I would only ever admit this in my own head—he was everything that I found attractive. I had found myself in almost nightly naughty dreams with him as the centerpiece once or twice since he had turned up. They started out as memories of a sort, reminders of those times in school where he'd beaten me down both mentally and physically, until they changed and became the type of dreams I'd never have expected Quinn Sanders to star in.

Heated ones.

Ones that resulted in my waking with my boxers soaked in my own cum.

In them, he was still a bit of an asshole, but I loved it.

Fuck, I practically begged for it.

I hated those dreams. Working so close to him was not going to help me chase them away any.

I suspected it was because I had been thinking so much about him lately. But that night, he appeared in my dreams again.

I was at the station after a call. It had been a smoke-heavy callout, but no one had been hurt. I often tended to linger a little longer in the showers after a call like that as I had figured out that the cat that occasionally visited my house didn't like smokey scents, so in order not to chase off the creature, I had taken to lengthening my time in the showers.

The water was hot and comforting, pounding down on my shoulders, which were sore from work. I rubbed at the muscles slowly, letting out a small groan. My fingers weren't quite long enough to reach my shoulder blades properly, but they had a decent level of strength to press into the knots near my neck and I breathed a sigh as I finally began to loosen them.

"Need help with that?" His deep voice was low and sultry. I didn't even have to look around to know it was Quinn.

"Piss off," I grumbled at him with half the effort I would use normally.

"You don't want that. Not really."

"Arrogant ass," I growled, though his strong hands on my shoulders, thumbs rubbing the aching flesh with a fragrant soap, made the growl quickly turn into a soft, breathy moan.

"Arrogant, but very good with my fingers." Quinn chuckled in my ear as he pressed up behind me. This was always the way. I never really saw him in my

dreams, he was always behind me, always in control, but I knew it was him. His height made it easy to curl over me slightly as his chest pressed to my back. I could feel the way his chest and arm muscles flexed as his hands continued to massage my shoulders, then down my arms.

I never fought back. Even if we were in the showers at work, somehow, that only enhanced my need. Leaning my head back against his shoulder, my eyes fell closed when his hands moved to massage my front.

"They are good fingers." I moaned softly. They were. I noticed them a lot when he was working with both heavy and delicate equipment. They were strong and agile, careful and precise. They were the kind of fingers I imagined could pick me to pieces easily.

I felt Quinn smirk against my ear, and soon his tongue was running along the edge of it. "You need to keep quiet, or someone might hear you," he whispered, his fingers and thumbs finding my nipples and giving them a teasing pinch.

I wanted to say I didn't care. I wanted to tell him that I wanted him to make me scream in pleasure and screw anyone who had a problem. But even in my dreams, I was terrified of anyone knowing what I was.

"I can't..." I whimpered pathetically.

"Don't worry, I'll help." Lifting his left hand to cover my mouth, he paused for a moment waiting for my nod of approval, before he trailed his right hand down my back between us.

I had not been with many men, but I knew I enjoyed being the bottom. It was something I usually felt ashamed of, but in my dreams, I was able to arch my back and press my ass into the hand that grabbed and squeezed at the cheeks with eagerness. Unable to speak, I nipped at the palm of Quinn's hand as an encouragement.

I heard nothing more than a chuckle as a warning before his hand left my ass, and I heard the click of a bottle. I hissed at the cool feeling of lotion or conditioner as his fingers ran over my tight hole. More gently than I imagined Quinn could ever truly be, he pushed one digit inside me and slowly shifted it against the walls of my insides, letting me get used to the feeling.

I wanted more. I was burning deep within for more. With his hand still over my mouth, the only way I could show him that desire was to push back on his hand.

"So needy..." he purred against my neck, not wasting any time by pushing another two fingers inside me. He pulled me back close against his chest as I shuddered and writhed at the pleasure of his fingers brushing against the most sensitive glands bundled up there.

I was needy. And in my dreams, I was allowed to be needy.

Lifting my arms to reach behind my head, I slid my fingers into that short black spiky hair and curled them against his scalp, mumbling against his palm. When he pulled it away just slightly, I heard myself whine out a plea.

"Fuck me." God. I wanted it so badly. And from the feeling of hard heat against my hip, Quinn wanted it to.

"Say please," he whispered teasingly.

"Please!" The word came easily, and I found myself being shoved forward against the cold tiles of the shower room. Quinn's hand splayed out against the tiles to support himself as his other hand withdrew from my body and held my hips in place.

My mouth was dry with anticipation, and my body practically trembled with want.

Fuck.

The sound of my alarm brought me

back to reality. Panting softly and glancing down at myself, I couldn't even begin to deny the evidence of my dream that was all over the inside of my boxers. I could see the wetness from the outside of the blue material.

"What the fuck am I, a goddamned teenager again?" I growled to myself as I got out of bed and peeled the boxers from my body, slinging them into the hamper. I needed to get laid. Perhaps it was time I went out of town for a long weekend and went somewhere no one knew me to let off some steam.

I'd done it a few times, not so far away that anyone got suspicious, but far enough that no one would recognize a firefighter from Baton Rouge. Usually, I drove over to Lafayette, where I could go to a club called Bolt, which was extremely relaxed and friendly for the queer community. They welcomed everyone from the extremely out to the quietly closeted.

I could barely remember the last time I had been. Probably not since Trevor had retired.

Glancing down at myself in the shower, already reacting to the memories of the last time, I decided I would definitely go on the next weekend when I didn't have plans.

That thought was only cemented further when I was at work later that day, and I had told Quinn that he could wash the truck. Hearing laughter from outside, I glanced out the window to see that Quinn had obviously slipped and dropped the hose, spraying water all over himself while Carmen laughed so hard that she had actually begun to snort a little.

If I could have been annoyed that they were getting along okay despite Carmen having been told about my issues with the man, I would have. But, it was heavily distracting to see Quinn's white shirt plastered to his body by the water.

Shit.

It was everything I imagined in my dreams when he was pressed against my back. Every inch of him was toned and well formed, and I could see the golden color of his tan through the wet, now see-through shirt.

"Quit fucking around! We have a call!" I yelled down from the window before storming back inside, hoping my blazing cheeks would calm in the time it took Quinn to change. It wasn't an urgent call, more along the "cat stuck in a tree" level urgency where they didn't really need anything but the ladder height we could provide. Still, it was a job, and the two-man team was being sent for it.

"Sorry, Jase," Quinn said as he jogged back out of the locker room with a fresh set of clothes on.

"Forget it. Just do the job." I rolled my eyes, still unable to give the man an inch of trust.

"Sure." He sighed. "What is the job?"

"Helping a couple down from a third floor as their stairs collapsed in," I replied, motioning for Quinn to get his ass in the truck so I could start the journey across town.

"Look, I get you aren't happy about being paired with me, but we can still do the job without needing to bitch at each other. All right?"

"Still calling people female terms to make them feel smaller?" I turned a glare at him briefly before looking back at the road.

"What?" Quinn sounded genuinely surprised. "No. I'm not misogynistic."

"Oh okay, just against feminine men... sure." We pulled up to the site, and I jumped out of the truck before Quinn could say another word.

I knew I was taking my frustration out on him even more so than I normally did, but every time he spoke, I heard the whisper in my ear from the night before, and at the same time, I also heard the younger version of Quinn calling me a girl because the hairstyle I had was longer and resembled one that was sported by a favored video game character back then.

By the end of the day, after snipping at Quinn after every single thing he did and listening to him growl in annoyance while biting back his own responses, I decided that I was just going to go to Lafayette at the end of this working period. I just couldn't wait any longer and I felt like I was about to explode.

"So, you aren't coming over for tea then?" My mother asked when I phoned her later that evening to let her know I wouldn't be by to visit as previously planned.

"Sorry, Ma. Don't get many days that Annie and my schedules work out so we can hang out," I explained, using my usual lie. Annie was a nickname for one of the drag singers at the club I wanted to go to, but it was also the name of a girl who used to live down the street who I got on with very well.

I was pretty sure my mother was under the impression that Annie and I had something going on, but we just never saw each other enough to make it work.

"I know, sweetie. I'll just miss you, is all," she sighed, her exaggerated disappointment making itself evident down the phone line as intended.

"Same. But I'll be there next time!" I reassured her with a smile on my face that I knew she couldn't see.

"Well, you better say hi to Annie from me and get me the latest gossip from her life."

I laughed loudly. "I always do, mom." Even if it was always made up. "I'll also bring some of that pie back that you really like and drop it off on my way back into town."

"Oh! The apple and cinnamon?"

"Either that or the blueberry, your choice."

"Definitely the apple and cinnamon." My mother chimed happily. "You're such a gem!"

After a little more talk about how her week had been and me attempting not to rant too much about Quinn, in case she realized I was talking about the old preacher's son, I hung up the phone with a soft sigh. I hated lying to my mother, but I just couldn't see her ever smiling at the idea of me bringing a man home instead of a woman. And the idea of losing my family seemed too high a risk just for the so-called romance of love.

Still, at least I now had a few days to look forward to. Jumping onto my laptop, I picked through a couple of hotel websites I had come to know over the years. Ones whose staff looked the other way if someone came back with you and who didn't comment when you asked for the name on your room to be altered to one that didn't match your ID. The ones that understood that being gay in the deep south of the USA wasn't always the easiest or the safest thing even in the modern day and were happy to help in any way they could.

I specifically liked one known as the Phoenix Inn. It was more of a B&B, but you didn't get woken up for the breakfasts if you said upon arrival that you would be having a late night. It was run by two men who claimed to be business partners, and both said they had wives who had died not long ago. Personally, I suspected that was a front, and the main reason they were so discrete was due to the fact that they had spent their whole lives doing just that.

Unfortunately, they were all booked up, so I ended up booking the run-down motel that obviously didn't care who came in and out so long as they paid. It wasn't the most secure, and usually, I took some portable locks to add to the inside while I was there as a precaution, but it was located close to the club, and it was cheap, so it would do.

Getting through the next few days of work was the hardest thing to do. Working with Quinn was annoying and frustrating and always left me both angry and in need of a cold shower. His ass just looked way too good in uniform. By the end of the week, I couldn't tell if I was angrier at him for being who he was, or at myself for finding him so ridiculously attractive. I had never fantasized about a specific person that wasn't some kind of airbrushed Adonis of a celebrity, and yet here I was doing just that over my bully from high school.

Just because he had grown up to be just my type, it didn't change that he was some homophobic piece of shit who would only torture me again if he ever found out I was really gay like he claimed all those years ago. Once the frustration was out of my system, I would be fine.

At least, that was the story I told myself all the way to Lafayette, with some classic 80's rock blasting from my pickup's radio. It was a pleasant drive, but I was antsy. I wanted to get there and find someone... anyone... to get me to stop thinking about Quinn.

CHAPTER TWELVE

Quinn

MY PATIENCE AND tolerance were wearing thin. Working so close with Jase and receiving the full brunt of his attitude was slowly but surely grating on all my nerves, and it was only a matter of time before my temper really snapped.

For fuck's sake, was the man really planning on holding a grudge from school for so long that he made the station a miserable experience for us all working there?

I knew that Johnson and Mark had Jase's back, but I refused to believe they wouldn't rather have a team that didn't cause tension so thick that you couldn't even cut it with a knife while waiting for callouts.

"You need to get out," Jared said over

dinner at the end of my working week. "You've got three days off now, why not make the most of it? Go out, get laid." Jared chuckled.

It wasn't the worst idea in the world, but I couldn't stop myself from pulling an unconvinced expression. "I dunno..."

Jared raised an eyebrow and waited for me to elaborate.

"I'm not sure how comfortable I am going out and trying to find someone to have sex with here... you know, in Baton Rouge, where I associate more people with religion."

"I suppose that makes sense. You haven't been back here all that long either," Jared mused. "You could take a couple of days in New Orleans."

"No," I replied too quickly. I hadn't told anyone why I had moved back to my hometown, but the memories that New Orleans held were still much too painful to consider returning.

What if I bumped into someone I had known, and they started to ask questions or make comments about the events back then?

That would definitely kill any buzz I might have managed to build up.

"Okay." Jared sighed. You could see what Lafayette has to offer, though it's a smaller town than here.

I remembered going to Lafayette on a school trip, but I could barely remember a thing about the town itself. Pulling out my phone, I decided to have a quick look on Google to see if there were any decent clubs for my needs. Normal clubs were fine, but I wasn't ignorant to the fact that my tall, dark, tanned look often caught the eye of women rather than men if I didn't place myself somewhere that made people think I was gay. After all, the likelihood of a good-looking guy being gay when found at a gay club was considerably higher than at a regular club.

"Well, there's one place with pretty good reviews," I confirmed as I clicked on the website link from the maps.

"One place is all you need," Jared stated, placing a couple of fresh beers on the coffee table and flopping himself back into the chair. I hadn't even realized he had left the room.

"You wanna come?" I asked.

"As much as I love a drag show and cheesy music, I don't need to be around while you get laid, kiddo." Jared barked out a laugh and shook his head.

"I'm not a kid."

"Always will be to me."

I rolled my eyes at him before calculating the route. "It's not that far... I could go tonight and use tomorrow to chill." It was only about an hour's drive, and it had been a long time since I got to drive on an open road with my music playing.

It didn't take long to pack a few clothes, toiletries, and bedroom necessities once I decided to go. I knew I wouldn't need too much, and I had some excess money, so I could afford a couple of lunches out or a hotel dinner if that was easier.

I hadn't booked anything yet, but it was midweek, and I suspected I would be able to walk into most places and be able to find a room.

Settling into my BMW was the easiest thing in the world. I knew it was an expense I didn't really need when living in a city, but for me to drive out of the city, my beautiful car was a blessing. Smooth drive, comfortable and supportive seats, and a damn good sound system.

Singing along to some 80's classic rock was always a successful way to make me relax. By the time I reached Lafayette, my mood was much lighter than it had been in days.

As I was not too fussy about where I

stayed, I simply decided to pull into whatever parking lots I came across and ventured into the closest hotel until I found one with an available room.

It was nearly midnight when I actually arrived at the hotel, so there was little point in going out that night. I decided to grab a quick shower and then get some sleep. It was always nice just to freshen up a little after a hot car journey.

I could explore the town a little in the morning so I knew my way around before going out to intoxicate myself and find someone to let loose with. It would be a lot easier to deal with a drunken night if I knew where I was on my way out of the club. Especially considering how bad my sense of direction was after a couple of drinks.

It was a cheap hotel chain about a ten-minute walk from the center of the town. It was not flashy, but the bed linens were clean, and that was all I needed. The room had two beds with a desk in between them, two lamps on the walls, a closet, and an attached bathroom. It looked like it hadn't been updated since the 1970s, but for one night, I didn't care.

I glanced into the bathroom and found I did care a little about the fact the shower looked just as old. As long as the water was warm, at least, coming out of those metal bars. It smelled like bleach and there were no fancy showerheads or anything else to make it look nice but at least it was clean.

I turned on the water, allowing the temperature to heat as I shucked off the clothes I'd worn to travel. Sliding under the hot spray, I sighed as I did a quick dash of shampoo over my hair, letting the hot water sluice over my skin for a minute, then rinsed my locks and grabbed the bar of hotel soap, lathering my body and making a half-assed effort to clean all the necessary crevices.

One hand braced against the slick wall, I closed my eyes as I wrapped my other hand around my sensitive head, spreading some of the soap along my engorged shaft. I moved down my length, gripping my cock in my fist, pulling and tugging slowly, building a rhythm. Faceless images flitted through my mind. Blond-brown hair, brilliant blue eyes, slick, tanned skin with freckles haphazardly speckled over the shoulders.

Then suddenly, the image changed.

Jase blushing before me on his knees, my fingers threaded through his hair as he looked up at me from under his lashes, his cheeks hollowed while he sucked me off, pushed to the forefront of my mind, and I groaned with pleasure at the thought.

Immediately, my cock twitched at the vision. I tugged harder, faster, as I imagined my cock hitting the back of his throat, his eyes widening and watering as he struggled to swallow my hardness. The sound of choking prevailing as I gripped his hair, my fists tightening in the strands, pulling him to me hard, burying myself in his warm heat.

My hips moved faster as my breathing intensified, and I thrust my cock desperately against my slick palm as I chased my orgasm through the clouds and haze of my imagination.

I pumped my cock, feeling the orgasm build to bursting nearly instantly and thick ropes of warm cum sprayed onto the wall of the shower as I reveled in the rush of sweet release, some sliding down over my hand as I fought to control the trajectory of my release and catch my breath.

I opened my eyes and stared at the ceiling with a mixture of remorse, regret, and desire that left me both sated and hungrier than I'd ever been before.

I turned off the water, feeling like an ass for even having thoughts like that of

Jase.

Where the hell had they come from anyway?

Stepping out, I grabbed a clean white towel from a stack above the toilet and dried myself off, dropping the towel on the counter as I flicked off the light and left the bathroom.

I pulled back the sheets of the bed closest to the bathroom and slid down onto the old-looking but surprisingly comfortable mattress, nodding off within minutes.

CHAPTER THIRTEEN

Quinn

WAKING FROM THE most decent night's sleep I'd had in weeks, I yawned and stretched, rolling out of the bed to hit the bathroom. I took a piss and brushed my teeth, then threw on the comfy clothes I'd packed in my duffel bag and grabbing the keycard, a light jacket, and my phone, I headed out into the bright sunshine.

Thankfully, while I wandered the streets, I discovered the town was fairly simple, and I noted that most of the roads would eventually lead me back in a circle to the central area where I was staying.

As the streets had not taken very long to work out, I decided that I could browse the shops and perhaps even catch a movie as a way to truly relax on a day off. Plus, if I happened to find a clothing shop or two I liked, there was no harm in having something new to wear tonight.

The day was a beautiful one. It was sunny but cool enough for me to want to keep my jacket on with the zip down. As it turned out, I didn't really need it for long. A little before lunchtime, I found myself overheating in the sunshine and having to carry the jacket over my arm.

I wandered through a few of the shopping areas nearby, looking at different stores and trying to imagine what I would buy if money were no object. There was so much I wanted but couldn't justify buying. I really needed some new shoes or boots. My old pair had seen better days, and I had been wearing them practically every day since moving to Baton Rouge. They were well worn now, and I realized that they probably wouldn't last another month without needing to be replaced.

Eventually, I located a quirky little charity shop that actually had some decent clothes on offer. I browsed around a bit and picked up a couple of things; a nice pair of jeans, a casual shirt, and a soft leather jacket which looked like it might have been pricey originally but had obviously been donated by someone who had too many jackets or just got bored with it. Along with the clothing, I actually found a decent pair of boots in a box of heavily discounted shoes. I actually felt like I had done pretty well and gave myself a mental pat on the back for it.

I trekked my way back to a movie theatre I'd passed in my wandering earlier, happy to note they were playing a matinee of an older Tom Cruise movie followed by one with Richard Gere.

Who could resist an afternoon of watching sexy-as-sin hot man bod on the big screen, right?

I paid my entry fee, snagged a big bucket of popcorn with double butter, some M&Ms, and a super sized drink before settling into a seat in the back row in the near empty theater for an afternoon of action, intrigue, and romance. This was definitely a great way to relax on a day off.

CHAPTER FOURTEEN

Quinn

DESPITE FINISHING THE entire bucket of popcorn and a bag of crunchy chocolate goodness during the movies, when I emerged from the theatre squinting at the bright light a few hours later, my stomach made itself known with a loud growl.

Before heading back to my hotel, I decided to stop at a small diner for food. It was reasonably busy for an early evening but not so busy that I couldn't hear myself think. Choosing a seat at the counter, I glanced over the menu. The diner was simple, but the details that were found in the decor and the presentation of the dishes that I could see suggested that there was great pride in the work here.

"Hi there, doll. What can I get for ya,"

the girl behind the counter chimed as she walked over to me. She was a beautiful brunette with a slightly wonky nose, cute little freckles, and green eyes that I had to admit matched mine in brightness. Her hair was cut short, which suited her and made her look more mature than the other kids her age. She wore a pair of jeans and a plain white T-shirt under the apron that was clearly the only uniform, but she looked like an expensive model rather than someone who lived in a small town like this and worked in a diner.

Usually, I'm more than happy to flash a charming smile at women to get them to settle into a conversation and provide information when I need it. But I had a feeling that I wouldn't need to do that with this woman. She seemed more than friendly already.

"What do you recommend?" I asked, flashing her a smile. "I'm Quinn, by the way. Nice to meet you."

"Katie." She smiled in return. "Are you here for a meal or just a snack?"

"Meal. I'm going out tonight, so something heavy enough to keep me going for the night, but not put me into a food coma, " I mused, glancing over the choices.

"Oh, a night out. I miss those." She

chuckled softly. "I'd go with the classic burger with a helping of our paprika chips. That way there's a lot of carbs to keep up with an exciting night but yet not overkill, if you know what I mean."

"I'll have that then," I decided. "And a coffee if you have vanilla syrups."

"A man with a sweet tooth. I'll have to tell my fiancé he's not the only one who likes coffee syrups."

"Oh, definitely not. I've always been partial to sweet drinks. Not so keen on a lot of deserts, though," I admitted. I had always been an appetizer and main course kind of person rather than a main and desert.

"Ah, not quite so alike." Katie chuckled, beginning to brew a new pot of coffee. "If it's a sweet snack, he'll finish it in seconds."

"My father was like that." I laughed, finding it nice to just relax and talk to someone new without having to think or worry about what they were going to say next. "Do you have to hide snacks just to make sure you still have some waiting at a later date?"

"That's a good idea. But we don't live together yet."

"Oh?" I had to admit, that surprised me. She spoke like they were so close that it made sense for them to live together.

"We want to. But we both study, so it's hard to get enough money saved up," Katie explained.

"Understandable. What are you studying?" I asked, finding myself getting lost in the conversation rather than waiting impatiently for my meal.

"I'm studying to be a nurse. He's aiming to become an astrophysicist."

"And you both work as well? Damn."

"I know. We barely see each other." She laughed as though reading my mind. "But we have our goals, and when we have enough money, we'll buy a place, and we can see each other whenever we are home." She almost sounded dreamy as she spoke. There was a familiar stab of envy in my chest as my smile softened while watching her eyes sparkle as she spoke of their plans.

I would truly love to find such a connection one day. To find someone who had my back while I had theirs, even if I couldn't be home at all the same times as them. It had taken me a long time to accept that it was okay to want that kind of future. After growing up believing that being gay was wrong, I never really thought I'd ever be allowed to find a love like that. But now, after finally living life a little in New Orleans and coming into the man I really wanted to be, I think it's more than worth trying for. Now that I'd finally accepted myself the way I am, that the past was the past and the only thing I could do now was make the future better—with no more regrets, guilty feelings, or second thoughts about what I deserved—maybe the right person was just waiting out there somewhere, ready to catch me when I fell.

Though I doubted I'd find the love of my life in a club in a town that wasn't even where I lived. Oh well, I supposed I hadn't come here for love, after all. I had come here solely to let out some frustration.

I could find love another time.

The meal was as fantastic as advertised, and I had to admit I probably ate more than I should have before a night out. My stomach poked out just slightly, but I hoped that by the time I was dressed, at the club, dancing, and had caught someone's attention, it would have shrunk back to my usual toned look with tempting hips.

Looking at myself in the mirror as I pulled on a black shirt that was tight enough to show off my arms, but not too tight, I smirked softly. I knew I was hot. I wasn't about to deny it. The dark jeans I wore curved around and highlighted my backside, and even though I wasn't usually a bottom in the bedroom, I did delight at it being grabbed in encouragement. I had to admit, I found it fun when a guy would stare at me like he'd never seen anything so delicious before. It didn't happen often, but every now and then there were those guys who couldn't take their eyes off of me.

The thought made my smirk grow and I turned away from the mirror. Okay, I was definitely more than ready for a night of fun.

CHAPTER FIFTEEN

Quinn

THE CLUB, IT turned out, may have been the only one in town, but it was kitted out for everything a guy might need. There were a few rooms, and one was quieter on the music front, so a conversation could actually occur without having to go and stand outside. I thought that was one hell of a good touch. The number of times I had had to go and stand in a smoking area just to have a conversation with someone, even though they didn't smoke either, was insane. Here I would be able to buy them a drink, stand comfortably in the warmth, and focus on them rather than the fog of smoke surrounding me.

The drinks on the menu were all named strangely, not one of them giving away what they would actually taste like until you read the small print of ingredients underneath. With a chuckle at the name *Buttery Nipple*, I ordered two of those plus a simple rum and coke. I would normally go for vodka mixes, but the buttery nipple contained a cream-based liqueur, so vodka would have been a bad mix.

"God, that's good," I said to myself after the shots were gone, and I was able to bask in the aftertaste.

Walking through the club, I glanced around, taking in just how many people were there, even on a weekday. There appeared to be some kind of drag show mixed with karaoke that night. There were already a few people putting their names down on the list along with what they wanted to sing.

I kept walking, checking out everyone and everything as I went. Some folks were clearly here for the drinks while others looked like they were here for whatever was going on upstairs. A couple of guys had others hanging off them, obviously on dates or at least trying to look like they were on dates. They didn't have much luck though, since every time one of them would look back over his shoulder, I'd see their partner giving me an evil eye. It wasn't hard to figure out why either. It seemed like most of the men in the place were looking at me.

I smiled widely and waved at several groups who gave me a friendly wave back but no more than that. One guy even tried to get my attention by singing off key and horribly at the top of his lungs. Oh, I did love a gay bar. It was the only place that I could truly enjoy men checking me out rather than women.

"Hey there, handsome."

I glanced around at the voice and found a beautiful blond guy smiling at me. He was young, probably in university for some kind of sports, if his body was anything to go by.

"Hi." I smiled lightly.

"You here alone?" he asked. "Want to come and dance with us?" He motioned to a small group of friends who were already on the dance floor.

I didn't even offer any subtlety as I dragged my gaze down from his face to his body. He was dressed in fashion brands he probably couldn't afford without student loans, but he looked good.

"All right." Draining my drink and placing the glass on a side table, I followed him out on the dance floor.

It became clear pretty quickly; however, it wasn't him who had been interested in me. Soon enough, he and all his friends had edged away slightly, leaving a small brunette with a shaggy fringe. I wasn't even convinced he was of drinking age, and as he smiled up at me and danced closer, I felt an ominous concern in my gut.

I felt like a predator.

The moment I got the chance, I smiled gently at the brunette and made a motion with my hand that I was going to go for a drink. I picked the timing for the center of a song he seemed to be really enjoying, and thankfully, he didn't seem too interested in following me. I felt a little bad for deceiving the kid, but I would have been plain and honest with him if he had followed. Not my scene.

The bar had increased its number of patrons queuing for drinks by the time I returned, and it took a while to get to the front. Taking three more shots of the same kind and ordering another rum and coke, I moved to step back and felt my heel press down on another's foot as my arm bumped into them.

"Oh, I'm sorry!" I called over the music, turning my head to face them and hoping they weren't going to take an unnecessary level of offense. The face I found there was one I recognized so very clearly. Gorgeous soft brown eyes, the gentle slope of the jaw, messy brown hair obviously styled more carefully for a night out.

"Jase?"

I had to be dreaming, right?

What in the hell would Jase be here for?

He was straight, wasn't he?

I had heard him talking to Johnson and Mark about women and laughing about times back in college.

Right now, Jase was looking at me with the most terrified expression I had ever seen on anyone. I could see the cogs in his mind freeze up and panic take over as he tried to turn and leave without acknowledging me.

Reaching out, I grabbed his arm to stop him from leaving. I'm not sure why I did, but the idea of him being here was mind-boggling, and I needed to ask.

"Jase... are you bi?" I asked slowly. Perhaps he was curious about men but not sure how to go about it, so he wanted to test it out in a city he wouldn't bump into someone he knew.

Oh, the irony wasn't lost on me if that was the case.

"What? No!" Jase snapped.

I raised an eyebrow at the defensiveness in his voice. Okay. He was definitely still in the closet then, whatever his sexuality.

"What about you? Come to torment some more gays?" Jase prickled.

"No. I am gay."

Jase seemed flabbergasted by the news.

"What?"

"I'm gay," I repeated. "A cumgobbler. Queerboy."

"But the shit you used to give me..."

I could definitely see why he would be so confused after how I was when I was younger, but I had never hidden it since coming back to Baton Rouge. I was sure I had made more than one comment about how I wasn't interested in women when the guys had accused me of flirting. But apparently, none of that had overwritten Jase's memories of me, and I realized that Jase would need more of an explanation here. Sighing softly, I dropped my hand to take hold of Jase's, leading him to one of the quieter rooms.

Convincing Jase to sit down at a table, I brought over two beers and slid into the seat on the other side of the table.

"Jase, I need to apologize to you. I should never have done the things I did and said back in school," I started. "I already knew I was gay. I even had a crush on a guy a year above me. I was terrified, and I was angry. Everything I used to call you, tease you about, that was me hiding my truth from myself and everyone else. My parents and our community had raised me to believe that what I felt and who I was, was wrong. It was a sin to like another boy, and so I hid it the best way I knew how... which, looking back, was a really stupid way." It was strange saying all of this without Jase even responding from across the table. He just watched me, his brown eyes wide and questioning as he took a couple of large gulps from his drink.

"I thought if I was big and tough and handsome and good at sports and spoke about God enough, I could point at other people and deflect any suspicion of sin away from me," I continued. "I hate myself for that. I really do."

Jase surveyed me with eyes full of scrutiny, looking for any kind of lie he could find. But he wouldn't be able to. Every word was the absolute truth.

"I came out to my parents when I was living in New Orleans. Yet, they *still* try to set me up with girls every time I speak to them." I rolled my eyes and let out a tired chuckle.

"Was it hard?" Jase finally asked.

"Coming out to them," he clarified as I looked up from my beer.

"One of the hardest things I've ever had to do," I admitted. "But I had some supportive friends in New Orleans who helped me through the six months where I wasn't sure if dad would ever accept it. I drank so much." I laughed, reflecting on the descriptive first few years of college. "At least I got it out of my system then, though."

Jase let out a sigh. "Well... I'm not straight, but no one knows."

Not straight.

That could mean anything, but the way Jase shifted in his seat, he was clearly uncomfortable with just admitting that vague statement. So I decided not to pry; instead, I nodded with a slight smile.

"I'm so very sorry for everything I did at school. That probably hasn't helped."

"It really didn't." Jase half-laughed, flashing me a shy smile, almost as though he couldn't believe he was having this conversation.

CHAPTER SIXTEEN

Jase

I COULDN'T BELIEVE that Quinn was gay. It explained so much... Actually, it kind of explained everything.

He also seemed to genuinely regret the way he was back at school.

I wasn't sure I was ready to forgive what he had done and the damage he had added to an already fairly intolerant school, but I felt something inside me change that night.

Perhaps it was the slightest bit of respect?

I couldn't deny the strength it must have taken Quinn to come out to his deeply religious parents. It was the courage I had never been able to find, and my parents didn't even tell me regularly that being gay or different was a sin.

"So, how come you decided to come to Lafayette rather than just go out in Baton Rouge?" I asked after a couple of moments.

Quinn slowly let out a breath and shrugged his shoulders. "I know I'm out as gay, but I still feel uncomfortable flaunting it in the same town as my parents."

Thinking over that, I couldn't say I blamed him for that. Going out and being seen with another man would only cause more tension in his family.

"It'd be worth it if I was dating them, but just for one night of fun, it doesn't seem worth it." Quinn chuckled. "So, what about you? I assume you are here because it's easier to keep not being straight a secret if you don't go out where you might already know people?"

I nodded slowly.

"Don't worry. I won't tell anyone," Quinn reassured me with a smile that was soft and believable, even if I really didn't want to believe the man who had bullied me so badly back then. But, I supposed there was nothing I could do now apart from trust him. Quinn knew the truth, and I couldn't change that fact. Either he would tell, or he wouldn't.

"I'll get us some more drinks," Quinn

finally said, probably realizing I was stuck on the same train of thought, unable to find a way to the end of it. "Would you like some shots? I've been having the buttery nipples."

I laughed quickly, having not expected such a phrase to leave his lips. "Buttery nipples?" I asked incredulously. "I think I'll stick with Jaeger."

Quinn laughed lightly and shook his head. "Sure, because that isn't just a cough syrup knockoff. You have absolutely no leg to stand on when judging me."

I soon discovered that just sitting, chatting, and drinking with Quinn was actually rather fun. He was quick-witted and sarcastic, which I already knew, but when it was paired with a man who was smiling, and it wasn't in response to something spiteful either myself or the others had said, it was a fun combination, and I found myself laughing a lot. Ironically, I was actually enjoying myself and I felt like a weight had been lifted off my shoulders.

"You've actually had the 'save a cat from a tree' callout?" I laughed after hearing one of the most stereotypical fireman stories in the books.

"Twice. The second time was because

the old lady wanted tea with my colleague." Quinn laughed brightly. "He reminded her of her late husband, so he felt bad and agreed to have tea while I hung out with the cat we'd saved the previous week."

"You hung out with a cat?"

"Hey, don't knock it. Cats are cool company."

"True. I have a stray one who visits my place almost daily now." I flashed him a smile. "She's a cute little grey thing, tiny as though she's not grown properly."

"Oh, poor thing."

"Yeah, I had her checked. She's not micro-chipped, so I figure I'll put food out for her and give her a worming treatment. Least I can do."

"That's good of you. Most would have just shooed her away or taken her to an animal shelter."

I shook my head quickly. "I thought about it, but they are such small cages, and she is used to being outside." I drained the last of my beer before adding. "Besides, sometimes she'll come and sleep on my bed if I leave the window ajar, which is very nice."

"Company in bed usually is." Quinn laughed.

I immediately raised an eyebrow, and

smirked.

"That why you are here?" I didn't think a man as masculine as Quinn could blush, but his green eyes blinked twice as the color rose on his cheeks, and he glanced away.

"Maybe," he grumbled, bringing a half-mocking laugh from my lips. This time it was obvious that my teasing was not in a cruel sense.

"Well, what are you doing spending the whole night with me? Unless you think I'd bend over for you." I flashed him a flirty grin, slowly, vaguely realizing what I had said just a minute too late. Clearly the alcohol had gone to my head a little much if I was daring to flirt with someone I worked with. Never mind the fact that he had been my high school bully. Even if I was finding myself not despising him quite so much anymore.

I watched as a mixture of emotions ran over Quinn's face, but somehow I hadn't expected the mix to include lust.

"You shouldn't say things like that," Quinn started. "I tend to imagine ideas when they are put in my head like that."

I arched a brow and the words flew out of my mouth before I could stop them. "Oh really? And is that image a good one?"

"A very good one, so I would suggest you change the subject unless you are actually looking to rile me up." Quinn sent a challenging look my way.

It was tempting to keep going, though I couldn't say why. Perhaps it was the alcohol and the resulting lowered inhibitions. Perhaps it was simply because he was the most attractive man I had ever met, or perhaps it was because of the dreams I had been having over and over. Thankfully, I had the sense to know I would regret pushing those boundaries once I sobered up, and self-preservation finally kicked in. I raised my hands in defeat.

"All right, I'll stop," I agreed. "But considering we are both here to find someone for the night, we should probably be talking to more people than just each other."

"I suppose. But you are a good conversationalist." Quinn flashed me a smile and a wink.

"Turn that charm on for someone else. Come on, we'll find some people on the dance floor." I shook my head, pushing myself up from my seat and motioning for him to follow. I didn't much like dancing alone, but I would happily dance with someone and socialize with the people I found around us.

It was easy when people seemed to gravitate toward Quinn. He was taller than most of the men here, and even in the dark clothing he had chosen for the night, his muscles and rhythm were obvious.

I found a burning acidic feeling bubbling up in my gut as a youthful redhead with cute freckles danced up closer to Quinn, gaining his attention more than anyone else had done so far. I shouldn't have been jealous of that, I had no claim on the man, but shockingly, I did.

He didn't seem too interested in anything beyond the guy's body, though. The way he moved and swayed, the way he ran his hands up and down his arm while they both danced... It made me want to take Quinn by the hand and lead him away from all this madness.

But that was crazy right?

He was a colleague. He was my old bully and I was supposed to dislike him. He could dance and flirt with whomever he wanted. I had no right to be jealous. None.

So, why did the idea of him pressed up against anyone but me fill me with a bizarre anger that I could barely contain?

I wasn't sure why I reached out a hand to wrap around Quinn's wrist. The way the dark-haired male turned to look at me suggested he was just as confused.

"Jase..." he started, but I didn't want to hear it. Instead, I glanced once at the indignant-looking redhead before pulling Quinn forward and crashing my lips against his.

Part of my own mind screamed at my actions.

What the hell was I doing?

Kissing a man in public.

Kissing Quinn in public.

Second-guessing what I was doing, I moved to pull away when his arm looped around my waist and pulled me closer. Quinn kissed me with a passion I could never have dreamed up. I went weak in the knees, moaning into the kiss as his tongue pushed into my mouth and explored.

"I told you not to tempt me," he growled against my lips as he pulled back just slightly.

"Better than them tempting you," I grumbled. Before I could think about what I was doing, I let myself act on what my body wanted. "Come back to my place?"

Quinn raised an eyebrow, his eyes

filled with questioning concern. "Are you sure?"

I hesitated for a moment, all the mocking and fears rolling around in my mind. I could back out now. Or I could actually have a connection with someone I knew, who knew me and who wouldn't look at me differently afterward.

"I'm sure." I nodded, beginning to step back toward the edge of the dance floor. "So, how about it?"

Quinn's eyes instantly darkened with a desire that lit my body on fire.

Fuck.

No one had ever looked at me that way.

"Let's go." I grabbed his hand and tugged him toward the door.

CHAPTER SEVENTEEN

Jase

IT DID NOT take long for us to get to the hotel I had booked myself into. Quinn chuckled a little at the awful 80s decor that made up the hallway, and once I pushed open the door, he smirked widely.

"You were hoping to get lucky in a room like this?" He chuckled, turning to me as my expression fell.

Was he about to leave me here?

"It's a damn good thing you are gorgeous enough that the room doesn't matter."

With that, he crowded me against the closed door and kissed me as though he was a starving man and I was the only meal in a million miles. My breath caught in my chest when he finally released my lips. He placed his forehead against mine before whispering, "I want you so badly."

"Quinn," I said on a soft sigh, not wanting to break the spell. He nipped my bottom lip, sending a bolt of desire straight to my core. His hand slid down my back until it wrapped around my ass and pulled me even more tightly against him.

"Do you want to be on the bottom or the top?" he mumbled against my lips.

Top.

I should have immediately said I wanted to be on top.

I moaned deeply as his leg pressed between my thighs, and his thick thigh rubbed against my already throbbing and engorged dick.

"Bottom," I panted out, surprising even myself.

"Really?" Quinn asked, astonishment lacing his voice.

I nodded eagerly. "Yes. I just... just... need..." God, I didn't know what I needed. Quinn seemed to think that there was something he understood in those words though, as he nodded and pressed himself tighter against my body, catching my lips with his once more.

Running my hands up his chest, I began to unbutton the shirt I had wanted to get under all night.

His body was as gorgeous as I had expected, but I didn't get much of a chance to admire before he pulled me back toward the bed, turning until he was able to guide me until I fell onto the soft mattress. As I lay there, my breaths coming quickly, I watched as Quinn towered over me, slowly pulling his shirt off.

"It should be illegal to look that good," I mumbled, licking my lips.

Quinn laughed. "Well, thank you. I think I prefer the sight in front of me." He smirked, making me feel almost self-conscious, like a meal spread out for him. Self-conscious but powerfully aroused.

"Well, I'm not here for you just to stare at me." I lifted a hand to beckon him forward, something he did more than willingly. "Take off your pants," I ordered.

Watching Quinn do as I told him was thrilling, and even though it left me fully clothed with him crawling up the bed in just his boxers, I felt alive. His lips met mine once more, and he ground his hips down skillfully against mine. I could feel his size and length through his boxers and groaned into the kiss as his movements provided enough friction to rub my jeans against my own cock. He was just heavy enough to make me feel pinned but light enough that I could thrust my hips upward for more friction and know he would struggle to stop me.

If there was going to be a physical power play, I doubted there would be a winner. But as I pulled away from his lips and kissed along his jaw, sinking the fingers of my right hand into his hair and forcing his head to tilt to the side, I realized that if I wanted a power play, I could probably win it.

He whimpered a little, then moaned deeply as I pressed my teeth down on the sensitive skin of his neck, his breathy sounds mixing with mine as his hips thrust forward.

"Fuck." He groaned, one of his hands running down my shirt and unbuckling my jeans to make room to slide underneath. "You've got some size to you..."

I smirked a little, raising an eyebrow. "Would you rather I fucked you?"

"Another time." Quinn chuckled darkly. "For now, I wanna see if I can take it somewhere else."

For a moment, my brain lingered on the phrase, another time. Warning bells tried to go off that maybe this was a bad idea.

What if Quinn really did out me back

home?

Those thoughts flew from my head when I felt a wet heat surround my length. Looking down quickly, I saw possibly the most attractive sight I'd ever seen before.

Quinn's mouth was stretched around my cock, very slightly pulled into a smirk as his green eyes watched my reaction. He was clearly well versed in the act as his tongue ran over every sensitive area. My head fell back against the pillow as he pulled moans from my lips over and over. He was too damn good at this.

"Quinn, I didn't bring you here for this," I whined after a short while.

"Feeling impatient?" he asked with a laugh as he pulled back and flashed a smile at me, his eyes filled with such need that I could feel reciprocated through my whole body.

"Yes," I replied instantly.

Quinn laughed. "Well, if you'd tell me where you put your prep stuff, I'd be able to do more than this."

I blinked up at him for a moment before I laughed and shook my head. "The drawer of the left bedside table."

"Gotcha." Once he knew where things were, Quinn took no time in fetching the lube and coating his index and middle finger with it. Pushing my jeans down to my knees, he slid his hand between my legs, and the first finger ran around the edge of my rim before slowly sinking inside.

Taking me apart was something Quinn didn't need much practice with at all. I was soon bare from the waist down, and my shirt unbuttoned so he could bite down on the skin by my ribs, which he had discovered made me shudder and moan.

"You sound good," Quinn whispered into my ear as he pulled his fingers from me. "Roll over."

Normally, I would have argued being told what to do, but I found myself rolling over to my front, my body pliant when Quinn's strong hands pulled at my hips to guide me onto my hands and knees. The sound of the lube bottle and a condom packet ripping made me lick my lips, whimpering in anticipation.

Groaning deeply as Quinn's length pushed inside me, I felt the burn of the stretch and the pulsing heat slowly filling more and more of me. I decided then and there that what they said about big men might have been correct. They weren't just tall...

Pausing once he had pushed in as far

as I could take him, Quinn draped himself over my back, kissing, licking, and nibbling at the back of my neck. "You're so fucking hot, Jase." My name on his lips was ambrosia.

As soon as he began to move, all sense was lost. I don't know how many times I moaned his name, I don't know when it was that I ripped the pillowcase with my fingers, and I honestly don't know if we had one round or two before I passed out from exhaustion and pleasure.

CHAPTER EIGHTEEN

Quinn

THE CURTAINS OF the musty old motel room did nothing to keep the sun off of my face the following morning. Normally, I liked basking in the sun, but even with my eyes closed against it, I could feel the light causing my head to pound.

Rolling over with a groan, I stretched out my arm, expecting to find a body, but I found nothing but empty space and cold sheets.

Bracing myself against the pain, I opened my eyes slowly as the light hit me square in the face like a hot poker. I was alone on the bed, naked except for the top sheet. I glanced around the room. It was completely empty... the only sounds were from outside.

"He left?" I asked no one, letting a sigh

leave my lips. As I pushed myself to a seated position, my head swam with a hangover I probably shouldn't have had.

After inspecting the bedside tables, I realized there weren't any of Jase's belongings left. Nor was there a single note to explain why he had gone. I felt disappointed and mildly irritated. I thought we had gotten to a better place the night before, even without the sexual events that followed. The fact he had been willing to get up and leave without a word was slightly hurtful.

With a huff of annoyance, I climbed from the bed to search through my discarded clothes for my phone.

"Fuck!" I groaned in frustration when my gaze landed on the time and the dying battery. I was late for my own checkout, which meant no time to charge my phone either.

"Could have at least woken me as he left, so this didn't cost me extra," I grumbled as I threw on the clothes from the previous night and rushed out the door, and as quickly as I could, made my way back to my hotel.

There was no time to shower. Therefore, I swiftly changed into a casual set of clothes for travel and checked out. I didn't enjoy the concept of sitting in my car for an hour smelling of sex, sweat, and alcohol, but I didn't have much choice.

It still bothered me that Jase had left without a word.

Was he angry?

Was he ashamed?

Did he regret what had happened?

He had definitely invited me back to his room, and he had been the one to ask for more than just a blowjob. I could not remember doing anything that he hadn't asked for... But perhaps it had been adrenaline and alcohol that had fuelled it. I had certainly had nights where I had regretted it, but I at least had the decency to stick around.

Finally, about fifteen minutes from Baton Rouge, I recalled the look of sheer panic that had dawned on his face when he had first seen me at the club.

Perhaps the answer was as simple as Jase had gotten scared when he woke up sober and realized he would actually have to face the man who had fucked him?

It could have been a hard hit from reality that made him freak out and flee before I awoke.

Thinking about it that way, I felt all the irritation in me fade. Now I only wished that he had stayed so I could have ensured he knew this was not something to be afraid of. It was a fun night, but if he never wanted to acknowledge it, then I would respect that. I had no intention of making the closet more difficult for him to be in.

Reaching home was bliss for me. Thinking so much about the situation with a hangover and not much sleep had left me exhausted. I needed food, water, pills, and probably a nap before I would be able to function properly. Jared wasn't in, which meant doing all of that was on the cards, and falling asleep on the couch was acceptable.

After popping two pain pills, followed by scarfing down a few pieces of left over pizza I'd found in the refrigerator, and guzzling a bottle of water, I went straight to the living room, closed the blinds behind me, and flopped onto the sofa face first. The piece of furniture groaned under my weight as I crawled over it, passing out before my head had even reached the other end.

CHAPTER NINETEEN

Quinn

WHEN I WOKE, I could hear the low drone of voices from the television and knew immediately that Jared was home and watching his nature show in silence so he didn't disturb me.
"You had a good night, I take it?" He chuckled once I had stirred enough for him to know I was conscious.

"What?" I asked stupidly, still groggy from sleep.

"You smell of sex, dude." Jared laughed.

I groaned slightly. I had been so tired after having food that I had completely forgotten to shower before falling asleep.

"Sorry," I mumbled as I sat up and blinked drowsily, glancing around the room. It was still light out, but that didn't mean much, as it was summer. It could have been eight in the evening, for all I knew.

"Don't be! I'm glad to know the night was a success."

"Hmm. Not sure about that."

Jared cocked his head to the side as his smile faltered. "What do you mean?"

I hesitated for a moment, unsure how I was going to be able to explain it without outing Jase. Not that Jared knew him or would say anything, but the principle of it was important. I had promised not to tell anyone what I knew, and I intended to keep that promise.

"I bumped into someone I knew," I began slowly. "We had such a laugh, and we ended up sleeping together, but in retrospect, it was probably one of my worst ideas." Even if it wasn't really my idea, sure, I had thought about it, but it was Jase who had acted.

"If you had fun, why was it a bad idea?" Jared ventured.

I sighed heavily before the main thought I had been stuck on for most of the day fell from my lips. "Because I want to do it again."

Jared laughed loudly. "That good?"

"No. Well, yes..." I admitted. "But it's not just that. I want the laughter, the conversation, and I'd like to actually wake up with him still there so I could make breakfast.

"Careful, sounds like you like the guy." Jared chuckled.

"Yeah, sure." I laughed it off, reminding myself just how long it had been since I had been in a relationship and justifying that that was the reason why I was fantasizing about those things. Usually, the daydreams were fine, but more often than not, I didn't imagine one specific person. Hopefully, the Jase addition to them would fade in time, and work wouldn't become awkward again.

Still, it was near impossible to forget the way Jase had looked spread around my fingers or how delicious his moans were as I drove into him harder than I thought I'd be able to. Once he was relaxed and aroused enough, he had even met my thrusts with each stroke, making the force that I tormented his insides with considerably higher.

It was a miracle I had lasted as long as I had, though I suspected the alcohol had more to do with that than anything.

In the shower ten minutes later, the memories of the night before joined my hand and me in a joyous self-pleasuring session.

CHAPTER TWENTY

Quinn

THE NEXT MORNING, I woke up from a dream of taking Jase against my bedroom door, where he cried out beautifully. By the time I got to work, I wasn't actually sure I would be able to look at him without feeling some kind of arousal.

I was the first to arrive for the shift, which at least meant I could get settled in and help myself to the worst coffee in the world before anyone else arrived. I had to put six sugars in it just to make it tolerable, but I needed something to do while I waited for the previous shift to leave. Otherwise, I was going to drive myself insane.

Carmen greeted me with a nod while Mark and Johnson gave the usual half-assed wave I had become familiar with. It was obvious they had worked with and known Jase for a long time and had his back automatically, even if they didn't know everything. In a way, I respected them for their loyalty, but that didn't mean it didn't piss me off too.

"Morning to you too. Hope you had a nice weekend," I called after them. I realized moments later that I shouldn't have let my irritation out on anyone. Carmen's raised eyebrow said that much. If I wasn't looking for trouble, I shouldn't go around starting it.

I shrugged my shoulders in response and turned back to my locker, which I had decided to deep clean during my wait. My coffee sat on the top of it so I could reach up and have a sip whenever I wanted. Though, every sip made me grimace in disgust.

"I thought I warned you the coffee here was shit?" The laugh that came from behind me was honestly one I didn't think I'd hear again. Turning around, I found myself looking at Jase's amused grin as he pulled a coffee from the carrier tray in his hand and held it out for me to take. "Here."

It wasn't exactly something huge. It wasn't an explanation of his disappearance or any form of acknowledgment that anything had even happened. But it was a very clear sign that Jase didn't hate me for what happened. As he walked away, I felt a tension in my spine release along with confusion.

Had I actually been that worried that Jase was going to hate me?

He had despised me since I stepped foot into this place.

Had one night of laughter really given me that much hope?

Lifting the cup, I took a sip of a sweet, almost buttery-tasting latte. It reminded me of the Buttery Nipples, and I laughed lightly to myself.

Maybe Jase *was* acknowledging what had happened. He just couldn't handle a conversation that was too serious right now. That kind of tone could easily freak anyone out. I understood that.

"Damn, coffees all around. You're in a good mood." Mark laughed.

I couldn't help but look across the locker room and watch what little I could through the open door.

"Bet he got laid while we were off." Johnson nudged Jase in the ribs, careful not to spill his own coffee but laughing loudly when Jase choked slightly on his.

"You're an idiot," Jase grumbled, his

cheeks darkening in color.

Damn.

He looked good when he blushed, and honestly, I found I liked that his cheeks grew a deep pink shade at the memory of what we had done together.

"You did! Ha! Was she hot?" Mark demanded.

"Was she good?" Johnson joined in.

"Bet he can't even remember her name...." Carmen's voice sounded from somewhere, sounding half amused and half bored. If the door opening and closing was anything to go by, she had probably just gone out for a smoke to get away from the typical guy talk.

"Oh, ignore her," Mark commented. "Come on, tell us. Was she blonde? You like blondes."

I frowned, a niggling feeling of annoyance in my chest.

"Actually..." Jase sighed. "She had dark hair, nearly black. She was hot as hell. Tall, long legs, muscles, and curves, in the right places. A mouth to die for, if you know what I mean."

The two men whistled and laughed at the comment. I was very glad to be in another room as there was no chance I would be able to hide the triumphant smirk that sat on my face as I continued to clean out my locker. Jase was definitely talking about me. Everything other than the pronouns fit.

They were still asking questions by the time I had finished my work on my locker, and I wandered back through to the main room. Jase quickly turned crimson as I entered, most likely assuming I hadn't heard anything so far.

Anyway," he started. "As it's a damn good day, I figured I would tackle the store room. If you guys need me, I'll be in there."

I almost laughed at the obvious stumble he made trying to turn around and flee the room so fast. It was definitely unfair that someone so hot was also that cute. The thought frustrated me. I was supposed to have gotten this out of my system, not developed some kind of stupid crush.

Shit.

Rolling my eyes at myself, I took a seat away from the others to go over some paperwork Captain Clarke had left for us. The coffee and the wordy rambling papers in front of me were at least able to distract me from the fact I was actually tempted to make Jase blush more.

Unfortunately, the papers and coffee only lasted so long. Quicker than I would have liked, I was walking through the station with the papers in hand to give them back to the Captain. I'd have to give him some feedback as well, but other than a few repeating rambles, the general flow was good.

"So what happened with you and Quinn?"

I paused as I heard Mark's voice from the male bathroom.

"What do you mean?" Jase replied.

"You brought a coffee for him as well this morning. Since when do you play nice with him?"

Mark had a point. Jase had made it pretty obvious that there was something different between us now. I felt bad eavesdropping, but I couldn't make my feet move. I wanted to know what Jase was going to say. He surely wasn't going to admit what had really occurred.

"I bumped into him at the coffee shop the other day." Jase sounded calm. I wondered if I was about to hear a cover story that he had been rehearsing. "We decided to have a chat and came to an agreement to be civil before we create enough of a war zone that it fucks us over in the field."

"Really?"

"Yeah. I mean, think about it. What

happens when we get a serious call out, and we all need to have each other's backs? If he and I are at odds and don't trust each other, it could cost someone their life." Jase sighed. "I still hurt from what happened in school, but it ain't worth destroying my future over."

Having heard enough, I forced myself to walk on through the corridor. If Jase was about to speak more of the personal pain I had caused him, I didn't want to overhear that. I wanted him to talk to me in person so I could try to rectify at least a tiny portion of it.

It was a good cover story, though. Even with trust, this job was dangerous enough.

"You all right, son?" Captain Clarke asked as I climbed to my feet after giving him some feedback about the document.

"Just thinking about New Orleans," I admitted.

His face softened immediately, and he nodded. "It was an absolute tragedy. You know, we have a trained therapist on site to help with stuff like this if you need to speak to him. I can set it up quick and discreet like."

It was touching that he would respond like that. Something in his eyes told me that he had seen the therapist once or twice in his career too.

"I'll think about it. Thanks, Cap."

He didn't press the issue. Instead, he just got up from his chair to give me a clap on my shoulder and tell me that the station had my back before motioning for me to get out of his office.

It was a slow morning, but around midday, we received a call out for a car crash on the highway. I hated callouts like this. Being a firefighter, we were trained to give emergency medical treatment, but that didn't mean it was always successful. We arrived before the ambulance and had to begin cutting a young lady from her car while keeping her neck supported in case there was major damage there. Thankfully, she was the only one injured, so Jase and I were able to focus until the paramedics arrived and got her strapped down with a collar on her so she couldn't move and injure herself further.

"Thank god it wasn't worse," I mumbled as we clambered into the truck.

"Yeah, I've seen some hellish crashes in my time." Jase sighed. "Makes you think about how short life is."

"It's what prompted me to come out..." I admitted, unsurprised by the raised eyebrow Jase gave me. "I was in a drunken crash when I was at college. My friend was seriously injured, but he pulled through. I had a massive crush on him, and suddenly I didn't want to hide that anymore because what if I missed out on something great?"

"So you told him?"

"Yeah, and he punched me in the face and told me to leave him the hell alone."

Jase's features scrunched up in both horror and disgust. "The fuck?"

I laughed lightly and shrugged. "It wasn't the end of the world. It made me realize I'd rather be rejected for who I actually am than loved for pretending to be something that made me miserable."

"You've got guts," Jase breathed after a moment. "I'm more scared of that punch and rejection than anything else."

"And that's okay," I responded. "Fear can keep us safe."

Jase smiled softly as though he had been worried that he was going to be reprimanded for being in the closet.

"If you ever need someone to talk to though, I can always listen." I flashed him a smile. "We could get it over coffee or something."

Jase arched an eyebrow, his look questioning.

"You know... like we did a couple of

days ago?" I prompted.

Jase gaped for a moment before sending a slight glare my way. "You overheard me?"

"I did. Though it may have been practical to let me know the cover story so I didn't blow it for you." I laughed.

"Shut up," he grumbled.

"Hey, I could have asked if the tall, dark-haired beauty was really as good in bed as you were describing earlier." I smirked widely, adding what I knew to be an evil teasing glint in my gaze as Jase turned his attention from the road to look at me in surprise.

"Asshole." Jase laughed as he shook his head and smiled.

He was considerably more relaxed around me. Perhaps it was because I had listened to the story of the girl without batting an eye or correcting him. Perhaps he had a little more faith that I wasn't going to out him.

Finally, I felt like I could actually settle into work and was able to relax and start to fit into the team properly.

Jase was fun to be on the trucks with. We spent a lot of time teasing each other and exchanging banter, much like Jase did with everyone else. But every now and then, I would say something a bit too playful, and a slight blush would creep up Jase's cheeks. Every time it did, I was plagued by the same annoying thoughts that he was just so damn cute for someone so hot.

CHAPTER TWENTY-ONE

Quinn

"ARGH, HE'S DRIVING me insane," I grumbled one evening as I flopped down onto the sofa.

"Who?"

"Jase!"

"Is he still being an asshole?"

"Does being so cute I want to kiss him and so hot I want to fuck him count as being an asshole?" I huffed as my roommate laughed loudly at me.

"Depends. Does he know he's doing it?" Jared asked, sniggering in amusement, and kicking my feet off the edge of the sofa so he could sit down.

"I think he knows he's hot, but I don't think he knows just how crazy he is driving me." I sighed. "I thought sleeping with him as a one-time thing would be fine, get it out of my system type deal, but I really just want to do it again."

Jared paused. "Quinn... was Jase the one you were with when you were in Lafayette?"

My eyes widened as I realized that I'd given myself away and he had figured it out fast. I'd also inadvertently broken my promise and outed Jase, much to my chagrin.

"So, he's not as straight as you say?"

Rolling my eyes slightly, I finally gave in. "No, he isn't. But he's very much in the closet and determined to stay in it."

"Damn. I'm sorry, man." Jared actually seemed to be sympathetic to my troubles. "Is the fact that you bullied him still a sore point too?"

Letting my head drop forward, I sighed heavily. "God knows, but probably, knowing my luck." I had been trying not to think about it, but there were still many moments when he shrunk back from me as something reminded him of our years in school.

I hated who I used to be. I had been such a stupid, pompous, and arrogant young brat who didn't think about his actions. If they had caused this much pain for Jase, I didn't want to imagine who else was still suffering from the things I had done.

"Okay, we need to get you in a better mindset. Let's go out!" Jared said after a couple of beats.

"I don't want to," I replied with a sigh. For some reason, I couldn't even muster up the energy to dress up and smile.

"Oh, come on. We'll go pig out on some junk food along with some good drinks." Jared nudged at my side in the same way that an annoying child might when they wanted attention. Turning my gaze to him, I made it very clear that I wasn't impressed by the action.

"Can you not?" I deadpanned.

"I know how to annoy you into doing what I want," Jared chuckled. "Sure you want to out-stubborn me?"

For a moment, I debated trying just that. But I knew that he wasn't about to give in, so I just let out a dramatic sigh and nodded. "Fine, you win. Let me change first."

CHAPTER TWENTY-TWO

Quinn

JARED ALWAYS MANAGED to make having drinks and playing pool a good laugh. He was the life of the party, but he didn't drink much, and his game never dipped. He somehow made friends with other patrons, and I soon found myself laughing easily and drinking my way through more pints than I perhaps should have. After another hour or two, I felt as though I couldn't keep up with Jared's pace any longer and decided to try and get his attention so we could go home.

"Yo, Jar," I slurred as I stumbled over thin air, trying to get through the crowd in the bar. "I think it's time for me to say goodbye."

Jared looked at me and chuckled at the way I swayed on my feet. "Damn, you are drunk," he said as we both laughed.

"Yeah, well, I've had a few too many tonight," I told him as he moved toward the exit so he could open the door for me. "Such a gentleman," I mumbled as we walked out into the night air.

"No need to thank me. You're welcome anytime," Jared replied as he held the door open for me. We walked down the front steps, Jared's arm wrapping around me as I slipped and nearly fell.

"You all right?" he asked me as he steadied me against his side.

"Yes. Thank you." I smiled up at him before I closed my eyes and leaned back against him. "I'm tired."

He pulled me closer to him and then wrapped his arm around my shoulder. "I'm not surprised. Come on, let's get you home."

We were halfway across the street when I heard someone yell out to us from behind. I turned to see who it was but didn't recognize anyone in the crowd. It wasn't until the guy started walking toward us that I realized who he was.

"Quinn, my man!" The guy yelled out as he approached. "How have you been, my friend? Haven't seen you in a while."

Jared looked at me with a questioning expression. "Who is this guy?"

"This is Harold. Used to go to my dad's church," I said slowly, wondering if I should pull myself away from Jared. I really needed to get home because my head was pounding again, and I just wanted to be alone.

"Oh, wow. Hey, Harold." Jared grinned at him before turning back to me. "I'll walk you home."

"That's some good friendship right there." Harold smiled. "But, I just... eh... wanted to warn you, Quinn. There are some pretty unfavorable rumors going around about you. You may not want to stumble so close to another guy on your way home."

"What?" I frowned at him. "Why? What did I do?"

Harold took a step back and looked me up and down. "They're saying you sin with men, Quinn. Horrid thing, really. I mean, I was at school with ya. I know you'd never do something that disgusting... but there's a lot of people who are starting to talk."

I felt a prickle of anger in my chest, and even though I couldn't stand straight, I still turned a glare toward Harold. "And what exactly is so disgusting about it?" I snapped at him.

Harold looked shocked for a moment.

"It's wrong. It's unnatural."

"Well, no one's asking you to do it..." I grumbled. These were the kinds of things that made people scared to come out. My mind went to my past, where I had said such things to Jase. No wonder he had hated me so. "I *am* gay, Harold. If you've got a problem with it, I'm happy to face you anytime."

Harold's mouth opened and closed like a fish out of water. His whole expression changed, and suddenly he was looking at me like I was the scum on the bottom of his shoe as opposed to an old friend.

"How could you?" he asked, as though he was somehow experiencing a betrayal. "Do you understand how sinful this is?"

The anger inside me flared, and I stepped forward, ready to tell Harold just what I thought of him. But Jared's hand on my arm stopped me, and I saw the look in his eye. It was one of warning. Not to fight with Harold but to put up a fight in another way. There was a gleaming look of mischief in his eyes that gave me an idea of exactly what other way the man was thinking.

Well, he was the one with a partner to explain it to later.

"Well, if it's that sinful, maybe you'll be corrupted if you stay and watch,"

Reaching out a hand, I sealed my fingers around Jared's shirt and pulled him to me, catching his lips with my own and kissing him hard.

Harold's eyes bulged out of his skull as I kissed Jared so hard he couldn't even speak or react much. I don't know why I did it. Maybe I was angry at the world, maybe I was drunk, or maybe I just wanted to show Harold that I just didn't care what he and the church thought of me anymore.

Once I had heard Harold storm off, I released Jared from my grip and smiled awkwardly at him. "I hope that's what that mischievous look was suggesting."

"Actually, I was going to suggest you kissed him, but that worked too." Jared laughed loudly, clapping me on the back and then catching me as I stumbled from the force of it.

"Okay, Drinkerella. Home to bed." Jared chuckled. "You need your rest."

I nodded, turning to head home. "Yeah, I think I better do that. Thanks for helping me."

"My pleasure," Jared replied as we finally made it through the front door.

I stumbled into my room and fell face first across my bed without even taking my shoes off. My last thought before I passed out was how I was going to regret drinking so much in the morning.

CHAPTER TWENTY-THREE

Jase

I HAD NOT expected to see Quinn out in town that warm summer night. It was after a long day shift, and from previous conversations, I knew he preferred to stay home. But there he was, standing by the bar with his back turned to me in conversation with his friend, who was laughing at something he'd said. My suspicions were confirmed when Quinn turned around, smiling so easily at the man he was with.

Was he on a date?

The very idea of it had an ill sense of jealousy bubbling up within me. While I didn't have anything against the two of them being together or even having a relationship, as long as they made sure not to involve me, it just seemed wrong for him to be with someone else, knowing how much I cared about him.

Wait.

He didn't know.

I had specifically made sure I kept any and all thoughts and feelings under control since our night together. I needed to keep my distance if I wanted things to remain platonic between us.

But now that he was getting close to another man, could I really let this go without saying something?

What would happen if I did?

No.

He was a bully and an asshole. I didn't want to be with him anyway.

Deciding to get out of the bar and head to another for the night to get away from the annoying circle of thoughts in my head, I soon bumped into an old friend from school. "Hey there, Callie," I greeted her happily, trying to push any thoughts of Quinn out of my mind.

"Oh my god, Jase! Hi!" She was a perky woman with a short pixie cut and a smile that had always been cute but a little lopsided. Her crooked teeth gave her face character, making her seem more approachable than most. "How are you? You look happy."

"Yeah. Things are good," I lied.

JASE

"You're a firefighter these days, aren't you?" Callie asked.

I nodded. "That's right. Been there almost ten years now."

Callie looked impressed. "Wow, so you pretty much went in straight after high school?"

"Well, I had a few years of changing jobs to see what I liked, but yeah," I admitted.

"I'm glad you found your calling. That is such a cool job. I ended up teaching." She laughed. "And now I drink more than I should admit."

We chatted for a while before she left me to go to her next destination. As I walked down the street alone, I couldn't help but think of Quinn again. The thought of him with another man made me feel jealous, angry, and strangely... excited. Though I knew I shouldn't be thinking about him like that, especially given how I felt about him, I just couldn't stop myself.

What am I doing?

Why am I jealous?

I shook the thoughts from my head. I should just go home.

As I rounded a corner, lost in my own thoughts, I spotted Quinn and his friend again. They were walking close, the man's arm around Quinn to keep him close.

Did they just leave the same place?

How long had they known each other?

Why was he paying attention to him instead of me?

I paused, knowing if I walked at my pace, I would end up having to acknowledge them. For a moment, I debated walking the long way home when I saw Quinn being approached by a man I had never liked.

Harold Wright.

He had been one of Quinn's friends in school, and he had been even worse of a bully. If anyone had ever crossed him, he would make their life a living hell.

He was tall, broad-shouldered, and had the kind of greasy hair that only comes from regular use of styling products. His eyes were brown, though the yellow hue of the streetlights made them look otherworldly and evil. He wore a Fred Perry polo shirt and lacrosse jeans with Timberlakes adorning his feet. He was a man of money and it was obvious he took good care of himself, having muscles that bulged through his shirt that I could see from across the street.

Whatever he was talking to Quinn about obviously wasn't pleasant. I could see the discomfort and anger in my coworker. Quinn's whole body was tense and even though I couldn't see his face, I knew his expression was probably tight while he tried to keep himself calm. A large part of me yearned to go over and comfort him.

But I didn't.

Instead, I watched.

Quinn gave a terse response, which I could hear even though I couldn't see his face. Then, he turned, and my heart sank. His lips slamming against the man he had been laughing with earlier sent lightning pain racing through my chest. My mouth dropped open, and I felt the sharp twinge of jealousy and hurt.

Why was he kissing another guy like that?

I quickly moved away, heading back the way I came. Not wanting to watch anymore, I tried to shake off my emotions.

Who cared if he kissed that asshole?

It wasn't my business.

Right?

CHAPTER TWENTY-FOUR

Jase

THE REST OF the weekend passed in a blur. I did my best to pretend I hadn't seen Quinn in public with another man. I knew it was wrong, but I couldn't help but feel a little wounded. I knew there was nothing actually between Quinn and me, and yet, I still felt rejected.

I spent Sunday in bed, alone, watching TV. Monday morning, I got up early, showered, and drove to work. I walked in, relieved to find the locker room empty. I didn't have the energy to deal with anyone right now.

I caught sight of myself in a mirror set next to the shower stall. My hair was still wet from my shower at home, so it looked even more like I'd been dragged through a jungle by wild dogs. My eyes were rimmed with dark circles and my skin was pasty white and covered in dry patches. I couldn't believe how bad I felt... especially after sleeping all last night. It must have been a really shitty night. I was glad I couldn't remember if I had any dreams on top of the frustrating thoughts of Quinn with another man. I pulled on my uniform and grabbed a cup of coffee before heading out into the hall.

"Jase! Hey, didn't wake up early enough to stop in for the good stuff?" Johnson asked, motioning to the coffee that everyone knew I hated.

I shrugged. "I had a rough night," I lied.

"Ah, yeah. I hear ya." He nodded. "Hopefully, the day makes it better."

I had to work with Quinn, so I doubted that there would be any kind of plus to the day. Especially if he decided to tell me about his boyfriend. The idea of hearing about someone else kissing him made me want to scream, even though I knew it shouldn't. It did.

"Morning, Jase. Good morning, Johnson," Quinn greeted us as we walked down the hall.

"Good morning, Quinn," I returned, trying to ignore the twinge of guilt I felt every time I thought about what I'd seen and how I was reacting internally.

Just because he has a boyfriend doesn't mean I can't be happy for him.

Or does it?

It was almost lunchtime when Quinn walked past me toward the break room. He stopped and gave me a quick smile. "Hey, Jase."

I smiled back. "You have a good weekend?"

"Yeah, thanks. You?" he asked, turning to look at me. There was an awkward pause where neither of us said anything.

"Um..." I stammered, unable to come up with something to say. "Yeah, good."

"Okay then. See you later, all right?" He turned to walk away.

I looked after him, feeling a bit disappointed that our conversation was over so quickly. He seemed distracted, and I wondered if his mind was preoccupied. I let myself think that maybe he wasn't thinking about his boyfriend at all but rather me. That he was interested in me too.

I knew it was wishful thinking, but I hoped anyway.

This was getting ridiculous. But more than that, I found myself jealous of how both Quinn and the other man had been able to just show their desire in public. Doing that was everything I wanted but everything I feared. I'd never acted on my desires before because I didn't want anyone to know about them.

And even if they did know, what would they think?

Would they tell others?

Would people laugh at me for thinking such things?

Would they judge me as a pervert or worse?

It wasn't worth the risk. Besides, it wasn't like I hadn't made out with girls before... But it had just felt so wrong.

Anything with girls always felt wrong. Even when my mother spoke about a young lady she had met at her yoga class.

"I think you'd really like her," my mother said to me over dinner one night. "She's very sweet but has a wicked sense of humor."

My mother always seemed to have these mysterious friends who were 'very sweet' and who she told me about every time we talked on the phone. It was rare for her to bring them up over dinner in person, though. Most of the time, I ended up feeling like I should duck and cover to avoid any further talk.

I thought about meeting the girl just to

satisfy my mother. But the image of Quinn kissing that other man flashed into my mind, followed by the memory of how he had kissed me at the club and the way his muscles seemed to shine with a small layer of sweat when we had slept together. The fact that he did not make me feel dirty only made my thoughts about him all the more confusing. I knew nothing could ever come from it... but my mouth opened before I could think anything through.

"Mom, I can't keep meeting up with girls. I'm gay. It'll never work out," I said, a sad and defeated tone overlapping the words.

Time seemed to freeze. My mother stared at me for a few seconds while I waited for a retort, some form of denial or anger that would indicate my honesty had been wrong. She was silent. Then she stood up and took my hand in hers.

"I don't care if you're gay..." she said simply.

I looked up in surprise, searching her face, which went from calm to mildly annoyed.

"Did you really think I would care? Boy, how little do you think of me?" she asked sternly, looking down at me.

"No, Mom! Of course, you wouldn't

care," I replied, suddenly wondering where I had even got myself concerned that she would. She had always been a supportive and caring woman.

She paused again, trying to find the right words, then smiled.

"You're right. You should have said something sooner. I feel bad having tried to set you up with so many women." She reached over and patted my cheek. "I'll just have to find a nice man for you instead."

I laughed at the idea of my mother trying to set me up with a man. But I couldn't help but smile back at her. I loved the woman, despite her oddities.

"Maybe there's someone at work?" she suggested with a raised eyebrow. "Firefighters are usually cute."

I blushed a little, ducking my head and taking a large mouthful of the apple pie she had brought out.

"Oh, there is... What's he like?"

"Taken," I grumbled, watching her face fall into something akin to sympathy.

"Oh, love. I'm sorry," she said, reaching over and placing a hand on mine. "It's hard to meet men without being obvious about your interests."

I sighed a little, feeling a bit embarrassed now that I had admitted to her that I was gay. "He knows I'm gay. He is too. But I've seen him with another guy, so I guess I'm a bit late to the scene."

"Well, if he didn't wait for you, then he isn't the one," Mom said.

I chuckled at her idealism.

"So, you are telling me Dad was *The One* for you?" I chuckled, glancing at the back door. As usual, Dad had vacated the table as soon as he had finished his meal and taken his dessert and a beer into his workshop.

"He has his moments where I wonder," Mom laughed. "But I do love him with everything I am."

My smile faltered slightly. "How do you think he'll take the news?"

"Oh, you leave the old grump to me. He'll be fine." She flashed me a reassuring smile before finishing off her pie.

I rolled my eyes, amused at the way she tried to pretend everything was normal.

CHAPTER TWENTY-FIVE

Jase

I SPENT MOST of the rest of the week working. It was harder than expected to stay away from Quinn and the memories we made together. I kept thinking of the things he'd whispered to me, the way he smelled, the way his skin felt against mine. We had such a good time together. And yet I was still conflicted about what he meant to me.

Was it lust?

Or something else entirely?

On Friday night, I practically crawled into my house after a long shift at the fire station. I was exhausted, but I couldn't stop thinking about Quinn. I wanted to see him again outside of work.

But what would happen if I did see him?

Would he reject me?

Stumbling into the bathroom, I turned on the water, allowing it to heat while I stripped down, tossing the dirty clothes into the hamper.

Stepping under the hot spray, I sighed as the water beat down on my sore muscles, my mind wandering back to the night with Quinn and my dick hardening instantly.

I grabbed some body wash, running my hand over my pecs and down my abdomen until I fisted my already hard cock, a moan slipping from my lips as memories flitted through my brain.

My body going pliant when Quinn's strong hands pulled at my hips to guide me onto my hands and knees. The sound of the lube bottle and a condom packet being ripped open and making me whimper in anticipation.

Groaning deeply as Quinn's hard length pushed inside me and I felt the burn of the stretch and the pulsing heat slowly filling more and more of me.

Quinn pausing once he had pushed in as far as I could take him, draping himself over my back, kissing, licking, and nibbling at the back of my neck. Pressing his lightly furred chest flush against my back as he whispered my name in my ear, making me cum again and again.

I moaned his name, my breath catching in my chest as I felt my release build up within me, pulling my balls up tight, heat rushing through my belly before long, thick ropes of cum painted the shower walls, mixing with the water and swirling down the drain.

Just as I stepped from the shower, tying a fresh towel around my hips, my phone dinged from across the room, and I quickly jogged over and snatched it up. My heart fluttered as I saw that it was a text from Quinn, with an invitation to come hang out at his place.

What were the odds?

CHAPTER TWENTY-SIX

Quinn

WELL, I'D DONE it. Inviting Jase to my place had been a challenging thing to do. I was very nervous about being behind closed doors with him, without anyone else around.

Jared had agreed to go to a friend's for the evening so I could have some space. We'd stayed up talking until well after midnight most nights since our night out and the backlash I had received from the church and my parents. Eventually, Jared convinced me to try to see if anything could develop with Jase. He said he wanted me to be happy and that he would support whatever decision I made. So, I texted Jase the next day and invited him over. I was honestly surprised he agreed.

I decided on an old-fashioned spaghetti

bolognese. It's one of my favorite meals and a true comfort food from my past. I'd also baked some bread earlier in the week as part of my new healthy eating kick, so I rustled that up into a loaf of garlic bread to go with the meal.

Shortly before Jase was due to arrive, I began second-guessing myself. I had put on one of my nicer shirts and a pair of tight black jeans that left little to the imagination... but I hadn't said anything about a date in the text.

What if Jase thought we were just going to hang out as friends?

Would he think I was being too forward or pushy?

Ugh, what if he didn't come?

I tried my best not to freak out, but it did make me feel a bit nauseous while I quickly changed into pants that didn't scream, 'Yes, I have size down here, and I want you to know it'.

CHAPTER TWENTY-SEVEN

Quinn

JASE ARRIVED RIGHT on time. I opened the door and let him in. His eyes lit up when he saw all the food I had prepared for us. "Wow, this is amazing," he exclaimed. "I was expecting takeout. I didn't know you cooked."

"It's not my greatest talent, but I can make a few dishes really well." I rubbed the back of my neck shyly, unsure why I was so nervous tonight.

Actually, that was a lie. I knew exactly why I was nervous. This was the first time since New Orleans I had actually wanted to try and have something date-like with someone.

"I've never been much of a cook myself," he admitted. "My family are very good cooks though, my Mom especially.

She taught me to make a lot of their recipes, but I've only really succeeded with her apple pie" He smiled fondly.

We sat down at the table and started chatting away. After a couple of minutes, I noticed he was watching me out of the corner of his eye. "What?" I asked suddenly.

He gave me a sheepish smile, looking down at the table. "Nothing..." he mumbled.

I frowned and cocked my head to the side.

"I guess I just expected something different?" He shrugged.

"What, like take out, beer, weights, and some porn videos on the shelves?" I laughed loudly as a look of guilt flashed across Jase's eyes. "Oh wow. Do I come across as that much of a stereotype?"

Jase grimaced. "Kinda? You come across as everything I pretend to be. All manly and nothing much to second guess."

"You don't have to act tough for me," I told him softly.

He looked up and met my gaze. "No, I do."

"Why?" I arched an eyebrow as I watched difficult emotions shine from him.

"Because if I'm not tough with everyone, then I'll let slip where I'm not supposed to."

Ah.

Yes, I knew that fear well.

Setting my fork down for a moment, I reached over the table to tap his forehead so those gorgeous eyes met mine. "You can be tough and gay. My ex taught me that."

"You've been in a normal relationship?" he asked, clearly intrigued.

"Yeah. It was awesome. Didn't last, though, but we are still really good friends."

"In New Orleans?"

I nodded as Jase asked his question.

"Do you see them much now?" Something about his voice was tight, as though he was holding something back.

"No." I sighed. "I can't."

"Why?" He looked at me carefully.

"Do you know what happened at my last station, Jase?" I asked, though I knew full well that none of my new team knew about it. I figured they would have treated me very differently if they did.

Jase's eyebrows furrowed in confusion, obviously thinking this was a strange change of topic. But, still, he shook his head. "I don't, no."

"Someone committed arson on a warehouse, and the only reason I survived was because my ex was there to help me. We worked together. He was my partner."

Jase's eyes went wide. "Holy shit. Did he..."

"He died in that fire, along with every single one of my other teammates. I was the only one who made it out." I felt the grief I kept so tightly under wraps well up in my chest, making it hard to breathe. Tears threatened from behind my eyes.

Jase was looking at me with heartache and terror in his eyes. I hated it when people heard the story because there was always so much pity and so many apologies for my loss.

"Did they catch who did it?" Jase asked. Not a question I usually got straight away. Usually, it took a while for the details to filter through.

"They found out who set the fire," I answered. "But they never tracked him down."

"Fucker," Jase growled, causing me to chuckle.

"My thoughts exactly."

"It sounds like you were very close with him."

"Very," I agreed. "We weren't just partners. We were best friends. The only real thing that ever made me feel safe or happy was him. He's the main reason I came out to the family because I hoped they'd meet him one day."

Jase's eyes were sad as he watched me speak.

Was he just feeling sorry for me?

Or could I be selfish enough to think that maybe he would like to be more important than that to me one day?

"Why did you break up?" Jase asked tentatively.

"We both quickly realized we were forcing a romantic love onto what was actually a deep solid friendship." I smiled. "We didn't understand just how many kinds of love there were... but I realized I wanted the whole shebang. Romance, sexual intimacy, laughter, closeness, trust. The whole thing."

"And you didn't think he felt the same?"

"No," I sighed. "He wasn't someone who was into romance and didn't ever think he would be."

"I can't understand that," Jase commented. "I'm scared of it, but I would love to hold hands in public and give someone flowers."

I laughed. Yeah, I could see why I was so drawn to this man. "Oh yeah? What kind of flowers would you want?"

"Promise not to laugh?" Jase pointed the finger at me as he cleared his plate. "Peonies. They are considered a sign of good luck and a happy marriage."

I snorted. "You're such a dork."

"Oh, shut up. I bet your flower choice wouldn't be any better," Jase grumbled.

"Hmm. Not, probably not. I actually like snapdragons." I shrugged and chuckled as Jase raised an eyebrow my way. "I know, strange choice, right."

"Not exactly cliché." Jase smirked and then leaned back in his chair, crossing his arms over his chest as he watched me.

"Well, I'm not exactly normal." I flashed him a grin.

CHAPTER TWENTY-EIGHT

Quinn

"WANT A DRINK?" I asked, picking up his empty plate and stacking it onto mine so I could clear the table.

"Sure, what do you have?" Jase asked.

"Well, beer." I chuckled at the earlier expectations Jase had voiced. "But we've also got some raspberry vodka which is very good with lemonade, whiskey, honey mead, and some peppermint schnapps somewhere." I opened a cabinet to show him the various alcohol bottles within.

Jase's eyes went wide in response to that list. "Holy shit!" He looked around again as if he expected someone to suddenly appear with a tray of drinks and snacks. "Where did you get all this?"

"My roommate tends to get given booze as presents from everyone but doesn't actually drink much," I explained, picking out the raspberry vodka for myself. "So we keep it here so we can have it when people come over."

He nodded understandingly. "I see." Then his eyes narrowed slightly as they focused on something behind me. "Is that a unicorn gin?"

I turned around to look where he was looking and found him pointing at a bottle labeled 'Unicorn Gin' sitting among the other bottles. "Yes..." I said slowly, thinking about how to explain what it really was. "We have yet to touch it."

"We should try it." He laughed, flashing me a cocky grin. "It sounds sickly."

"That's because it's not meant to be consumed neat." I flashed him a smile. "You need ice with it or something to make it taste better."

"Maybe." He shrugged and then pointed to another shelf. "Tell you what, I'll have an Elvis juice ale, please." He motioned to the cans at the back of the cupboard.

"Coming right up." I smiled, grabbing a couple of the cans and leading Jase through to the living room. He sat down on one of the couches and looked around curiously while I set the drinks down on the coffee table in front of him.

He snapped open the lid on the first drink, his eyes narrowing slightly as he sniffed it before taking a sip. "This tastes weird..." He frowned after swallowing the first mouthful. "But interesting."

I snorted, smiling at him. "Good?"

His eyes widened a little at my tone. "Yeah." He reached for his second drink. "The thing is...it doesn't taste like I thought it would." His eyes were bright and clear as he stared at me. "Elvis juice sounds like it should be... I don't know... salty?"

I laughed loudly at the obvious innuendo. "No, no saltiness." I shook my head, grinning at him. "It's just a fruity-tasting lager, you silly man."

Jase laughed a little and settled back on the sofa. "Let's call it an American IPA beer and leave it at that." He grinned at me. "So, um, what do we do now?"

I raised an eyebrow at the sudden change in topic. "What did you think we'd do?"

He shrugged. "Whatever you wanted to do?"

I rolled my eyes and leaned forward to rest my elbows on my knees. "Well, if you want to watch TV, there are a few things on at the moment. We could also play video games."

"Video games?" Jase repeated, shaking his head. "I didn't think you'd be into those."

"I'm not." I sighed theatrically. "But, sometimes, when my roommate goes out, I feel like I have to entertain myself somehow."

"Oh." He seemed to consider this. "I guess that makes sense, then. Though I think a movie is probably a good call. Have you got any good sci-fi films?"

"Sure." I nodded. "We've got a lot of them." I gestured toward the cupboards fulled with Dvds around me. "You can take your pick."

Jase picked one out, and handed it to me with a grin. It was a movie I hadn't seen before, so I wasn't sure how I felt about it. But I knew Jase would enjoy it, so I couldn't complain.

As the film started, I noticed a small smile playing across Jase's lips. He looked relaxed and happy as he drank his beer and munched on the snacks I'd brought out. I liked seeing him like this.

CHAPTER TWENTY-NINE

Quinn

"WOW, THAT WAS intense," Jase murmured. "Who directed it? That guy's good."

I shook my head in amusement. "It was only his third feature film." I pointed out. "I'm surprised you haven't heard of him, it's been getting rave reviews everywhere lately."

"Huh. I must live under a rock." Jase chuckled. "I'll have to check him out online later."

I smiled lightly as he jotted the name down on his phone. I noticed that we had moved closer together during the movie. I thought about asking him if he minded if I put my arm around his shoulder, but I hesitated. I wasn't sure whether he might find it too intimate, even though I wouldn't mind doing it.

In the end, I decided against it. Instead, Jase said something I had not expected. "I came out to my Mom."

I turned to him with wide eyes. "Really? Did it go okay?"

"She told me she loved me regardless of who I am," he explained. "And then she hugged me tight." He smiled warmly. "We decided to not tell my father yet, though. He's an old traditional Texan, so Mom is going to work on him for me."

"That's amazing!" I exclaimed. "Congratulations! Your mom seems really cool. I'm somewhat jealous. I wish my mother had taken such a viewpoint." I sighed. "Mine hasn't talked to me for a few weeks now."

"Why don't you talk to her?" Jase asked, concern darkening his expression.

"I've tried," I replied, my voice soft and sad. "She's blocked my number since it became public knowledge that I'm gay. Seems now that everyone at the church knows about it, I've been pushed out."

I was surprised when Jase leaned forward and wrapped his arms around my shoulders, and pulled me into a hug. I leaned my cheek against his chest and inhaled deeply, feeling his warmth. "I'm so sorry, Quinn," he whispered softly. "Is there anything I can do?"

I shook my head. "No, I don't suppose there is." I rested my head back against his shoulder. "I just need to get over it."

Jase stroked my hair gently. "I know it's hard, but you're a strong guy. You'll make it through this."

I nodded slowly. "Thanks, Jase."

He gave me a little squeeze. "If you ever want to talk, I'm here."

I smiled wryly. "I know. I'll definitely take you up on that."

As I pulled back, I realized just how close his face was to mine. His lips were inches away from mine, and I could smell the scent of beer on his breath. I felt a sudden heat begin to burn inside me, and my heart beat faster.

My hand was still on his shoulder, holding him in place as he held me. Slowly, I moved my gaze up to meet his eyes. They were full of warmth and desire, and his lips parted slightly on their own accord. I saw the intensity of his feelings mirrored in my own, and I was suddenly filled with the urge to kiss him.

I found myself leaning forward, bringing our lips together tenderly. At first, he resisted, but after a moment, he followed suit and closed his mouth over mine. We kissed tentatively at first, but the longer we did it, the more passionate it became.

Our tongues danced gently against each other, tasting each other's flavor. I felt a surge of excitement run through me as my hands explored his body. My fingers traced the muscles of his shoulders, feeling them tighten under my touch. Then I slid my hands down his chest, feeling his warm skin beneath my fingertips. As my hands reached his waistband, he lifted one arm to wrap around my shoulder. The contact sent electricity zinging through me, shivers racing down my spine.

His tongue finally entered my mouth, making me moan softly. It wasn't long before I felt him move his other arm so that they both wrapped around my shoulders. The more passion we expressed, the more I wanted him to do it again. After kissing for several minutes, I pulled back with a smile on my lips and looked into his eyes. "Want to go to the bed?" I asked him.

Jase nodded and let me lead him by the hand, pulling him up the stairs behind me. Once there, I turned to face him. He was looking at me with a serious expression and I worried he was having second thoughts.

"You okay? You have any questions or concerns about this?"

"No, never," Jase said quickly.

I smiled at him and slowly began unbuttoning my shirt. For some reason, I didn't want to look away from his eyes. His gaze seemed to be focusing intently on my chest, which only made me feel even better. When he finally tore his eyes away from my chest, he gazed into my eyes once more, this time with an almost pleading look.

I gave him a gentle smile and then slid my hand under his shirt to feel the smooth skin of his abdomen. He gasped when I touched him, and I could see his erection growing in his pants. This wasn't what I had planned. I hadn't actually *planned* anything, in fact. But something about Jase just set me on fire and I couldn't control the desire and heat that I felt as soon as his lips touched mine.

Slowly, I removed my hand from his stomach and moved down his body. I could feel his breathing getting heavier as I went further down. By the time I reached his belt, he was practically gasping for air. I unhooked his belt and undid his button. I heard him gasp as I took his zipper down.

A smirk pulled on my lips as I slid my

fingers beneath the waistband of his boxers and cradled his dick. He was already half-hard, and I knew that it would grow even more if I continued to touch him. I slid my hand back up and then ran it along the length of his shaft, causing him to groan and shudder.

Grasping the waistband again, I slipped his boxers off of his hips. His cock sprang free, springing toward me like a hungry predator. I stared at it for a moment, mesmerized by the sight. It was thick and long, standing out from his body. The head was dark red, and I could see the veins running through it. I dipped my head to take the tip between my lips.

Jase moaned and leaned his head against the wall behind him. I could feel his hands grip the back of my neck tightly as I sucked on him. I began bobbing my head, sucking him deeper and deeper.

"Oh, fuck!" His voice was muffled when he spoke.

I smiled around his dick and then took more of him into my mouth. He was still wearing his clothes, and I had to remove his belt properly before I could pull his jeans down further to give me full access to him. Once I got them off of his feet, I tossed them aside and resumed giving him pleasure.

His legs trembled, and he had difficulty holding himself up. I felt his fingers tighten in my hair, holding my head closer while he chased the pleasure I gave him. I began moving my mouth faster, taking him deeper each time I sank down onto him. I felt him throb in my mouth, and I could hear him moaning as I worked.

When I felt him tense, I pulled him out and licked the tip. He whimpered and tried to push my head back down, but with a sudden burst, he came all over my cheeks and chin, covering me with his hot seed. I swallowed him again eagerly, licking him clean. I loved the taste of his cum.

"Don't stop," he gasped, and I smiled.

I rose up and kissed him again, tasting the salty residue left from his orgasm. His cock was still hard as steel, and I could tell that he was ready for more. I didn't hesitate to kiss him again. I grabbed his hand and led him further into the bedroom, pushing him onto the bed. Then I climbed on top of him and straddled his lap.

"You're going to make me come again," he said, smiling at me.

I laughed and brushed the hair from his eyes. "That's the idea." I chuckled wickedly.

CHAPTER THIRTY

Jase

I SUCKED IN a breath of anticipation at the wicked chuckle. His eyes promised a pleasure I could only dream of.

"I'm going to fuck you, Jase." He sat up and grabbed my thighs. Leaning forward, he kissed me with an intensity that stole my breath. "This time, I want to see your face when you come for me."

There was something in the back of my mind saying that I shouldn't be doing this with Quinn again. But whatever it was, it was lost in the haze of want and pleasure that I felt as he began to unbuckle his belt. Pulling down his jeans, he kicked them off before sitting back down between my legs again. A rush of cold air filled the space left by his movement, and I shivered from the sensation. The bulge in his boxers was obvious, a small damp patch showing just how turned on he had become from sucking me off.

Fuck.

A man who enjoyed giving just as much as he enjoyed getting himself off. It would take a lot of self-control not to reach over and tug him out into the open.

Quinn's fingers were slick and warm against the skin of my inner thigh as they massaged my skin before his lips trailed after them. Biting and nipping at the sensitive skin, I could feel his stubble brushing against my length, stimulating and tormenting me to a half-hard state.

"Quinn..." I whimpered. I hadn't noticed the way he had reached to his bedside for lube, and so it surprised me when his fingers began tormenting my hole. But there was something about the warmth and wetness that made me relax as he pushed two fingers inside. My whole body clenched tight around him as I tried to stifle the cries that tore through me.

"Shhh," he hushed against my mouth and then slid his other hand over my rigid cock. "I want you to get ready for what's coming."

Fuck.

I didn't know if it was the pain or the pleasure that was making my head spin.

Quinn's fingers moved faster and deeper inside me. He added a third finger before using his other hand to start stroking my shaft. I knew he was only trying to prepare my ass for what was to come. But that didn't stop me from coming undone. Waves of pleasure crashed over my body, and I let out a guttural moan as Quinn found the sensitive bundle of nerves within me.

"You're so fucking beautiful," he growled against my throat.

His words sent a shudder through my body. "Please... please, don't tease me like this..."

He chuckled against my neck before moving up and kissing my lips. "I won't tease you unless you ask me to."

And all I wanted was *more*. That was the problem. So many times, I'd been close to begging him to fuck me. But every time I thought about asking, I knew I couldn't do it. I wasn't sure how I could be intimate with him without feeling guilty.

Why was I feeling guilty?

My mind flickered with the image of the man I had seen Quinn kissing in the street.

Oh.

Shit.

Yeah. This would be cheating.

Or maybe they weren't together properly yet, and I still had a chance to win him over?

The thought should have made me laugh. Instead, my heart sank. There was no way I could compete with someone else. Not only was I a pathetic middle-aged man stuck in the closet, but the guy I had seen in the club was gorgeous.

"I want you so badly," Quinn whispered into my ear, his breath sending shivers down my spine. He sounded genuine, and his eyes were filled with awe as though I was the most beautiful thing he had ever witnessed.

Lifting my hips, I guided him toward my entrance. I wanted to give him everything. Every part of me, my mind, and my soul. I couldn't say no to a face like that. If there was still a chance I could have him, then I should take it.

It took a moment of pressure before I felt him pushing inside. I moaned as he stretched me wide open. "Yes... Oh fuck... Ungh"

I gasped as he settled inside me. His whole length was buried deep inside me, and I felt myself stretch to accommodate him. It hurt, and it felt amazing. We both groaned as he began to move, slowly at first, before building speed and force. Every thrust was met by a gasp or a moan from me. The constant rocking motion was enough to send waves of pleasure rippling through my body. I gripped onto his arms, digging my nails into his flesh.

"Jase... Don't hold back," he begged as I tightened my grip around his muscular shoulders.

I shook my head. "I can't. I want to feel this... so bad."

As soon as I said the words, he began to move harder and faster. I heard myself screaming his name as we came together, our bodies pressed tightly against each other. Quinn kept on moving until he finally came to rest against my chest.

I buried my face into the crook of his neck and breathed him in. He smelled divine, of sweat and spice. I kissed the top of his head and whispered, "That was amazing."

He pulled away and looked down at me. "Thank you."

I smiled up at him. "For what?"

"Everything."

I laughed. "Vague, much."

He grinned. "Sorry. But honestly, thank you. You've given me more pleasure than I've ever experienced in my life."

I blushed at the statement, my heart

lightening at the idea. If I had really been able to give him something so good, maybe I could actually have this. Maybe we could have a relationship.

Kissing the tip of his nose, I asked, "I feel like we should have coffee and then go for another round?"

His eyes twinkled with mischief as he slid his length from me. "We can do that... Black with two sugars, right?"

I nodded, unable to help the grin spreading across my face. "Sounds perfect." Pulling my boxers back on and adjusting the shirt he hadn't gotten around to removing from my shoulders, I followed him through the apartment.

As he switched the coffee maker on, he pulled me close to him to steal kisses while we waited. When he finally turned around and handed me a mug, I tried not to stare at his near-naked body. A quick glance confirmed that he was completely hard again under his boxers.

"Wow..." I whispered.

He shrugged. "You're too tasty for your own good."

A blush crept into my cheeks at the compliment. I sipped my coffee before I heard the front door open.

"Oh God," I groaned as I covered my mouth with my hand. It was the guy who

Quinn had been kissing in the street. He had a set of keys in his hands, and he obviously lived here too. His dark hair fell over one eye, and he wore a white shirt with some kind of blue tie underneath.

"Shit."

I glanced at Quinn's obvious state, walking around in just his boxers, and then down at myself in an open shirt and boxers with hair that clearly looked as though I had been fucked thoroughly.

By Quinn.

In the apartment that these two shared.

Quinn wasn't just taken...

He was living with the guy.

Mortification and anger flooded through me. I wanted to run, but my feet were rooted to the ground. All I could do was watch as the man walked further inside and closed the door behind him. I watched as he flipped the lock on the door, and then he headed for the bathroom as though we weren't even there.

Fuck this.

I turned a glare at Quinn. "What the fuck is wrong with you?"

Confusion marred his expression, but I didn't stop to talk about it further. Tossing my half-filled coffee mug at him, I stormed through the apartment to grab my trousers and pull them on before picking up my phone and turning for the front door.

"Jase? What's wrong?" Quinn asked, trying to reach out to take my arm as I walked past him.

I snatched his wrist from the air, my fist locked around his wrist so that he couldn't touch me. He pulled back and stepped away quickly. "Don't ever fucking call me again." I pushed the door open and practically ran down the stairs.

"Wait!" Quinn called after me.

I ignored him.

The guy who had come home hadn't blocked my car with his, thankfully. I got in and slammed the door shut before I started the engine. I just needed to get away.

Away from him.

Away from everything.

I needed to be alone.

I needed to think.

CHAPTER THIRTY-ONE

Jase

I DROVE STRAIGHT to my apartment, trying not to stomp loudly as I rushed up the stairs, though I did slam my door behind me a little too heavily for the time of night.

Kicking my shoes angrily from my feet into the entrance hall wall, I grabbed my head in my hands and let out a long, muffled cry of anger. Needing to scrub off his heavenly scent, I rushed through to the bathroom.

I stripped naked and hopped in the shower, letting the hot water wash over me. I didn't cry or scream. I just stood there, hoping to just melt away into the tiles.

How could I have been so stupid?

Why didn't I even ask about the other

man?

Had I truly been that desperate to feel Quinn again?

Was all this just a massive mistake?

When the hot water eventually ran out, I stepped out of the shower and dried myself with rough towels. Even though it was late, I knew sleeping tonight wasn't going to happen. I couldn't sleep knowing Quinn was at home, possibly getting ready for bed as I sat here stewing in the aftermath of my own stupidity.

I padded quietly through my bedroom and grabbed my phone. I wasn't going to text him.

Not now.

Maybe not ever.

My anger overrode logic and my hands were shaky as I opened his number and typed out a quick message:

You're an asshole.

And then I hit send and turned my phone off. I stood there staring at it for what felt like hours before I finally left my room and walked into the livingroom. The TV was on, but I couldn't really focus on anything else.

Strolling into the kitchen, I reached into the freezer and pulled out a tub of ice cream, snagging a spoon from the drying rack. I plopped back on the couch and proceeded to snack on spoonfuls right from the tub while I watched some terrible reality show. I ate the whole thing, finishing it off with a few chocolate chips and a mouthful of melted ice cream. By the time I'd cleaned up the dishes, I realized it was three in the morning. I sighed and looked around my apartment. It was so empty.

So lonely.

It took me forever to fall asleep. When I did, my rest was fitful, plagued by nightmares that involved Quinn. I woke up several times throughout the night, and each time I found myself reaching for my phone to check if I had any messages from him, only to remember I had specifically left it turned off.

CHAPTER THIRTY-TWO

Jase

I SLEPT TILL midday, awoken suddenly when I heard someone knocking at the front door. I groaned as I rolled out of bed, running my hands over my face and carding my fingers through my hair. I hoped it wasn't Quinn. I was in no state to deal with him right now. But the person on the other side of the door was one of my neighbors.

"Good afternoon, Jase. I was heading to the food market out of town and wondered if you wanted some of that chili cheese I got you before?" She smiled brightly.

I smiled lightly. Mrs. Jenkins was a sweet old woman who I had bumped into a few times in the local grocery store before she had started to offer to pick up stuff from the farmer's market her son took her to every couple of weeks. "Sure, that'd be great," I said. "Do you want to come in and grab some coffee first?"

She looked shocked but nodded enthusiastically. I led her back inside, and we spent half an hour catching up. Having something other than the previous night to focus on was a blessing, and I immediately felt the weight of the pain settle back in my chest as Mrs. Jenkins left to meet her son.

I poured myself another cup of coffee and settled down on the couch to watch some more mindless TV.

By four o'clock, I was bored. I realized I hadn't eaten since breakfast yesterday, so I decided it was time to make myself something to eat. I opened the fridge and stared at the contents for a moment before deciding I had nothing worth eating. Settling for some scrambled eggs and some bacon, I wolfed it down, hardly tasting a bite.

I figured it was about time to turn my phone on and face the music. If Quinn was trying to contact me, there would be a message. But there weren't any texts, only a couple of missed calls.

The one from the station from only minutes prior caught my attention.

JASE

Dialing through to my voicemail, I held the phone to my ear and heard Captain Clarke's voice.

"Jase, are you okay? You haven't checked in all day, and the shift is already underway. Please call me ASAP."

I hung up and put the phone back on its charger.

Fuck.

I had forgotten I had work today. Running my hands through my hair, I glanced at the clock. There was no point going in now. I'd have to make my excuses tomorrow. Moving to place my phone back on the charger, I nearly jumped as it went off in my hand.

Looking at the screen, it showed it was the station. With a tired sigh, I lifted it again and answered. "Yeah?"

"Jase!" The Captain half yelled. It wasn't angry, just urgent, and I immediately stood straighter. "We need you at the station. There's a huge fire in the central apartment blocks and its spreading fast. Every available unit is being called in. Get to the station and on a truck now!" With that, the line went dead.

What the fuck?

My mind was racing as I ran for the door.

What could have happened so quickly?

Something huge would have to happen to cause a fire like that these days. I didn't bother even tying my shoelaces as I ran out of my apartment and down to the parking lot. I drove like a maniac to get there, not really caring if I got pulled over. I had a valid reason, at least.

CHAPTER THIRTY-THREE

Jase

I PULLED INTO the parking space and raced inside.

"Oh good! You're here. Get in," Carmen called as she tied her boots and shrugged on her protective over-layer. Kicking off my shoes and trousers, I left them in a heap on the floor to save time. I was still fumbling with buttons and ties as Carmen screeched out of the station, my body sliding in the passenger seat at the speed at which she took corners. The lights and sirens were going, and I could hear others converging toward the same place. We turned onto the main road and roared toward the scene.

It was like something from a movie. The building we approached was completely engulfed in flames. Plumes of black smoke billowed into the air, and embers rained down from above. Police cars blocked off roads leading to the area while fire trucks and ambulances were parked outside. A helicopter hovered overhead.

"Holy shit," I muttered under my breath as the first responders all began arriving. Fire crews were running to their trucks as others arrived at the scene. I saw Carmen's face go pale as she spotted the truck I usually drove in near the front with Mark fighting with the hose that just wouldn't reach any further. She immediately switched lanes and sped toward it, the brakes squealing as she skidded to a stop.

I grabbed my kit bag as she threw herself out the door and rushed over to help.

Mark looked up at us as Carmen dropped to her knees beside him to help him unhook the extra length of hose.

"Carmen! Oh my god," he said as he turned around to look at me.

"Are you all right?" she asked, brushing his hair away from his forehead.

"Yes. Just getting a bit old for this, I guess." He smiled weakly.

I tried to smile but I was too busy watching the firefighters battle against the flames as they raced upward.

"I'm going in to help!" I called over the noise of the scene and jogged over to the Captain who was directing teams to different points. When he saw me approach, he gave me a grim look.

"This place is coming down fast but there's still people inside. By my count, there's still a kid on the fourth floor who hasn't been brought down or sent for."

I nodded in response. That was where I needed to be.

"On it!" I pulled my oxygen mask from my side and situated it over my face.

"You'll need to hook up your air supply before you go in, Jase," the Captain called out.

I took the regulator and attached it to the tank on my back. Once the tanks were connected, I pulled the straps tight and hooked the mouthpiece into place.

I couldn't believe I was doing this. I hadn't done anything like it since I was in my twenties. My heart started pounding in my chest as I turned away from the Captain and charged at the building.

There was no way I was going to let anyone die.

I ran in through the windows and kept low to the ground as I made my way up the stairs. I was terrified at what I might find waiting for me when I reached the fourth floor. Every thought and prayer in my mind went out to hope that the kid was still okay. I continued my ascent until I finally reached the top of the stairwell.

The smell hit me hard as soon as I opened the door and stepped into the hallway. Flames were shooting out from the third floor and billowing smoke filled the corridor in thick waves. The walls were already starting to melt and there was a heat haze all around. It was almost like the whole floor was on fire.

I sucked in a deep breath and pushed forward, pulling my breathing mask tighter over my face. The air was hot and heavy on my skin, stinging and making my eyes water. I held them closed for a moment, and then opened them and continued to push forward.

When the hallway ended in front of me, I found myself looking down a large open space that led to other rooms beyond.

Where was this kid?

I took another deep breath and moved forward. My eyes started to tear up again but I clenched my jaw and pressed on. The flames were growing stronger by the moment as they tore through the ceiling and began to spread out across the floor.

CHAPTER THIRTY-FOUR

Quinn

THE BLAZE THAT swallowed the apartment building in the center of town was worse than anything I had witnessed since that day in New Orleans. It went up so fast, a few seconds at most, and then it burned hot enough to melt metal on the ground below.

The whole block caught fire all at once, and the flames leaped into the night sky, illuminating the entire city. Flames licked out from every window as though a giant bonfire had been set inside the building.

A column of black smoke rose high above the surrounding buildings, almost reaching the heavens themselves. Whatever had happened to cause this was serious, and the age of the building meant it didn't have the same safety features as the newer ones being built further away from the center.

I shuddered as an eerie sense of déjà vu stole my breath for a moment before I shook my head and pushed it aside. I pushed past the fear and memories choking my throat, determined not to relive the past. This wasn't the same.

I had backed the public up as best as I could to give the other firefighters plenty of space to work with their hoses, but the scale of the fire limited what they could do about the flames. They were forced to douse the building from the outside, and it wasn't long until the roof began to collapse.

"Is everyone out?" Captain Clarke yelled over the roar of the fire. "We're going to have to contain it rather than stop it!"

"Jase is still in there!" Mark called, bundling a small child from around the side of the building and carrying him over to the medical specialists.

"Shit!" The Captain turned his head to his radio to try and contact the man within the building, but my blood had already turned to ice.

Not again.

Images of the New Orleans warehouse drenched white-hot in flames erupted before my eyes. The scent of burning wood permeated my nose and I swore I could hear the screams of my coworkers from that fateful day.

I couldn't handle it happening again... Not when the last thing that had happened between Jase and I still confused the life out of me. I still didn't understand why he had been so angry. After the evening we had had, I thought that perhaps we had a chance for something real.

This time everyone was getting out alive. I'd make sure of it.

Without much thought or care for the yells of shock and warnings from my colleagues behind me, I flipped my breathing mask down onto my face and ran for the building. My boots slipped and slid on the broken pavement beneath the scorching asphalt, and my hands stung under my gloves from pulling myself through the splintered and melted front entrance with the sheer force of will. But I made it inside.

My heart pounded in my chest as I took in the scene. It was chaos. In the middle of the room, I glanced up through a gaping hole where the ceiling used to be.

Fuck.

What if Jase had fallen through somewhere?

Kicking at the burning debris with my boots, I made sure there was no one beneath it before heading up the stairs. I could hear the Captain over the radio telling me to get my ass back outside, but I refused to even acknowledge him.

"Dude!" Carmen's voice sounded through the radio. "Cap says he was headed to the fourth floor! If you are going to be this level of idiotic, at least you know where not to waste time!" She sounded frustrated and worried. It warmed me a little to know that she understood what would actually help right now. I wasn't coming back out without Jase, so telling me where he was supposed to be was the only thing that could have come over the radio waves that might have just saved my life.

I moved up the stairs two at a time, ignoring the searing pain in my feet and shins as I went. The heat of the flames was so strong I could feel the burn of them through all my protective gear. When I reached the fourth floor, the heat and smell from the fire was so intense I found myself panting heavily through my mask.

"Jase!" I half yelled half coughed.

"Jase, can you hear me?"

There was no reply.

He wasn't dead. He had to be alive. I felt sure of it. I pushed through the door and raced toward the end of the corridor.

"Jase, where are you?" I shook my head when I saw the remains of the wall that had collapsed across the hallway.

Fuck.

I was beginning to think this might have been a suicide mission. Then I heard him.

"Fucker!" His voice echoed off the walls. "Get out!"

I climbed over the remains of the wall and kicked open the door on the other side of them. Inside, through the smoke, I could make out a figure on the floor.

"Jase!" I ran through the room and came to a halt next to him. He was struggling with his leg, which had gone through the floor below. There was a great deal of blood and an awful lot of fire surrounding him.

"Fuck!" I said, running forward and trying to lift him up. "Come on." I tried to get him to stand, but his leg was stuck fast. "Goddamn it, man!" I shouted.

The more I struggled to free him, the more obvious it became that he was beyond any help I could give him here.

"Jase," I said, placing my hand on his arm. "Brace yourself." I only had one possibility left, and it was likely going to harm us both. Standing up, I lifted my leg and brought it down heavily on the wooden boards that kept Jase trapped in place. He cried out in pain behind his mask, but the wood splintered. It was so weak from fire, and the water that had been used in the attempt to fight said fire, I had to hope it would give way easily. It was our only shot.

I stomped my foot down on the same spot on the floor a few times before a loud crack sounded around us, and the old floor gave way, dropping us both through to the floor below.

I grabbed Jase tightly as we fell. We landed hard and rolled to our sides, tumbling into a pile. I lost my breath momentarily as Jase's weight pressed down on me and I knew we didn't have time to waste. I knew the entire building would go at any minute.

I quickly pushed him off me and stood up. I searched the room quickly to make sure there was an exit before I leaned down and pulled Jase up, and tossed him over my shoulders. He wasn't going to be able to move quickly enough with that injury.

I glanced back at him, gave him a nod, then turned away and ran through the room. He didn't argue, and I couldn't help but wonder if I was carrying Jase's unconscious body.

"I need a medic!" I yelled as soon as we cleared the front entrance.

On the stretcher, Jase was still out of it. They took his helmet off and checked his pulse. His breathing was ragged, but the paramedics were focused on his leg after a new oxygen mask was placed over his face.

"What happened?" Newt, firehouse twenty-one's paramedic asked as he examined the wound.

"He fell through the floor upstairs," I replied.

"All right, we've got it from here. You can meet us at the hospital later." Newt flashed me a knowing look over his shoulder as the two paramedics made their way across the road, and my gaze followed them as they loaded Jase into the ambulance.

I wanted to go with him. I wanted to get into that ambulance and make sure that Jase was okay, but with the fire behind me, I knew I still had a job to do. With a mild curse, I turned and rushed back to the scene to help contain the fire.

EVIE RILEY

CHAPTER THIRTY-FIVE

Quinn

IT TOOK HOURS to control the flames, and by the time we did, there was little more to the apartment than a charred shell.

Most firefighters went home exhausted at the end, but our team and Captain Clarke all ended up trudging to the hospital to find out how Jase was. He was stable, and we were told his lungs would be fine, but his leg would take a lot of physiotherapy before he would be able to work again.

"It will take a lot of effort from him." The doctor sighed.

"He'll do it. He's stubborn enough," Mark commented, a rippling of agreement sounding from the rest of us.

Not wanting to bother the doctors any

more than they already were, everyone decided to leave and come back during visiting hours the following day.

At least, everyone else did.

I mumbled an excuse that I needed to visit the restroom so I would see them at work the following day, but I did not leave the hospital. I couldn't. I needed to know that Jase was okay. I needed to see him when he was conscious, to make sure he knew that everyone was there for him through the therapy he would need. I needed... Oh, I don't know what I needed. I just needed to see him.

The images of him surrounded by fire played in my head over and over.

What if I had been slower?

What if I had listened to the Captain and not gone back inside?

The idea of losing Jase from my life made me feel physically sick to my stomach, and twice I did have to visit the restroom to unload my stomach.

Once I felt better, I found myself wandering around the hospital corridors aimlessly until I finally saw him. His face was pale and bloodless, his eyes wide and terrified, and his hair matted with sweat. They wouldn't let me talk to him yet, though. The nurse said he was being taken into surgery to fix his leg and someone would let me know when he was in recovery.

I took to pacing in the waiting room and about an hour in, I recognized Jase's parents as they finally arrived at the hospital. It looked like Jase's father had literally run across the city, and now he was striding up the corridor like a man on a mission, his wife half running beside him. They were older than I remembered them, but I recognized them instantly. Jase shared so many of their features.

"Mr. and Mrs. Turner," I called, jogging over to them.

"Sorry, we're in a rush."

"Jase is still in surgery," I called after them, watching as they came to a stop and turned back to face me. "They are making sure his leg is as clean as possible, so recovery is easiest. I paid the bill in advance. I just wanted him to have the best chance at getting back to work."

Mr. Turner's eyes narrowed at me. He was a beefy man with a mustache adorning his upper lip and a receding hairline. He had a nose that stuck out slightly too far, which only served to give him an even more intimidating look. His wife, on the other hand, looked like she was about to burst into tears at any second. She was petite and pretty, with dark brown hair that fell down her back in ringlets. Her eyes were sad and puffy, and I could tell she was afraid. Mr. Turner moved forward then, stepping between her and me.

"And who exactly are you?"

"Quinn Sanders, sir. I work with Jase." I glanced from Mr. Turner to his wife, who looked at me with a slight curiosity in her sad eyes.

"Sanders? The preacher's son?"

"Yes, sir."

"Hmm." He hummed in deliberation before sighing. "Well, thank you. It's nice to see a member of that family actually helping out someone else."

I chuckled darkly. "Yes, well, my father and I see things very differently."

He smiled grimly at me as if he knew exactly what I was referring to. The knowledge of my sexuality, despite my upbringing, was probably a rumor that had spread far by now. "Yes, I imagine you do. Now, I must find a doctor to find out what's happening."

His wife gave me a look that said 'thank you' as they turned and hurried away. I smiled softly back at her, deciding to give them space and venture to the cafeteria for some coffee. There was no chance I was sleeping tonight until I knew Jase was awake and okay.

CHAPTER THIRTY-SIX

Quinn

WHEN I RETURNED to the floor where Jase was being treated, I saw a familiar figure sitting outside his room. Captain Clarke was leaning against the wall, looking tired and drawn. I sat next to him, sipping at my cup of instant coffee. "I thought you went home," I commented. "How are you doing?"

He laughed bitterly. "Like shit. I'm used to seeing people injured, but this time it was one of mine, and I've never seen anyone's leg torn up so badly."

"You're allowed to be angry. I know you care about him a lot."

He shook his head. "No, no. I know that. Just... I keep going over what happened in my mind. I can't believe I almost stopped you from going in for him." He took a deep breath before continuing. "I'm sorry, Quinn. I really am."

It was my turn to laugh, albeit weakly. "Don't apologize to me. You did nothing wrong, Cap. You were following the guidelines, and there was every chance me going in there would have killed me too."

"Maybe. But I should have trusted you. I should have trusted your instincts. I just..." He sighed and rubbed his face. "This has been the worst day of my career."

I felt for him, and with a hand on his shoulder, I squeezed slightly. "At least he is alive, and he will be fine."

Captain Clarke nodded but didn't say anything. We sat quietly for a while, drinking our coffees in companionable silence.

CHAPTER THIRTY-SEVEN

Jase

I WOKE UP from dreams of fire, brimstone, smoke, and ash. The smell was still heavy in my nose, and the taste was on my tongue. There were no birds, no animals, nothing alive that I could see. It looked like the world had been destroyed by some terrible natural disaster. The ceiling I focused on as I drifted back to the world of the waking was a dingy off-white, and I recognized the rhythmic beeping of a hospital. I tried to sit up, but pain shot through my head, and my stomach clenched with nausea.

"Shit," I grunted and fell back onto the bed.

"Easy!" A nurse was hovering over me, pulling out an IV drip and peering at the readout. She tapped something into a small computer pad and then turned back to me. "You're awake, good."

I nodded. My memory was fuzzy; I couldn't remember very much about what had happened or where we had ended up. "Where am I?"

She smiled. "The doctor will be down soon to talk to you. He's just finishing up another case."

As she walked away, I noticed her name badge said 'Lisa'. I closed my eyes again, trying to get more rest before the doc came. After a few minutes, the door opened, and a man in a lab coat entered. He glanced at me briefly, then moved around the bed, examining me. "Well, looks like you've come through all right this time. You got pretty banged up, though. How do you feel?"

I grimaced, feeling the dull aches in my body, trying not to move too much. "I feel okay?"

"Well, that could be the drugs," the doctor admitted. "I'm just going to check on your leg, then get the nurse to redress it. After that, you have visitors." He patted my shoulder. "Try and stay awake for them."

I nodded. I didn't want to sleep anymore anyway. After a minute, the nurse returned and began unwrapping the dressing. My eyes widened as I saw the stitched-up wound on my shin. I remembered the pain of falling through the floorboards as they splintered and ripped and dug into my leg. I winced as she pulled the gauze clear of the gash.

"That looks painful," she said, cleaning it with antiseptic soap and bandaging me again.

"I suspect that it would be if I wasn't on the meds," I mumbled.

"But it's looking good. No signs of infection." The doctor smiled. "I'll check on it again tomorrow."

With it all dressed again, they left me alone in the room. I watched the door as it closed, blocking out the multitude of hospital sounds. I sighed and lay back, feeling drained, waiting for my visitors to come.

After a little while, I heard footsteps and saw the door to the room open. I sat up, keeping my legs tucked under the blankets, as my parents walked in. My mother quickly launched herself across the room to hug me, pressing kisses to my forehead and mumbling over and over how glad she was that I was okay. It made me smile.

My father stepped back and looked me over carefully. "You look better now. God knows how you survived that fire."

"Now?" I asked. "How long have I been here?"

"Three days," my father said, taking a seat in the chair beside my bed. I rubbed my face with my hand, and I realized just how much my beard had grown in that time. I could remember the heat of the flames surrounding me, the feeling of not being able to get myself out of that hole, the fiery pain from my leg, and the sinking feeling in my stomach that I was going to die there.

And Quinn.

I remembered him appearing just as I was starting to give up.

Glancing from my parents to the door, I wondered if I had imagined it. He wouldn't have been stupid enough to come looking for me in a fire like that.

But if he didn't, then how did I get out?

"He had to go home for a shower," my mother said with a smile as she noticed my gaze hovering on the door. I glanced at her with a raised eyebrow.

"Quinn. He's a lovely young man, but he was starting to smell quite badly, having not washed after the fire for three days."

"He was here?"

"For all three days, yes," my father grumbled. "I'll admit, if you have to be gay, you could do worse than him."

My face flushed immediately, and I shifted uncomfortably, which made my leg twinge in pain. "You know?" I braced myself for a lecture or worse, but the man merely rolled his eyes.

"Your mother told me. And frankly, I'll take you gay and alive over straight and dead if that man loving you was what saved your life." He crossed his arms over his chest, obviously not one hundred percent comfortable with the idea, but still, as an old-school Texan, I wasn't sure I could have ever wished for better.

"He doesn't love me," I grumbled, remembering the man he lived with.

To my surprise, my father barked out a laugh. "Oh, please. There are only two people I'd run into a fire for, and that's you and your mother, let alone a building that is literally falling in on itself because of those flames."

"We're firefighters, Dad. It's what we do." I sighed.

"Your Captain said he ignored direct orders not to enter that building because it was so bad."

"And we are so grateful he did," my mother added, reaching over to take my hand and squeeze it. When they put it like that, it did make me feel a sliver of hope. Surely it said something if Quinn had been the one to ignore orders and run in when even my long-term colleagues Mark and Johnson hadn't.

Still, even if he didn't, I knew my father was accepting of my lifestyle now as well. The weight lifted from my shoulders by that very idea made me feel exhausted to my core. Or perhaps it was the drugs.

CHAPTER THIRTY-EIGHT

Jase

I SPENT THE next few days in and out of sleep. The pain meds and anti-nausea injection they gave me a few times a day so I could eat made me feel as though the world was spinning, like I'd had a hundred drinks too many before I fell asleep again. Every time I was awake, I seemed to have missed Quinn. But according to the nurses, I was only allowed a couple of visitors at a time, and when my parents were there, he would step aside and wait down in the cafeteria. Apparently, he had practically been camping out there, and every time a nurse who knew my situation went down, they gave him an update.

I wanted to see him so badly, but it was a week after my surgery that they finally allowed me out of my room with strict instructions not to put any unwarranted pressure on my leg.

Eager to see him, I managed to get myself into a wheelchair and then rolled through the halls and down to the cafeteria. It didn't take me long to spot him.

He had his back to the door, which meant he hadn't seen me yet. He was bent over the table with one hand propping his head up while the other absently stirred the coffee in front of him.

Carefully weaving my way through the tables over to him, I noticed dark rings around his eyes and that his hair was still damp from a recent shower, one he had likely rushed if his unshaven appearance was anything to go by.

I stopped by his elbow with a sigh. I'd missed his face more than I was willing to admit.

His arm twitched as he felt me there. He turned to face me and his eyes widened comically before he grinned. "Jase," he exclaimed. "Hi! Erm... Are you okay? How is your leg?" He fumbled a little with his coffee as he half-rose in his seat, not knowing whether to embrace me or not.

"It's fine," I answered, giving him an

apologetic shrug of my shoulders. "The doctor said you didn't get too hurt coming in to get me. That true?"

Quinn smiled softly, his eyes full of a soft emotion that made me melt. "Twisted ankle, nothing that I couldn't walk off." He chuckled. "I'm just glad I could be here for you. The medical staff said you'd probably need someone to help you out when you were up and mobile again."

I positioned my chair up against the table, and Quinn continued. "I know your parents will help, but I just want to say that I will too, if you need anything."

I tilted my head to the side as I watched him. "Why?"

He looked at me with confusion clear on his features.

"Why are you going so far for me?" I asked.

Quinn laughed bitterly. "Oh, come on, surely you know why?"

"No, I don't," I replied. "One minute, I might think you like me, then I find that you live with your partner."

"What partner?"

"Don't mess with me, Quinn," I muttered irritably. "I saw you kissing him in public. I can't believe you slept with me in the same place he lives."

Quinn flushed slightly, and his cheeks

grew redder as he took a deep breath, realizing what I had seen and what I was talking about. I expected some kind of defense, but instead, I was met with a mildly hysterical laugh from him as he hung his head.

"God, what a clusterfuck of a misunderstanding," he mumbled before turning his beautiful eyes to look me directly in the face. "There's nothing between Jared and me. He's got a long-term girlfriend he's planning on proposing to."

"But, I saw..."

"Me kiss him. Right. Which means you saw a guy from my parents' church giving me grief too, right?"

I nodded slowly.

"Well, he was giving me crap about rumors of me being gay and telling me he knew I'd never do something so disgusting and all that shit. So I kissed Jared to prove a point and make him fuck off."

Thinking back to the view I had seen, it had made sense. Quinn had looked very uncomfortable with whatever had been said to him, and the man had quickly stormed off when Quinn had kissed his friend.

"So there's nothing going on with him?" I questioned carefully.

Quinn shook his head vehemently. "Nothing. We're friends like we always have been, but there's no more to it than that."

"Oh..." I whispered.

"Is that why you left so angrily the other night?" Quinn asked. "You thought I'd cheated on him with you?"

Heat spread over my cheeks as I looked away from him in embarrassment. "Kinda," I admitted. "And that I thought maybe there was something between us, but suddenly I just felt like a bit of fun for you."

Quinn looked horrified. "Absolutely not. I don't think you were even 'just a bit of fun' back in Lafayette. I was gutted when I woke up, and you were gone."

I looked around in surprise. "Really?"

"Yeah." He smiled.

"I was so scared about how good it had been and that my secret would be out for good."

"I promised I wouldn't out you..."

"I know..."

Silence fell between us. I didn't know what that conversation meant. From the way Quinn sipped his coffee, I could tell he wasn't sure what to do or say anymore either.

Slowly, with a lot of courage, probably

from the drugs in my system, I reached over and linked my fingers with his. His hand was warm and strong, and I immediately remembered how they had held me steady while he broke the floorboards to free me. I remembered how he pulled me close to keep me from further harm as we fell through the floor, and I remembered how he had grunted a little as he threw me over his shoulder right before I passed out.

"You saved my life," I whispered.

"I couldn't bear to let you die," he whispered back. "When you passed out, I thought I'd lost you. I couldn't do anything else in there, so I just pushed it all aside and focused on getting you out safely."

I swallowed hard, looking up at him. "Thank you." At that moment, my father's words rang in my head, 'Better gay and alive,' and I reached forward to take hold of Quinn's chin, holding him still as I leaned across the table to kiss him.

He let out a sound of surprise, which was honestly adorable, before he kissed me back eagerly. After a moment, he pulled back.

"You do realize this is public, right?" He chuckled.

"Yeah, I know." I could feel myself

flush a little when it was pointed out. "But I could have died. All of a sudden, being out as gay doesn't seem so scary."

Quinn looked at me for a long moment, then said, "I'm glad you're safe."

The sincerity of those words made something inside me flutter, and I felt like I needed to say something more. "I'm glad you are too." There was silence again as we finished our food. When we were done, I wiped the crumbs from my lips, and put my napkin down on the table. "Thank you, Quinn."

"Don't mention it," he replied. "Though, if you want to thank me; you'll let me take you on a date when you get out of here." He flashed me a grin.

"Actually, I was hoping you'd come and stay with me for a bit... you know, make sure I don't strain my leg around my apartment." I raised an eyebrow, knowing he had already offered to help once but amused at the surprise on his face nonetheless.

"I can absolutely do that," he promised, flashing me a megawatt smile and leaning across the table to kiss me once more.

CHAPTER THIRTY-NINE

Quinn

I MADE GOOD on my promise when Jase was let out of the hospital to return home. His parents had wanted him to move in with them for a while, but he was adamant that he would be fine in his apartment because I would be there to help him. I honestly wasn't sure if his father was going to be okay with that, the man hadn't been the most friendly toward me whenever I had seen him in the hospital, but Jase told me that was just what he was like. A surly old Texan who didn't really like to show too many emotions. The fact he had shaken my hand and told me that if I didn't treat Jase well, he would shoot me in the face with a shotgun was apparently a good sign.

The drive back to Jase's place took about an hour due to traffic, and taking it easy since I didn't want to aggravate Jase's leg. Once we arrived at his building, I climbed out and got Jase settled in a wheelchair on the sidewalk, then parked the car down the street and walked back over to the front door. It was now dark outside, so I couldn't see much of anything, but when I reached the door, I could hear some sort of commotion inside.

"Welcome home," came a yell as I opened the door to his apartment. "Glad you're here! We were beginning to think you weren't coming."

Jase looked up from where he was sitting in his wheelchair to find the rest of the crew from the station waiting inside. He glanced up at me, and I gave a half shoulder roll shrug. Of course, I had known this greeting would be waiting for him, but I hadn't wanted to spoil anything.

He wheeled himself over to the group and flashed me a smile before turning back to them.

"What's all the fuss," he asked as he maneuvered himself into the middle of the room. "It's not like I nearly died or anything." He smirked and chuckled as

Mark reached over to smack his head lightly before hugging him.

"Yeah, yeah," Mark said as he stepped away from him. "But you *did* almost die, my friend. But that's not why we are here."

"Huh," Jase asked.

"We saw you snogging Quinn at the hospital," Johnson laughed. "We wanted to make sure you knew we were all cool with it, and you didn't have to worry about telling us."

Jase spluttered at the bluntness of the message, his cheeks turning a shade of red that I was starting to adore.

"And by the way," Gage added. "We all agree you're the hottest between you two, even though you can't walk right now." That got another laugh out of everyone except Jase, who gave him a look like he had lost his mind.

"Well, I can agree with that." I laughed.

"Gross." Carmen laughed from the sofa. "No sappy shit on shift, though, all right? I like keeping my food in my stomach," she teased. It was such a light atmosphere, and the way they had addressed the news of Jase being gay was almost like they weren't taking it seriously, or really didn't care one way or the other. But I could see from the relief and the smile on Jase's face that this was the best way for him to be received. His sexuality would change absolutely nothing about his relationships with his coworkers. They were still teasing and laughing with him, which was most likely exactly what he'd feared losing.

"That's actually the second thing we wanted to talk to you about," Johnson said after giving Jase a quick glance that was mildly serious. "We have a bet going at how long it'll take you to be back on your feet, and if I don't win, I'm going to put you back in that chair." His face changed to a cheeky grin as Jase rolled his eyes and reached out to swat his friend's arm.

"Don't go betting on my injuries!" He laughed. "I'm already feeling better than I have been all week, so I say I'll be walking again within a week."

"A week?" Johnson repeated. "That's pretty optimistic."

"Damn straight, but you know me." Jase flashed him a cocky grin.

I just shook my head, a smile gracing my lips at my stubborn man.

Quinn

THE BANTER AND laughter went on for a couple of hours before the visitors decided they should probably head off as they all had to work the next day. I had already booked the time off to ensure Jase was supported when needed. Once silence fell through the apartment, Jase looked up at me with a raised eyebrow. "You knew they'd seen us?"

"Of course." I smiled. "They all gave me a similar speech to one that your dad did. If I hurt you, they'll make sure I get stuck in the next fire-filled building." He blushed slightly at the protectiveness of so many around him. "I told them that if I have hurt you, I'll walk into that building myself," I assured him, stepping over to him and leaning down to catch his lips with mine. This kiss differed from our first one. He held onto my waist and pulled me close, and a soft moan escaped his mouth.

After a few moments, I felt him loosen his grip and then pull back to look into my eyes. "I want to explore more with you," Jase whispered. "Not just tonight, but whenever we can. I want to feel you against me. I want to know every inch of your body." He traced a finger along my jawline before I heard him chuckle.

My heart thudded heavily as I nodded slowly, stepping toward the bedroom. Jase wheeled himself in there first, but the door didn't even close before I strode over to him, pinned him into the chair, and crushed my mouth against his. I moved my hands down his arms and across his chest before reaching up to grab his hair and pull his head back, deepening the kiss.

His fingers wrapped around my wrists, and he pushed my hair away from my face with his other hand while I continued to suckle on his tongue and nip at his bottom lip.

"Fuck," Jase gasped as I broke away.

"That's the idea..." I purred, slipping my arms under his legs and lifting him enough to move him from the chair to the bed, where I crowded him against the mattress.

"God, I love you," he breathed.

I stopped for a moment, pulling back and gazing down into his eyes as the words echoed in my ears. They were genuine and honest, full of emotion I could see clearly in his features.

"I love you too," I replied, pressing my mouth against his again.

This time, Jase wrapped his arms around my torso and held me tight as I explored every inch of his mouth with my tongue. When I slipped my hands inside his shirt and cupped his hard, firm chest, I felt his hands glide down my sides and grab hold of my hips. I moaned softly against his lips when he thrust his tongue into my mouth, swirling it around mine before pulling away. He attempted to shift his leg and hissed slightly in pain.

"Fuck." Jase groaned.

"You shouldn't move," I whispered. "Leave this to me."

He nodded, letting go of me and allowing me to remove his shirt. I tossed it aside and began unbuttoning his pants, pushing them and his underwear past his knees, making sure to be careful of his injury. I watched him from under lowered lashes as the head of his cock sprung upward, wet and glistening with his arousal. I ran my hands between his thighs and then around his ass, squeezing gently. He shivered at the touch, and I chuckled.

"I think you like being touched," I said between kisses as I made my way down over his belly, my tongue teasing his furry treasure trail downward.

His gaze flashed up to meet mine, and he nodded slightly. "I do..."

I leaned down and licked along the length of Jase's shaft, tasting the salty pearl of fluid that leaked from the tip. I swirled my tongue around the head, lapping up the precum before pressing my lips against his skin. A low, guttural sound escaped his throat as I slid my lips along the length of him, teasing him with my tongue. I picked up the pace, taking him halfway into my mouth and then pulling back, working him rapidly with my mouth. He was moaning and panting by the time I took his entire length into my mouth, letting it bump against the back of my throat before once again pulling upward and hollowing my cheeks, sucking hard on the last inch or two.

I pulled back from him with an audible pop and sat upright, looking up at him with lust-filled eyes. "Do you want to fuck me?" I asked softly.

"Yes," Jase hissed. "Please."

Pulling my clothes from my body quickly, I crawled onto the bed and straddled his lap, watching as he blindly reached to the side of the bed and fumbled with a small box. As he pulled it open, I smirked as I saw lube and condoms. "I knew you weren't going to be shy about this," I teased.

"I'm not," he growled. "And neither are you... right?"

I laughed softly, running my fingers across his cheekbone and down the column of his neck. "Right."

"Let me touch you," Jase urged, his voice husky.

I obliged, keeping my weight off his thighs as he sat up beneath me and spread lube over his fingers. His teeth nipped and bit at my chest, leaving small marks behind as his first finger invaded my body from below. I groaned deeply as the digit moved inside me, exploring me in a way no one had ever done before. I had never been the one on the receiving end, but as he touched me, I couldn't help but burn for him. I wanted everything I could get from Jase, and the idea of riding him and watching his pleasure made me hotter by the second.

"Fucking hell." He sighed, and I felt his fingers leave my body as he worked the condom onto his dick. He eased himself into position, and I lifted myself from the bed, taking care to avoid jarring his leg. I moved closer to him and reached for his hand, threading our fingers together as I positioned myself above him.

Jase looked up at me with wide eyes, and I smiled as I lowered myself onto his hard erection. The sensation was incredible. It was a tight fit, and I wiggled against his body, enjoying the feeling of his hardness and warmth.

I placed my hands on his shoulders and leaned down, kissing him once more. Then I slowly started to move, rocking my hips back and forth as I impaled myself upon him, the initial burning stretch turning quickly into an unbelievable feeling of fullness.

"Oh god..." Jase groaned, his head falling back onto the pillow.

I rocked slowly, feeling his hands slide down my waist and grip my hips as he tried to pull me closer to him. There was a slight pain that accompanied my movements, but his hands on my hips kept me from speeding up while I got used to his size.

I felt my muscles tense as he hit my

deepest parts, brushing again and again over my sweet spot, and I sighed in relief when there was nothing but mind-boggling pleasure left in my body. I felt him tighten beneath me, and I leaned down further to kiss him again. He tasted like salt, and I smacked my lips against his, unable to stop myself from biting his lower lip. I reached up and grabbed handfuls of his hair, holding his face still so I could devour him as much as possible.

My body was on fire, and I needed more. I rocked harder, increasing the pace. Soon, I was slamming my hips against his, feeling his hands dig into my hips as he forced himself not to thrust up to meet me in case it strained his leg. I didn't mind. I could feel every movement of his body as his breathing became labored, and his voice grew louder with each passing second. I leaned down and buried my face against his shoulder, unable to take any more.

"Fuck. Jase, you feel so good inside me," I groaned against his skin.

He held my hips tightly in his grasp while he kissed the side of my neck. "You're so tight, baby," he growled.

I moaned at the sound of his husky voice, digging my nails into his shoulders as I continued to ride him. My body was ready to come. I wanted to let go and scream my release. But I wanted Jase to come first. I needed to see him lose control. I needed to hear him say my name while we both came undone.

I slid my hands down his strong arms, moving my hand between us until I found the base of his cock, stroking him hard and fast even as I rode him. I was almost there. I could feel it building inside me. His breath was ragged, and I could tell he was close too. I gripped his thighs tighter, holding him firmly in place as I felt the pressure of his swelling cock build within me, pressing against the walls of my body, as my own balls pulled up tight and heat coiled in my belly.

I dug my nails into his thighs as I cried out, my back arching, feeling my orgasm take me over completely. I watched as Jase stiffened beneath me as my body clamped around him and sent him over the edge as well. I felt his body tense as his release caused him to jerk beneath me.

Slowly, I began to rock my hips, milking every last bit that he had for me before I finally stilled my hips and leaned forward to capture his lips again. The kiss we shared was slower, sensual, and loving. Heavy breathing merged together between the kisses, and for a while, we just stayed there, enjoying the aftermath and losing ourselves in the emotions that filled the kisses.

We were quiet for long enough before I pulled away and slid off him, lying alongside Jase. We lay side-by-side, and I wrapped an arm around him, pulling him into me as I snuggled him against my chest.

"I love you so much, Jase," I whispered.

His fingers traced circles along my arm as he turned onto his side to look up at me. "I love you too, baby."

For a moment, time stood still. We simply stared at one another, understanding what had just happened. I knew I loved him, but this was different. This was more than I'd ever thought it would be. Jase had shown me everything I hadn't known about myself. And now I understood just how deep my feelings ran for him.

Jase pulled me closer, kissing me softly as he rested his hand on the back of my head. The warmth of his body seeped through my skin, and a smile touched his lips when I pressed mine to him in return.

He pulled away from me then, looking up at me with those bright eyes that seemed like they could see right inside me. He brushed a strand of hair behind my ear, then leaned over to kiss my neck, making me shiver underneath him. My heart began beating faster, and my breath quickened. His hands moved down my sides, slipping between us to explore my abdomen and toy with the dark trail of hair there.

"I'm not a young man anymore," I warned him. "But if you keep roaming, I'm going to want to do you again soon enough."

Jase smirked a little. "Is that a promise? Because I could really do with the feeling of you inside me as well."

I raised an eyebrow, shifting so I could roll him onto his back and place my arms on either side of his head to box him in.

"Oh really? You think you're up to that? What about your leg."

He nodded. "To hell with my leg."

"And here I was trying to be nice." I chuckled. There was something about Jase that made me feel like an excited teenager again. I could feel the blood in my body running south in an attempt to have more as soon as possible.

"I want the night we should have had if

I hadn't misunderstood," Jase grumbled, reaching up to bury his fingers in my hair and pull me down for another hungry kiss.

My entire body trembled as our tongues tangled together. I felt my control slipping by the second, and I wanted nothing more than to lose myself inside him. It wasn't just the sex, though. I'd never been with anyone who was so open and honest with me. He showed me things I didn't know existed within myself. But more importantly, he showed me how much I truly cared about him. How much I needed him.

I reached down and grasped his cock beneath the sheets, stroking him slowly until he moaned and rolled his hips against my touch, growing half-hard already. Jase growled low in his throat, rolling his hips more forcefully.

"You're killing me," he groaned, and I laughed, knowing exactly how he felt.

I sat up and pushed his legs further apart, so I could see his bare ass and the thick length of his shaft standing proudly from between his legs. I loved the way he looked.

"Spread your knees, baby," I ordered, and he complied immediately. He moved carefully with his injured leg, and I propped a pillow beneath it so he could rest it in that position easier.

I dropped my mouth to his balls, licking and sucking them gently before I teased his opening with my tongue until it softened and fluttered under my ministrations. Jase let out a deep moan, and I could feel my own length hardening by the second.

"Fuck," Jase swore, his voice rough and strained as I licked the underside of his shaft. I nipped his sac with my teeth and sucked on his ball sack, enjoying the way he bucked against my face. I worked my way up the base of his cock, licking and sucking along the way until I got to the tip. I swirled my tongue around the slit, coating it in my saliva, then wrapped my fist around his base and stroked him up and down a few times.

"Mmm, you taste good," I murmured.

"I need you inside me, now," he demanded.

I grinned, slicking up my fingers before pushing a finger through the tight ring of muscle past his entrance and sliding it in and out, watching his stomach muscles tense and relax as I did. I loved the way he tasted as I kissed along his hips, the musky scent of his skin.

I slipped two fingers into him now,

thrusting them in and out. He clenched tight around them, and I added a third, moving them in and out of him with slow, deliberate strokes. He was so fucking hot and wet. Every inch of him was slick with his arousal.

"Shit, you are so fucking gorgeous," I hissed as I pulled my fingers from him and surged up to slam my lips against his. Lifting his healthy leg up onto my shoulder, I pressed the tip of my cock to his hole and paused, smirking into the kiss as he whined and attempted to push down onto me. Pulling away from his lips briefly, I ran my tongue along his jawline. "You want me that badly?" I whispered.

"Yes," Jase panted. "Come on. Fuck me."

I smiled, pulling my hand from his hip and grabbing a condom from the bedside table. I tore it open with my teeth, rolling the latex over my hard, throbbing cock in one smooth movement. I gripped his hips tightly, lifting him off the bed slightly so I could drive into him. His legs were still spread wide, and I moved my hand to hold his thigh against my chest, keeping him steady as I slid to the hilt with a single thrust.

"Ahhh," Jase let out a long breath, tilting his head back. "God, yes."

I held him in place with one arm wrapped around his waist while I pumped my hips, working my length in and out of him with slow, easy thrusts. I leaned forward and brushed my nose against his neck, inhaling the warm scent of him. He was so fucking sexy and delicious. I couldn't get enough of him.

His breathing grew heavier as I began to move faster, pounding his ass roughly with each thrust. I bit down on his shoulder, and he let out a throaty groan.

"More," he begged.

I chuckled, biting down a little harder, making the most of the moment and creating a mark that would surely last for days. The feeling of possession ran through me as I pulled back to inspect my work.

"Mine," I growled a little, shifting my hips to piston against the sensitive bundle of nerves within Jase that made his back arch and his mouth fall open in silent moans of pure pleasure.

He was mine. And I was his.

CHAPTER FORTY-ONE

Jase

THE FOLLOWING DAY, we slept late, waking up only when the sun had begun to rise. We showered together, thoroughly washing each other's hair and bodies but avoiding anything more intimate. I was stuck in a shower chair for some of it. For other parts, Quinn held my body close to him to support my weight so we could share kisses and feel the heat of each other's bodies close. When we were both clean, he helped me out into the livingroom, where we sat on the couch and watched television.

He had left his phone charging on the coffee table while we were asleep, and he didn't seem worried about it that morning either. It was bliss to lose yourself in the company of someone, and I still couldn't believe he had actually said he loved me. Even though I'd never been one to be romantic or emotional, there was something special about being with him, knowing that he wanted me.

Even better was the fact that my parents and my coworkers knew about my sexuality and hadn't cared.

Over the next few weeks, my father often came over to take me to the clinic at the hospital where my physical therapy would be held. He was retired and knew that Quinn needed to return to work, so he had been the first to offer to take me to my appointments. Each time, my mother stayed at my apartment to clean and cook so Quinn did not have too much to do after a twelve-hour shift.

Quinn was sweet and understanding, and even though he was always tired from working nights, he tried to help as much as possible. He went grocery shopping for us, made sure I ate right, and cooked meals for me every night. The only downside was that I no longer had access to the gym or any of the machines. Still, I got plenty of exercise with the routines my PT, Frankie, provided. And my appointments were easy to manage.

"Look, Jase..." my father said on the first day I was given a crutch to use instead of a wheelchair.

I glanced over at him where he had stopped before getting in the car. He looked uncomfortable.

"I just wanted to say... I'm so fucking proud of you."

My eyebrows shot up at the genuine softness in the old man's voice. "That's really nice, Dad," I replied, reaching across the car to squeeze his hand.

He squeezed mine back, smiling. "But look, this whole thing isn't exactly easy for me."

I knew he meant the sexuality thing, but I stayed quiet.

"I mean, yeah, it makes sense. You're a good guy. But it still feels weird..." he trailed off.

I sighed and rubbed my forehead. He was so nervous about things like this. I thought it was because he was afraid of what people might think of him or his family. My father wasn't very religious, but he was still raised in a very different era. He expected certain behavior from those who lived in our town. He had grown up in an area where it was illegal to see two men holding hands or kissing in public and where gay marriage was never going to be accepted.

"It's okay, Dad," I started, but he

raised a hand to cut me off.

"No, let me say this, okay?" He sucked in a deep breath and looked down at his shoes. "I love your boyfriend," he admitted, looking up at me again. "I know he's not my son, but he's doing everything right by you, and if it weren't for him, I don't know... I definitely couldn't have afforded your surgeries. He's a good man, and I'm just glad you have someone who cares so much for you."

I smiled at the compliment. "Thanks," I told him. "And that's all I need to hear. I just never wanted to lose you and Mom."

"Idiot. You'll never lose us." He flashed me a smile. "You're my boy."

After that, I did a lot of thinking about my father. I realized how lucky I was to have grown up in such a loving home and how I should be grateful to have had the upbringing I did. It also made me think about Quinn and the way his parents hadn't spoken to him once since he came out publicly. He never spoke about it, but there must have been pain deep within him, knowing that his parents couldn't love him enough to get past something that their religion condemned. Their actions were a sign of their lack of understanding and acceptance. They just didn't understand that they needed to change, not Quinn.

I thought back on all the times that I'd read about someone who was persecuted because of being gay. The stories always left me feeling sad and scared. Once more, I was struck by the level of courage Quinn had despite the actions he had performed in his youth due to fear. If only other people could find the same strength in themselves, then maybe things would start to change for everyone.

CHAPTER FORTY-TWO

Jase

THE NEXT DAY while Quinn was at work, I caught myself staring into space as I stared at the TV screen. Something was bothering me. As I sat there waiting for Quinn to come home from work, I tried to figure out what it was. After a few minutes, it hit me like a ton of bricks—I felt guilty.

Since being together, Quinn had been so affectionate, working hard to fix any remaining wounds I might still have from his actions at school, but I had not once acknowledged his pain in return. I knew that Quinn's family had hurt him deeply, especially when he was young, but I didn't want our relationship to be built off one-sided guilt from the past.

"You all right?" Quinn asked as he

walked through the door with a smile on his face. He was such a beautiful man who had changed so much from his youth. His skin was now smooth and clear, without a single blemish or scar. Those eyes of his were now the most expressive part of him. Whenever he looked at me, I felt as though we were the only two souls in the world.

With a small smile, I took hold of my crutch and used it to get to my feet, hobbling over to where he had unpacked his backpack in the kitchen.

"Getting better every day." I flashed him a megawatt smile.

He laughed softly as he shook his head, then held out something to me. "I picked you up a treat," he said.

As I looked at the object in his hand, I smiled lightly. It was a specific brand of non-alcoholic beer, which I enjoyed but couldn't get at the local shop. Being on the medications that I was, I couldn't drink anything with alcohol content, and it had been something I missed. Even after a long shift, he still thought about me and expressed it in small but meaningful actions.

"Thank you," I said softly as he placed the can on the counter and then wrapped an arm around my waist, pulling me close to him.

"Are you sure you are okay," he asked.

"Yeah. I was just thinking about you," I admitted. "I want to say I forgive you for everything from when we were younger. You are an amazing person and so brave for coming out the other side of that fear instilled in you by the church."

Quinn tilted his head to the side as I spoke, his eyes glistening a little with emotion. "That's why I love you. You always see the good in people, despite what they do. I'm happy that you feel like I have changed for the better. I would never be able to forgive myself if I hadn't." He chuckled. "Although, there is one thing I can't forgive myself for."

He glanced down and took hold of my hand, lifting it up and pressing his lips to the faded scar that lingered on my wrist from that awful night I had wanted out of everything.

"I will spend the rest of my life making sure you never feel that bad ever again, and I'll never forgive myself for being a factor in that decision, in making you feel the way you did."

It was true. Since he had been living here with me, Quinn had made me happier than anyone else alive. The pain I had lived with was finally beginning to fade away. We were both free men now, and neither of us was going back.

I kissed him gently before reaching over and snagging the beer can off the counter. I opened it up and took a sip. "I'll hold you to that." I smiled, liking his promise to be around for the foreseeable future. I had no idea how the future would turn out, but knowing I wouldn't be alone was nice.

With a soft kiss to my forehead, Quinn carried his things into the bedroom, and I watched him go, feeling a sense of pride in myself for having managed to live this long. I had left the past behind, and even if I was now facing a few months of therapy, I had grown stronger in so many ways, and I had someone by my side.

Life was changing, and I was starting to accept that it really could change for the better.

EPILOGUE

Jase

IT DIDN'T TAKE long for Quinn to move in with me permanently. I had a bed that was big enough for the both of us, so I offered it up, and he accepted without hesitation.

Of course, there were some moments when I felt like we were moving too fast, but those times passed quickly as well. We would spend hours talking about our favorite things or just sitting around watching TV while occasionally playing video games together.

Being open about who I was allowed me to deepen the friendships I had with my coworkers too, and my social life expanded as a result. Johnson and Carmen had ended up getting together and took to joining me for walks and jogs as my leg got stronger. They even brought their dog, Maxim, along once or twice, which made them all laugh when he started growling at Quinn.

It was when I was sitting on the floor with my back leaning against Quinn one evening when everyone was around for food that I realized that I didn't think I could be much happier with my life. Everything was just that much brighter with Quinn by my side.

"What are you thinking?" Quinn asked after a few minutes of silence between us. He had been nuzzling into my hair and it felt nice.

I smiled and looked up. "Just that everything is going really great."

He raised his eyebrows. "And that's a problem why? It always should feel good when you're happy."

My smile grew bigger. "No," I said, grabbing him around the neck and pulling him to me. As he leaned down, I kissed him on the cheek. "Things are perfect for me right now. You make me feel so safe, protected and loved. Those feelings are what happiness feels like to me," I paused, and then blushed. "Well, they do anyway."

Quinn smiled down at me and pressed a kiss to my forehead. A kiss that felt full

of promise for this happiness to continue
for as long as he had a say in my life.

Thank you for reading Jase and
Quinn's story.
Continue the series with Gage, book 4
in Smokejumpers!

OTHER BOOKS BY EVIE

Federal Protection Agency

Mason

Rafe

Ryzen

Cooper

Noah

Damien

Sebastian

Gabe

Logan

Ruthless Empire

Courting Danger

Chasing Danger

Kissing Danger

Smokejumpers

Hawke

Cyrus

Jase

Gage

Jackson

Xavier

EVIE RILEY

Jasper Springs
Cade
Dawson
Drew
Grayson
Riley
Mitch

From The Edge
Shattered
Runaway
Jaded
Rescue
Hidden
Tormented

Gray Vale Pack
His Fated Mate
His Wounded Warrior
His Healing Heart

ABOUT THE AUTHOR

Evie Riley is a prolific, neurodivergent author known for her captivating MM romance novels. She has gained a significant following and topped the LGBT+ action and adventure bestseller charts with her series.

Evie's writing style often explores dark and gritty themes where her men must overcome difficult obstacles in their search for love, but she has also ventured into sweeter small-town romances, incorporating tropes like enemies-to-lovers, friends-to-lovers, age-gap, and forced proximity. She is known for crafting engaging romantic suspense novels and has a knack for creating interconnected series worlds that keep readers invested.

Interestingly, Ms. Riley has hinted at exploring new genres, such as Alien Omegaverse Romance, in the future.

Outside of writing, she enjoys spending time at the beach and has a quirky personality, described by her partner as ranging from cute to deadly, depending on her blood-chocolate levels.

Evie spends her nights writing bad boys in love, and her days wrangling the sweet boys she loves.